A Warner Communications Company

WARNER BOOKS EDITION

Cover illustration by Franco Accornero
Cover design by Jackie Merri Meyer

Warner Books, Inc.
666 Fifth Avenue
New York, N.Y. 10103

A Warner Communications Company

Printed in the United States of America

This book was originally published in hardcover by Warner Books.
First Printed in Paperback: June, 1989

10 9 8 7 6 5 4 3 2 1

Death is one of the states of the soul, but slavery is the soul's abasement.

—NAPOLEON BONAPARTE, A CORSICAN

In Corsican eyes, to accept forgiveness is as humiliating as to offer it.

—DOROTHY CARRINGTON

Acknowledgments to:

Lawrie Mackintosh, Father Richard O'Rouke, Cobus Smit, Peta Sokolsky, Greg Morris, and Nellie Swindells.

With my thanks to Larry Kirshbaum for his inspired editing.

I am deeply indebted to Dorothy Carrington, whose magnificent book, *Granite Island*, provided me with both inspiration and the background to write *The Corsican Woman*.

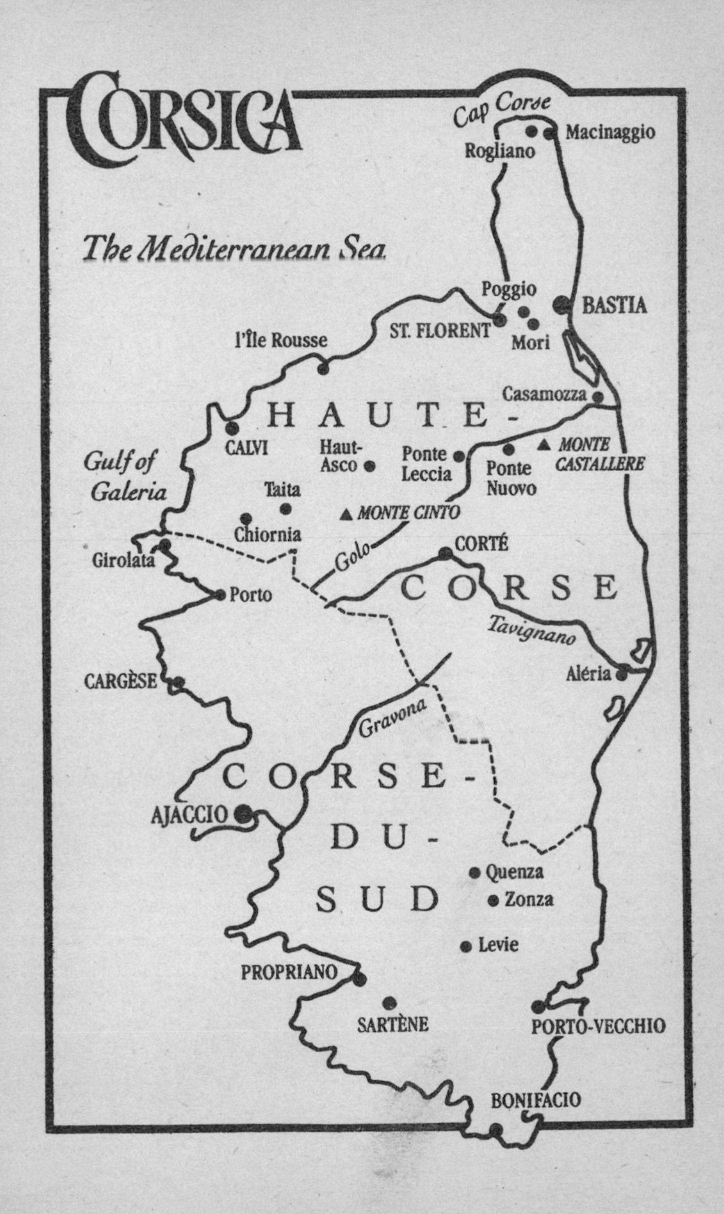
CORSICA
Cap Corse
Macinaggio
Rogliano
The Mediterranean Sea
Poggio
BASTIA
ST. FLORENT
Mori
l'Île Rousse
Casamozza
HAUTE-
CALVI
Haut-
Asco
Ponte
Leccia
Ponte
Nuovo
MONTE
CASTALLERE
Gulf of
Galeria
Taita
Chiornia
MONTE CINTO
Golo
CORTÉ
Girolata
Porto
CORSE
Tavignano
CARGÈSE
Aléria
Gravona
CORSE-
DU-
SUD
AJACCIO
Quenza
Zonza
Levie
PROPRIANO
SARTÈNE
PORTO-VECCHIO
BONIFACIO

PROLOGUE

Taita, Corsica, August 11, 1960

Sybilia Rocca sat motionless in a high-backed chair. Only her fingers gripping the table's edge and the unnatural hunch of her shoulders betrayed her tension. The windows were shuttered, but beams of light shone through the wide cracks, lending the stark room a deceptive mellowness. Sunbeams shone on the yellow varnished table, reflecting on the woman's upturned face so that she resembled a golden statue of the Madonna. Her stillness accentuated this impression, and so did her features, which were classically correct. Her deep blue eyes, usually warm and laughing, were glazed and swollen, but even then she was lovely, with a bruised, sensuous beauty that incites male aggression and the rancor of unfulfilled desires.

In the village Sybilia was known as the *putana,* the whore, and she was despised, but she bore her reputation with dignity and a certain nobility that infuriated the men and drove the women to envy her. But here, in the solitude of her room, dignity had fled as she clung to the table and tried to stifle her sobs.

Abruptly Sybilia stood up, flung back the shutters, and leaned out. It was noon: the sky was a luminous blue behind jagged peaks. Snow-streaked and sun-drenched, the mountains were a shimmering backdrop of brilliant glare against purple shadows. Below was the deep, dank green of ancient forests—pine, chestnuts, cork oaks, stretching to the distant azure sea.

Beneath the window was a narrow terraced garden with an old stone wall where the land fell a sheer three hundred meters to the lake. Narrowing her eyes against the glare, Sybilia searched the garden, but it was deserted: straggling flowers, weeds, rubble, and a broken shed.

Crossing the wide room, Sybilia flung open the shutters on the western side, which overlooked the square. The village of Taita had been hewn from an almost inaccessible cliff between the mountain and the lake. Granite against granite—a cluster of gaunt fortresses around a cobbled square. To one side of the square was the Church of St. Augustine, and a statue of the Taitan patron saint stood in the shade of a dense chestnut grove, beside a fountain where mountain water trickled into an old stone trough.

Sybilia turned as if sleepwalking and trancelike walked down the stone steps to the living room. She shuddered as she took the rifle from the peg on the wall, but after only a moment's hesitation, she loaded it and went outside.

The air was oppressive, the trees motionless, the village lay becalmed. Even the birds were slumbering in the shady branches of chestnut trees. The throb of cicadas and the tinkling church bell were muted, almost inaudible in the sluggish heat. Dogs sprawled over cobblestones, and a sow with seven piglets grunted blissfully in a mud pool at the edge of the trough, where cool water from mountain streams gurgled lazily in deep, grassy gutters.

On a bench in front of the church a man sat dreaming. Even in his sixties he was still handsome with his harsh but regular features, his shock of wavy white hair, and his bushy white mustache curled at the ends as if in a perpetual sneer. His was a powerful torso with bulging biceps and strong mountain legs. Over the years he had grown arrogant, and this showed in the curve of his mouth and the glint of his eyes.

He heard footsteps, yawned, and sat up blinking and regretful. When he saw his daughter-in-law, Sybilia, approaching, his face became a trifle sterner.

Father Andrews, who was climbing the steps to his church,

paused and watched her. A strange tenseness emanated from the woman as she walked across the square, carrying a rifle awkwardly. The priest paused and then went on into the porch.

At ten paces Sybilia swung the rifle to her shoulder. She took aim, but her hands were shaking and the image in the rifle's sights swung wildly from the man, to the trees, to the cobbles. She saw him frown, open his eyes, and jerk forward. Sybilia gasped, steadied her hands as she held her breath, and pulled the trigger. The bullet shattered one arm he flung up to protect his body. She moaned softly. "Oh, God! Oh, God!"

The man fell sideways across the bench, then pushed himself up to his feet and lurched toward Sybilia. Sobbing, she struggled to control her shaking hands and find the courage to pull the trigger again. Another shot rang out, and a crimson stain appeared upon his snowy-white shirt. He staggered but kept on his feet. There was a look of shock and anger on his face.

"No, Sybilia. Don't do it." Father Andrews came running out of the church and down the stone steps into the square. He felt as if he were in a nightmare; it seemed to him that he was hardly advancing as he threw himself forward—but too late.

He saw the woman fire again and again. At each loud report the man shuddered and jerked like a puppet with a clumsy manipulator until he collapsed spread-eagled on the cobblestones.

The priest reached the woman and grabbed her, but she did not resist. "Holy Mother of God," he swore in his native Irish tongue without even realizing.

Sybilia stood staring at the corpse and the blood, her mouth working as she gasped for breath. When the priest took her arm it felt icy cold. Suddenly she flung the rifle away and ran sobbing into the church.

Father Andrews bent over Xavier Rocca to give absolution. Too late, he knew. By now Xavier was in God's hands—or the devil's.

PART I

CHAPTER 1

August, 1960

Looking back, it's hard to recall the events that enmeshed me with the destiny of the Roccas. I suppose it began years ago at Boston University, when I first broached my ideas to the head of the anthropology department, Professor Don Miller. Archaeology was a new science in the faculty, and I was regarded with a certain amount of skepticism. I wanted to link these two social sciences in a single project that was unorthodox and therefore suspect.

I argued patiently for weeks: "What do we know about Stone Age man in Europe? We know his tools, homes, burial sites, pottery, but very little about the guy himself—his beliefs, politics, ideals. We transfer data from contemporary primitive societies: aborigines, bushmen—degenerate cultures. A far better method would be to find an isolated European group, cut off for centuries by geographic barriers, and study their roots, aided by an on-site archaeological excavation."

"It's speculative, Dr. Walters," Miller told me time and again.

I shelved my project. Then one evening I found an old book gathering dust on the library shelves: *British Essays in Favour of the Brave Corsicans,* by James Boswell (1768). More research convinced me that Corsica was my goal.

Isolated for generations, the islanders' unique culture and beliefs had no parallel in Europe. I should be able to find traces of Stone Age man in the community's legends and superstitions—a living legacy to study and record. Now that I was more sure of my objectives, paths were smoothed, doors were opened, and before year's end I had a five-year grant to finance my research.

I'd been right.

My research had been even more successful than I'd hoped. The village I'd chosen, called Taita, consisted of a cluster of ancient stone houses, gaunt and enduring, built on a precipitous rocky cliff. On the mountain slopes above I'd found an ideal vantage point: a granite boulder whose concave top was smooth enough to sit comfortably and high enough to see over the tangled undergrowth. From here the village appeared to be spread-eagled beneath me, neat and convenient as a living frog pinned for dissection: its heart the cobbled square, its soul the church, its conscience the indomitable Irish priest Father Andrews.

This satisfactory project was now completed. My published theories had brought me international acknowledgment. Two quasi-scientific books had made me financially independent. I had no cause for regrets. I was about to quit the island because I'd been offered the chair of anthropology, due to Don Miller's early retirement. Yet that summer morning, as I gazed down at Taita, I felt regretful. I didn't want to leave. Forcing my mind away from vague longings of what might have been, I considered the future.

Professor Jacklyn Walters! (Jock to my friends). It sounded great, and I'd worked hard for it. I wondered how I would cope with wearing suits and ties. For the past few years I'd lived in shorts, hiking boots, and a watch that doubled as a compass. I'd miss the free and easy life-style; I'd miss Taita and the villagers. Most of all I'd miss Sybilia Rocca. We'd been close friends for the past year, and I had to admit I owed her a great deal. I'd never have found the ruins without Sybilia's help. They'd been completely hidden by the maquis, that dense thicket of myrtle, lavender, thyme, cistus, and wild fig trees that covers half the island and chokes the torpid air with its heady, bittersweet aroma.

I knew that she, too, was feeling sad. Did she regret my leaving? She had said very little on the previous evening when we had discussed my new appointment. This morning she had arrived at the dig with our provisions, as usual. She'd been excavating in the cave for most of the morning, but she had left just before lunch. I'd noticed how tense she looked. What was it she'd said just before she hurried down the hill?

I wish I had loved you more . . . I'm sorry I left it so long and wasted so much time.

Strange that she should say that. It had sounded like a promise, but one that had come too late. For the past five years I'd lusted for Sybilia, but in spite of our friendship she had never acquiesced, never let down her defenses.

From the monotonous clang of spades against rock-hard gravel, I realized the diggers were slacking off for lunch. God, it was hot. If it weren't for the workers, I'd take the afternoon off and go spear fishing. This was just the day for it. I could see the Gulf of Galeria twinkling in the distance. I grinned as I gazed at the distant blue sheen, remembering yesterday's chase after a giant ray that had flapped halfway round the bay like a grotesque, hideous crow before I finished it off.

The digging stopped, and there was silence. Siesta time! I glanced at my watch. It was noon. The men began opening their lunch baskets. I was hungry, too.

I climbed down from the rock and walked toward the cave, one corner of which I'd converted into a small office. Sybilia had left my lunch there. Pausing at the entrance, I gazed back toward the site for which I had searched so painstakingly. I gloated at the statues: hewn from granite, they were three times larger than life, their features blunted, their eyes bored holes set close together as they glared down with sinister intensity.

When the first shot rang out I was eating my sandwich. I wasn't particularly startled by the shot. Almost every man, woman, and child in Corsica could handle a rifle, and hunting was the national pastime.

When a second shot rang out it seemed that the sound echoed from the village square. Then I heard shouts. I raced back to my vantage point and grabbed the binoculars.

Three more shots rang out in rapid succession.

I focused on the cobbles through a gap in the branches and saw the victim prone on the ground. Who was it?

I was snagged by a moment's indecision. This was my last

chance to witness a traditional vendetta. My view was spoiled by the trees, but if I were to run down to the village, I would miss the next ten minutes' vital observation.

The priest ran down the steps from the church, and the villagers began to gather. Then a woman ran across the square toward the church. Her familiar stance sent my heart thudding against my rib cage.

Could it be? No! Impossible! Not her!

The woman stumbled and sprawled over the steps. Momentarily she looked back. It was Sybilia.

"Oh, God!" My mind was in a turmoil. It couldn't be happening—not to people you know. *But Sybilia was Corsican.*

Why? Why had she done this terrible thing?

As these thoughts flashed through my mind, I dropped the binoculars and raced down the slippery slope through the maquis. In spite of my panic, I was ironically aware that a lifetime's discipline in detached, scientific observation was in danger of being hurled to the wind.

CHAPTER 2

By the time I reached the square I was too late to help anyone. Father Andrews had hidden Sybilia in the church and run back with an altar cloth to cover the corpse.

The villagers were hurling abuse toward the church in a vitriolic outpouring of pent-up emotions that, I knew from experience, could turn them into a punitory mob within minutes. There was a sudden, high-pitched keening from the mourners: "The whore . . . the shameless hussy . . . may she die in agony . . ." The *voceri*, or professional mourner, was singing, with a voice like an angel. The drumming was louder now. Oppressive!

Father Andrews hurried over to me. "I've locked Sybilia in the sacristy," he mumbled. "I don't know what we're going to do." The priest hurried back to Xavier's corpse:

"Lord have mercy, Christ have mercy, Lord have mercy, Holy Mary pray for him." His voice was in fatuous combat with the mourners who were giving full vent to their talents, their hair disheveled, their dresses rent. Soon they would carry Xavier Rocca to his house, but the mourning would last all night and well into the next day.

I stared down at the solemn, waxed features and the massive corpse of Xavier Rocca, war hero, leader of the local Nationalist party, and village headman. To the authorities he was a wanted murderer who hid in the maquis when police squads arrived; to the villagers he was a "bandit of honor," revered for upholding Corsican honor. What a magnificent figure of a man Xavier had been! Now his body would be reprocessed into this endless earthly resurrection, as his soul would be.

"Lord have mercy, Christ have mercy, Lord have mercy, Holy Mary pray for him."

Angry cries for vengeance mingled with the monotonous thud-thud-thud of rifle butts slammed on cobbles.

Suddenly my arm was gripped. Father Andrews looked defeated. Glittering eyes revealed his panic. "It will take the police two days to get here," he muttered close to my ear. "What can we do? They'll be coming for her tonight. She won't see the light of day if she stays in the church."

"Someone must hide her?"

He shook his head angrily. "Who in Taita would shelter the *putana*?"

For a moment I couldn't think. I felt dazed. I knew Sybilia as a warm and sensitive person. I couldn't be wrong. Goddammit, we'd worked together for months. I knew her well enough, didn't I? Yet I couldn't refute the evidence of my own eyes. Shafts of panic kept penetrating my guts. With this terrible act, Sybilia had put herself beyond help. She had shot down a man in cold blood in front of most of the villagers. What would they do to her—the villagers or the French authorities?

"Listen to me," Father Andrews whispered. "They'll use this vendetta as an excuse to kill her. There are many people in this village who would sleep easier if she were dead. Without help, she won't see morning. The poor lassie," he added to himself.

"I'll try to get her out of here," I said without much hope.

I didn't think we stood a chance. Every villager was a superb marksman, and they knew the territory intimately.

"After dark," I promised. "I'll come to the sacristy door at nine. Have the donkey ready. Meantime, keep Sybilia locked up."

Eight hours to go. I decided to push personal considerations to the back of my mind, but my scientific excitement was sadly lacking. Here was the real Corsica, I told myself. This was what I had come to witness—the pageantry of a code of justice as old as man was about to unfold. I tried to record what I could.

Work has always been my opium. Grabbing my notebook, I tried to describe the scene. *A vendetta gives the* voceri *(otherwise known as a* voceratrici*), or singing mourner, full scope for her talents,* I had written. *She works herself into a trance as she hurls accusations and insults at the killer and calls upon the victim's relatives to avenge the murder. This ancient ritual, handed down . . .*

I could go no further. How could any words convey this ghastly scene: the tangible anger that scorched me like heat from a fire; the sonic shrapnel of abuse exploding in my ears; the rhythmic smash of rifle butts on cobbles; church bells numbing my senses? The women were scrambling to touch the corpse and tearing their clothes. Was it women—or tatty vultures—flapping and screeching, rummaging in blood?

Eventually I took the priest's advice and waited in the presbytery, where I passed the time reading his research on local vendettas.

The last recorded vendetta began with a fight over a straying donkey, I read, *and led to three prison sentences, five murders, and wholesale street fighting.* And then: *To a Corsican, a vendetta is a "misfortune" imposed by destiny. Its execution is the sacred duty of the victimized family. A man who shirks his duty is disgraced and ostracized. He has to kill or live in exile. If there is no man available, a woman must take on the role of executioner in order to uphold the honor of her family.*

Was this a vendetta? Had Sybilia killed to redress some grievance, real or imagined? Absurd. I was out of my depth. Foolishly I had imagined that her Corsican ways had been extinguished together with those ugly black clothes I had persuaded her to burn in the furnace at the bottom of her garden. Until now I had seen only the fair side of her: a sweet and generous woman who endured her humble role with dignity and patience. She was intelligent, cultured, and kind, but she was also Corsican, and in her blood ran the intense passions of her race.

It was a long day as I weighed the pros and cons and speculated on her possible sentence. Against all reason, I had a strong instinct of Sybilia's right. Somehow I had to get her through the mountains to safety. She deserved a fair trial, and I intended to make sure that she got one.

CHAPTER 3

I'll never forget that god-awful evening as I waited for Sybilia, crouched uncomfortably on the marble edge of a grave among the tombstones and the waxed flowers in glass domes. As nine o'clock became ten and then ten-thirty, I became increasingly frightened. I was about to flee from a scruffy, vengeful mob—armed to the teeth—through the maquis, dragging the village whore, now a murderess, on the priest's bad-tempered donkey. For Christ's sake! It should have been funny, but instead it was tragic.

Why? Why had she done it? Pointless to waste time in fruitless conjecture, yet these questions plagued me, and the priest's words kept ringing in my head like a disturbing melody that could not be banished. For the first time, I felt acutely aware of the sinister and oppressive quality of the mourners' cries. When the villagers' identities merged in anger, I feared them. This trait in the Corsican psyche was like the dark side of the moon: ancient, unknown, an untamed wild creature, always there, lying dormant, waiting for the call. Satan's beast! Right now it was lusting for Sybilia's blood. Strange how mutual hate could bind men irrevocably, yet love could not.

Eventually the village elders lifted the corpse onto their shoulders and walked toward a house at the end of the square, the mourners trailing behind.

At last they were gone. Peace! I could hear the birds singing. It was a glorious evening, fitting recompense for the intolerable heat of the day. The soft breeze was carrying the fragrance of sea air mingled with the pungent scent of the maquis, while the musky tang of dew on earth and grass drifted toward me, wafting away the stench of blood. From a nearby house came the welcome odor of spiced mutton boiling in olive oil to remind me that I had not eaten since early that day.

The full moon was rising. Chunky granite peaks were silhouetted starkly against the brilliant moonlit sky. The full moon would not help us. I began to feel increasingly scared of the journey ahead. But why was she taking so long?

Time to get on with it, I decided. I would prise her out of the sacristy. I stood up, walked slowly to the door, and hesitated there. It was then that a brick hurtled past my head and chipped the plaster beside me. I dived headlong into the church.

Sybilia was inside. White and drawn and obviously terrified, she was struggling with the priest, who was showing a ferocious strength. Her forehead was damp with sweat, her long brown hair had come loose in the fight and was tumbling about her face and shoulders.

"Thank God you've come," he gasped. "She wants to go out there onto the steps. They'll kill her, and she knows it."

Sybilia was clawing at the pew, trying to free herself.

"For the love of God, help me get her through the sacristy door. The donkey's waiting. There's no more time . . . they're coming back to kill her." The priest broke off as a brick smashed through the stained-glass window. From outside came ominous shouts, marching feet, and the rhythmic hammering of rifle butts.

"Leave me," she wailed, drowning out his voice. "I do not want to be rescued. If I did, there's nowhere to go."

"I'm not rescuing you," I said softly. "Only escorting you to the nearest police station." Then I saw the terror in her eyes, and I understood. She had welcomed oblivion in the guise of rough and ready Corsican justice, quickly administered. The prospect of prison, a public trial and the guillotine waiting at the end of it, appalled her.

Compassion touched me. I cupped her face in my hands and forced her to look at me. "Sybilia, listen to me. You have one murder on your conscience. There'll be more unless you come now."

Too late! The church door crashed open. As the mob surged forward we thrust her through the sacristy and onto the donkey.

I heard an owl cry, and for a split second there was an uncanny hush as frogs and cicadas were silenced. Then shots cracked around us. The donkey reared up and bolted across the yard into the maquis.

CHAPTER 4

There sat Sybilia, drenched in moonlight, a moving target that bumped and swayed on the galloping donkey while I skidded behind on the dew-wet path, slippery as moss. The noise was alarming: the donkey braying with fear, the clip-clop of its hoofs on crackling sticks and tumbling stones, and my own heavy footfalls. The volley of shots fired toward us every few seconds seemed like physical blows.

At a steep turn in the track Sybilia fell. For a horrified moment I thought she'd been shot. I flung myself beside her, searching for blood, but she was only stunned. I dragged her into the dense maquis and clapped my hand over her mouth. Shortly afterward the villagers rushed past after the fleeing donkey, which was out of sight, thank God.

I waited, listening. There was no one around. I had a plan of sorts. We would deceive the villagers by avoiding the only road out of Taita. Instead we would double back and climb the mountainous slopes through the maquis toward the forest. From there on the going would be easier as we skirted the trees. Later we would have to cross the rough mountain pass to the east. There was a new road ten miles beyond it, and from there we'd probably be able to hitch a lift to Bastia.

If this should fail . . . The thought was chilling, but I had another emergency plan as a last resort.

Eventually I pulled Sybilia to her feet, and we began to force our way through the tangled undergrowth. At first it was not too bad because we were following the route of my earlier exploratory digs, which roughly encircled the lake and village. Higher up the bush became all but impenetrable. We had to stumble around huge boulders and crawl through thickets. It took longer than I'd expected. Several more shots rang out, but in the distance. I was sure that the villagers were firing haphazardly into the maquis. After a while the shots came toward us again. Presumably they'd caught up with the donkey and worked out what we had done. That was too bad.

After an hour we saw the lights of Taita far below and realized we'd made pretty good headway. We'd both gotten our second wind and weren't so breathless as when we started out.

Then, toward midnight, I heard the pounding of feet on the path below. They were too close. I flung myself down, pulling Sybilia with me. There were angry shouts, a great deal of whistling, but no one seemed to know where we were, so eventually we kept on climbing.

By two A.M. a cold front had risen from the sea and thick clouds covered the western sky. It would take some time before the clouds concealed the moon, I figured, but when they did it would be safer.

Sybilia was looking dreadful. Even in the moonlight I could see that she was completely bushed. Her face was smeared with mud, and her arms and legs were scratched; there was a long tear in her skirt, and one heel had been torn off her sandal. She was drenched, and her hair was tangled with twigs and leaves. I knew I should try to push her harder, but instead I wrapped my arms around her and tried to comfort her. I pulled the twigs and leaves out of her hair, rubbed her cold hands, and whispered words of encouragement. I didn't succeed at all. It seemed that nothing would ever comfort her again. I, too, was filled with a sense of impending doom.

There was a tall boulder nearby. I pushed her into the shadows and climbed up to check our route. What the hell was going on? For a moment I couldn't figure it out. The maquis was brilliant with lights strung out in a semicircle below us. Then I heard the thuds and realized the villagers were beating their way through the maquis, just as they hunted wild boars. There were no lights above us. Safety seemed to lie that way, but for how long?

Slithering down, I grabbed Sybilia and hurried her forward. In spite of her exhaustion, there was no fear on her face, only a passive acceptance of death. It was that expression more than anything else that alarmed me. I grabbed her arm so tightly she winced, and I thrust her forward. "Faster," I muttered.

An hour later we reached the upper limit of the maquis. From here on the shrubs and trees gave way to bare granite slopes and boulders. Sybilia wanted to rest, but that would be suicide. I was about to push her ahead when I noticed a torch flickering behind a rock. As I pulled her back behind a bush, I heard the low hoot of an owl, but no bird ever called quite so melodiously. The sound set my heart hammering and my skin crawling.

We'd been seen! I was sure of that. Who were they? Perhaps shepherds? But no. We were too high for grazing. Besides, shepherds slept at night. There were no predators here, except men. Glancing uneasily at Sybilia I realized that she, too, had seen them.

"They seem to know where we're heading," I said softly.

"They hunt boar, don't they?" She shrugged helplessly and buried her face in her hands.

"We'll go back. . . ." I gestured behind us vaguely. "Deeper into the maquis. They'll never flush us out."

Sybilia caught hold of my arm, pulling me back toward her. "Jock! Save yourself," she whispered. Her eyes were glittering with fear, her face white and wretched. "Please go ahead. Yes, do that for me. I implore you. I shall give myself up to them. It's best. Listen to me, Jock. I don't want to go to prison. Besides, we can't escape from them, and all this has nothing to do with you."

"You're wasting time. Keep moving." I caught hold of her arm and hauled her along behind me.

It was almost three A.M. Our clothes were in shreds from pushing aside a multitude of thorny bushes. For the past few hours we had been moving through the maquis in a northerly direction. If we did not make the pass tonight, Sybilia would be exhausted by the following evening. We'd gone some distance since I saw the lights. I decided it was time to take another look. When we passed the next tall rocky hill, I hauled myself up the slippery side of a tall rock to set their bearings, pausing there to catch my breath.

The first gunshot was thunderous. It shook the night like a thunderclap. The rock beside me exploded in a spray of earth and dust. A second shot followed. For a split second I was completely paralyzed with shock. Then I flung myself down and half climbed, half fell to the ground.

Sybilia cried out. Looking down, I noticed blood spurting down my shirt.

"It's only a scratch," I gasped, pressing one hand over my arm. Scratch or not, it hurt like hell. "They're moving in. We're almost surrounded. We'll have to go back."

We ran headlong down the path, tripping, falling, gasping as shots peppered the bush around us. I was more frightened than I had ever been. We were being hunted like animals, and desperate like animals we retraced our footsteps, time and again, hour after hour, as we tried to elude the hunters. I lost all idea of time. I only knew that we must keep moving away from the noise of men firing and their shrill whistles, toward the only place of safety I could think of.

Later—I had no idea how much later—immense thunderclouds obscured the moon as the storm moved overhead.

At long last I slowed our pace. It would be almost impossible to take reasonable aim in the darkness, I reckoned. I felt we stood a far better chance now that we were no longer so exposed.

A sudden streak of lightning transformed the darkness into daylight, and in that split second I saw the site of my excavations. The towering, massive faces of ancient warriors looked down on me, lifelike and menacing in the weird, surrealistic light. If I could only reach the cave, we'd stand a chance, I thought gratefully. The site had been chosen by primitive man to withstand all types of siege, and who was I to argue with their sense of self-preservation? I had a rifle and ammunition in the cave, which I kept for the occasional chance sighting of wild boar. If only we could reach the ruins, I could keep her there in safety for days until the police came for her.

So close! *But we still had to cross the river, and there was no cover. We'd make an easy target.*

That thought brought the blood hammering in my chest.

It was then that I heard the pounding of many footsteps close behind us. I grabbed Sybilia's arm, but she would not move. She seemed to be frozen to the ground.

Frantic now, I picked her up bodily and flung her over my shoulder, plunged into the ice-cold river, and began slipping and slithering over the pebbles and boulders. Twice I almost lost my footing against the force of the stream but managed to catch my balance again.

We were exposed, horribly vulnerable! I heard another shot. It came from below this time. Crouching over, I stumbled through the deepening water. A sudden terrible chilling pain slashed across my thigh. I lurched forward and almost collapsed, but if I fell now, we would die. Was I to be hunted and shot down by the very people I was writing about? This was madness. Insane! A burning anger kindled in me and flared up as I stumbled on through the rushing water.

Providence or coincidence saved us. I've never known which, but as we reached the riverbank the rain fell, a solid mass of water that poured over us. It pulverized the ground, beating on bushes and rocks, churning the earth to mud in seconds.

The villagers were firing haphazardly now. Visibility was almost nil, but I knew the way to my excavation blindfolded. As I climbed the last bank, I remembered the priest's words: "There are many people in this village who would sleep easier if she were dead. They will use this vendetta as an excuse to kill her."

I reached the safety of the cave, dumped Sybilia on the floor, grabbed my gun, and began firing into the maquis. I reloaded and fired again. At last the lights began to move away. The villagers were leaving.

Sybilia was shocked but unharmed, and I'd escaped with only flesh wounds, although they hurt like hell.

A disturbing thought came to me as I bandaged my wounds: I realized I'd been deceived by the picturesque nature of the terrain. Now I saw the island with a new awareness. It was a harsh, unforgiving land, not to be underestimated, and I had violated its hidden places. In return I was being drawn into the danger and the deep emotional content of a Corsican vendetta.

CHAPTER 5

The funeral service had been held in a packed church with half the mourners overflowing into the square. Now it was over, and as Father Andrews led the coffin to the graveyard, his face was pinched and gray. He looked a broken man, and I knew why. He had christened, married, or buried most of the villagers; listened to their confessions, healed their quarrels. He thought they trusted him. But Sybilia, whom he loved as a daughter, had committed murder and put herself beyond redemption with her refusal to confess or repent.

Thrust forward by the momentum of the crowd, I, too, emerged from the whispering alcoves into the sun. The grass glittered with a billion dewdrops, flowers thrust out their petals to welcome the bees, and the air vibrated with gratitude.

Relieved to be outside, I breathed deeply. Suddenly I was overcome with sadness for Sybilia. It was she who had given me this sensuous love of nature. She had her vision of the earth—a fruitful, living mother, suckling the seeds of flowers and man, lending them substance to grow into forms of infinite beauty. She loved life. She would never kill any living thing, not even a caterpiller or an ant. Was all that a sham? Did that gentle face harbor the mind of a killer? Surely not.

"The bones that lie in the dust shall thrill with joy before the Lord," the priest read as he led the throng.

Children raced around the flower beds until they were brought to heel by scowls and threats. Then they too tagged along at the back of the procession.

I watched the villagers file past me: black-clad figures with stony faces and angry eyes.

They all know why she killed Rocca. That's why they want her dead.

I gazed at them each in turn as they took their places

around the empty grave. Maria Rocca, Xavier's widow, pale and sorrowful, was sobbing into her handkerchief. Earlier that morning she had told me that she despised Sybilia for bringing disgrace and grief to the family.

The bearers set the coffin at the side of the grave to a chorus of angry mutters. With a piercing shriek the *voceri* launched into her own sermon of vengeance and blood, but Father Andrews silenced her with a scathing glance. I could not help admiring him. His flock were a stubborn, obstinate people, forever harking back to ancient superstitions and their own brand of sledgehammer justice. They were all practicing Christians, but they were also Corsicans.

As the mourners stepped forward to nail down the coffin, I gazed at Xavier Rocca for the last time. In an island renowned for bravery, he had outshone them all. As the village headman he had ruled the villagers according to his traditions. It was men like Xavier Rocca who had made the work of the Catholic church and the French police a nightmare in Corsica.

Footsteps on cobbles! As the priest commenced his sermon an icy shiver of fear ran down my back. I scanned the mourners. Not a rifle among them, nor a knife, as far as I could see. Father Andrews had refused to perform the funeral service until they heeded his plea to come unarmed. They had grudgingly agreed.

"We ask Thee, O Lord, to show mercy to Thy servant who is dead, that he be not made to suffer for any wrong he may have done; for he always desired to do Thy will . . ."

The priest did not falter as Inspector Hiller crossed the cobbled square. He was on time, just as we had arranged, but accompanied by six well-armed policemen. Hiller had never been known to take a chance. The villagers turned their backs on the inspector. Their eyes registered contempt. Not a man in Taita would lift his hat to Rene Hiller. Hiller, however, pretended not to notice the subtle insults as he hung around behind the mourners.

A murmur of rebellion ran through the crowd, but Father Andrews quelled it with a frown and a gesture.

"Grant, O God, that while we lament the departure of this Thy servant, we may always remember that we are most certainly to follow him . . ."

I glanced across the mound of flowers to Sybilia's son, Jules Rocca, who was staring moodily at his feet. Jules had arrived from Ajaccio that morning. He and I were the only ones not wearing black. Like me, he had tied a black scarf around his arm. Jules was a good-looking boy, but he was scowling furiously, and his lips were pulled into a tight line. He looked agonized. The boy had adored his grandfather, and in other circumstances he would have gone after the killer. There was no sign of Ursuline, his half sister. She was a novice in a French convent, and presumably she had not yet learned about Rocca's death.

"Have mercy on me, O God, as Thou art ever rich in mercy; in the abundance of Thy compassion, blot out the record of my misdeeds. Wash me clean, cleaner yet, from my guilt, purge me of my sin."

Father Andrews ended the service, but the mourners hung around as if sensing there was more drama to be wrung out of the morning. There was a sudden silence. A tensing in the crowd. All eyes turned as Sybilia appeared dramatically at the edge of the trees. I moved closer to the rifle I had hidden in a neighboring grave earlier that morning and watched for any sudden movement in the crowd.

Smoothing the leaves out of her hair, Sybilia walked slowly through the long grass, past the gate, the flowers, and the trim graves, unhesitatingly toward Hiller. She was wearing the same blouse and skirt she had worn when she'd fled into the maquis. Crumpled and bedraggled, she retained her innate dignity.

The mourners parted reluctantly as she approached, leaving a path through the crowd. The police, who were clearly nervous, fingered their guns.

"I am here," Sybilia said to Hiller, "to give myself up to your French justice."

Angry mutters from the crowd; eyes blazing hatred; there was a sudden shout, shrill and violent, from the *voceri*: "Death to the whore."

Against the mourners' grumbles, the priest could hardly hear Hiller's mumbled arrest, but he heard Sybilia's answer, which rang out loud and clear:

"I did not murder Xavier Rocca. I executed him." Then she swept past, looking proud and uncompromising, as she always did.

I noticed the brave, squared shoulders, her head held high, and her last imploring glance toward her family as they led her away.

* * *

Later, when the crowd had dispersed, Father Andrews and I leaned over the stone wall at the perimeter of the square, watching the distant wisp of dust from the police vehicle that was taking Sybilia to Ajaccio.

I said: "I have to know why she did it."

Father Andrews shook his head. "Jock, my friend"—he put his hand on my shoulder—"I can't reveal the secrets of the confessional, not even to you."

"Without a defense she doesn't stand a chance," I told him angrily. "Can't you see it's your duty to help her?"

"I'll do all I can," he said. "The poor, poor lassie." He broke off and ran his hand over his face in a gesture of despair. "She has no chance anyway. Or so Hiller believes."

While the priest's voice droned on, I was trying to come to a decision. I had finished my work here. Ahead of me lay the rewards of years of hard work. Was I to throw away my career to help a woman whom I could only call my friend? Looking back, I'm ashamed that it took me so long.

"Sybilia will be made an example to deter islanders from resurrecting their age-old system of retribution," the priest said. He sighed. "Hiller says the prosecution intends pressing for capital punishment."

How can I return to Boston as I planned and leave Sybilia to her fate? She's alive because of me. When I handed her over for trial, I promised to do my best to help her. But how? With sympathy and false hopes while the conveyor belt of French justice bears her inexorably to the guillotine?

"I may delay my departure a little after all," I said slowly. "But I don't know how I can help her."

"You'll have to dig up the past." Father Andrews gave a sly smile. "After all, that's your trade, isn't it?

"Funny how you get reminded of things," he went on after a long silence. "That look on her face when Hiller took her away . . . defiant, haughty, but terrified nonetheless, that's just how she looked when I welcomed her to Taita as a young and frightened bride."

As he turned away, I heard him mutter: "Oh, heavenly Father, when is the twenty-year-old past to be allowed to die?"

PART II

CHAPTER 6

Taita, July 13, 1939

Sybilia felt light-headed that morning as she set out for Taita from her home in Chiornia. Not sad, really, or even scared, she comforted herself. Why should she be scared? This could not be happening to her, not to Sybilia Silvani, favorite of the nuns at the convent, school prefect, soloist in the choir, top student in English, aged sixteen years and two months. Oh, no, this nightmare journey on the back of an evil-tempered mule could not be real. She felt safe inside her cocoon of unreality.

As if in a dream, she glanced from side to side as they passed through the Tetti forest. Images flashed past, blurred by her veil: dappled light among patches of mist; thick glades of chestnut trees that darkened the road with their dense foliage; a family of fat pigs, gorged on nuts and berries, wallowing in a mud pool.

People were calling. Laughter flashed among them like sunlight through the branches overhead. She heard her father's voice, and he too seemed to have nothing better to do than to joke with his friends.

Blessed Mary, help me. Make all this go away.

Only a week ago she had been so blissfully unaware that her world could turn upside down. She had been looking forward to another year at school. Mama had insisted. Then, only last week, Papa had informed them of his plans. Mama had cried, but Sybilia had stood there dry-eyed. The truth was she had felt too stunned to cry. Until then she had imagined that her father loved her. From this day on, Sybilia vowed, she would never speak to him again.

As for Michel, her bridegroom, she did not even know what he looked like. When she'd met him for the first time early that morning, she had been too depressed and too shy even to glance at him, but she knew he was there behind her, trudging along in this ridiculous wedding procession, together with her mother, her four brothers, six aunts, and their husbands and children, each carrying a part of her trousseau.

I mustn't cry. It's not real at all. Just a bad dream. It will pass.

Shortly afterward the winding gravel road left the forest and zigzagged steeply up into the mountains. Now at last the mist seemed to be lifting as they reached a higher altitude. It was becoming hot, for it was nearly noon. The jokes and gibes had ceased; in turn there was panting breath, an occasional curse as a foot slipped on loose gravel. As for the women, they winced and crackled in their Sunday black and kept their eyes fastened on the treacherous path. Best shoes were never made for walks like this, they grumbled quietly.

To the French born and bred Madame Silvani, the long walk was a torment. She could hardly bear to look at her poor daughter, dangling on the back of that obscene donkey. Sybilia was a tall girl with fine bone structure and delicate features that belied her strength. Until last year she had been as thin as a beanpole, but lately her breasts had grown and her hips had become rounded, her glance more womanly. She had been so proud of her, and then, at the very first glimpse of womanhood, her husband, Claude, had used her as a bargain to curry favor with Xavier Rocca, a local leader in the powerful National Front party. It was so bitterly unfair. She should never have married a Corsican. Corsica was a man's world, and she hated it. She had always borne the restrictions and humiliations of being female with fortitude and compliance, but there must have been a spark of rebellion there, all the same, she thought guiltily, for she had encouraged her daughter, Sybilia, to think for herself and to expect no less from life than her four brothers. They were all so much alike: fiercely independent, outspoken, proud, headstrong, brave. Each quality was a virtue for a boy but a tragedy for a girl.

She had not spoken to Claude for days. Not since he had returned drunk to the house to announce his evil plans. He and his hunting friends had sealed her daughter's fate without even consulting her. She had stormed and pleaded for hours, but Claude would not give in. He had given his word, he said. And that was that. "It's a good match," he had muttered in the face of her fury. "Xavier Rocca is a big landowner, he's headman of the village and highly regarded in the Nationalist movement. He only has one son, and so he wants to ally himself to our family." There was a trace of satisfaction in his voice. "Rich in men" was a common-enough phrase to find in Corsican documents, and God knew she had the four best sons in Chiornia.

"But you have no right to send her away so young and unprepared," she had persisted.

"And what did six years in a convent prepare her for, may I ask?"

"She wants to be a teacher. . . ."

"The boys get an education—she gets a dowry," he had said, and that was that.

There was no point in arguing. Men controlled the family. Personal inclinations had no place in the Corsican concept of marriage, and young people were frequently called upon to sacrifice their feelings in the interests of the family.

She had betrayed her daughter. She knew that. Sybilia was strong and fearless enough to cope with almost any calamity, except being female.

The sun broke through the mist, and the village of Taita was suddenly visible high above: a cluster of stone houses clinging to a ridge poised over a yawning chasm of granite rock from which a waterfall, shining like a ribbon of light, fell to the moon-shaped lake below.

Below the village, narrow strips of terraces had been hewn out of rock. They were separated by thick walls of stones, now overgrown with weeds and shrubs. The strips between had been haphazardly cultivated, so that patches of farmed land were interspersed with weeds, olives, citrus trees, grass for the occasional donkey, or simply abandoned to the maquis.

Winding up through the terraces was the only road, providing a tortuous ascent to the village. Unexpectedly the mist thickened and Taita was lost to sight. The members of the wedding party rubbed their eyes and wondered if they had been victims of a mirage. God knew they were tired enough and thirsty enough, but then Xavier Rocca, who was several paces ahead, called out: "That's it, then. That's Taita for you. The loveliest village in all of Corsica. Today she's shy, she's hiding behind a veil of white, just like this young bride. It's an omen to welcome her. That's what it is."

He slapped his mule, Pierre, on the rump, and the animal lowered his ears and kicked his back legs in temper.

Sybilia shuddered. It was becoming impossible to avoid reality in the face of so many physical discomforts. When they had seated her on the mule dressed in her family's satin bridal gown and veil, she had prayed that she would die of misery, that she would never reach the hated village, never see her miserable bridegroom, never endure the coming night with the humiliation and pain that she had been warned about. But now, compared with her awful aches and pains, even her grief and dread had taken a backseat. The gown was too tight around her bust, too close under her arms, it pulled and pinched and made the heat intolerable. A cloud of horseflies buzzed around her veil and bit her bare legs, but far worse was the wretched blanket, which had rubbed blisters on the tender skin inside her thighs. At this moment it felt as if she had been set alight there, and she wondered dismally how she would endure another hour of it. She kicked out as another fly landed a stinging bite on her ankle, and Pierre laid back his ears and brayed angrily.

It was a good six-hour walk from Chiornia to Taita. The wedding party had left at eight that morning, and now they were all tired and irritable. Only Xavier Rocca felt happy as he half pulled, half coaxed the obstinate Pierre with his precious bundle toward home. Xavier was a giant of a man, towering head and shoulders over the other villagers, strong as an ox and twice as cunning. He was the best hunter in the district, and for endurance no one could touch him. When he was young he had joined the French navy and quickly learned that he was what women considered handsome, with his crystal-clear blue eyes, wavy black hair, and regular features. Now, at forty-three, his hair was slightly gray, but he looked much the same as he always had. Or so he thought.

His hand strayed up to his mustache, and he gently twirled the end of it. Plenty of hard work, plenty of fun, plenty of women, but he kept his secrets away from Maria. Scandal had never touched the village of Taita.

He was smiling, blue eyes twinkling, and he felt the good humor and love of his fellow men bubbling out in great waves. He wanted to embrace every member of the wedding party. Right now he could embrace the whole world. He had pulled off a coup, and he knew it. The Silvanis owned a long strip of land next to his own, higher up the mountain, where their flocks were pastured in the summer months. It bordered a small mountain lake, which he had viewed with a covetous eye for many years. Silvani had not taken much persuasion to let it go with his daughter, only too glad to ally his family with that of the powerful Roccas. Then there was the girl herself to be considered. She was well educated and a rare beauty. Just the girl for his son. If anything could turn Michel into a man, she would.

For a moment his smile faded as he thought about the boy. Bad blood, he muttered. He had known when he married her that Maria was wrong in the head—a *mazzeri*, they called her in the village—harbinger of death, and some believed the cause of it. Huh! Superstitious nonsense. Xavier did not believe in witchcraft, nor in second sight, nor in his wife's endless conversations with the dead, but he had endured her babbling for these past twenty years with remarkable patience. When Xavier struck a bargain, his word was his bond. He had married Maria in full possession of the facts, only too pleased to lay his hands on her extensive inheritance.

He shrugged off his dismal thoughts and quickened his pace. This was not a day for gloom. It was long past drinking time, and he was thirsty. The celebrations would start right after the church ceremony. Yet another waste of good drinking time. He knew the villagers were astonished that he had given in to this earnest young priest from foreign parts who understood so little of Corsican ways. Well, he had, and with good reason to do so, which he was not about to divulge.

The sun was breaking through again. Armfuls of wildflowers lined their route, the chestnut harvest was bountiful this year, and the pigs and goats were bursting their bellies. There was no better place than Corsica, no place so beautiful. He should know. Hadn't he traveled the world?

CHAPTER 7

The Church of St. Augustine was only two hundred years old, an infant in terms of Corsican architecture. It was built of solid stone blocks, faced with expertly cut slabs of yellowish granite, meticulously fitted together. With its vaulted ceiling and superimposed arches and little domed lantern atop, the church was a masterpiece of mathematical precision in stonemasonry. It was a small church. There were no famous works of art here, but several lovely old wood carvings and statues painted in blue and white and gilt, and an ornate altarpiece by some long-forgotten master sculptor. Finest of them all was the painted statue of St. Augustine of Hippo, symbol of sinners, severe and imposing in his bishop's robes, his face as white as chalk.

Today the church was decked with flowers in readiness for the wedding, and Father Andrews was wearing his gold alb, cope, and stole that set off his black hair and his dark skin. In spite of his coloring no one could mistake him for anything other than Irish. His features were too angular, with pointed nose and chin and wide cheekbones sloping to a full, sensuous mouth. His eyebrows were black and bushy, and they almost met over his deep-set, serious eyes, which were of an indeterminate shade of brownish green that seemed to change with the light. At times he looked shy and young, and then his eyes could flash with indignation and he would look years older and downright intimidating.

Father Andrews had been in Taita for just seven months, on an eighteen-month visit to further his research. While here, he was supposed to act as assistant to the Taitan parish priest, Father Delon, but four months ago the old man had suffered a stroke, and now the work had fallen on the young priest's shoulders. There was little time left for his research. He was young and idealistic, and he reckoned that the practical experience he would gather here would be invaluable. Perhaps this was the only chance he would ever have to work with real people, for, as a brilliant scholar, he was destined for a research job at the Vatican.

This was his first wedding, and he was overanxious. It was past one P.M., and for the fifth time that day he climbed the old stone spiral staircase to the bell tower, where there was an uninterrupted view for miles around. Now that the mist was drifting away, he could see a cloud of yellow dust hovering over the start of the last steep climb to Taita.

"To be sure it's them," he whispered gratefully. Only the villagers came this way, and no other large group was expected. As he made the sign of the cross, he admitted to himself for the first time that he had never believed the wedding would take place at all.

In Taita he had quickly learned that the head of the family was far more powerful than either the Church or the French authorities. Xavier Rocca was a man of considerable influence. He had not attended church since his mother's funeral. Rocca had intended that his son and bride would be married in the traditional Corsican manner, where the girl was simply summoned by her father to meet her groom in the house of her parents. At this meeting they would kiss in the presence of relatives, the girl would hand the groom a plate of fritelli (fritters made from chestnut flour), and shortly afterward the wedding party settled down to munch fritelli while the groom led his bride into her room and promptly consummated the marriage.

This was indeed a coldhearted, heathen practice that offended Father Andrews's sentimental Irish heart, so he had waylaid Rocca one afternoon some distance from Taita and trailed behind him pleading for a decent marriage for the young couple. Inexplicably Xavier had put up very little opposition, and the wedding had been arranged for noon that day.

Ah, well, Father Andrews smiled as he looked at his watch. Pointless to expect the Corsicans to be on time. Lucky they were coming at all.

When he clattered down the steps to the church, he was surprised to see Rocca's wife walking into the nave with an armful of tatty shrubs that were dropping bits of bark and dried leaves on his spotless flagstones. She was touched in the head, he'd decided from her strange, babbling weekly confessions, yet she had her moments of lucidity. Presumably this was not one of them. He summoned an altar boy to take care of the mess and grabbed the bundle.

"It's really kind of you, madame," he said in his slow but accurate French. Then he paused suddenly and looked at her, really looked at her for the first time. She had the most extraordinarily beautiful yet piercing eyes of bright blue, deep-set in an ugly face with skin the texture and color of gravel. He felt he had caught a glimpse of a once beautiful woman trapped in the shell of an old and ugly hag. For a moment he was quite stunned with compassion.

"Wildflowers," she was stammering. "So much more beautiful than the cultivated ones—they are natural, you see, whereas these . . ." She gestured contemptuously toward the magnificent floral arrangements that he had personally supervised.

"Maybe you're right," he acknowledged grudgingly.

For a moment Maria forgot her shyness and smiled winsomely, but suddenly remembering her discolored teeth and the gap on one side, she clapped a hand over her mouth and backed away.

"This is a big day for you, Madame Rocca," Father Andrews began again more jovially. "They'll be here within the hour."

Within the hour! The thought appalled Maria. Was everything going to be all right? What about the cat? she thought. Why had she forgotten the cat when she laid the food on the table? She had worked so hard for days. She had no daughters to help her, and lately she kept forgetting what she was doing. Her mind wandered around like a butterfly, stopping here and there but never anyplace for long enough. She seemed to remember her mother saying the very same thing, yet surely she was much older then—in her eighties—at that great age you can be excused for a wandering mind. She broke off, remembering the day her mother forgot they were going to the plot to dig onions and instead picked a huge bunch of lavender and brought it back to the kitchen. How they had laughed at her, but she had pretended it was to keep the flies out of the kitchen—and it worked.

"It really does work," she said earnestly to the puzzled young priest. "Lavender keeps the flies away. I've proved it myself many times, but there now, I've forgotten the cat again."

She hurried away, and Father Andrews watched her cross the square, a frown on his forehead. How would she cope with a daughter-in-law in the house? Was she really as batty as she seemed, he wondered, or just shy and absentminded?

The Rocca house was an imposing fortress of granite, four stories high, towering on the edge of the precipice that overlooked the lake. Like the rest of Taita, it had been built five hundred years ago by the industrious Genoese, with walls two feet thick and huge timber doors and shutters.

From the outside it looked wretched, with peeling plaster, badly discolored paint, and the doors and shutters in an advanced state of decay. Maria never looked at the outside, but only at the interior, which was always spotless. She gazed with satisfaction at the wooden floors polished to a mirror surface, freshly painted walls, hand-embroidered muslin hung at every window, and the well-made furniture. She had time for a last-minute inspection, she decided.

The basement, which was the ground floor at the back, contained a wood stove for heating water, for here they did the washing and bathed in a large copper tub. Directly above, up a broad flight of stone stairs, was the kitchen.

The kitchen led into the parlor, which was Maria's pride and joy. It was a big room with an oval cherrywood dining room table, inherited from her mother, and twelve chairs of pine. Cushions of her own embroidery were placed on the seats and on the long blue couch. Family photographs hung on the walls around a framed reproduction of a painting of Mount Cinto by Edward Lear, which she had once found in an antiques shop in Ajaccio and bought because it so resembled the view from her bedroom window. On the marble mantelpiece was a statue of the Virgin Mary. An old upright piano that had belonged to her mother stood next to the door. Today, however, the room was crowded with trestle tables laden with food.

The floor above the living room contained two rooms, one huge main bedroom and Xavier's private den. Above that was the attic of two large rooms, which had been converted into a flat for Sybilia and Michel. All the ceilings of the house were of yellow timbers, which shone golden at night in the glow from the oil lamps.

Maria gazed lovingly at the attic flat, which looked so inviting. There were two rooms. The first was the couple's own parlor, with a big couch she had bartered for with the Pinellis in return for oil and a sheep. There were also two hard-backed wooden chairs with cushions she had made to soften the seats, a small oak table, a desk, an open grate, and a bookcase for Michel's books. The bedroom was filled with the furniture from Michel's room, except for the bed, which was a double brass bedstead covered in knobs with a thick mattress of goose down and a feather bolster. She had even given the bride her own dressing table, reasoning that it would give her pleasure. The girl would bring her own linen, naturally, but meantime she had loaned some of her own, only the best, of course. She had filled stone vases with fragrant herbs gathered in the maquis, and the rooms were filled with their pungent scent.

Would she be happy here? Would she be good to Michel? Maria knew very little about this young girl, Sybilia, who was about to be thrust into her household, other than listening to Xavier boasting about the fields she was adding to the family fortune.

Marriages were arranged among the men of the family, and she had not expected to be consulted. Xavier kept his peace. He was not a man to confide in anyone. Happy-go-lucky with his friends, he acted out the part of the brave, reckless Corsican. Brave he was, she admitted, but reckless? Never! Behind the genial grin was a devious, closemouthed man whose first consideration was keeping up appearances.

Well, she had no cause to complain about arranged marriages. Suddenly she was tossed back in time. She was a young and prudish girl, not yet eighteen but strong-willed and determined to enter a convent. It was springtime. A lovely spring. Xavier Rocca, on leave from the navy and looking dashing in his French pom-pom, had grabbed her, pulled up her veil, and kissed her on the church steps in full view of the entire village. An unforgivable act in Corsican society, which had compromised her entirely and should have cost him his life. He had pleaded ignorance, having been abroad for so long. He had forgotten he was in Corsica, he had lied.

So they were married at once. How her mother had cried, while her father had raged at the dowry Xavier had cheekily demanded. Later, of course, she had discovered that Xavier Rocca never made mistakes, but she had not regretted marrying him.

Oh, her head! If only it did not ache so much. These blinding headaches to which she was so prone filled her with anxiety, for they often led to her nightmares. Oh, God! Surely not today? She must pull herself together.

All of a sudden she remembered the food and clattered down the stairs in a rush. Yes, she was right, there was a chicken missing, and only a short search revealed the greasy trail where the cat had dragged it into the garden. Fortunately there was plenty, but if the evidence of the theft was still around when Xavier arrived, the cat's head would leave its shoulders.

On the spur of the moment she decided to throw the carcass farther away from the house, but the cat, snarling and angry, fled with it into a corner of nettles. Maria shrugged and hurried back to the house.

She was about to cross the square to the church when she felt a sudden surge of pain in her temples. The light seemed blinding, and as she gasped and clapped her hands over her eyes, she heard the sudden beating of a drum.

She winced, clasped her ears, and hurried faster. *Mary, Mother of Jesus, help me. Help me. Not today. Not on my son's wedding day.*

The sound of the drums encompassed her, all-embracing, inescapable. It seemed to originate from the mountains, but it was echoing in her head. The echoes hurt, and there was no escape. She groaned quietly and collapsed on the old stone bench by the fountain. *Oh, God, help me!*

But there was no help for her. The spirits were calling to her, and she must obey the drums, omen of death. Groaning quietly, she stood up and stumbled toward the edge of the square. The weird, gray, misty substance that always accompanied her dreams was drifting down from the mountain slopes, and soon she was able to make out the dim shapes of people walking solemnly through the mist.

She saw Xavier leading the small band of village elders who were carrying the coffin. Their faces were set in lines of anger, not grief. Why? She had to know. They looked tired, unshaven, and unkempt, as if they had all spent several nights in the maquis.

Who was it? She did not want to know, but she was no longer in control. Her feet carried her forward as if sleepwalking, and peering down into the coffin, she saw her son, Michel. She screamed quietly. He was horribly mutilated, his face swollen and disfigured, his eyes blackened. Staggering back, she had time to see his widow, a beautiful girl, in men's khaki jacket and trousers, carrying a rifle, as a man would, and she too was crying. Her sobs were the last thing Maria heard as the vision faded.

Suddenly she was alone.

She staggered back to the fountain and pushed her head into the stream of ice-cold mountain water. "A dream, it was nothing . . . just the ravings of a mad old woman," she muttered, wiping the tears from her cheeks. "It's not real. Never! Never! I should be put away."

She remained there, peering fearfully toward the church, her face filled with dread.

CHAPTER 8

It was after two P.M. before the footsore relatives from Chiornia felt sufficiently refreshed by the fresh fountain water to be shepherded into the church. Shortly afterward the bride was hustled across the square by her parents and brothers. Clutching her skirt and her veil, she hesitated on the last step of the porch and turned toward the west, as if snatching one last glimpse of the forests and valleys of her home. Then she genuflected and with a bowed head walked up the aisle.

Watching her, Father Andrews felt compassion for this trembling figure in the elaborate wedding dress, which was clearly too tight and hideously uncomfortable. She was unusually tall, he noticed, with square shoulders, now drooping disconsolately, a narrow waist, and slender hips. He could see her long, tapered fingers, fidgeting nervously with her bouquet, but the rest of her was a mystery. Her face was hidden under a thick bridal veil. Nevertheless, he noticed her hand stealing up to brush her cheeks dry every few seconds, and beautiful hands they were, too.

Poor lass, he thought, to be married at sixteen when she's never so much as set eyes upon the bridegroom before this morning. "God give her courage," he muttered under his breath. She'd need all she could muster and then some.

He could not help frowning at the groom, who was waiting beside the altar. At twenty-two Michel Rocca was a strange, introverted boy who never came to church and had few friends. He spent his hours wandering alone in the maquis or working on the Rocca land. Some said he had inherited his mother's second sight, but the priest did not believe this. He had certainly inherited her strangely hooded eyes, which no doubt reinforced the rumor. He had long, straight black hair. His features were curiously sharp, with a short pointed nose and sharp high cheekbones. His pale skin, straight black brows, and thin, expressive mouth gave him a strangely elfin appearance. The priest scowled until his brows met across the bridge of his nose, and unexpectedly Michel looked straight at him suspiciously, as if sensing the priest's thoughts. Then his eyes shied as he flushed, and gazed desperately around the church, anywhere except at his bride.

The guests were fidgeting noisily, clearly impatient to get on with the celebrations. With a sigh, Father Andrews launched himself into the marriage service and his sermon. "The art of loving," he began confidently, for his sermon was based on several days' earnest thought and meditation, "is an art which is sadly neglected in this day and age, and strange that it should be so, since love is a word much bandied around by young people the world over nowadays. The young couple standing before us today are here to unite their two families in bonds of kinship, in a marriage which has been arranged for them by their parents in their wisdom. Now, as they set off to build a life together, they should make love their first target, for without love their separate existences will be lonely and barren. But with love even the lowliest task each day will be a joy and they will be truly united. So I say to you, Michel and Sybilia, love God, love the world, and then I promise you this love will flow into your relationship. . . ."

Love, Xavier thought scornfully as he listened to the sermon. Such nonsense this fool of a priest was stuffing into their heads. What part did love play in a Corsican marriage? Romantic love, which he had learned about to his astonishment in his travels, was one of the many sicknesses that was seeping into Corsica from the outside world. There was no such awareness in Corsican traditions. A girl was the property of her husband and his family. All her energies and her desires would be channeled into serving the family. She would expect protection, food and shelter, children, but love? Well, what could you expect from an Irish priest? He could have done without this ceremony, but Michel being the way he was . . . He shrugged off unwelcome thoughts and shifted to a better position on the hard pew.

Sybilia listened to the words in dismay. Love him? How disgusting! It would be a miracle if she did not die of shame. All the world knew what would happen to her tonight. She would have to open her legs and . . . Oh, God—oh, Virgin Mary, save me, help me. . . . Her mother had just told her, in hushed whispers while she rearranged her veil, what she could expect, and not too long after the ceremony, either. Would it hurt too badly? Worse than the donkey ride? Mother had said that it did. But what did the pain matter compared with the shame of it? How would she ever lift up her face in public again?

She was the only person in church that day who was not longing for Father Andrews to finish his long-winded sermon. Let it go on forever, let this ceremony never end, for when it ended . . .

When the priest pronounced them man and wife a few minutes later, the girl stiffened and seemed to shrink into herself. But she recovered and lifted her veil, offering her cheek for the traditional kiss.

It was the priest's turn to be astonished. For the first time in his life he saw real beauty, and he gaped with his mouth open. Her features were lovely: the nose and chin in perfect harmony, the long, graceful sweep of her cheekbones, the lips full and perfectly formed, her eyes set wide apart, huge and candid, like a fawn's. But most remarkable of all was her flawless golden skin, characteristic of the Corsican mountain people. Her hair was brown, shining with reddish glints in the candlelight, but her beauty was more than the sum of these things. It had a great deal to do with the sweet and loving nature that was so clearly stamped upon her face. Truth, beauty, and love personified were standing here before him.

As the organist, Vannina Susini, began the "Wedding March," Sybilia tossed her head proudly and gazed scornfully at the priest and the congregation and all her new relatives. It was a good try, but she could not conceal the grief and fear that were brimming out of her.

CHAPTER 9

Just before the ceremony ended, Xavier slipped out to search for Maria, who was missing as usual. He found her huddled by the fountain, face gray as ash, her eyes haggard.

For once his anger swept over her without any visible effect.

"I heard the drums," she began in the strange, chanting voice she affected after her uncanny visions. "I saw them coming down from the maquis, as real as you stand here now, but in the distance. You were there. . . ."

Xavier stepped back and turned white as death. Maria had never once been wrong, and he had learned to fear her second sight.

"No, not you. You were carrying the coffin on your shoulder as well as a gun. I saw you weeping, and her . . ." She gestured toward the church. "I saw the bride. She's lovely, isn't she?" She bit back a sob. "It was Michel, he'd—" She crumpled.

With a bellow of rage, Xavier caught Maria by her shoulders and shook her violently. "Will you kill your own son, woman?" he cried.

"Not me," she whispered. "Them! It was horrible. . . ."

"You're mad. Pull yourself together, Maria. I tell you this.

If you breathe one word of this nonsense to anyone, you'll be sorry. Now tidy yourself. Be quick. Our guests are coming."

By the time the wedding guests had slapped each other on the back and emerged from the church, Xavier was standing in the square to welcome them to his home.

He flung open the doors with a flourish. The guests trooped down the wide stone passage into the front room and gasped with pleasure. The sight of so much food and wine arranged on the gleaming tables put everyone in a good mood.

Then Vannina Susini fluttered dovelike across the square, and after strutting and cooing and pecking around the table, she puffed out her voluptuous bosom and began pounding out a waltz on Maria's piano, as arranged. Everyone was far too busy eating and drinking to begin dancing. The plates were half-empty and Xavier half-drunk before he grabbed Sybilia and whirled her round the circular space cleared between the furniture.

Xavier Rocca was an excellent dancer, but Sybilia's fear had turned her legs to wood. Besides, she was hampered by her unaccustomed long skirt, so she stumbled and tripped and turned very red in the face, but Xavier kept smiling.

Her thoughts were in turmoil, but uppermost was anger. *I'm not real to him, not real at all. I'm just a thing. A possession, bartered to this monster and tossed to his horrible son like a toy or a doll. Yes, I'm a wooden doll, and that's just what I feel like.*

Doll-like, she handed around the plate of fritelli; woodenly she shook hands with her new relatives, but all the while she hardly knew what she was doing, for she was still in a state of shock.

"Take care of Maria Rocca. She's a witch, a *mazzeri.*" Her brother Dominique grabbed her by the shoulder and hissed in her ear. Then he gave a sly chuckle. "She can order your death whenever she wants. Just whenever you make her angry. That's what the boys here swear. As for your husband . . ." He giggled at the hated word and ducked instinctively, but Sybilia was too shocked to cuff his ears. "He's got his mother's evil eye. He's like her. Better make sure you please him, too, or we'll have to walk all the way back to Taita again for your funeral."

The party was a nightmare: thick-set, sweating bodies were

leaping into each other's arms; the women were kicking off their shoes and fanning their faces; the room was odious with smoke and the smell of sweat, tobacco, and brandy. The jokes were coarse and embarrassing. The older men were eyeing her lecherously, and her mother, who had drunk too much wine, kept pulling her aside to whisper words of advice in her ear. Then her eldest brother rushed outside and vomited loudly into the bushes. Oh! The awful shame of it.

Sybilia fled to the back garden. There was a bench set among some rocks beside a stream that was rushing noisily from the mountain. Shuddering, she noticed that the garden was an overgrown mess of weeds and wild herbs, yet it was pure and beautiful in a way. Sybilia felt like an intruder in her soiled wedding gown, with her sweaty hands and dirty feet, and her mind obsessed with the fears of the shameful night ahead of her.

As she hid there, two doves flew down to the grass beside the river. The male strutted around in circles, preening its tail. Suddenly the two were a shuddering, circling oneness. Sybilia watched intently, her stomach a fluttering echo of each movement they made. Quickly they parted and began pecking among the grass.

Was that how it would be? It did not look so painful. Oh, if only she could think of something else, but she was obsessed with the stories she had heard and the scenes she had imagined.

After a while a tan-and-black shaggy dog ran up to her and wagged its tail. Behind it strode Maria Rocca, lithe as any man. She was tall like a man, too, and when she stood staring down from the other side of the stream, Sybilia could not help trembling. The woman looked so intimidating with her curved nose and her hooded eyes. Her hair was still black, but her skin was horribly eroded, and Sybilia shuddered and wondered if she would grow as ugly in time. *Is she really a witch? And if she is, did Papa know about it when he married me into this family? Did he care?*

"I understand what you're going through," Maria said in a voice that was surprisingly soft and gentle. "I shall try to help you. You can count on me as your friend—if you want to, that is. I saw you weeping, you see. I saw you as plainly as I see you here in front of me now. I could see that you cared for him, and I was grateful."

Whatever was she talking about? Sybilia did not know how to answer her. But obviously she meant well, and Sybilia felt grateful and tried out a timid smile.

"In all the world you won't find a kinder boy than my Michel," Maria went on. "I hope you will be good to him."

Just as good as he is to me, Sybilia thought, but she simply bowed her head and stared at her scuffed shoes.

There was a sudden commotion as her cousins came rushing up the slope. "There you are," they shouted in a chorus. "We've been looking everywhere for you. You've been hiding." They giggled as they pulled her back toward the house.

Her brothers had struggled to carry the wooden trunks containing her trousseau and her possessions up three flights of stairs, and now they were heaving up buckets of warm water. Flushed and guilty, they tried to bid her good-bye, but she would not look at them. She could not even reply because of a painful lump in her throat.

There were her possessions: her hairbrushes, handkerchiefs, toilet water, and knickknacks laid out on the dressing table with her toothbrush and ribbons as if to demonstrate the irrevocable and unbelievable truth—she was not going home.

She wanted to die as her mother and her cousins pulled off the hateful gown and thrust her into a tub of scented water. Simultaneously giggling and weeping, they scrubbed her and dressed her in a frilly muslin nightdress. Then they fled. Her mother crumpled on the bed and buried her face in her hands. "Oh, Sybilia, my poor little child."

"Mother, please go," Sybilia whispered.

"Sybilia, I've never talked to you about being a woman —or a wife," she added hastily. "I never liked to . . . and God knows I thought it would be years—" She broke off and sighed. "Never let him see you naked," she said, pulling out a handkerchief to wipe her eyes. "That way you lose respect, you see. Tonight, remember that it only hurts badly the first time," her mother prattled on. "With any luck, he'll only do it once and then sleep until morning. I found that if you push hard, it doesn't hurt so badly."

Sybilia longed to throw herself into her mother's arms and beg to be taken home, but she was a married woman now, and it would be futile to beg. Instead, she hung on to her dignity, since it was all she had left, refusing to answer and keeping her eyes averted. At last her mother left.

CHAPTER 10

It was nine o'clock, and Sybilia was alone. She knelt at the window in prayer, but the words would not come, perhaps because she was so angry. Eventually she said the rosary, and the familiar touch of the beads was some small comfort.

Ten o'clock passed. Would he never arrive? Like a condemned man, she dreaded the coming ordeal but longed for it to be over and done with.

At half-past ten the door of the bedroom was flung open and Michel staggered in. There was muffled laughter from his friends, whispered hints on what he should do, a strong whiff of brandy, and then the door slammed shut behind him.

Sybilia stared coldly and dispassionately at her husband. She noticed for the first time his large blue eyes and black hair, which kept falling over his eyes. She could feel the sensitivity of the man, the shyness and the hesitancy that was so un-Corsican. It gave a certain delicacy to his bearing and a gracefulness to his appearance. He's not a monster, she thought. No, he's more like a poet, really. There's no reason to be afraid of him, but he's not a boy, either.

No, Michel Rocca was a man of twenty-two, and he was staring at her with something close to despair in his eyes. Yes, she thought, remembering her brother's warning. He did look a little like his mother with her strange, hooded eyes, but that was all. Admittedly his hair was black like his father's. But for the rest, his face was entirely his own, with a short nose, a puckered forehead, and an intelligent, cynical expression he was trying so hard to maintain. He's more scared of me than I am of him, she thought.

"Are you Michel?" she whispered timidly, for this was the first time she had plucked up the courage to look at him.

"Shit!" he swore. "Are you simple-minded, or what?

Welcome to the Rocca household. You'll fit in well with my mother. She's a maniac, or hadn't you heard? You can go hunting souls with her in the maquis."

Sybilia's chin jutted out defiantly. "You can be rude to me if you like, since you're my husband and from what I've seen husbands are always rude to their wives, but I don't think you should talk about your mother that way. She's not mad, she's just . . ." She searched around for an apt description. "She's kind," she said.

Michel looked dumbfounded by her show of spirit. His cheeks flushed, but his eyes lingered for a moment over her face and her hair. Then he turned away and laughed. "Wait and see," he said. Sybilia could not think of anything else to say. She stared at her hands and turned her wedding ring round and round. It was so unfamiliar and intrusive, and it bothered her all the time. She listened to Michel walking across the floor toward their sitting room.

He paused in the doorway. "I pity you," he said softly. "A husband is all girls think about, or want, but you've got nothing. You've been cheated. I didn't want to marry you. He made me. Now I feel sorry for you."

Sybilia flung herself facedown on the bed and pulled the sheet over her head.

Michel turned off the oil lamp. Then he kicked off his shoes. The springs of the settee squeaked rustily. Was he sitting down or lying, perhaps? Was he going to sleep there? She saw the flare of a match and the dull red glow of a cigarette, and soon the smell of pungent tobacco wafted into the bedroom. Am I supposed to sleep in this fog? I shall complain. But to whom? This was not home. After a while the butt was ground out, and Michel settled deeper into the couch.

For Sybilia, this was the worst part of the night. Nothing happened! Yes, for sure this was the worst part. She felt wretched and unwanted. In the dark the slightest sounds took on fearful importance: the tick-tock of the clock on the mantelpiece, ticking away her life, and the wind whistling through the trees. How loudly the waterfall thundered in the night. Even the cries of the night birds in the mountains were unfamiliar. From time to time there came the sound of shouts and singing from houses around the square. The wedding guests were taking a long time to settle down. They would be tired tomorrow when they were faced with their journey home. But oh, if she could only go with them, she would not mind how tired she was.

This was not how wedding nights were supposed to end. Of all the terrible stories her friends had whispered, surely this was the worst of them all. Loneliness and rejection set the seal on her nightmare, and for the first time she burst into tears. Curling into a ball, she buried her head under the blankets to muffle her sobs.

Michel, who was not a cruel man, clapped his hands over his ears, but her dismal sobs went on and on. In spite of his determination to ignore her forever, it was all he could do to swallow. Women made him feel soiled and slightly nauseated. The knowledge that she was to live in his house and sleep in his bed was unendurable. You disgust me, he wanted to say with real loathing in his voice, but how could he hurt her so? She was, after all, an innocent victim in this tragedy.

Why am I crying? What do I want? If only I knew. I'm lucky that he leaves me alone. Well, aren't I? If only it weren't so horribly dark. If only I weren't so completely alone.

"I'm so cold," she called out, and began sobbing again.

Eventually Sybilia crept across the floor and tapped Michel on the shoulder. "I'm so cold," she said, but as she stood there she began to feel burning hot with spasms of pain shooting through her stomach. She stared at him with frightened eyes. Then she reached down and touched his shoulder.

"Please stop crying," he said. "It's no use. You see that, don't you? Nothing can be put right now, and there's no one to comfort you. We're trapped, but never mind. Life is a matter of endurance," he said when he had calmed her by holding her hand.

"Endurance?" she cried out bitterly. "What about happiness? What about love? What about all the things the priest said at the wedding?" She bent over swiftly and tried to ease herself under the blanket next to her husband, but with a vicious push he shoved her back.

"What a baby you are," he said bitterly, trying to ignore her gesture. "Happiness? In this house? I have never been happy, but I would be ashamed to make the noise you are making." After this there was silence, and he felt he had gained a brief respite, but shortly afterward she began again.

"You're my husband," she sobbed, sinking to her knees beside the couch.

"Unfortunately, yes," he said.

"So you didn't want to marry me either?"

"Don't take it personally. I didn't want to marry anyone."

"So why . . . ? Was it for the land?"

"Not only for the land, but because I wanted to go away—I wanted to study in Paris."

"Why, what would you study there that you can't learn here?"

He shrugged. "I'm an artist," he went on after a small hesitation. "One day I will be famous, but first I have to get to Paris—and study."

"So what stopped you?" she asked.

"Him!"

"Your father? Are you so afraid of him?" she asked softly.

"Let's not talk about it," he said. "Please go back to bed."

For a moment she hesitated, but when she fumbled for his hand she felt Michel quivering. Why? Disgust? Or was it desperation?

In some strange way she wanted to be violated, longed to find out about the strange mystery of physical coupling between men and women. But Michel had no such desires, and the knowledge of this was like falling into a lake of ice-cold water. Feeling heavy with anguish, she tiptoed back to bed.

Poor Michel, she thought when at last she could think rationally. They were both victims. With this thought came a strange sense of bonding, but the realization brought no comfort. Sinking into this strange family was like being sucked into a noxious bog. She would never escape, never . . . never . . . and neither would Michel, for all his fine talk.

CHAPTER 11

July 14, 1939

Sybilia awoke from a deep sleep to a light tap on the door. Such a lovely dream, she thought, stirring languidly. She had been feeding the birds in the school's aviary with her favorite teacher, Sister Agnes, who had taught her English and German. Opening her eyes, she gazed at the unfamiliar ceiling of oak beams sloping to eaves. Embroidered muslin curtains shimmered in the breeze. Was it a dream? When she moved her head she saw Maria standing smiling in the doorway holding a jug of steaming coffee on a tray.

Maria's smile faded when she saw her son, fully dressed, sleeping on the couch.

Maria turned as if to block her husband's view. "Let them sleep," she said urgently, but Xavier saw the boy and let out a bellow of rage.

"God almighty! What do I have to do to turn this slinking cur of yours into a man?" he growled. Thrusting Maria aside, he scowled at Sybilia until she felt less than human. Was she goods in a shopwindow, then? She sat up angrily, forgetting that her frilly muslin gown was almost sheer.

Intuitively she had divined his thoughts. A blemished apple, Xavier was thinking. There must be something wrong with her, but as he deliberately scanned her body, he could see no faults. Above the sheets her breasts were full and thrusting forward, the nipples erect in their brown circles of flesh. Her shoulders were smooth and square, and from them her neck rose slender and exquisitely formed. Her eyes were wide with fear, but they were still lovely. She had clamped one hand over her mouth, and the other was clutching the sheet. She was like a chamois disturbed by the marksman one chilly mountain dawn, just as startled, just as tragic. The male huntsman's instinct was aroused; he wanted to shoot his bullet straight into the quivering, seductive flesh.

The thick muslin frills of her gown, crumbled now, hung around her neck like the garland of dying flowers he had once seen around a Hawaiian girl. The memory of that far-off night of bliss thrust his body into turmoil.

Shit! If this girl could not provoke his son into some semblance of maleness, then there was no hope for him. The guilt and horror of his own lust heightened his anger.

In a split second Xavier was across the room. He grasped his son by his tie, hauled him upright, and shook him.

"No! Oh, God, no, you're choking him," Maria called out.

Sybilia watched dumbfounded as Xavier rained a dozen blows on Michel's face and shoulders with his right fist, while his left hand held him upright. Michel looked terrible. His usual sardonic expression had changed to a look of resigned acceptance. For an insane moment Sybilia imagined that he was enjoying the battering.

With a low moan of pain, Maria rushed forward and tried to grab Xavier's arm, but her efforts were as futile as a blackbird fluttering at a windowpane. Sybilia was rooted in shock for a few seconds. She had never seen such fury. Xavier's face was contorted into an unrecognizable mask of rage.

"Stop," Sybilia cried. "Stop!" She bounded out of bed, pushing Maria aside as she picked up a chair and brought it down with a crack on Xavier's head.

The chair shattered, and Xavier yelled with pain. He held his head and sagged onto the couch, stunned with surprise more than the blow. Feeling bemused, he watched Sybilia lead Michel to the bed. His lips curled into a grimace of chagrin and amusement as she grabbed a leg of the broken chair and sat guard over the frightened boy.

"Look what you've done," she cried out. "He's bleeding. You've broken his nose most likely, and you've split his lip. Look at that," she said, pointing at the deep red stain spreading over the sheet. "My God, what sort of a man are you? What sort of a family is this? He needs stitches." Brave words, but her heart was pounding and her breath was coming in short, sharp gasps. *Don't let him see how scared I am,* she prayed.

"Stitches!" Xavier snorted contemptuously. "He needs a splint to prop up his cock. That's what he needs." He stood up, rubbed his head once more, and staggered toward the bed.

Sybilia brandished the chair leg in front of his nose. "I'm warning you, don't come any closer. I'm not afraid of you," she said.

He glanced briefly at his son and then averted his eyes. It was too painful a sight. "His mother's son," he muttered. "Bad blood. Now you, Sybilia. You should have been my son. You've got spirit." He stared down at her, his eyes slowly examining her body.

Sybilia flushed and grabbed the sheet, hauling it up around her neck.

Xavier reached out and took hold of the chair leg, and although Sybilia pushed with all her strength, Xavier's grip was like a vice. She could not move it one way or another. He smiled gently. "I won't touch him again, I promise," he said. Gently he pulled the chair leg away from her. "Feel here," he insisted. "Feel my arm."

He took hold of her hand and placed it on his upper arm. "D'you feel that?" he asked. "Solid muscle."

His flesh was like rock. It was like touching a granite statue. Sybilia could not resist poking at his back, which was like a steel board.

"I'm the strongest man you're ever likely to see," he said slowly. "Don't try to fight me again."

"Even the strongest men have to sleep, Monsieur Rocca," she said quietly, "and if you ever touch Michel again, I will get you back."

His eyes narrowed, teeth glistening in a grimace of a smile. He looked like a wolf, she noticed, but a handsome one. If only Michel were more like him. Suddenly he smiled and stood up.

"Papa! Call me Papa," he said, and ruffled her hair with his hand. "Now listen to me well. Your children will be my grandchildren, so get pregnant, Sybilia, and make it soon, or by God, I swear I'll show your queer husband how to do it."

He grabbed his wife by one arm and pushed her out the door. Sybilia heard Maria arguing tearfully outside the door, and then they went away.

Later that morning, when the family had given up trying to persuade Sybilia to leave her bedroom and at last she was in peace, she lay on her bed and heard through the window the voices of women gathered in the square around the communal washing tub. Snickers and laughs and oohs of admiration floated up as they gazed at the sheets bloody from Michel's nose. The fools! She could hear every word they said quite clearly, and she marveled at her mother-in-law's easy deceit. "Ah, yes, what passion," she heard Maria say. "He is, after all, his father's son."

CHAPTER 12

July 22, 1939

It was Saturday night after mass, and the church was quiet. The candles flickered low in the candelabra, and the air was heavy with incense and the sadness of old women's prayers. Only a few worshipers remained, those who wanted to be among the last into confession. From time to time the heavy curtains parted, and a figure slipped out and hurried away in a whisper of footsteps on flagged stone.

Sybilia sat in the back row of the pews half-hidden in shadow, her body hunched with misery, her beautiful face swollen and red. She tried to stifle her tears in her handkerchief, but she felt sure everyone could hear her. She must stop crying, but how? So she too had waited, hoping to be the very last. She had to be quite alone, apart from the priest since he did not count as a real person.

This was the first time Sybilia had been to church since her wedding over a week ago. It had taken her hours to pluck up courage and pummel her face with cold water into some semblance of normality. But when she had crept into the church, the familiar sounds and smells had brought a vivid recall of her childhood church and of the family's Sunday mornings together. The smell of incense, the polished wood slightly dusty and slippery under her fingers, the prayer book yellow with age, the painted, gilded statues in flickering candlelight were all so sickeningly dear, a part of her happy childhood.

She had crumpled into the pew and begun to pray, but in spite of her best intentions her prayers turned to vengeance. "I hope Papa lives to regret his selfishness. I hope Mama is lonely without me. I hope they never forgive each other. I will never forgive them. Never."

For the past nine days Sybilia had cowered in her attic rooms, pretending to be sick. And she was, too, she told herself, with shame and homesickness, in spite of all her family had done to her.

Each day Maria brought her meals up, knocked, and eventually left the tray on the chest of drawers outside the door. At first Sybilia had ignored the food, but eventually hunger won out.

She could not neglect her need to wash and visit the toilet, so she had listened to the sounds of the household and crept down when everyone was out. Finally, that morning, when she could no longer bear her own company a moment longer, she had decided to attend mass and confession on Saturday night.

Footsteps disturbed her gloomy thoughts, and she looked up with a start. The last person hurrying out of confession was the dovelike Vannina. Now it was her turn, and her stomach lurched. For a moment she thought of fleeing back to the attic, but that lonely place had become unbearable, so she crept up the aisle into the box, sweaty palms clutching her handkerchief.

She knelt by the curtain, clung to the polished wooden bar, and gazed desperately at the profile of the priest. Although he could not see her, she sensed that he knew who she was.

"Bless me, Father, for I have sinned."

She waited while the priest blessed her.

"I missed mass and confession last Saturday," she confessed. "I was sick." A surge of guilt overwhelmed her. Lying in the confessional was unthinkable. "That is, sick with shame and grief," she added more truthfully. "These are my sins," she added glibly. She had spent the last hour in church trying to clear her mind, but she felt confused and angry. She must have been very wicked in her past to be so wretched now. What was she to say? "Oh, dear, I have sinned so much since the last time I went to mass," she began haltingly. "Of course that was in Chiornia and only two weeks ago, but it seems more like two years."

"It is a mortal sin to miss mass, my child," the soft voice with the strong Irish accent murmured. "But under the circumstances, I am sure your lapse is forgiven."

"I really don't think I should have come at all. I can't find it in me to repent for hating them. I feel as if . . ." How could she explain to this cold profile outlined against the whitewashed wall? "As if I am not myself. I mean, I was so happy being Sybilia Silvani. I would have been head girl next year, the nuns told me so. I was top in languages—English, German, and Italian. I was going to be a teacher. Papa promised. Dominique and I . . . he's my youngest brother and closest to me," she confided in a rush. "Well, we were planning to climb Mount Cinto during the summer holidays. I was given no warning, you see. Just dumped here. Just like that. I remember how I used to feel when I woke up in the morning. Like I couldn't wait for the day to begin. Now it's as if I'm in someone else's shell. I don't know who I am anymore, or what I should do."

She waited hopefully, wondering if this strange priest would help her sort out her confusion.

Father Andrews felt equally confused. She was such a child. What a tragedy! How cruel to treat this lovely girl in such a crude manner. He yearned to be able to help her. Instead he tried to wipe the emotion out of his voice as he said:

"You are a young wife in a strange situation, and it is only natural that you should have certain . . . conflicts." Would she understand him? he wondered. "Now you must try to build up strong bonds with members of your new family," he added.

"With them?" She knew she was being proud and scornful, and this was not the way to talk in the confessional, but she did not care. Suddenly she found it hard to speak coherently as her feelings tumbled out: the sorrow of dreams lost, the rejection, the impossibility of bearing her present circumstances. Eventually she burst into tears.

Father Andrews wanted nothing so much as to comfort her. "Patience, my child," he said. "God's mission for us all is sometimes hard to understand, but he has one for you, you may rest assured of that."

"I'm beginning to hate God," she said. "I've been left to rot in this horrible place and I shall never escape. No, never. How can I, since my name is Rocca and I am one of them?"

"Hush, child, you are a married woman, and you must behave as one."

"I am married, yet not married. Married in name only."

"In God's good time, in God's good time. Love grows. . . ."

"Love. Don't talk to me of love. I disgust Michel, I swear I do, Father. He doesn't like women. He told me so."

As her miserable story poured out between the sobs, Father Andrews found himself clenching his fists and trying to stem his anger.

"I hate my father-in-law," she went on passionately. "Yes, I hate him. One of these days I am going to break his head open, if he ever looks at me like that again."

"My child, you must calm yourself. That is no way to talk about your father-in-law."

"He saw me next to naked, Father. He couldn't look away, and I was so ashamed. But there's worse to come, Father. I dreamed about Xavier Rocca. I dreamed that I had married him. It was . . . it was lovely," she stammered. Oh, God. What was she saying? But the relief at speaking those words was indescribable. Last night she had relived her wedding in her dreams, floated across the square in a diaphanous flimsy wedding gown, saw, as if in slow motion, her bridegroom reach out and take her hands and pull her toward him. But when she looked up to see his face for the first time, it was Xavier Rocca who gazed at her with his strange, slanted ice-blue eyes, his handsome features, his jet-black curly hair. "You see, I am damned. There is no help for me."

"But he is an old man," the priest burst out with all the wisdom of his twenty-six years.

"He is a man," she said simply.

"And Michel?"

"He is a coward."

"A coward!" In his brief stay in Corsica, the priest had learned that there was no more damning label here than that. Searching desperately for inspiration, he said, "You are his wife. It is God's will."

"No!" she exploded, and gasped at her own foolhardiness. Lowering her voice to a stage whisper, she said: "It was Xavier's will. He wanted me because he hoped I would turn his son into a man and give him grandchildren. He despises him. I can't help feeling sorry for Michel," she went on more gently. "He's too sensitive for a man. He is even too scared to come to our rooms. He sleeps on the couch downstairs. I have not seen him since our wedding night. His father has been away on business,'' she went on in a low voice. ''I don't know what will happen when Monsieur Rocca returns. Papa!'' She laughed harshly, and the sound of her voice upset Father Andrews. ''He said I should call him Papa. He told me . . .'' In low whispers she recounted Xavier's threats.

The young priest felt stunned. He had never before felt such a warring between the man and the priest inside him. He longed with all his heart to be able to protect her. Instead he took refuge in rhetoric. ''The Roccas' sins are their own affair, my child,'' he said eventually. ''It is not for you to judge them. You must be concerned only with your own behavior. Be brave, God is with you, and''—he paused and went on recklessly—''I promise you I will speak to your father-in-law. No doubt he was trying to annoy Michel.'' His voice trailed off.

''Is that what you believe?'' she asked scornfully.

Father Andrews bowed his head in prayer, but his mind was in turmoil as he searched for words of comfort. ''My daughter, think of yourself as a child at a Christmas party. You have been given a box covered in fancy paper. You don't like the look of the paper, so you want to throw away your gift. You haven't even opened it to see what's inside. Open the box, Sybilia, before you throw the contents on the rubbish heap. Take a good hard look at what it is you are discarding. Remember that your husband is a creation of God and much loved by his Creator, so who are you to deem him worthless?''

He ignored Sybilia's sobs and tried to introduce a sterner tone into his troubled intonation, reminding himself that his main responsibility as parish priest was to the flock as a unit, while giving sympathetic attention to the mavericks.

''Sybilia, just step down from your high-and-mighty stance and listen to my words, not as a priest, but as a friend. You've been the victim—yes, I will say victim—of an arranged marriage. I don't agree with this custom, but it's the habit here. In God's good time it will be abolished, I'm sure. Your parents felt they were doing the best for you. They've married you into a good family—Rocca is the most powerful name around here. They are also a proud family, and they will not tolerate your antagonism. You will destroy yourself with your hatred and your contempt.

"There's nothing else waiting for you at the end of the rainbow, Sybilia," he went on with a rush. "Whatever your dreams were—let go of them. Michel is all you're going to get. It would be wiser to make the most of your life.

"Think of me as your friend, Sybilia. If things get tougher, you can always come and talk to me. It doesn't have to be here in confessional. We can talk in the sacristy.

"As a priest, I say to you: My child, for your penance you will attend the early service every morning. You will spend your days working diligently, like a good daughter-in-law, in the household, but besides your work you will be looking for good words to say about each member of your family. By next Saturday I want to hear ten good points about each one of the Roccas. That is your penance, my child."

"I would rather kill myself," she blurted out.

"And condemn your soul to everlasting hell?" he roared. "No, Sybilia. Do as I say and put your faith in God."

Was that really what God wanted? Was God so unfeeling? Sybilia closed her eyes and tried to swallow a lump in her throat. "I will try," she whispered, meaning it. Automatically her lips voiced the traditional plea: "Oh, Lord, be merciful to me and restore me to Your friendship. . . .

"Ten good points about each one of them?" she murmured incredulously as she hurried across the square. In all her life she had never been given such an impossible task.

CHAPTER 13

After Sybilia had left the confessional, the young priest listened to her soft footsteps fade across the square. She was gone, and the warmth and light seemed to have gone with her. The church had never seemed so empty before.

Confused and unhappy, he knelt in prayer. "Oh, Holy Father, this is a strange, harsh world you've sent me to, where women are treated like possessions and disposed of just as their fathers feel inclined. Her tragedy has touched me, and I long to help her. This is wrong, and I know that.''

Since the day he was ordained, Father Andrews had always prayed to forget the secrets of his parishioners the moment they left the confessional box, and he nearly always succeeded. But now? Guiltily he acknowledged that he would never forget Sybilia's anguished whispers.

He was feeling shaken as he locked the church and walked across the square to his tiny cottage beyond the graveyard. How beautiful the night was. The balmy, voluptuous air caressed his face as softly as a woman's touch. There was a strong scent of lilies, tobacco flowers, and the fragrant wild fig trees in the maquis. Cicadas throbbed, frogs croaked, night owls called in the forests. The world was alive with all that was natural and thriving and fertile—while he? His treacherous thoughts hit him like a blow, and he stopped short in his tracks, amazed that he could have entertained such an idea, even if only momentarily.

Twice in one night. He must give himself a vigorous penance. Man or priest? Priest or man? He felt tormented by his doubt.

He retraced his footsteps and sat on the old stone bench in the square under the statue of St. Augustine. Symbol of sinners, he reminded himself, and this brought him some small comfort.

A few candles flickered behind the windows of the homes around the square; most were dark, but not necessarily sleeping. Murmurs in the night! Good, wholesome sounds: a bed squeaking violently in the attic of the Castellis—Carlo, the cobbler, was wasting away with tuberculosis, but his children kept emerging at regular yearly intervals. A small light flickering in the attic room of Louis Padovani, the cabinetmaker. Since his young son had contracted scarlet fever, Louis's nervous twitch and his stutter had intensified. There was a baby whimpering in Jean Pinelli's bedroom; he heard the father yell at the mother to feed it and shut it up. The Lecas' windows were all shuttered, for Madame Leca had just died in childbirth. Strains of an accordion and the pounding of feet came drifting up from the Roccas' cafe below the square. It was run by Xavier's brother-in-law, Pierre Bonnelli, but Xavier kept a shrewd eye on the takings most nights. They were open late tonight. No doubt they were plotting political maneuvers or another hunting expedition. There was very little else of consequence to the village headmen.

Suddenly Father Andrews realized how lonely and homesick he was. He had a sudden vision of his mother and of his home in Killala, on the west coast of Eire. Memories crammed into his mind in rapid succession, but over and over again came a vivid recall of the day he had been ordained—of how his best friend, Sean, had come to him with tears in his eyes and called him Father Andrews. Then his mother, too, had looked at him shyly and called him Father. That was the day real loneliness began. No, not loneliness, he corrected himself. He had his faith, which was always with him. Aloneness might describe it better.

Suddenly he was jolted by the sound of footsteps. It was Xavier returning from the cafe. He saw him lurch toward his house, walk inside, stand there in the hallway for a long time staring up the stairs, and then gaze at his son, sprawled on the couch. Then, abruptly, he walked out, slamming the door behind him, and set off down the mountain trail toward Chiornia again. No doubt he intended to visit the widow Lucette, who lived alone on the outskirts of the town. He knew because Maria had revealed the affair to him in her confession, when she had poured out her jealousy and despair at her encroaching age.

At that moment his responsibility as their parish priest seemed almost more than he could shoulder. He felt inadequate to cope. A wave of panic washed through him, and he prayed for the swift recovery of Father Delon. Since his stroke the old priest had showed no sign of change, either for the better or worse.

CHAPTER 14

Remembering her promise to Father Andrews, Sybilia was dressed and ready to go downstairs by dawn next morning, but she could not find the courage to take the first steps.

How can I? I'm a stranger here. No one wants me. What good am I to anyone in the family? Even my husband hasn't spoken to me since our wedding. It was all a trick to get Papa's land. And now they plan to starve me to death.

The truth was, no breakfast had arrived that morning. Usually Maria carried up her food each day, knocked at the door, waited, and eventually left the tray. Later she returned and collected the dirty dishes. At times Sybilia felt a little guilty about causing her mother-in-law so much trouble, but in her present state of resentfulness she was simply not prepared to meet anyone halfway. Instead she wallowed in her misery. She felt sure that by now the whole family regretted the marriage.

By noon she was still sitting at the window, her head in her hands, when she heard a brief knock on the door.

It was Michel. What a strange, intent person he was, she thought, watching him anxiously. Because he was not slouching today, she noticed that he was quite tall, but too thin. His hair was falling over his forehead, while his shrewd blue eyes were gazing suspiciously around the room. She caught a glimpse of his resentment at having a stranger pushed into his life . . . and his bedroom.

"I haven't spoiled anything," she said softly.

His face became a trifle colder, if that was possible. "Would you care to come down, madame?" he said, fixing his eyes on the wall above her head to avoid looking at her.

"Yes," she snapped. "I was just coming anyway."

Michel turned abruptly and clattered down the stairs.

Sybilia glanced nervously in the mirror and smoothed her hair. "Please, wait for me, Michel," she called, but he pretended that he had not heard her.

A few minutes later she walked hesitantly into the kitchen, but there was no one there. Obviously they were expecting guests, for there were dishes of food laid out on the long oak table, and a large pot of stew was boiling on the coal stove. It was a pleasant kitchen, far larger than the one at home. She had not been in here on her wedding day, but now she had time to notice how scrupulously clean it was and to admire the copper pots and dishes on the oak dressers.

Sprawled on the rug by the back door was the dog, part collie, part Labrador, and goodness knows what else, she thought. He was sizing her up. When he made up his mind, he wagged his tail and ambled toward her.

Feeling grateful for any form of recognition, she stroked the dog until she heard footsteps behind her. It was Madame Rocca, and she was blinking nervously.

"We've been longing to see you," she began awkwardly, "but we didn't want to intrude on you." She had a strange, halting manner of speech, as if she had difficulty finding the right words. "You've been sitting up there overlong. How thin you've become, child. People will think we're starving you. Well, you see we don't normally eat breakfast on a Sunday because we have a big meal at noon. But today we're expecting Xavier's brothers and their families, and they're late."

She paused as if tongue-tied and then went on with a gush of words. "It's a fine day today. I thought it would rain, but the sun's come out. Really hot. I remember another Sunday, just so warm, but when was it, now? . . ."

There was a sudden roar from the next room. Xavier's voice! "Stop babbling, woman, and bring her here."

Sybilia followed her mother-in-law into the sitting room and flushed hotly. Xavier Rocca was sitting at the end of the table in his shirt-sleeves and suspenders, a carafe of wine at his elbow and a half-empty glass in front of him. Michel was sitting beside him. Xavier had been reading the paper, but now he folded it and pushed it away politely. "Well, come and sit down," he said. "We'll have some wine to celebrate your emergence. It's a little overdue, but never mind."

He pushed out a chair for her, poured the red wine into her glass and Michel's, filled his own, and held it up to her. "You're very welcome here," he said, "and the sooner you get to feel at home, the happier we'll all be."

Sybilia had been prepared for almost anything—except kindness. As her eyes began to water, she bent her head over to sip her wine. It was too sweet, and it tasted like medicine. Two big tears rolled down each cheek, and she hoped no one noticed as she brushed her hand against her face.

Xavier had noticed, but he decided to pretend that he had not. His oaf of a son was doing very little to help her, so he picked up the newspaper and began to read the news to the family.

Sybilia remained silently staring at her glass, hoping that no one would speak to her again, but after a while she became aware of Michel's intent appraisal. He was not looking at her directly, but she sensed that all his attention was targeted on her. When she moved her hands, his eyes flickered. If she sipped the wine, he shot a swift glance of disapproval. If she looked away, she could feel his glance on her. When she turned her head, he was suddenly studying his hands or the table. After a while he leaned back and made a show of lighting his pipe and discussing the war news with his father. He was showing off.

Later, when the dog ambled in and laid his heavy head on her knees, Sybilia noticed how jealous Michel became. Evidently it was his dog. "Gus," he called angrily. The dog shifted over obediently.

What strange hands, she noticed. They seemed to be the strongest part of him. His fingers were long and blunt and callused. Was that from farm work? She had not seen him on the terraces, although she had looked often enough. She watched him stroking the dog with soft, sensuous movements. Eventually she stretched out timidly and fondled the dog's ear. Surely he would remove his hands in another fit of pique, but he did not. A strange warm glow seemed to be flowing from his hand into hers, although their fingers never touched. A tingling feeling burned in her stomach and moved to every extremity, until she was gooseflesh all over.

Xavier looked up and noticed the two of them so intent on stroking the dog. He grinned and filled their glasses. Could it be possible that he's not queer after all? he wondered hopefully. Glory be! His eyes scanned Sybilia slyly. Without doubt she was the loveliest woman he had ever set eyes on, and he'd seen the best. Fucked the best, too, and all over the world, but you can't beat Corsican women, he thought smugly.

Unaware of his scrutiny, but feeling warmed by the wine, Sybilia leaned back, her mouth slightly open, her eyes fixed unseeingly on the wall. What a strange morning it was. Sitting there, confused and sleepy, with one hand on the dog and the other on her lap, and listening to Xavier's voice drone on and on, Sybilia had the strangest sensation that her soul was merging into the Roccas. It was as if their bodies were only a part of them, the part you could see, but the essence of them flowed into the room in waves, and she was merging and joining, flowing headfirst, like a small stream into a river.

She pushed back her chair in an abrupt gesture as Madame Rocca hurried in with a plate of olives and bread and cheese. "You'd best eat something, since you're drinking on empty stomachs," she grumbled. "The family's late, as usual."

"I must help you," Sybilia mumbled.

"No, no," Xavier said in his deep, gruff voice. "Stay here beside me. Today you are our guest. Don't worry about a thing, just enjoy."

Suddenly the spell of warmth was quite lost. Michel scowled and withdrew his hand, and the dog walked back to the kitchen.

It's all very well for Monsieur Rocca to say that, she thought critically, but it was Madame Rocca who was doing all the work. Mama, she thought desperately. I really must start to think of her as Mama, or I'll never say the word. She looked around guiltily, but Madame Rocca nodded her approval and pushed a plate of olives toward her. "Eat," she said. "Eat! Put on some weight, for goodness' sake. You're as white as a spook. You'll be frightening the life out of Michel one of these nights."

"She does that already," Xavier said, and laughed heartily at his own joke.

Michel flushed and grabbed his pipe again, while Maria frowned at her husband and then hurried back to the kitchen. That was my fault, Maria told herself. Why am I so foolish as to give him openings like that? The boy will never be a man while Xavier's sitting on him. Something stirred in her mind, some sadness connected with the boy. A sense of time closing in on her. She stirred the simmering pot of mutton stew, thick with vegetables and barley, and tried to remember what it was that was making her sad; but she could not. She had forgotten her vision on the day of the wedding, as she always did, but she was left with a sense of foreboding that she could never quite define.

The lunch was ready, but first they would eat smoked ham and sausage, with tomatoes and raw onions swimming in the unrefined olive oil she made each year from their own olives. If only the family would come. Anxiously Maria checked the homemade cheeses of ewes' milk, nuts, and small sweet melons that grew so well on the eastern terraces and which she had laid out on a large dish with slices of homemade bread.

It was past one when her brother-in-law, Pierre Bonnelli, arrived with his wife, Carlotta, who was Xavier's sister, and their three sons and daughter. Maria heard them greeting Xavier and her husband's booming response and then Carlotta's heavy footsteps approaching along the stone passage.

Carlotta was a well-built, compact woman of unusual strength. Surprisingly she had not run to fat, for her bulk was muscular and shapely. Her skin was olive, more like the coastal people, and her prominent nose and full lips were a permanent reminder of the many Saracen invasions. Her black, wavy hair was cut short, and although she wore peasant black, she wore it stylishly. Her expressive, heavy-lidded eyes flashed affection, or contempt, or envy, but usually with a trace of amusement in them. Today her lips were twisted into a forced smile that was more of a sneer.

"Why is *she* not helping you?" she hissed in a stage whisper. She clasped Maria and kissed her on both cheeks. "Why does *she* sit languishing in the living room with the men? Who does she think she is—a *queen*?"

"She's our guest yet," Maria retorted promptly. "She hasn't really settled in."

"Ten days! That's time enough, unless of course she thinks *she's* too good for the family. Poor you! You'll have a permanent houseguest on your hands."

Carlotta flounced into the living room and placed a plate of homemade bread on the table, slinging a meaningful glance of approbation toward Sybilia, who was still hunched beside Xavier sipping her glass of wine.

"There's a *fine*, haughty lady for you," she muttered to Maria seconds later. Carlotta had noticed that Sybilia's beauty, added to her youth and sensuality, seemed to fill the room with an electric charge, and the men were vibrating with it. They couldn't forget her for a moment, none of them could, not Xavier, nor her husband, Pierre, nor her three silly sons, who were showing off madly. She'd lay her hands around their ears if they didn't stop gaping at the girl. Even Xavier was red-faced and beaming like a dog that had brought down a boar. You'd think he'd married the girl himself, instead of that queer boy of his. No point in his trying to turn Michel into a man; he never would. Well, Xavier had married Maria for her fortune of land, and he'd gotten exactly what he deserved—land and nothing else, while she was rich in sons and only had one daughter, thank God.

"Maria, darling," she whispered loudly in the kitchen, "you're too patient by far. She'll sit on you, just like the rest of the family. You mark my words, Maria. You're becoming a long-suffering donkey carrying a load of ticks."

Sybilia heard her stage whispers and shuddered inwardly. A queen? Could anything be further from the truth? She felt bewildered, foreign, homesick, and scared. Just when she was feeling faint with desperation, Michel leaned over her head as if to grab an olive and murmured: "Take no notice. She's jealous of you."

She felt amazed. She could not quite believe that Michel had said that. Xavier pushed a dish of canistrelli, dried cakes flavored with aniseed, toward her and filled her tiny glass with Maria's homemade liqueur in which whole grapes floated. She was beginning to feel quite dizzy from it all. Or was it from joy? Michel had said something kind to her. She felt like a starving dog that has been tossed a crust.

She sat up and began to take more notice of the family. Carlotta's three boys were so alike that it was hard to tell one from another; they were stocky, swarthy, and flamboyant, and they were all making a great deal of noise.

Their father, Bonnelli, had only one eye. He looked surly and behaved churlishly, as if he had a chip on his shoulder. Perhaps because he worked for Xavier, Sybilia thought. Their daughter, Anna, seemed so different from both of them. She was slight and lighter in coloring.

After a while Anna sat next to Sybilia and told her about her vocation. She was to enter a convent as a novice soon. She hoped to be sent to Africa eventually. "So much leprosy . . . need for service . . . our deprived black brethren . . . the plight of the poor . . ." Her voice went lightly on and on, but she never finished her sentences, merely tripped from one idea to the next, like a butterfly in a garden of flowers.

Sybilia was overcome with envy. Anna would be free. She was escaping from marriage.

At that moment Carlotta blustered in: "Why, Anna, what's

got into you, child? Come help in the kitchen or you'll grow corns on your backside.'' She shot a meaningful glance at Sybilia, who flushed and stood up.

Sybilia followed Anna to the kitchen. She felt quite intimidated by the flamboyant Carlotta.

''Just mind the milk,'' Carlotta snapped at Sybilia.

Maria hurried over, but Sybilia told her rather abruptly that she was quite capable of minding the milk. She stared at it for ages, and it showed no signs of boiling, but then, just as she turned to find a spoon for Anna, there was a horrible hissing and burning smell, and the milk ran onto the coals.

''Heavens girl. Just what did they teach you in that high-class convent?'' Carlotta shrieked, making sure her words were heard next door.

Maria was too busy mopping up to notice Sybilia's burning cheeks.

Then she heard Xavier shouting from the living room. ''Hey there, ladies. You've too many cooks in the kitchen. Ask Sybilia to come here and play the piano.''

''How vulgar,'' Sybilia murmured. ''Now I'm to be paraded in front of the family.'' She flushed and walked unwillingly to the piano. Was she a little dog? When Xavier snapped his fingers, would she jump through the hoop? Underneath her resentment, she realized that in some subtle way Xavier had come to her defense. He was not going to allow her to be criticized. Why? Because he liked her? Or because she was a part of his family, and he wanted to be proud of her? Yes, that was it. She was being drawn into them, for better or worse, like a new skein of silk being threaded into Maria's embroidery. She would be stitched and blended, and eventually she would be so much a part of the whole pattern that there would be very little of her left. No, she thought rebelliously. No, no, no.

''She's a talented girl,'' Xavier roared, giving her a hearty smack on her shoulder.

Maria rushed to her rescue. ''What, after all that wine you gave her? Leave her in peace.''

Xavier's disappointment was so blatant, Sybilia decided to try her best. Something simple! She sat down in front of Maria's piano and strummed her fingers over the keys. As she played an old Corsican lullaby, she was gratified to notice that Carlotta's boys stopped shouting and sat quietly. Glancing up, she caught Michel's glance. He was looking at her, really looking at her for the first time, and he looked puzzled. She tried harder. She missed her music, but fortunately there were a few pieces she knew by heart: *Clair de Lune*; the Moonlight Sonata; Chopin's Nocturne in E-Flat; she had played them all at school concerts. She tried her best, wanting to show the family that their pride was justified.

The first course arrived, and soon they were seated around the table. Sybilia was fussed over and found a place opposite Michel. In no time they were all discussing Corsica's problems.

"Western civilization," Xavier explained patiently, "has damaged our traditional customs and all but destroyed our way of life. Corsican virtues will soon be forgotten when the modern world's loose ways come flooding in."

Watching him, Sybilia sensed his fears. He was a traditionalist who lamented the passing of his culture. Nearly all the changes he had seen in his lifetime were for the worse, he explained, wars, mobilization, inflation, the exodus from the countryside, the neglect of the land. And what were they getting in return? "A lump of dung, Sybilia dear."

Western ways had infiltrated the coastal cities, he said. Nowadays there was no time for friendship. Everyone was obsessed with profits and self-interest, but the result of their busy life-styles was the gradual erosion of man's dignity and honor.

There was only one person prepared to argue with Xavier, and that was Michel. Sybilia was surprised. Michel was loud in his scorn of his father's opinions. No doubt the wine was giving him courage, she decided, and he was showing off. He was French, he told them. He was born French, and he would die French, and let no one say otherwise. He despised everything Corsican.

The mutton stew was still delayed. They were waiting for Xavier's elder brother, Francois Rocca, and his wife, Lucilia, who were coming in a donkey cart from Asco. When they arrived the old woman had to be helped down from the cart, she was so weak. They were so thin they seemed almost translucent, but their manners were impeccable, and they kept smiling and nodding politely. Francois was a gentle old shepherd who, she discovered, guarded the Rocca clan's flocks. His voice was soft, his movements curiously graceful, and he had a long white beard.

Lunch was over, and the dishes were washed. The men were still arguing about Corsica's plight. Only Francois had fallen asleep on the couch, a gentle smile on his face. Maria had abruptly disappeared.

Sybilia wandered outside to the south side of the old house. Here the garden sloped steeply down for a hundred yards until it reached the cliff's edge, where it fell to the lake below. It could be lovely, she thought wistfully. Once, long ago, some industrious people had terraced the steep slope with waist-high stone walls. Now the weeds and wild bushes had claimed almost all of the garden, but here and there was a cultivated piece planted with garden herbs and vegetables. She found rows of onions where the ground was cleared around the base of the fruit trees, and almost toppling over the edge was a row of olive trees.

In time I will make this garden lovely, she thought. It will be brilliant with flowers, as beautiful as the cemetery.

She walked around to the north side of the garden, where the ground sloped steeply up toward the maquis and the mountains. On the garden's eastern boundary a stream rushed toward the lake, bubbling over boulders and falling in a thousand small waterfalls past rushes and reeds. Tall strelitzia and flags were still blooming, although past their best. There was hardly any sign of cultivation here, for the ground was rock hard in places. Thistles and myrtle and wild fig trees burst out of granite cracks, and there was a wide strip of cultivated land with small melons ripening in the sun.

Suddenly she came across Madame Rocca, sitting on an old garden chair, gazing out over the valley. Her face showed her surprise.

"To be honest, I'm not too fond of the Bonnellis," Maria explained, her eyes twinkling. "That's a secret, you understand. When I've had enough I sit up here among the shrubs and the birds, and then I get a sense of peace. It's better than getting cross."

"I was wondering, Madame Rocca, if you would allow me to have a piece of the garden for my own."

"Have it all, Sybilia," Maria said. "I'm getting very stiff, and Michel has no interest in gardening. But Sybilia, won't you please call me Mama?" the woman asked courteously. Then she flushed.

Mama? Sybilia watched Maria cautiously. She was so ugly, but so kind and considerate, and she had such beautiful eyes. Will I ever get that old? Sybilia stole a furtive glance at the gravel face that had fallen in pouches as Maria bent down, and at her legs, which were gnarled with varicose veins, like an old oak tree burdened with creepers. Her hands were misshapen and covered in arthritic bumps, but how eloquently she spoke.

Sybilia went a little way down the hill and began poking around the flowers, removing weeds and grass.

Maria watched her anxiously. She understood all too well what her daughter-in-law was suffering. For Corsicans, whose roots fed deeply into the rich loam of intense family loyalty and love, transplanting was a painful process. It could even be critical. If only she and Michel . . . She sighed. Well, they were progressing. The child had a piano, a garden, and her own apartment. Perhaps she would take root.

CHAPTER 15

Sybilia was up early next morning. For the first time since her wedding, she had slept well. Michel had spent the night downstairs and was sitting at the kitchen table eating breakfast: black coffee with sour bread. There was no sign of his parents.

"Where's Madame Rocca?" she asked shyly.

"Talking to spirits in the mountains," he answered rudely without looking at her.

Sybilia frowned. Later she would do something about Michel's unkindness to his mother. "And Monsieur Rocca?"

"Hunting, of course."

"I see." She stared at him in silence, not wishing to start a fight. He seemed embarrassed by her gaze. His neck reddened, and he began to fidget with his hands.

"Have some coffee," he said grandly. "I must be going." He jumped up, knocking over the sugar, and fled.

Sybilia washed the plates and then wandered outside. This morning she was determined to feel at home. Perhaps she could weed the vegetable patch. She had big plans for her garden.

When she was hoeing the weeds from the melon patch, near the maquis, she heard plaintive mewing coming from an old stone shed on the other side of the stream. She crossed the stepping-stones and tried the door, which was unlocked. As her eyes became accustomed to the gloom, she saw that the room was swept and dusted as clean as the house. There were onions and wildflowers hanging from rafters to dry. Bulbs were spread out on a table, together with all kinds of herbs, among the hoes, spades, and scythes. Chopped wood was stacked along one wall of the shed. On top of the logs was an old basket from which came the sound of mewing. Sybilia looked over the rim and saw three ginger-and-white short-haired kittens and one beautiful tabby. It peered up at her with angry, questioning eyes.

"Oh! You! You sweet thing, you." Sybilia almost burst into tears, for the little tabby was a miniature of the cat she had left at home. She picked it up, and after a plaintive cry it began to suck at her thumb. Its mother came rushing from the garden and rubbed itself anxiously around her legs.

A sudden shadow appeared in the doorway. Sybilia spun around and saw Maria in the doorway.

"So you like cats," her mother-in-law began shyly. "You can have one, that is . . . if you like. Xavier was going to drown them; so Michel hid them up here. Of course Xavier's right," she said, excusing him. "There are so many wild cats around. But Michel's always been a sensitive boy. He can't bear anything to be killed or to be in pain. He's afraid of pain. Always has been, not so much for himself, but for others. . . ."

She rambled on while Sybilia petted the cat. Her own cat, she reminded herself. She would call him Tim-Tim.

"Thank you, Madame Rocca," she began shyly, suddenly terse and mindful of her awful situation.

"Poor old thing," Maria was muttering. "She knows we're

going to drown them again. We always do, but still, this time you'll have the tabby. One will be enough for her. One was enough for me." She looked round sadly. "You're a good girl, Sybilia. You're going to love Michel. Be patient."

Sybilia looked up and said bravely, "Why did you go up into the mountains this morning?"

"To be honest, I love the mountains and the maquis," Maria said, her eyes sparkling. "They are my refuge."

"It's rumored you are a *mazzeri*. That you can foretell death. Is that true?"

Infinite sadness glowed in eyes as deep as the lake. "I see death in my dreams. Sometimes I dream when I'm awake. I don't like what I see. I don't like what I know." Her voice took on the quality of a sleepwalker.

Like chanting, Sybilia thought as Maria gazed up toward the mountains.

"They will be hunting up there, just as they always do, but they will be hunting death—and a living death for you—I see it all so clearly."

Sybilia took hold of her arm and shook her. "Stop it! Please! Don't say these awful things."

Maria pulled herself together with a start. The girl looked so frightened. Had she had another turn? If only she could stop her foolish babbling, but it came and went of its own volition, and she had no control over it.

"Was I rambling on again? I'm sorry, Sybilia. You are frightened. I will try not to frighten you. You see, I like you so very much, and I hope that we will be friends," she whispered. "They say I am a *mazzeri*, but most times I don't really know what I've said. It's like a dream that you can't quite remember."

Sybilia smiled shyly. She didn't understand, but she was glad of her mother-in-law's confidence and her offer of friendship. "I'll take Tim-Tim upstairs to my apartment and give him some milk—Mama," she added as an afterthought with a shy smile.

From then on Sybilia grew closer to her mother-in-law. Maria was a warmhearted, generous woman, and Sybilia was grateful for her support. It was Maria more than anyone else who helped her to adjust to a life that was so different from what she had expected. Sybilia knew how to train a servant, but she had never scrubbed floors; she was an excellent cook in the French style, but she had never gathered chestnuts and ground the kernels into flour to make dough and bread. She did not know how to press olives or make goats'-milk cheese, but she was willing to learn. Maria was glad to teach her and fond of her company.

In the halcyon prewar days, there was nothing deprived about the Corsican peasant's life. The Roccas were among the luckiest, as Sybilia soon realized. Working haphazardly on their eighteen acres, spread far and wide, on terraces and fields and mountain pastures, they were practically self-sufficient.

Some of their land was fit only for grazing, but they also owned acres of old olives, big as oaks, alongside the cemetery. Down by the lake they had several rows of the best irrigated terraces on which Xavier grew barley, wheat, and maize when he felt like it. Sybilia soon took over this chore.

Together the women planted vegetables and put in some new fruit trees. Maria seemed to have found more energy and enthusiasm now that she had someone to work with her. She showed Sybilia how to collect the honey from their beehives in the maquis and how to protect the bees from the ants. The poultry were kept around the north side of the house, the pigs and goats roamed at will on the communal grazing land, stamped with the Rocca brand. Francois herded the sheep, spending five months of the year in the summer pastures high up the mountain slopes and four months farther down near the coast.

Except for hard cash, they lacked very little. There was a vineyard that provided enough wine and eau-de-vie for the year. They made cheeses from goats' milk, they had pork and mutton. When Xavier shot a hare in the maquis, Maria cooked a pot on the open fire with olive oil and whole cloves of garlic. Sometimes they killed a sheep and lived like kings for a while. Xavier kept the bistro's cash in his tightfisted grasp. He could only be coaxed to part with some of it for an emergency.

Every day Maria and Sybilia finished the household chores and gardening in four or five hours. Afterwards, they sewed or spent their afternoons sitting on the little terrace overlooking the magnificent sweep to the Gulf of Galeria, hardly speaking, glad of the rest and the peace.

When they needed coffee, sugar, or fabrics, Sybilia learned, they would take their olive oil or cheeses to the next village and barter with the villagers. She enjoyed these outings. They would leave after breakfast, before the sun was up, and walk along the village track bordering the cliff around the lake, with frequent stops to admire the flowers and the view. Sometimes they would stop at shady fountains and drink the cool mountain water or pass some time with old men and women sitting on logs in front of their homes. Their bartering would take place with great decorum in the best parlors of the houses they were visiting. Apart from exchanging produce, they would also swap gossip and news. They never left a house without exchanging small gifts.

In the afternoon they would start their home journey, stopping at sunset by a fountain, where they would eat some of their new bread, sausage, and wine tomatoes with olive oil. They would watch the sunset and discuss it and the people they had seen, and Maria would sketch in the background of each family for Sybilia. Eventually they would trudge home in the dusk of purple shadows and mountain mists, tired under their heavy burdens.

To Sybilia it was new and strange, but she was determined to do her best and not be depressed. The Roccas understood and tried to make her welcome. Even Michel was polite and fairly amiable toward her.

Nevertheless it was an anxious time for everyone. Underneath the deceptively calm exterior of summer days were hidden tensions. Everyone was preoccupied with their own worries. For Maria it was a time of dread. Night after night she woke sweating with fright. She would light her lamp, scramble out of bed onto her knees, and try to banish her nightmare in a tumult of prayer. But she could never forget the horror of the First World War, where thirty thousand of their young men in the Foreign Legion died in the trenches. Because of this, many of their mountain villages were still depopulated. Now war was coming again. There was no escape from it.

Michel's fears were for his career. He was on the point of running away from home. He had nothing against Sybilia. He even liked her. But the web of Taitan peasant life seemed to be binding him closer. Soon no escape would be possible. But if he went to study in Paris and war came, he might be killed. If the Foreign Legion didn't get him, the Germans would.

Xavier's anger made life difficult in the Rocca household.

Daily he harangued the family with his fears. The British and French governments were cowering from a confrontation with Hitler's armies. Their policy was appeasement. This was no way to run a country. In Xavier's opinion Hitler would soon overrun Europe, and who would stop him? French forces were inadequate even for their own domestic defense. Britain had begun a rearmament program in 1936, but she was hampered by lack of funds. The British Expeditionary Force, which comprised the only two divisions capable of fighting on the continent, was badly equipped for modern warfare. It was well known that they had no infantry tanks, very few up-to-date machine guns, and little mortar ammunition. Europe would be occupied quite soon, Xavier told them gloomily. Then it would be Corsica's turn. "Here we sit like a juicy plum waiting for Mussolini to gobble us up," he would say. Then he would explain his reasoning. As if it needed any clarification, Sybilia thought, since he voiced his fears at the supper table night after night.

The Italians had always coveted Corsica. In the past year Mussolini had openly voiced his intentions to annex their island. This coming war would give him the chance he needed. Any day now the Italians might hop across the water and invade Corsica. There was nothing to stop them. That was the most hurtful part of all—Corsica's helplessness. Most Corsicans despised Italians, calling them "Macaronis." To be called "fit for a Macaroni," with reference to manual labor or a fallen woman, was the ultimate insult.

One evening, to Sybilia's surprise, Maria joined in. "At least let the war stay off for another few weeks," she grumbled. "The olives are falling from the trees, and we can't afford to let them rot. After that we'll soon settle the hash of those upstart Bosch. As for the Macaronis . . ." She went off muttering to herself.

So the long summer idled on, and nothing much seemed to happen. Sybilia's days progressed smoothly enough, working a little, resting a little, trying her best to adjust. She was like a patient convalescing from an operation. There was still little direct contact with her husband. But the shock of her marriage, and her changed status, was slowly diminishing. She needed time and peace to rehabilitate herself.

CHAPTER 16

September, 1939

September was a long hot burden of a month. As the days dragged by, Sybilia became increasingly lonely. She missed her brothers, her dog, her cat, and her home. She would not admit that she missed her parents. Not for anything.

Maria was feeling the heat, but she was resting most of the time. Xavier was canvasing support for his party in neighboring villages. The autumn work was mainly finished, the olives picked, the chestnuts gathered, and their neighbors were providing both food and company for Maria. It took Sybilia a few hours to complete her household chores, and then she had nothing at all to do and the hours dragged by. For a while she practiced reading English, and then she played the piano, but she had no enthusiasm for either of these activities.

A sense of futility seemed to have invaded her body. Why bother to clean her teeth or comb her hair? Did anyone care what she looked like? she would ask herself bitterly. Most afternoons it was an effort to put one foot in front of the other, so she sat around listlessly doing absolutely nothing.

She was not at peace. She was tormented by her fears about Michel. He always ignored her, and she felt strangely empty. Not sad, not angry, she told herself repeatedly. Just sort of empty.

For the past two nights he had not slept at home. So where was he? The question was tormenting her. Perhaps he had a mistress in a neighboring village? Or was he sleeping in the mountains?

One morning after she finished the washing at the communal trough, she listened at the window to the older women discussing her plight with a good deal of scorn. The bloodied sheets had not fooled anyone for long. No one could agree on what was wrong with Michel, but they liked to air the possibilities. He was a *mazzeri*, like his mother, and hunted souls in the maquis, Vannina Susini insisted in her soft voice. Anyone could see he was more woman than man, Germaine the weaver proclaimed. Francoise Cesari, the *voceri*, reported that Michel was crazily in love with a goat. This was the story they all favored the most. Francoise had seen him carrying the beast up into the maquis for several mornings in a row. Nightly it ran back to the fold, frightened and hungry. Madame Rossi, the midwife, with her man's mustache and soulful black eyes, said he had a secret lair where he practiced black magic. And so on.

None of it was true. It couldn't be true! There must be a reason for Michel's long absences. Sybilia decided to speak to Maria, but it was hard to find the right opportunity. The day dragged by so slowly. Huge blue-black cumulous clouds gathered overhead at noon, and by midafternoon the air was heavy with humidity. The kitchen became so dark they lit the lamp. The gloom seemed to invade their thoughts as the two women worked at their different tasks in silence. Maria was dressed in black, as usual, with a checked apron. Her hair was straggling down from the bun, and her face was red and perspiring. From time to time she wiped her brow with her apron, and then she continued to knead the dough.

Sybilia, in revolt against black, wore an old school dress she had discovered in one of the chests. It was of pale blue linen with white cuffs and collar. With her hair braided she looked the child she was. She was bent over the ironing table when Gus appeared at the door, wagging his tail and begging for food.

"Well, at least the dog comes home for supper, which is more than one can say for your Michel," Maria grumbled as she filled its bowl with scraps from the stew.

"Do you know where Michel is?" Sybilia burst out, near to tears.

"Yes, I do, although he thinks I don't," Maria grumbled.

"Oh, Mama, what am I going to do?" Sybilia began hesitantly. "Is this to be my life?" Desperation brought the words tumbling out. "Will I never be a real wife, never have children? Will I grow old here, like a spinster aunt, helping in the kitchen and bored to tears? Oh, what's the matter with Michel? I heard the women talking—they say terrible, vicious things about him."

Maria collapsed in a heap on the kitchen chair and dabbed her eyes with the tea towel. Watching her, Sybilia felt so ashamed. She knelt beside her and wrapped her arms around her shoulders.

"Oh, Mama, I've hurt you. I'm sorry, really I am, but I'm so . . . so empty. I have nothing to replace all that I have lost. I mean I have you, and I'm grateful, but it's not enough. No, not nearly enough." She buried her face in Maria's lap.

"I know, child," Maria said, stroking her hair. "Those wicked women, they've always misjudged my Michel. He's different, but only because he's so sensitive. He's shy, you see, and he's never had much to do with women. You know, Sybilia, one always thinks that it's the man who does the chasing, but in many cases it's the women who have to take over. If they want their men, that is. If you want children, Sybilia, I think you're going to have to woo Michel. Try to get him on your side. Try to tempt him, Sybilia. I mean"—she wiped her face, which was damp with embarrassment—"that's just the viewpoint of a silly old woman, but in your place that's what I would do. Some men don't know what's good for them, not until it's rammed down their necks. I reckon Michel's one of them. He's proud and stubborn, and he didn't want to be married. It's up to you, Sybilia. You're a beautiful girl."

Sybilia was glad her face was hidden. She could feel herself burning with embarrassment. "How would I do that?" she murmured into the woman's lap.

"Oh, I don't know about those things. Xavier was always—" She broke off. "That is, until he met that other woman. But there, I mustn't fill your head with my problems, and besides, he thinks I don't know. I remember the day I found out. . . ."

She rambled on and on, but Sybilia was not listening. She was remembering a book she had seen once. A terrible book! One of the girls—yes, it was Miriam—had found it in her father's library and brought it to school. Photographs of such ghastly women, milky white and plump as Christmas geese, with deep red paint on their lips and nails and other places, in various stages of disgraceful undress, gazing slyly toward the camera. Oh, no, she could never do that.

She was brought back to the present by Maria tapping her shoulder. "Why don't you go up there?" she added with a smile. "Take him some food."

"How would I find him?"

"Keep Gus on a lead, and you won't go wrong. I'll lock that dog up for the night, or he'll be off as soon as he's finished his food."

Early next morning Sybilia dressed in her best black dress and set off up the mountain carrying a rifle, cheeses, bread, and a flask of coffee. What could be more reasonable than for a wife to take her husband some coffee? All the same, visions of herself dressed like those dreadful women in the dirty pictures kept floating into her mind's eye. Michel would not take kindly to that.

It was still cloudy; wraiths of mist were drifting in the valleys below. But the maquis was a blaze of autumn flowers, yellow broom, and wild chrysanthemums, lavender, and rosemary. Bumblebees, fat as plums, were gathering the last pollen, and the birds were lingering and swooping and twittering before their long southward flight.

Sybilia was in no mood to admire the morning. She regretted wearing one of her good dresses and wondered if Gus was quite as good a tracker as Maria claimed. Together they raced around boulders and through thickets, along a narrow goat track. In places the undergrowth was four meters high, and she burrowed through it until her dress was soiled and her hands scratched and bleeding.

Suddenly the maquis came to an abrupt halt at the edge of a slight incline. She would have fallen if it were not for the dog, which sat on its haunches and whined. She paused and stared in surprise, for she could hear the unmistakable sound of hammering.

Ahead the ground flattened into an old, disused quarry. Or was it a quarry? It was only slightly concave and more like a platform halfway up the mountain. On the edge of the platform, overlooking the mountain slope, huge blocks had been placed on top of each other to make a crude fortress. It looked as if a giant's child had played with building blocks.

Triangular slabs of granite lay on the ground. Some were weirdly shaped into the crude outline of a face. Whoever did it must have lived a long time ago, she thought wonderingly, for shrubs sprouted from every crack.

The dog was bounding toward a large cave in the mountainside. Sybilia followed more slowly, acutely aware of her ragged appearance. As she hurried after him, she heard a curse while she stood blinking in the sudden gloom.

"Shit! Sybilia! Why are you spying on me?"

Michel was sitting on a sliced tree trunk, his legs straddling a large rock that he had been attacking with a hammer and chisel. He was wearing only his corduroy pants. His thin suntanned body gleamed with sweat while his hair hung damp and disheveled over one eye. He looked pale, exhausted, and caked with grime.

"Spying on you? Good heavens!" She flushed with anger. "Spying, you call it? I was worried about you. I want to know what you do all day. Why shouldn't I? It's natural for a wife to worry," she added.

As her eyes adjusted to the shadows, she saw that the rock Michel was hammering was being chipped into the shape of a naked girl. Was it supposed to be her? It was hard to tell, for the surface was full of chips and the body was only crudely emerging from the waist upward.

Sybilia was speechless. The cave and the ledge behind were cluttered with statues of people and animals. Among the debris she saw a half-finished image of a goat, shockingly real and life-size, rearing up to paw the air. Then she remembered the stories she had heard about Michel, and she began laughing almost hysterically with relief.

Michel threw his hammer on the floor and swore. "So! What is there to giggle about? This is art. Something you wouldn't understand, you ignorant peasant girl."

"Do you know what they say in the village? They say you make love with the goats."

He sighed, pushed his hair out of his eyes, and stood up. For a moment he seemed undecided. Then he dropped his chisel on the ground and stretched. "And what else do they say?"

"That you are a *mazzeri*."

"Do you believe their stories?"

She shrugged. "I came to see for myself."

"Now that you've seen, you can go home," he said irritably. "You will tell all your prattling girlfriends, and Papa will find out."

He did not look angry, she decided, watching him intently. In fact, he looked quite pleased to see her, but wary, like a wild animal, half-tamed and hungry.

"My only friend is Maria," she said sadly. "And she knows—" She broke off. "What is it?" she said, pointing to his work.

"It's you," he said. Then he stood up and gazed down at her so searchingly that she frowned.

Michel turned away quickly. He did not know what it was about her that disturbed him so profoundly. He only knew that he had to re-create her with his own hands. It would be enough simply to capture the essence of her in stone or wood, but that very act of creation seemed to elude him. This was his third attempt, but when he looked at the real thing he was overcome with humiliation. Why was she so lovely? He noticed how the light from the entrance made a halo around her hair, how her face had a strange, brooding expression as she gazed at him. There were shadows under her eyes, and her cheeks were thinner. However much she frowned, she could never disguise the yearning in her face. She longed for a kind word, but his only defense was cruelty. He sighed, picked up his chisel, and began chipping away at the shoulders of the statue.

"You're not very good at this," she said after she had examined several pieces, "because you're not as realistic as the statues in the church. But there's a sense of power in your work. I feel the goat's fear, and its desperation. Yes, I feel it here." She pressed her stomach.

Michel looked pleased momentarily. Then he scowled and shrugged. "What do you know about it, little peasant girl?"

"I know what I feel, and the statues give me goose pimples. Oh!" she exclaimed, pointing toward a cleft in the wall where a life-size bust had been placed. "Just look at Carlotta there." She burst out laughing—a childish laugh that reminded him of her deprived youth. How wicked of their parents to force her into marriage.

"You've turned Carlotta into a grinning demon," her voice babbled on nervously.

"That's how I see her," he said.

"And is this how you see me?" She forced herself to turn back to the offending statue, which brought the blood rushing to her face. "One side is larger than the other," she stammered, "and I am not that fat."

"I can't do it—that's why." He flung his chisel on the ground in a fit of temper. "Since you're here, let's see what you've brought to eat."

They sat outside in the sun drinking coffee with homemade bread and strong goats' cheese. After a while Sybilia flushed and blurted: "Will you be my friend? I am not the silly peasant girl you take me for. You will be surprised yet." She held out her hand in a gesture of conciliation, but Michel made no move to take it.

His blue eyes were gleaming, his lips twisted into a crooked smile. "How can a man be friends with a woman?" he said. "That's a ridiculous idea. We have different interests. Besides, you would bore me."

Oh, how cruel! She would get him back for that. She longed to control and possess this disagreeable man. How else would she ever have any power or be able to do anything? Only through him. An idea was forming in her mind, taking her breath away with her audacity. But hadn't Maria said . . . ? And hadn't she seen in the book . . . ?

But no! Never! Her prudish convent upbringing, her shyness, and her virginity sent the blood racing to her skin until she was throbbing and flushing all over. She shook her head at her own boldness.

Instead of scowling, she smiled teasingly. "Would I bore you, Michel? Are you sure? Maybe I'll surprise you yet."

He lay on his back, put one hand over his eyes, and dozed in the sun.

"Michel," she persisted, "why did you drag the goat into your cave?

He sighed. "I'm sleeping," he said.

"Was it to help you make your statue? Can't you work from memory?"

"No," he snarled. "Even top artists have models. Didn't you even know that, you silly goose?"

She stood up and tiptoed into the cave. It seemed to go back a long way, and then she saw a hole leading to another dark cavern that she was too frightened to enter. "Shall I go now?" she called.

"Oh . . ." He sounded pleased. "So you are not going to surprise me, after all." He propped himself on one elbow, and his moody blue eyes met hers. They were so inscrutable, so uncommunicative, that she had a fleeting impression there would never be another chance to get through to him. She shuddered slightly, bit her lip, and unbuttoned her blouse. "I will be your model," she said. "Then perhaps you will be able to make your lump of rock look like me. That's what you want, isn't it?"

"Oh, God," he groaned.

"Or would you prefer that I didn't?" she called out, a new imperiousness in her voice.

Michel stood up and hurried into the cave. He stared miserably at his chipped rock with the dumb, uneven features and then back at her.

"Yes. You're right! That's what I want more than anything else," he admitted hoarsely.

"And we shall be friends? I shall be your model and help you with your work?"

"Maybe just this time." He sounded unsure of himself.

Sybilia walked slowly out of the cave again. How could she? Never. No, never. Part of her wanted to flee from Michel and not come back, but another unknown, pristine part of her womanliness knew that she must conquer him.

She tried to unbutton her dress, but her fingers had turned to jelly. At last she let the garment fall slowly to the ground. She looked around coyly at Michel. Why did he pretend that he was ignoring her when she could feel his intense awareness soaking into her like summer rain?

I'm his wife, she told herself as she lost her courage. It's not a crime to take off my clothes. What had her mother said? *Never let him see you naked.* Yet hadn't they dressed her in that silly, transparent nightgown? But here? In a public place? She knew there was no one around for miles. Gus would bark if there were.

She unbuttoned her bodice. Her breasts thrust up and out like birds freed from a cage. Then she noticed how silly she looked in her black boots and slip and glanced to see if Michel was looking, but his face was turned away from her, and he was still chiseling.

Hastily she kicked off her boots, her slip, and, last of all, her pants.

The breeze on her skin was like a gentle caress. Her body vibrated with the pleasure of it, and her nipples grew until they were erect. She tried to speak, but her mouth was so dry only a cracked whisper came out: "Where do you want me to sit?"

He glanced her way so briefly. "Oh, on that rock," he said as casually as he could.

"Can I sit on my skirt? The rock hurts me."

"If you wish."

Covered with shame and humiliation, but determined nevertheless, she sat, hunched and dejected.

"If you could sit more like this," Michel said in the manner of a polite stranger. He walked up to her and tried to move her shoulders around, but when he touched her skin he pulled his hand back as if he had been burned. She flushed deeply.

"Don't be a baby," he said angrily. "Married people do this all the time."

Whom was he snarling at? Himself? Or her? She smiled inwardly and tried not to think about her own body. She had never examined herself naked, and she tried not to look down. Instead she gazed out at the mouth of the cave. She could see a hawk soaring on an upcurrent. Suddenly it dived into the bushes, and a second later it rose, clutching a small creature, a rat or a mouse, in its claws.

Oh, Michel, she thought. I wish you had the courage of that hawk. I wish you would soar down on me and carry me helplessly away.

For the first time she became aware of herself as a physical being and not just a walking, moving hive of thoughts. She became aware of her breasts rising and falling with each breath, of the blood coursing through her body, of her heartbeat, which was surely much louder than usual.

She had the strangest sense of the present moment, as if it were a precious drop of moisture, and she, dying of thirst in the desert, must make the most of it.

"You're very beautiful," Michel said suddenly, breaking in on her fantasy.

"Am I?" She had never thought of herself as beautiful or not beautiful, nor as anything physical in her life. Merely as herself.

"When I have finished this, I shall use you as a model

for a statue of the Madonna. It will be far more beautiful than the one in church."

"Hush! That's blasphemy," she said, crossing herself quickly.

He chuckled. "What a little goose you are."

She looked around at him, feeling angered by his indifference. "How silly," she called out, pointing at his statue. "I am not wide like that. And my ribs are not all knobbly. Come. Feel how soft my skin is. And my breasts are round, not square."

Michel put down his chisel like a man in a dream. He walked slowly toward her and pushed his hand at her, as if into a fire. She caught hold of it and pressed it over one breast. How rough his skin was, how hot his hand—like burning coals.

She gasped and stood up. "You see," she murmured. She was not quite sure what she meant, but she could feel his hand trembling and hear his breath coming in short, sharp gasps.

Then her courage fled. She leaped away. Grabbing her clothes, she scrambled into them outside the cave.

"That's quite enough for one day, thank you," she called out in a high-pitched voice. "My back's aching, my neck is stiff, and I'm shivering cold all over."

"You will come back, won't you?" she heard wistfully behind her as she fled.

CHAPTER 17

October, 1939

An autumn heat wave held the island becalmed.

Xavier had organized a hunting trip for his political colleagues and rivals, and they were meeting in a glen on the outskirts of the Bonifato forest, under the slopes of the Ladroncello mountain peaks.

He was early. As he reined to a halt at the edge of the glade, he saw a chamois doe leap up and stand transfixed with shock, staring bolt-eyed at nothing. He pulled up his gun, aimed, and put it down again. It was too soon and too easy. There was no point in a kill without a chase, and it was too early to burden the hunt with meat.

What a morning! Dew fresh and new, the sky was washed by the rain into a pale, translucent blue. The crystal-clear mountains loomed over the forest. Chestnuts and oaks were turning gold and red. A sudden gust of wind sent the leaves spiraling into the sodden humus of countless leafy harvests, where brambles sprawled thick with berries and mushrooms sprouted. There was the sound of a stream gurgling in the thicket behind the glade.

Xavier let his horse go free to graze the fresh grass. He reached for his saddlebag and took out a bottle of brandy, which he would share. Meantime he took a swig, wiped his mustache, and sat on a tree trunk.

The hunting party arrived in twos and threes. They passed the carafe of brandy around and sat discussing the news quietly among themselves. They seemed to sense Xavier's mood of introspection, and they let him be. A month ago, Britain and France had declared war on Germany. Corsica, as a province of France, was at war. That was all they could talk about. As yet there was no visible sign of the war. You could say that nothing had changed, yet underneath everything had changed. Take this morning's hunt . . . that had changed.

Take fat old Rene Guerrini, groaning quietly on his old mare, red and swollen with exertion. He was here because he was too scared to stay away. Why was he scared? For the simple reason that he had canvased support for unity with Italy for many years, but now he had to show he was one of them—a patriot—a true Corsican—ready to do whatever had to be done with the rest of them. What better way was there than by joining the boys in the morning's hunt?

Take Maria! She had it firmly fixed in her mind that there would be shortages. For the first time, she and Sybilia had gathered every single fallen olive and with gritty determination squashed each one in the homemade press. She had exchanged the oil at the village store for coffee and sugar—enough to last them a year. Now she was walking around clutching her back and claiming she had slipped a disk with all that effort.

Take Michel! He had joined the hunt, and that in itself was remarkable. There he sat with a supercilious look on his face, as if humoring a crowd of overgrown children. When Michel put on that look, Xavier longed to wipe it off with the back of his fist. He had long since given up persuading his son to come hunting with the men. Come to think of it, he had long ago given up on Michel—full stop. But now Michel wanted to find out which way the land lay with the Nationalist movement—so he had tagged along. Xavier had never agreed with Michel on politics. He couldn't understand the boy's contempt for Corsica, his longing to be French. Nevertheless, they would be political allies at least until the war was fought and won.

The Bertoli twins were there, together with several other fugitives from the Marseilles crime syndicate. They were both diminutive men in their forties with identical faces, like cherubs, but with minds as savage as wildcats. They had opted out of their very profitable beat in the smuggling ring and the Lord knew what else in order to sit out the war years in Corsica. They would fight like demons if they had to, but only to protect their beloved island.

Antoine Romanetti had tagged along, too. The shepherd was a loner who never joined their hunts. Xavier had always considered him to be slightly demented because he hated any creature to be killed. Many evenings, after a good shoot, they'd had to listen to Romanetti's lectures, thinly disguised as poems, which he'd sung to them in the bistro. He must have changed his views because he wanted to join the Resistance. He'd come along today to make sure he wasn't left out.

And the rest . . . The shepherd Ambrosini was there because he was a tough fighting man. Normally he wasn't invited along. He stank, and there was something vile about him. Marcel Leca and Carlo Castelli were there, naturally. They were his aides in the party, but temporary allies only, for they were communists. Right now they had need of each other.

Xavier mounted his horse and gave an impatient wave to the rest of the party. They were all good men, he knew. With the exception of Michel, they were utterly dependable for bravery, if not for logic. In an argument their emotions won every time, yet they were courageous, loyal, and proud. Each one was fiercely independent, yet together, when hunting or fighting, they formed a composite body of men who could act as one without instructions. Curious, that. A sort of mental telepathy, a sense of oneness, born of centuries of hunting, fighting, and living in close confinement in their isolated villages. It was something he had always taken for granted until he had joined the French navy and found that it was a Corsican trait.

As he led his hunting party into the mountains, some of his excitement was transmitted to his horse, which was bucking nervously and working up a lather. The dogs were in a frenzy. They'd caught the scent of game. Xavier was in no hurry for that special moment when he sighted his quarry down the barrel of his gun. It wasn't the killing that fired his enthusiasm for hunting as much as the chance to get up in the mountains, away from roads and newspapers and the mucky invasion of the outside world. Then his heart sang with the earth and the wind. His mind moved in sync with that of his prey and plunged with it on the wild, canny flight into the maquis, even at its moment of death.

At seven thousand feet, after they had lost the trail of the boar and even missed a hare, they camped for *casse-croute*, a heavy meal of ham and cheese, bread, and wine with a great deal of eau-de-vie to drink.

It was cold and fresh, but even the mountain scenery could not pull Xavier from his morose mood. "We'll win the war, of course," he told them, "but we won't win the peace. The postwar era will bring changes we'll all have to accept. . . ."

Xavier's vision was not a pleasant one, but he held them spellbound as he explained his premonition. It was of roads and trains and airstrips, and all the paraphernalia of the modern world—the rape of Corsica, he told them several times. Of tourists flocking to Corsican beaches, for in all his worldwide travels he had never seen beaches to touch those of his island. Of the gradual erosion of Corsican morals and mores. Of divorce, women lying naked on beaches, of mass entertainment and the loss of crafts and patience. The property developers would come, and the money-makers and flocks of expatriates from every nation in Europe, coaxing the Corsicans to sell their houses for high prices, not realizing that inflation would whittle away at their capital. In the end they'd be the poorer and homeless, too. "Everyone in the world will want a slice of this paradise, once they find out about it," he told them. "It'll be up to us to hang on to it."

But that was another fight for another day.

His words were received with gloomy silence, each man unwilling to show his feelings.

"In the meantime we pull together," they all agreed. "Let's drink victory," they roared. "Victory or death!"

"Victory or death!" Their voices echoed around the glade.

They discussed what they would do when they were invaded. They would join the Resistance fighters—that was taken for granted—but each had a specific skill to offer.

"We'll be ready for the Macaronis. They'll be so shit scared they'll run back across the water," one of the men crowed.

"They won't come yet." It was Guerrini who had spoken, and a sudden hush fell over the rowdy men.

"You think that? Or perhaps you know. Perhaps you have special communication. Out with it, Guerrini. We all know you're a fascist. What'll they make you when they come—a commandant?"

Guerrini shook his fist under the nose of Castelli. "Don't joke about something so serious," he snarled.

"What's so serious about those bastard Macaronis?" Bertoli yelled.

"There's something serious about accusing me of treason," Guerrini murmured, fingering his knife.

"Knock it off." Xavier's quiet voice was enough to bring instant silence to the gathering. "I don't like to hear you talk like this. We've come here today to consolidate our unity. That's what this hunt is all about. We're going to sort the men from the boys. Let's face it, we've all got our ambitions for Corsica, but we've always stuck together when she's threatened."

A murmur of assent ran around the crowd.

"So it stands to reason that for the duration of the war, we'd be wise to put our differences aside. We'll sort them out later, when we've shown the French how to fight, and sent our enemies packing."

* * *

Michel watched and wondered. He had been on these hunts before. They were merely an excuse for a get-together. Corsicans were all highly skilled hunters, and so were their dogs. They knew the terrain intimately, and game was plentiful. So there was no need to become serious about the killing until an hour or so before sunset.

The rhetoric went on and on, and it seemed to Michel that they would sit there all day repeating themselves and assuring each other of their manhood and bravery. There were more roars, more toasts, more backslapping. So far Michel had not totally agreed with what his father had said, yet he had been stirred by Xavier's passion. There was no mistaking the power of his leadership. Michel had many contradictory feelings toward his father, part admiration, part hate, part jealousy, but never indifference. Impossible to be indifferent to a man who could stir such loyalty from his followers.

Primitives, all of them, Michel thought as he leaned against a tree looking bored and superior and watched the hunters leaping on their horses with bloodcurdling cries. Then they were off up the mountain, driving their mounts to extremes.

Michel followed more slowly. By tacit consent he was always left to bring up the rear. Were he not Xavier's son, he would not be included in the hunt. What a bloody bore it was, but he had to come, for he intended to join the Resistance.

An hour later he was still climbing. By now the sea had turned a deep peacock blue, and the sun was a glowing orange ball as it dipped slowly below the horizon. Far above he heard the frenetic baying of the hounds and the men's shouts.

He had no intention of driving his horse to near extinction, but after a while it seemed that the chase was moving southward and it occurred to Michel that he could take a shortcut. He climbed onto a nearby boulder and surveyed the territory. It must be a buck of some sort, for a boar would dive into the thicker bush and head uphill. It seemed to be making for the river. It would probably come downstream, to try to throw the dogs off scent and pick up more speed. Well, if he could cut across the bush here and make for the river, he might save himself hours of riding.

It would not escape. Night was falling, and the huntsmen

would be intent on their kill. A feeling of depression fell over him. The trees bending over the track seemed to be menacing him, the interplay of shadows in the thicket was like fleeting glimpses of spirits haunting the maquis. However much of a Francophile he might feel himself to be, Michel could never shake off his superstitious fancies. Age-old fears kept him hurrying through the bush.

By the time he reached the river it was darker and weirdly silent. He climbed on a boulder overlooking the waterfall and clutched his rifle.

He saw now with a sudden shock of dismay that it was all but over. A huge roan antelope stood at bay on a rock, foolishly hesitating when it should plunge into the torrent. Safety lay that way.

The huntsmen had moved up in position around both riverbanks, and the buck was surrounded. The dogs were baying on the shore. As if by tacit consent among the huntsmen, the final coup de grace was to be administered by Xavier. Michel could see him on the crest of the hill, down on one knee, his rifle on his shoulder as he took careful aim.

Still the antelope hesitated. Michel could see his magnificent antlers, see the fear in his eyes, and almost smell his frenzy, although he was at least eighty yards upstream, much closer to Xavier.

One shot! Just one shot would frighten that beast into taking its plunge for freedom into the river. To hell with Xavier. Without a second thought Michel flung up his rifle and fired over the beast's head.

It dropped. Oh, God! It dropped! He had never been a good shot, and now he had hit the antelope clean between the eyes. Time seemed to go into slow motion as he watched the poor beast crumple from the knees. It was still jerking and sliding down, about to slither into the water, when the first huntsman clambered up, knife in hand, and grabbed its antlers.

"Goddammit! Why? Why?" Michel hurled his rifle onto the ground and clambered down, blinded with tears of remorse.

He tried to keep his face devoid of expression as Xavier, roaring with approval, clapped his shoulder over and over and told the men proudly that Sybilia had turned his boy into a man.

It was an excellent shot, they told him repeatedly. Clean through the brain. The meat would be superbly tender because the beast had died before pain had tarnished it. Its brains had been blown clean through the back of its skull, they told him excitedly. They had never seen such a good shot—clean through the eyeball. What a sly, dark horse Michel was, leading them all to believe that he hated hunting.

Michel silently leaned against his horse and tried to choke back his nausea.

CHAPTER 18

She found him in the woodshed, stroking the cat. She would never have known he was there, but for Gus patiently waiting outside. He smelled of sweat and dirt, and his face was muddy and tear-streaked.

"Oh," Sybilia said. She took a step backward and began to tiptoe away, but what was the point since Michel had seen her? He was crumpled on a pile of sacks in the shadows, and he looked at her as if he hated her, along with the rest of the world.

"I thought you were the big hero, but I find you crying like a small child," she said. She hated hunting and had been appalled to discover that Michel was as thoughtless as the rest of the village men.

"Hero!" He spat the words out. "Any fool can kill. The cretins! If I were a hero, I would sabotage their damned hunts. Oh, Sybilia! I tried. I fired to frighten the buck into the river and I missed. Oh, God! It was such a beautiful animal. Magnificent, powerful, free. Now it's supper."

"I won't eat a mouthful," Sybilia said simply. She sat beside him and attempted to wind her arms around his shoulders.

"Don't be sad," she said. "It's over. There's no point."

"Oh, for goodness' sake, take your trite words of comfort and water the cemetery with them."

"Why do you hate me so?" she said.

"I don't hate you," he murmured. "I hate what you represent. You are my jailer; the key that was turned on me, locking me here in this hell they call Taita."

Sybilia sat thinking about that for a while. She looked as dejected as Michel, sitting cross-legged on the sacks with her head in her hands. Then she said: "You've never learned to be honest with yourself, Michel. You always blame other people, but you are your own victim. Look at the Bertolis and the Lecas. They left Taita after they were married. They only come home to spawn children. They make their money in Marseilles."

"Don't hold them up as examples. They're criminals."

"True. But if Bertoli wanted to be a sculptor, he'd be right there in Paris doing just that, I promise you." She folded her lips into an obstinate line and waited for her words to sink in.

"It would be years before I made any money."

"Not 'would,' *will*. You don't seem to have any faith in your dreams. Don't worry, Michel. I am much stronger than you. I will get a job—after the war. I'm sure it will be easy for me, because my English is excellent. My German is good, too, and I speak Italian fluently."

"Who doesn't?" he murmured. "You'd be a drag on me."

"Then go by yourself," she retorted, finding it hard to be patient with him. "Give yourself five years. If you haven't succeeded by then, come back and be a farmer. You'd do better with me," she added thoughtfully. "I could keep you."

"You crazy child. I'm supposed to keep you."

"You're so conventional," she said. "I thought artists were different. Anyway, we'll have to wait until after the war. Who knows, it may be over by the end of next year. That's what everyone's saying."

"A year! It might as well be a century."

"No, it will pass quickly. If only you had some optimism."

"Life has knocked it out of me."

She stood up abruptly and moodily kicked at the sacks. What a martyr he was, never happy unless he felt victimized. "If you were my brother, I'd tell you what a coward you are," she said at last.

"Why bother? Everyone else has told me already."

"But you don't believe them, do you?"

"No."

"The poor, misunderstood Michel."

"Something like that. Oh, all right, maybe I'm a bit scared. Not of going, not of starving, nothing like that, Sybilia. I'm scared I may find out that I'm no good."

She looked at him in surprise. He wasn't often so honest with her. "Yes, I can see that's a terrible fear," she said. "Perhaps we should stay here all our lives and never know what might have been. Just pretend that you're a great artist who never had a chance."

"You're a bitch," he said, standing up and brushing down his clothes. "I don't know why I bother to talk to you. Other husbands would beat you."

"Michel." She caught hold of his shoulders and shook him violently and could not help noticing his passivity at her touch. "Listen to me, Michel. Give it a chance, give your talent a chance, and please, Michel, give me a chance. You're all I'm ever going to have. I'll work myself to death for you to succeed."

He bit his lip and stared away over her shoulder toward the house, where noisy shouts were coming from the parlor. Xavier's posthunting party was a great success.

He sighed. "You want all this? This rooting and rutting, spending your life in backbreaking work just to survive, growing a little food, cooking, getting pregnant every year?"

"We won't be like that," she said bravely. "We'll be fashionable, and you'll be a famous artist, and we'll entertain and have a lovely flat in Paris."

Michel's depression seemed to be lifting under the force of her dream. "I never thought of you that way," he said, "but you could be an asset, I suppose. You can come home at night and cook supper and then model for me."

"Of course," she said. "That's how it will be."

Not far below them the antelope was turning over the spit—a delicious smell was wafting toward the house.

"Are you hungry?" she asked.

"Starving."

"I'll bring up some bread and cheese."

"If you want to eat . . . that," he said with a nervous gesture, "don't bring it upstairs."

"I would never," she vowed.

"I always thought I'd fall in love one day," Michel said, and this time it was her turn to look surprised. "I imagined a beautiful girl with long blond hair, walking barefooted along the beach, the wind blowing her hair and her skirt. The reality of women is rather different." He caught hold of her hands and held them close. "We're victims of the system. Two strangers tied together for life, for other people's convenience. Do we bow to the system? Do as we're told? Sex without love? Is that what you want? Like beasts?"

"Father Andrews says love grows," she said. "I'm getting to like you because I understand you better," she added softly.

"Well, that's a start, my beautiful Sybilia. Now I'm going to wash this filth off me. I stink worse than them."

"I've lit the copper. It's full of hot water for a bath," she said, and watched his eyes light up at the prospect. "I told you I'd be useful." She smiled.

The storeroom was full of steam, the stove was boiling merrily, and the tub was full of warm, soapy water. Michel was about to step into it when Sybilia returned carrying a clean towel and some fresh clothes.

His eyes were suddenly hostile as he grabbed a cloth and held it in front of him. "I can manage, thanks," he said. "Put the towel there."

She ignored him and bustled around the storeroom, shutting the vents to put out the stove.

"Sybilia, I'm waiting to bathe."

"Yes, you'd best hurry, or the water will get cold."

"Well, go, then."

"Why?" She turned and smiled winsomely. "Why are you so old-fashioned? So scared to be seen? Are you deformed?"

"God, no."

"Well then. Do you know that Japanese women scrub their men in the tub?"

"We're Corsican."

"I thought we weren't going to be Corsican."

He shrugged, scowled at her, and stepped into the tub.

"You've such a nice neck," she said, running her fingers

over his throat. "And a lovely profile. Did anyone ever tell you what a lovely profile you have?"

Once again that terrible passivity was there. He leaned back, closed his eyes, and his face took on a dreamy, sensuous expression. Was he never going to grab her? She took the sponge and began to rub away the grime on his shoulders, moving down to his chest.

Was it only curiosity? she wondered. She had wanted to see what he looked like for weeks, but now there was a burning need to know. The wanting began in her stomach like a warm sting and moved out to the tips of her fingers, turning her skin to gooseflesh.

"Does this feel nice?" she asked, running soapy hands over his chest and ribs. "Oh, Michel, how thin you are."

There was no answer from Michel. His eyes were closed, his head was lolling back against the edge of the iron tub, his mouth hung slack and slightly open. He was gasping slightly.

"Stand up," she said eventually. "You're only half-done."

To her surprise Michel stood up, and she gasped with amazement at his changing shape. She ran her soapy hands over his body, enjoying the feel of his flesh, the bristly pubic hairs, the sight of his taut thighs and smooth white skin.

"It's a pity to waste this nice warm water," she said, and feverishly took off her clothes, throwing them on the floor. "I feel so funny," she whispered. "As if I could split clean down the middle, like an overripe banana. Do you feel like that?"

"No."

"What do you feel like?"

"Why must you always put things into words? I'll show you what I feel like." He caught hold of her around the waist and pulled her against him. Then he slipped on the soap, and they collapsed in a heap in the warm water.

Sybilia felt languid and burning hot. She wanted to lie back somewhere, but there was no room. She hardly had the strength to toss her legs over the tub and slither onto his lap. His arms were snug around her waist and hers were wound around his neck. Her legs straddled his thighs. She felt an acute sensation of pleasure as Michel slithered and slipped against her skin.

"Oh," she gasped. "I think we're doing it."

Michel remained prostrate, his head thrown back, his eyes closed as if in a trance as she moved her thighs gently forward and backward.

Sybilia felt a dull pain almost lost somewhere among the urgency of her mounting tension. Then suddenly there was nothing at all, merely Michel groaning and the water staining red.

She felt disappointed. Why had he stopped? "Can't you do it again?" she asked.

"No, I don't think so," he said. He was intent on looking away and avoiding her eyes. "Maybe later. Right now definitely not. Did I hurt you?"

"No, it was nice," she lied. "Was it nice for you?" He grinned and then laughed. Surprisingly, he wrapped his arm around her shoulder. "Come on, time for bed, you little seductress," he said. "I hope you're going to find all that worthwhile."

Michel seemed to have lost his shyness with his virginity. He raced into the kitchen with a towel around his waist, took some bread and cheese and a carafe of wine, and brought them up to their rooms. He threw the towel on the floor and sat naked, munching hungrily. Then he smiled sleepily, kissed her on one cheek, climbed into bed, and fell asleep almost immediately.

There must be something wrong with Mother, Sybilia thought, remembering her whispered advice and fears at the wedding. It didn't really hurt. One couldn't call it wonderful, either, but at least they had done it. Now they were truly married. She sat by the window for a long time, feeling too restless to sleep.

CHAPTER 19

Michel stood in the doorway of the living room and gazed at Sybilia. The oil lamp suspended from a slender chain above the table reflected red glints in her dark hair. Her face seemed paler, her eyes unnaturally large. She gazed up at him and smiled shyly. As she bent over her book her dress fell forward, revealing a part of the sweet swelling of her breast where a crucifix twinkled. She was reading aloud to Maria and Xavier. The doors to the patio were wide open, and behind her he could see the full moon, as lustrous and sensual as Sybilia, bathing the earth and the blue night sky with a golden haze. Was there evèr such a night? His perceptions were sharpened beyond endurance, the mountains close enough to touch, like a theater backdrop, unbelievable but exquisitely beautiful, each tree and rock highlighted by moonlight.

He forced himself to look at his father in his chair, filling his pipe, the Corsican patrician, handsome, robust, virile, and deadly. Maria was stitching away at her cloth, black hair gleaming, blue eyes smiling, gnarled hands moving nimbly. She was amused by Sybilia's words and mumbled quietly to herself from time to time. They were all enriched by Sybilia's presence; she lent them grace and beauty and brought her own special peace to the household. He should paint them just so—a Corsican family bathed in Sybilia's golden glow.

Yet something was missing. The picture was incomplete. Of course, it was himself. If he were to walk into the halo of light from the lamp, how would he fit into the picture? Who was he? What would he look like? Her husband? Or an impostor? These questions shocked him. He had difficulty visualizing himself. He had never thought of himself as a person before, least of all as a member of a Corsican family or as a member of this family. He had always been an outsider.

He looked down and stared at his hands and the hairs on his arms and the muscles—a sculptor's muscles. He was wearing brown corduroy trousers and a checked mohair shirt. His mother had made it two years ago, and it was rather short in the arms, so he kept the sleeves rolled up. Now he consciously imagined himself walking into the room and standing behind Sybilia, placing one hand on her shoulder and saying . . . ? What would her husband say? "It's late. Shall we go to bed, my dear?" How trite and bourgeois! How desirable! But how impossible.

As if on cue, his father leaned forward, placed one hand on her wrist, and said: "It's late, Sybilia. You'll strain your eyes in this light."

"Yes, Papa," she said dutifully. "I'll finish the chapter. That is, if you like," she said, turning to Maria.

"What are you reading?" Michel asked. They all looked surprised, but each showed their own emotions: Sybilia pleased to see him; Maria anxious, as always; his father contemptuous. There was a strange silence, but Gus stood up and flopped over, rubbing his body against his legs.

"She's not reading," Xavier said with a tinge of peasant pride. "She's translating Mark Twain from the English for your mother."

"Of course it's not the first time I've read it," Sybilia said hastily. "We did it at school, so I know it very well."

"It's sad," said his mother. "The poor boy didn't have a real mother."

Xavier snorted contemptuously. "It's not sad at all. The boy's going to be a man. Some mothers can ruin their sons."

"Oh, come on, Papa," Sybilia said gently. "Don't start grumbling again. You'll spoil the story."

Xavier frowned and then smiled at her and sank back onto his chair, content with his pipe and her voice. She began reading, and Michel wondered at the ease with which she twisted his father round her finger. Even Maria seemed to have become saner and her ghostly visions less frequent lately.

A large brown moth fluttered against the lamp and fell on the book, and Sybilia flinched.

Xavier leaned forward, caught the moth in his great paw, and squeezed it shut. Then he dropped it into an ashtray.

Sybilia breathed, "Oh," in a slight implosion of air.

"You never think! . . ." Michel began angrily. "You just killed something that was rather beautiful."

His father looked up, one eyebrow raised dangerously high, wolf eyes narrowed to slits.

"You never think for a moment about life . . . what it means . . . about creation . . . about beauty," Michel went on carelessly, intoxicated with the splendor of the night.

"Oh, I think all right," Xavier began softly. "I think about bringing food to this table, about planting and plowing and milking the goats, about reaping the wheat, shearing the sheep. I think about survival—and we all survive. But not without this. . . ." He flexed the muscle of his right arm and hammered it with his left fist.

"I graft and I plan and I hunt when the meat's short. But you, you moon around the mountains all day, dreaming about beauty. What good does that do? Does that give your wife food in her belly?"

"No," Sybilia said firmly, putting down her book. "No more of this. I won't have it. Look, Papa. Look at his hands. And his arms." She reached forward impulsively and caught hold of Michel's hand. "See the calluses . . . feel the muscles. Not the arm of a man who does nothing. He's working, but he's working in his way. He's going to be a famous sculptor one day. You'll be proud of him, I promise you."

Michel stood transfixed with horror at her betrayal. And she had promised . . . he had trusted her . . . but she was innocent, because she did not know.

"Sculptor," Xavier roared, and flung back his chair. He towered over the table, black brows knitted, mouth drawn back in a sneer. "Is that what he tells you? Well, I'll tell you something. It's his excuse for dodging work and responsibilities. It always has been. He uses art as an apron to hide behind. He's afraid of life, afraid of other men, afraid of putting his hands to hard work . . ."

"No, no, I won't hear you say these things. He's got talent!"

"A talent for weaving lies."

Michel crumpled onto a chair.

Sybilia gazed at him incredulously, then turned angrily to Xavier. "Why do you hate him so?" she shouted. "Why do you want a cretin for a son? You resent his talent. Yes, I can see that it is so," she said sharply as Xavier shook his head. "You should be proud of him, but you despise him. Michel—" She turned tearfully to her husband. "You must believe in yourself. It's hard for your family to believe that you could be different from them. Don't base your self-regard on their opinion."

Xavier flushed with anger at her patronizing tone.

"Naturally I would be glad to be proud of him. Why else should I have taken a cartload of his damned statues to Ajaccio, to an art dealer? That was four years ago. I would have sent Michel to study in France if he had shown any sign of promise. They told me to tell him to take up plumbing." His voice rang with contempt.

"They were wrong," she cried out sharply, on the verge of tears.

"And his teacher? Was she wrong? And the art gallery in Nice?" He went on in a quieter voice, rather ashamed of his outburst, "He's had every chance. We would have paid. We would have pawned our fields. Anything! But if he hasn't got what it takes, then he must find some other outlets for these talents that he feels he has. He can't be a parasite forever. He's a married man now. My God, he can't even slaughter a pig."

Sybilia shuddered and heard Michel groan as if in agony.

Xavier stared at the table. "I'm sorry, Sybilia," he said. "I'm sorry for you and I'm sorry for him—and myself and Maria. But that's the way it is, and he's got to come to terms with things the way they are. Just as you had to come to terms with marrying him and living here. You did it. You're making the most of what you've got. Well, so must he."

"You're right. I aim to make the most of Michel," she replied tartly and too quickly, still smarting from the hurt. "He'll never amount to anything here. You'll make sure of that."

She saw Xavier turn red and then white with shock. He clenched his fists and stared at her with his mouth open. For a moment she thought he would strike her.

Then Michel leaned over the table, clutching a knife in his hand. "Leave her be," he whispered. "Or I swear I'll kill you."

Suddenly Xavier smiled crookedly. He shrugged and turned to Sybilia. "Maybe you'll turn him into something," he said. "If you keep your feet on the ground and your head out of the clouds. I have no fight with you." Then his fist shot out. Quick as a snake he knocked the knife onto the table. He picked it up slowly and handed it politely to Sybilia. "Of course, you have some way to go yet," he said.

That night Sybilia tried to comfort Michel, but he seemed listless and apathetic. When at last she succeeded in convincing him that they would throw all their efforts into making his dreams come true, he seemed slightly comforted. Later, when they tried to make love, he could not get aroused. Eventually, he fell asleep, but Sybilia lay for hours staring at the ceiling.

CHAPTER 20

November, 1939

Inside the confessional, Father Andrews kept his face averted as he heard the rustling of starched fabrics and felt the heat from yet another body in the small, confined space. From the smells and the sounds, he was learning to recognize most of the older women. He dreaded the sweet, cloying odor of female sweat, was none too fond of garlic, either, although he was getting used to it. But most of all he hated the smell of age. It reminded him of corpses. In spite of his training and his beliefs, he still dreaded death.

It was late, and he was tired. The sins, peeled off and abandoned there, seemed to fill the confessional with a poisonous odor. Pettiness, cruelty, spite, and envy—their venom spattered his feet like drops from deadly tropical flowers. He battled daily with his intolerance, and he prayed nightly for God's grace.

Was she the last? he wondered. He listened carefully. No, soft footsteps were approaching, the chair squeaked. There was a strong smell of eau de cologne, a sharp intake of breath, and then a young girl's voice whispered:

"Bless me, Father, for I have sinned."

Sybilia! There seemed to be a tight band around his chest as he gave the blessing. "What are your sins, my child?"

"It is many weeks since my last confession. I have omitted to come to mass or to confess. I know that I have committed a mortal sin, but Father, I was too shy to come."

"My child, omitting to come to mass or to confess is a most grievous state of mortal sin. There is no point in being shy before the Holy Father, since He sees all things and knows all things. You have committed a grave error, and you must make amends."

"Father. Oh, Father."

Her voice was hardly more than a whisper as Father Andrews tried to block his ears to her vivid description of modeling naked for Michel in the mountains.

What sort of a ninny was this husband of hers? he asked himself incredulously. And why had his own compassion slipped away, just when he needed it most? Wasn't Michel one of his flock? Sybilia was describing her physical needs in detail and leaving nothing back. Father Andrews's hands were shaking as he clutched the crucifix.

When she came to the day of the hunt, her voice was taut with emotion. "Oh, Father, we did it, right there in the tub. I was shameless. It was all my fault. I led Michel into doing it. I had to turn him into a husband, you see. How else will I get any children? The next day in the cave, I modeled for him again, but I could see he did not have his mind on his work, and later we lay down on the sand in the sunlight . . . right there in the open, Father. I'm ashamed to say that I enjoyed"—she paused—"*it*. Mother said that decent women never enjoy it, they simply have to do it, like a sort of a penance, and that I should never let my husband see me naked, but I did. And Father, Michel said I have the most beautiful body he has ever seen, and I enjoyed hearing that, too." She sighed. "I fear that I am beyond all help, Father. And I still do not love Michel, but I like what he does to me, although I wish . . . I wish . . . well, I wish he were more like a man and less like a boy."

"Have you finished?" he asked, and cleared his throat noisily.

"I wish I'd never been married to him. I will never love him, but I will grow to be his friend. But I have the ten points you asked me to bring," she went on in a rush. "He's tender, and a very good artist, I'll swear he is, and he's kind to animals. At the same time, he's a coward and he's not strong."

"That's enough!" He felt as if he were strangling.

"Father, Father Andrews, are you ill?" her voice called in alarm.

"I do not want you to repeat his virtues to me, merely to

yourself, daily. Physical strength is not a virtue, bravery is a doubtful one," the priest cut in. "So think about goodness, mercy, charity. Keep trying, my child," he went on, feeling calmer as his self-control returned. "You are a good and virtuous person, and you will make your marriage succeed in time."

"But there's much more," she persisted. "The night before last Xavier and Michel had an argument. Xavier told me that Michel is no good as a sculptor and that he's been told that many times. Papa was so cruel to Michel, yet I had the strangest feeling that . . ." Her voice faltered. "How can I explain? It seems to me Papa is afraid to have another man in the house, so he keeps Michel down. As for Michel, I felt that he enjoyed being humiliated. Is it wrong to say these things? I have no one else to talk to. What shall I do? I'll never turn Michel into a man while he's living in that house."

"My child, come into my garden tomorrow morning and we'll talk about your family. But for now, let's talk about you."

"About my last penance, Father. I . . . I found it easy to find ten good points about Maria. She's so kind, and good, and clean. You'd be amazed how hardworking she is. She's humble, God-fearing, she never misses mass, honest—"

"Yes, yes, I'm sure she's all of that," the priest said. "What about Xavier?"

"Well, he's courageous."

"I've never been able to find a reference to bravery being a virtue in the Bible," Father Andrews said. "Although I've tried, particularly since coming here."

"I'll keep trying," Sybilia said doubtfully. "Forgive me, Father, I am truly sorry."

A voice that whispered, soft and contrite. Sorry for what? For being forcibly married against her wishes? For trying her best to be a good wife the only way she knew how?

"You are a married woman. God has joined your two bodies as one. What you do is not wrong, my child." He broke off. She was prostituting herself for the sake of convention. God damn the lot of them. His righteous indignation was bubbling up and threatening to boil over.

"Your only sin was missing mass, my child," he whispered. "That was wrong. For that you must gather some flowers every morning for two weeks and bring them to the church and arrange them lovingly under the statue of St. Augustine, our patron saint. And remember, Sybilia, St. Augustine was a sinner, too." He broke off and took a deep breath. "I'll see you in the garden at nine tomorrow."

"Lord God . . . restore me to Your friendship and to full fellowship in Your Church. Amen," the soft voice intoned. Then he heard gentle footsteps . . . silence.

The following morning at nine, Sybilia walked hesitantly into the walled garden of the priest, situated between the cemetery and the forest. She sat on a bench and waited—a demure figure in her blue-and-white school dress. Father Andrews was raking leaves at the other end. He was dressed in dungarees and boots, and he looked happy. The garden was overgrown with weeds. There was a broken statue and a disused fountain sprouting moss, but there were signs of recent hard work in the neat piles of leaves and stones. A few of the beds had been tilled.

She was not really interested in his garden, Father Andrews could see that. She had brought him one of Michel's statues. It was of a bird trying to take off from the twisted bough on which it perched. The bird's feet were stuck fast to the gnarled branch. It was a simple thing, and not clearly defined, but the message of its agony and terror could not be overlooked. A strange piece of work in both wood and marble. For a moment he forgot about the artistic merits of the statue and thought about the bird's plight. How he hated that cruel Corsican habit of painting the branches of trees with glue, so that migrating birds were snarled until they were pulled off, legless, and cooked into a traditional pâté.

"What do you think, Father?" she asked anxiously.

"I'm no expert, my child, but it seems to me that he has the power to convey emotions and feelings through his art, even though the finish is rough and the bird is not very well proportioned."

He put it down, folded his hands, and said, "Just talk. Let it all out."

An hour later he knew that he must help her.

"Leave the statue with me," he told her. "I know a stonemason in Bastia. He's well established and a good Catholic, too. I'll talk to him next time I'm that way on a buying trip. Maybe he could offer Michel a job. A few years away from Taita might do you both a world of good. Bring me a few more examples of his work, not too many and not too heavy. It's a tough trip, as you probably know."

She went off happily, eyes shining with gratitude, but as Father Andrews watched her leave, his mind was clouded with confusion. Was he doing the right thing? If she were unhappy, she would have no one to turn to in Bastia.

Once again he knelt in prayer and remained on his knees for a long time.

CHAPTER 21

January, 1940

Two months later Father Andrews returned from Bastia with an offer of work for Michel from Angelo Serra, the stonemason in Bastia. The pay was low, the hours long, but it was a start. At least Michel would be learning a craft, Sybilia reminded herself. If their dreams did not materialize, they would always have this to fall back on.

In addition, the priest had spoken to Maria's cousin, Pierre Gaffori, a fisherman who owned a house in the old city, and the young couple could have the attic for as long as they liked, in return for Sybilia's help with the laundry.

"Pierre's mother is a bit of a dragon," Father Andrews had told her, "but you'll win her over, as you always do."

So they set off early one morning in midwinter, accompanied by the priest's pack donkey and a small boy who would lead it home later. They dispensed with good-byes to the villagers, reasoning that the past few weeks had been one long good-bye. Xavier, smarting at their show of independence, was sulking and had spent the night in Chiornia, while Maria was tearful and apprehensive.

It was a tiring journey, for their route was a steep, curving goat track worn into granite rock. Below them sheer slopes fell away into blue mists. Above, ancient pines flattened by the wind grew between granite outcrops.

On the very lip of the pass, Sybilia insisted on stopping. She opened the hamper and produced bread and sausage and a Thermos of hot coffee. She wanted to look back for one last time. This was a mistake, she soon realized. She could see her old school and the roof of her father's house, and the church where she had been christened and confirmed. But what was Chiornia, after all? Merely a cluster of roofs lost in an immense forest. Once she had felt so secure. Oh, what a fool she had been, believing in the sanity of her world, feeling loved, protected, and safe. As for Taita, which she could see clearly on a protruding rocky outcrop, she neither loved nor hated it but accepted it as her fate. She knew she was not escaping. Taita would always be there, lying in wait for her.

What am I crying for? she wondered, wiping the tears from her cheeks. Am I leaving anything worth crying for? Perhaps Maria, who was her only friend, she decided. So she sobbed into her handkerchief for her lost childhood, her school, her hopes, and for poor, forlorn Maria.

Michel became impatient with her and went on ahead, so after a while she packed the food and hurried to catch up with the donkey, which was slithering and sliding down the steep goat track toward the bus stop.

At the nearest bus junction a village had sprung up to cater to travelers en route to the coast. A friendly man directed them to a cafe owned by an Italian who made delicious pizzas. The whole place smelled of simmering olives and pastry. Behind the counter his wife was stirring a luscious mixture in a copper caldron. Michel spent some of their precious money from Maria's hoard on a pizza and two glasses of raw red wine, and they sat there feeling extravagant and very adult.

The bus to the north passed in the early afternoon, so they sat in the sun to wait. It arrived three hours late. Anxious to make up for lost time, the driver accelerated recklessly, and soon they were racing through villages, dazed by a flash of pink roofs and white walls, past bays of turquoise, rocky creeks and briar-tangled hedges.

By the time they reached the junction, where they would

spend the night, the sea had turned from turquoise to oyster pink, and the sun had fallen like a ball of molten steel, spreading over the purple-hazed sea and finally disappearing into it. Sea and sky merged into a gray haze as the bus disgorged its passengers under a chestnut grove.

They were met by a hefty girl named Anita, one of Michel's cousins, who led them toward the cafe she ran with her father. Sybilia followed, feeling light-headed and bewildered.

No sooner had she put down her boxes and bags than Anita called them for supper. They ate langouste, with homemade bread and olives, washed down with sour red wine, followed by goats' cheese. Anita's father was at the bar all evening, and Anita was serving at the tables, so she had little time to talk to them. After the journey and the strong wine, Sybilia was too sleepy to talk but merely ate her food hungrily and listened to a little wizened man crouched over his guitar playing an old Corsican lament with strong, skillful fingers. It was a love song, full of burning passion and melancholy passages, and it disturbed Sybilia.

She began to pulsate with the music. She was filled with strange yearnings and needs that she could neither recognize nor overcome. What was she longing for? She did not know; she only knew that she felt like crying. She wanted so much more than she had. She felt like their cow at home when it had not been milked, overfull, bursting at the seams, desperately needing someone on whom she could pour her excess of love.

She studied Michel speculatively. If only she could fall in love with him, but he had been particularly irritating all day and was even worse now. She understood him and knew that he felt threatened. The peasantlike surroundings, the hassles of the crowded bus, had all conspired to threaten his fragile ego and his misplaced sense of his own artistic excellence. So he had been showing off all day, affecting a jarring Parisian accent, and hardly bothering to be polite. He had lied quite shamelessly to Anita on the short walk from the bus stop, telling her he was en route to Bastia to begin work as a sculptor. He would soon be famous, he had told her, but she had not looked all that impressed, and Michel had been disappointed. Right now he was looking bored and ashamed of his uncle.

"What's so superior about us when we depend upon them

for our supper and our bed?'' she whispered. Michel pretended that he did not understand her.

If only they were in love. How wonderful it would be. Imagine the excitement of starting a new life together. Imagine the joy. She pictured a tall, strong, handsome man gripping her to his broad chest and making passionate love somewhere upstairs on the strange feather mattress bed that awaited them.

The fantasy was so thrilling that she reached out and took Michel's hand, but he pulled away and frowned. A public display of affection was not his style. It would spoil the world-weary, superior air he had adopted.

They ate and went upstairs. The bed was a four-poster with a thick feather mattress. No sooner had Sybilia's head touched the bolster than she fell into a deep slumber, only to be awakened by Anita's impatient shouts. Strong sweet coffee and a roll lay beside the bed, and there was hardly time to wash and dress before the bus left for Bastia.

Most of the travelers settled themselves down for the day. They had homemade bread, garlic, wine, onions, sausages, cheeses; one woman had three live chickens she was taking to her cousin, another a small goat. Children sprawled over the floor with their dogs, and the travelers shouted to each other about the war, the crops, and their neighbors. By mid-afternoon Sybilia was feeling extremely sick. When she threw up into a paper bag, helpfully supplied by a neighbor, Michel went to sit at the front of the bus, as far away as he could get.

Suddenly she was longing for her mother and for school and Sister Agnes, who was her favorite of all the nuns. How clean and fresh they had always been! The premonition of doom, which she had been fending off since her marriage, seemed to be hovering over her head. ''Oh, sweet Mary, mother of Jesus, help me,'' she prayed. ''How can I ever endure Bastia with that silly, stuck-up boy?''

Their route across the hinterland to the east coast was hazardous yet breathtaking. A gravel road had been carved along one side of a deep ravine cut by the San Colombano River. They were driven Corsican style, at breakneck speed, over ruts and bumps on the narrow, curved highway. On their right sheer cliffs of granite fell to the wide river over a thousand feet below. On their left the harsh granite peaks of the Mutereno and Pinzali mountain ranges loomed high above them. They passed countless holes in the low wall bordering the pass, where vehicles had smashed into the ravine, and from time to time they saw the rusty wrecks of trucks and buses that had fallen down and been abandoned.

In the late afternoon they suddenly came in sight of the sea. Around a bend in the road they saw Bastia. Sybilia felt overcome with awe at the size of the city. It was ugly, admittedly, but it spread for miles: a tangle of gray houses and streets under the low, hazy sky.

It felt claustrophobic. She had to open the neck of her tight black dress to breathe. Down and down they went along a winding road, through narrow cobbled streets of granite buildings, some peeling and neglected and some painted in beige or pink or rose. The familiar sight of washing billowed from every balcony.

The streets were bordered with aloes, camellias, oleanders, hibiscus, and wild shrubs blown from the maquis. The busy city center seemed to be intermingled with waterways of the old harbor, teeming with steamers, fishing boats, and the occasional yacht. The pavements were crowded, but, more than anything else, the women caught her attention, for they were not wearing black. She had never seen married women wear anything but black, and she could hardly control her astonishment. The entire city was lined with cafes, and everyone was sitting around on the pavements drinking. Didn't anyone work here?

The main square, where the bus came to a halt, was lined with palms. The passengers tumbled out, crumpled and dazed by the sudden change of environment. So many packages and no donkey. How would they manage? Somehow they did. Doubling back for the extra cartons and cases, they made their burdensome way up alleys almost too narrow for a laden donkey to pass, up more steps, past gardens thick with wisteria until they reached the Gafforis' house. It was old and worn, with a strong smell of garbage.

"Oh!" Sybilia gasped. "How awful." Gathering her skirts around her knees, she stepped up among the rotting vegetation on the steps and knocked on the old but solid wooden door. Maria should just see this filth, she thought. A middle-aged woman, worn looking but with merry brown eyes, opened the door.

"Madame Gaffori?"

The woman grabbed her and hugged her. "So you are Father Andrews's little waifs. Come in, come in, both of you." She smelled strongly of garlic, but there was no mistaking the warmth of her welcome. She kissed Michel on both cheeks, then drew them into a large room, shabbily furnished but comfortable, and plied them with coffee, pastries, and questions.

Sybilia left most of the answers to Michel. After all, it was his family they were describing, while she pondered her impressions of the Gaffori family.

Madame Gaffori, who insisted she should be called Aunt Lucilia, had once been very pretty, that much was clear even now. Although she was past fifty, she gave an impression of elegance. Her hair was naturally wavy and jet black with only a few strands of gray, and she wore it cut very short. Her brown eyes were always shining, and even when serious she seemed on the point of bursting into laughter. She was plump but well shaped, and she was obviously proud of her curved, slender legs, for she wore her skirt shorter than she should. Her blouse was red and frilly, and Sybilia could not help admiring it. "You'll have to get out of those awful black peasant clothes, my dear," she said to Sybilia. "I'll see if I can find a few old things you can use."

Sybilia also took to Uncle Pierre immediately. He was a short, wiry man who gave the impression of great strength. His was a fisherman's face, deeply lined and tanned by sea and sun. They had two pregnant daughters-in-law living in the house with them, for their sons were in the French Foreign Legion. Both were short and dark and pretty, but openly antagonistic toward their country cousin. Granny Gaffori was a slim, vivacious woman of seventy-odd who resembled her son, Pierre. She had a crippled leg and walked with a stick.

"She'll put you to shame, Lucilia," she said in a loud voice, for she was deaf, while waving her stick at Sybilia. "That one's a worker, I can see that, in spite of her beauty. She'll have this place spotless in no time at all, you mark my words."

My goodness, Sybilia thought fearfully. Was she expected to be the maid?

"Don't take any notice of Granny," Lucilia whispered

when they were carrying her belongings up the stairs to their flat. "She's an old dragon, but no one bothers with her."

Their attic apartment was the worst shock of the day. There were two small rooms, plus a cupboard-sized cubicle with a small window that Lucilia called their kitchen. It was a mess of peeling plaster and rotting wood under sloping eaves. There was a four-poster brass bed with a dirty mattress in one room, and an old table and four cane chairs in another. Nothing else. The floors were bare boards that had not been polished for centuries, while broken windows overlooked the street.

Sybilia could not disguise her disappointment and despair, but Lucilia patted her on the back.

"Don't fret, Sybilia. Tomorrow we'll go down to the secondhand shop and get a few bits and pieces for you. Pierre will lend you the money, don't you worry. We've got a few cans of spare paint in the basement. If you work hard, you can turn this into a home."

Michel and Sybilia stood in awkward silence after the Gafforis left them alone. They held hands for the first time that day and sat on the bed side by side.

"Let's go back," Michel said. "How could we endure this place? I'd rather live in my cave, or under a bush. Any damn thing, rather than endure this."

"All it needs is some paint and a bit of furniture," she said without much confidence in her voice. "You'll see, it will come right."

"Do you really think so?"

"Of course. You're the artist. Can't you visualize it after we've finished with it?"

"No," he said miserably.

"Well, I can," she said defiantly. "But not now. I'm so tired."

"Me too."

"Do you think we should go down for supper? After all, they invited us."

"I couldn't face another Gaffori today."

"Neither could I," Sybilia said staunchly. "Let's go to bed. Do you know which box our bedding is in?"

Eventually, with boxes strewn open and no place to put anything, she found pillows and an eiderdown.

"Where d'you think this leads?" she asked, pointing to a door at the other end of the living room.

"God knows."

It was not locked. Sybilia opened it gently. She peered out and then gave a whoop of joy. They had a balcony. Not just any balcony, but one twice the size of their tiny flat. Admittedly it was a shambles now, filled with old discarded tins and boxes and dead plants, but what a view! They could see right over the row of houses opposite to the sea. There was the fishing harbor and the main port with the ferry making its way into berth. The old town was laid out like a map beneath them. In the distance was the square where the buses stopped. Suddenly Sybilia's spirits soared. With a balcony like this there was hope for their apartment.

She went to sleep feeling optimistic, filled with ideas for improving their quarters. It might take a while, maybe as long as a year, but this was exactly how it would be. *I'll make this place look divine, and I'll make my marriage work, too.* Determinedly she snuggled closer to Michel. At least he was too tired to move away.

CHAPTER 22

A few months later some of Sybilia's dreams had come true. She was almost happy and almost self-supporting. She had two new dresses that were only calf length, and she had three pairs of smart, lace-up shoes.

Her excellent English had become an asset. Apart from giving daily lessons, which brought her a small income, she also listened to the BBC each evening at six and translated the news to friends. Lately their flat was crowded each evening, and her visitors always left a gift: a melon, flowers, or a few cakes.

She had to admit that their apartment looked as lovely as she had imagined on her first dismal day in Bastia. Their two rooms were small but no longer shabby. They were freshly whitewashed, while the secondhand furniture had been sandpapered and painted light gray. There were vivid splashes of color everywhere: some bright pictures Michel had painted hung on the walls, and she had made cushions and rugs and chintz covers for their old couch. Several good pieces of Michel's sculpture stood on the mantelpiece and table. It was charming, and Sybilia was proud of her home.

The best part of the flat was their balcony. She had transformed it into something really stylish, copied from pictures of penthouses she had seen in magazines. She had bought an old table, which she kept covered with a red-checked tablecloth, and she'd reupholstered the chair seats with the same fabric. Against one wall were whitewashed pots with a variety of brightly colored tropical plants and creepers that trailed up to the roof. Her favorite was a rampant rubber plant that covered most of one corner. Bamboo blinds hung along the southern exposure, but she kept them rolled up except in the late afternoons. Unless it was raining, they spent most of their leisure hours on the balcony, even sleeping there when the nights were too hot to bear inside.

She had come to love this old part of Bastia with its rich mingled scent of the maquis and the sea. In the evenings came the fragrance of lemon, magnolia, and orange blossom. Below them the sea was always changing, sometimes a deep azure, invitingly beautiful, and at times gray and treacherous. Then the building would tremble from the force of the surf on the rocks below.

Her days were quite enjoyable. She still paid their rent by washing Lucilia's laundry, but that was usually finished by midmorning, and she ironed on the balcony in the early afternoons. At three she gave English lessons to her students, and at six she cooked supper for Michel. He seldom came home before midnight, and she dreaded the long, lonely evenings, but if she became desperate, she could always spend time with the Gafforis.

So her days passed quietly but constructively. She was neither happy nor unhappy but poised somewhere in between. It was a period of waiting, of vague worries, some of which were caused by the war. They had become used to the shortages, and that was the only sign that Corsica was in any way involved. Sometimes they wondered if the war would pass them by altogether. Sybilia hoped that it would.

Her biggest worry was her marriage. She and Michel had

grown apart. She did not know why this was, but she had her suspicions. Michel's working hours and his evenings were happily spent with his boss, Angelo. On the rare occasions when he came home, he would talk to her of Angelo, whom he idolized. "Angelo is my best friend; the brother I never had," he confided. He seemed so happy that Sybilia felt ashamed of her jealousy.

One night when she was desperately lonely and needing to be loved, she set about seducing Michel. He was in the bedroom dressing to go out when she walked in and locked the door.

"You seem to have forgotten I exist nowadays," she complained as Michel's smile turned to a scowl. Oh, God, what was she saying? Was this the way to woo him?

"Is something wrong?" she demanded.

"Only with you. There's nothing wrong with me, but you seem to be full of complaints nowadays."

Sybilia felt agitated and bloated. Even worse, she felt rejected and angry that he could make her feel like this. How unfair he was. *It's been too long. I'm not old yet, and I need to be loved. But why am I thinking like a whore? What's the matter with me?* Inexplicably, she burst into tears.

"Don't cry, Sybilia," Michel said. He put his arm around her. "I hate to see you like this. I'm very fond of you. Surely you know that."

"But you're never home. I'm so lonely, and it's been so long," she sobbed. "I need to be loved. Not always, but sometimes. Everyone needs to be loved. I'm not unique. Just normal."

Michel sighed and began to unbutton his trousers.

This is all wrong, Sybilia thought. Can loving be a duty? Nevertheless, she began to unbutton her blouse. It will come right when we make love, she promised herself. She could feel the blood throbbing through her veins. Her thighs ached. Her fingers, flutteringly impatient, fumbled with the buttons of her skirt, while her eyes locked into his. She saw tenderness there, some embarrassment perhaps, but no passion. She did not care. She had rights, she told herself miserably.

Michel took off his vest. In a fever of impatience, Sybilia tore at her stubborn buttons, heard them fall on the floor as she caught hold of her underpants and frantically pushed them off. Her nipples stood out, aroused and urgent, and her voice was hoarse. "Come, then," she muttered. "Stop fighting me. Stop fighting us."

"Oh, God, Sybilia," she heard him whispering into her neck, "I'm trying."

Her body was in a turmoil; icy fingers of delight stabbed her stomach, her breasts were swollen and sore. There was a great urgency to have him right inside her, but then the exquisite sweetness of his naked flesh against hers was calming, soothing, hypnotic. She seemed to be falling back and floating away as she felt him move inside her.

"Too long, too long," she murmured. She felt quite helpless in the grip of her need. She was incapacitated by the intense spasms of ecstasy rippling from her womb to every part of her body. She could only give little sharp yelps of pleasure, clamoring for him to do more, more, and still more. She gave a long, low moan of fulfillment and the next moment felt him withdraw.

Something was missing. She opened her eyes and looked up, feeling puzzled and somehow cheated.

"Was something wrong?" she queried.

"I'm sorry." He stared at her impassively. "You came. Isn't that enough?"

"No. What is it? What's happening to us?"

"I said I'm sorry. I mean it. I'm so sorry for you. I wasn't in the mood. Next time it will be better, I promise."

Sybilia turned away, feeling shamed and loathsome. There will never be a next time, she promised herself. But a week later she stubbornly seduced Michel. Afterward she felt hurt by his lack of passion and vowed she would never again be the aggressor.

It was June, 1941, when she discovered that she was three months pregnant. Later she always remembered that summer as a particularly dismal time. When she told Michel she was pregnant, he flew into a rage and did not come home for three days. The weather was hot, she felt sick most of the time, and when friends and neighbors crowded into her tiny lounge for the nightly news bulletin, her translations were always discouraging. The Allies were retreating on all fronts, both in Russia and the Far East. Closer to home in the Mediterranean area, Tobruk had been encircled by German troops and the enemy had taken the main airfield at Crete.

She felt so helpless. There was no enemy to fight in Corsica and that was frustrating. In 1940, when France had fallen to Axis troops and signed an armistice with the fascists, the Vichy administration had begun its policy of cooperation and appeasement with the occupation troops. The Vichy administration was now the legal government of Corsica, although most of their leaders had voted against it. Corsicans identified with General Charles de Gaulle and the Free French. Many of them were fighting with him. For the rest, it was a time of waiting helplessly as more of the civilized world fell under the Nazi boot.

On December 7, the day of Pearl Harbor, Sybilia gave birth to a baby son, Jules, at the Bastia General Hospital. Michel came to see her, but the baby had broken their tenuous bond. What had happened to her relationship? Did it deteriorate because she was providing most of the cash for their living, as Granny Gaffori said? Her own feelings were rather more frightening. She knew that Michel loved Angelo. If it weren't for Angelo, her husband could at least have been her friend, but Angelo had taken everything. He had not even left a father for Jules. She could not calm her jealousy, or her shame.

A week later she returned to her normal duties, but her days were irrevocably changed. She was no longer an observer of life, she was inextricably involved because of her son. She had a stake in the future of the world. She cared! She began to voice her opinions more vehemently as the war news became more threatening on all fronts.

Was the enemy invincible? Clearly it was only a matter of time before Corsica was occupied and then annexed by Italy. Her son a slave to the fascists? Never, she swore daily as she watched Jules sleeping peacefully in his cradle on the balcony. He would be free, and he would be Corsican. Was there ever a child as lovely as her Jules?

CHAPTER 23

August, 1942

By the time Jules was eight months old, he had deep blue eyes like Maria's and Xavier's curly black hair. He was so lovely that passersby would stop her on the pavement to tell her that they had never seen such an infant. He was big for his age, too, with chubby cheeks, beautiful hands, and a ready smile. She loved him desperately. Jules made up for everything she lacked. What more could she expect out of life? she consoled herself nightly as she rocked him to sleep.

August 7 was a day of intense heat and unbearable humidity, but to Sybilia nothing else counted except the wonderful progress in the Allies' war efforts. It was the date of the first American landings on the Pacific Islands. There were rumors of British and Russian cooperation. In the Middle East British and Commonwealth troops were defeating the enemy. The entire world was taking up arms against the fascists.

Wearied by the heat, Sybilia put the ironing aside for another day because Jules was so fretful. Finally she decided to take a cold bath. Then she glanced at the clock. At five she gave English lessons to a young engineer, Jean Perrier. It was almost half-past five, and he was late. No doubt he would expect his full hour's lesson. Then she would not have time to cook supper. She sighed. Not that she was expecting Michel to come home to eat it, but at least she always had a meal ready on time.

When she heard a knock on the door, she took out her handkerchief and wiped her forehead.

It was Perrier. He was holding a bunch of lilies and looking amused.

"You're late," she snapped.

"Forgive me." He handed her the flowers with a wry smile.

Sybilia eyed him suspiciously. Lately she had discovered that his English was even better than hers. She had never understood why he wanted to take lessons. In the beginning she had suspected that he would make a pass at her, but his behavior had been irreproachable.

He puzzled her. Why was he always switching to German or Italian to question her? Even trying to teach her phrases and expressions. He wasted hours discussing the war news. When she objected he said that he was practicing his English, or German, or whichever language he had been speaking.

"Where are your books?" She felt awkward about accepting the flowers.

"Excuse me, madame. I was late. I didn't want to waste more time fetching them." He smiled. "Then I thought the flowers might recompense you for your wasted time. Please, put them in water. They are lovely, aren't they?"

"They are," she replied in English without really noticing that he had switched languages.

"Sister Agnes was right about you," he said, smiling strangely. "Your grasp of languages is truly a gift."

She dropped the flowers and to hide her confusion spent a long time picking them up. "Sister Agnes? Do you know her?"

"She recommended you to me. And she sent her love," he added.

"Oh." Impossible! How could Sister Agnes exist in this day and age? She belonged to another lifetime, didn't she? To a young, idealistic girl who had set her heart on becoming a teacher. "How is Sister Agnes?" She could not disguise the quiver in her voice.

"She's well. She's working in a convent outside Paris," he explained.

"And you saw her recently?"

"I did."

The conversation was frightening her. What had Jean been doing in occupied France? How had he escaped? Who was he, and why was he here?

"I thought we might try a little Italian conversation today," he was saying.

"Italian," she faltered. "Why? Whatever for? You asked me for English lessons."

"I think my English is about as good as yours."

"I would say better," she replied. "But why are you here?" she asked, switching to the Corsican dialect. She glared at him.

"I've been sizing you up, Sybilia," he replied in their dialect as he followed her to the kitchen.

Sybilia felt a sudden surge of relief. He was definitely Corsican.

"The Resistance is looking for young, attractive female linguists. You, madame, are exactly what we need."

"Intelligence . . . spying . . . ?" She stared at him and took a few steps backward, nearly dropping the vase.

"Me? A spy! I have a child . . . and a husband," she added as an afterthought. She thrust the lilies into the vase. They really were lovely. For a moment she buried her face against the blooms. Then she looked up. "You don't know what you're asking. You're forgetting I'm Corsican." She frowned. "Sister Agnes sent you to me? . . ."

"She said you might say yes. 'Patriotic, idealistic, determined, and gifted in languages.' Those were her precise words, Sybilia. I would like to add that it is your duty to help us."

"Duty?" she queried. "I will decide exactly where my duty lies. It could be to look after my son and my husband." She ignored his sarcastic smile and hurried back to her sitting room. She felt uncomfortable with him lounging against the kitchen table. "What exactly are you asking me to do?"

"Learn to operate a radio transmitter and the Morse code; broadcast information to the Free French in London and Algeria. Sometimes we would give you this information. In addition, you would act as liaison between the occupied coastal towns and the Resistance in the mountains. Relay information . . . that sort of thing."

"What sort of thing?"

"When enemy ships come in; what troop movements are taking place; details of enemy convoys in and out of Bastia . . ."

"How would I know?"

"From this balcony you have an excellent view of the

harbor. An intelligent girl like you could pick up a great deal just by walking around the city."

"Is that all?" she asked, guessing that she had only heard part of the story.

"You're not making this very easy for me. How do you feel about it? Are you enthusiastic? Frightened perhaps?" He smiled sympathetically. "You usually give me tea."

"Please . . . please. You're bombarding me with all this. It's not 'no,' it's not 'yes.' I don't know. I feel . . . well . . . shocked."

"We have a position for you at the Hotel Bastia. Enemy troops are coming. We know that. They will be lonely." She noticed that he looked embarrassed. "They'll be talking in the hotel. A good-looking girl could pick up useful information if she kept her wits about her. They would never guess that you have such an excellent grasp of their language."

Unthinkable for a Corsican woman to work in a hotel at night. Her reputation would be irreparably tarnished, and her marriage would be over, but would that be so bad? a small, irrepressible voice was whispering at the back of her mind.

"Unthinkable," she said.

"In wartime the unthinkable becomes necessary. We all have to make sacrifices. Many people will die."

"Better dead than disgraced." She stood up and went to put on the kettle. "You are Corsican, aren't you?" she called.

"Yes," he said after a moment's hesitation, "but I have lived most of my life in France."

"Perhaps you have forgotten what it is like in our mountain villages. My mother was French," she went on. "She never really understood Corsican ways. Besides, your plan sounds a little absurd. The fascists know how close our dialect is to Italian. Everyone will be able to understand them."

"And German?"

"Germans! Here?"

"There's no doubt about that."

A shiver of apprehension ran through her. "They won't get far," she said. "They won't penetrate the interior. I promise you that."

"Not if we all work against them," he said. "Of course, it would be disastrous for you to keep your baby here. I mean, if you should be found out. You must take Jules back to your mother-in-law. You do understand that, don't you?"

Sybilia let out a cry. Glancing at Jules to reassure herself that he was sleeping in his crib, she turned to Jean.

"Stop talking as if I will work for you. I must think about it. My answer will probably be no."

She turned away, feeling safer now. Jean went on arguing.

"I'll discuss it with my husband," she said angrily. "I think you should leave now."

"Michel is a member of the Communist party and the Resistance. You know what his answer will be."

"But he's also a man and I'm his wife."

"Very well, Sybilia. Until the next lesson." He stood up and gave her a strangely cynical look.

"You're still coming? For lessons?" she asked incredulously.

"Italian next time. What d'you say?"

"Who's teaching whom?" she asked sourly.

"We're learning together, but I'm paying, as usual. Or to put it bluntly, Sybilia, you've been in the pay of the Resistance for some weeks."

"Oh, you bastard," she muttered, surprising herself, for she had never sworn before.

It was a long, lonely evening as she waited for Michel. At twelve Jules awoke and wailed. She breast-fed him while sitting at the table reading the newspaper. Much later, Michel came creeping in with an apologetic smile on his face.

"I thought you'd be sleeping."

"As you can see, I'm not. Supper's on the stove, but you'll have to wait until I've finished with Jules."

He hardly glanced at their baby. Surely that was strange, she thought, feeling sad. How was it possible Michel could be so disinterested in them both? He was not against them. No, nothing cruel, no anger or spite, just his apologetic disinterest. Perhaps that was worse.

"I'm not hungry," he said.

"You must eat. You'll get sick if you don't."

"I went out for a bite. As a matter of fact, we went down to the new harbor cafe. Quite a joint. Hell of a crowd."

"We?" she queried.

"Angelo and I."

The name of his employer always brought a feeling of unease and vague, undefined jealousy. Absurd to think this way, she lectured herself.

Carrying Jules, she walked across the kitchen and switched off the stove. "That was a wasted effort," she grumbled as she took out the food.

"Strange that you should spend so much time with Angelo," she blurted out. "After all, one would think you had enough of each other's company, working together all day as you do." Why could she never keep her mouth shut? Michel's lips were pursed into a thin, tight line. His eyes flashed with anger.

"My friends are my business," he said curtly.

"I'm entitled to ask. I sit alone night after night. I'm your wife."

"Wife," he spat at her. "How you love that title. You try to goad me with it. Quite honestly I'm sick of it. Leave me alone, Sybilia. I'll try not to interfere with your life, if you keep out of mine."

Strange talk from a husband. She put Jules into his crib and sat at the table. Suddenly she felt overcome with a curious apathy. She was so tired, almost too tired to go to bed. Sadness makes you tired, she thought. She tried to pull herself together as she told Michel about Jean Perrier's strange request.

"Oh, come on, Sybilia. You can't expect me to make your decisions," he said. "You must do as you feel best."

What a letdown! She felt anger welling up. "Oh, you miserable imitation of a man," she said bitterly. "As if you cared. I'm just the fool who married you. All your feelings are for Angelo. Don't think I don't know about you two," she went on, noticing how shocked he looked. "I might have been naive when I married you, but I'm learning fast. I listen to the women downstairs. They know all about Angelo and his past affairs."

Suddenly she crumpled, her rage spent. She buried her face in her hands and wept.

Michel knelt at her feet and laid his head on her knees. "Oh, God," he moaned. "I'd rather die than hurt you." He gave a long, convulsive sob. Then he reached up and shook her shoulder.

"I'm not like you think. Maybe it's true about Angelo—I mean, his affairs. You're probably right. But not with me. I'm fighting it," he added lamely. "Help me."

She looked down at him and frowned. Even the way he clung to her was more like a woman than a man. What hope did they have? When she saw the anguish on his face she flung her arms around him. "Of course I'll help you," she promised. Intuitively she sensed the depth of Michel's confusion. The poor boy was so frail and oversensitive. A girl's mind thrust into a boy's body. She was so much stronger than he. Never again would she ask him for more than he could give.

How old she felt as she made love to Michel that night. He wanted to be wooed, so she wooed him. She kissed him gently, reassuring him, seeing his face, so virginal, while she straddled his shivering, passive body.

You won't get him, Angelo, she vowed. You never will.

Later she whispered, "I'm sorry, Michel. I didn't understand. Don't worry about anything . . . I mean, about Jean Perrier. I can make my own decisions. I'm strong. Lean on me."

Was she really so strong? she wondered when she awoke next morning. She had dreamed of a tall, handsome man whose body she worshiped and whose strength she relied upon. "If only . . . if only . . ." she muttered as she fetched Jules from his cradle.

CHAPTER 24

October, 1942

"We never see you anymore. I've been longing to see my little Jules."

It was Maria's voice.

Sybilia laughed happily, and the sound rippled in her throat. She paused in her long climb to Taita and shaded her eyes as she peered toward the top of the ledge. The sun was almost at its zenith, and against the glare she could see only the dark green outline of the cliff and the brilliance of the sky.

"Where are you?"

"Here, above you." The soft voice caressed her. Sybilia smiled happily and looked back for Michel, who was carrying their baby, but there was no sign of him. "Your son is a lazy layabout," she called out. "I left him far behind."

She glanced back toward the sea, twinkling china blue beyond the forests. Splashes of autumn colors blazed around her. The scent of the maquis was bittersweet, like her memories of Taita, soothing as incense, heady as mountain wine. She took a deep breath and murmured, "This is Corsica. The real Corsica. Not Bastia! Never Bastia. It's like a foreign city."

For a moment she forgot her aching legs, the blister on her heel, her thirst, and the flies that were tormenting her. "Just listen to that waterfall," she cried out. "I'd forgotten how lovely it is."

"You should come home more often." The soft, girlish voice was slightly reproving.

"We're here, aren't we? Well, almost."

She lurched forward, panting and pushing her shaking legs up the last steep slope. Her face was red and swollen, sweat trickling down her clothes. "Oh, my, it doesn't get any better."

She clasped her mother-in-law tightly and then pushed her back for inspection. It was always a shock to look into Maria's blue eyes, so vivid that you forgot the rutted skin and eroded teeth, like finding violets set into a crack of a granite mountain face.

"My, but you're so thin," said Maria. "Just look at you. Are you ill?"

"No," Sybilia said, smiling wistfully. "It's good to be home." She meant it, that was the strange part. She had not forgotten the vow she had made on her wedding day, and she had never returned to her parents' house in Chiornia. Taita was her home for better or worse. During the past year, she had longed for the old house. It had something to do with the peaceful atmosphere, the strange twilight of mellowed stone and seasoned wood, the perpetual gurgling of the mountain stream in the garden. Or was it Maria and her kindliness? Sybilia never really knew. She had been looking forward to returning for her son's christening. Now that they were here, she felt happier than she had for months.

"Here's Michel with Jules," Maria cried out.

"Enjoy him, and your son. I'm going to rest." Sybilia hugged Maria again and went to change.

Their tiny attic flat was always ready and waiting. There was a stone jug filled with wildflowers on the table, the linen was starched to crackling newness, floors and furniture gleamed from Maria's stout efforts. A new quilted eiderdown, handmade from tiny remnant squares, lay on the bed. Even the curtains were freshly laundered. Sybilia flung down her bags and opened the shutters, then drew in deep breaths of mountain air. She rummaged in her bag for clean clothes and went down to the basement to bathe. Of course Maria had the bathwater steaming on the old copper, with the tub taken down from the wall and standing ready on the floor with soap and towel and lavender essence. If Maria was mad, then let the whole world be mad, Sybilia thought, sinking into the steaming scented water.

A little later Maria knocked on the door. "Can I come in?"

"Of course you can come in. I didn't hurry. I thought you'd want the chance to talk to Michel."

Maria looked at Sybilia. She noticed with silent pride her daughter-in-law's breasts swollen with milk and slightly misshapen stomach.

To Sybilia she said, "Michel's gone with Xavier to the meeting, and they've taken Jules with them. Xavier's so proud. He wants to show off his grandson to the whole world. How you've changed him, Sybilia, and how pleased I am with both of you."

As usual, Maria seemed freer and more talkative in Xavier's absence. While Sybilia dressed and accompanied her to the living room, she babbled on about the cat's new litter, the bad season for the vines, the chestnuts which were better than last year, their record tomato crop from the garden.

Then she turned a little sad as she recalled how Carlotta had broken her hip and had to be carried down the mountain on a stretcher, groaning all the way. She would never see her home again, Maria knew that. She had seen her face in a nightmare and then she had found a dead cat in the stream, so she knew for sure that the poor woman was going to die.

"But you told no one about your premonition. You promised me. Remember?" Sybilia chided her.

"Of course I remember," Maria said. "But I have told you, so when she dies you will stop thinking of me as a mad old woman."

"I never think that, Mama," Sybilia said.

As they sat talking and the shadows deepened, Sybilia noticed that crowds of people were gathering in the square. "Why, look! Half the village is down there," she said, peering through the muslin curtains. "What's going on?"

"It's the war, but what has it to do with us?" Maria's voice was flat with anger. "The villagers are divided. Tonight, Xavier will chair the meeting, and several party men from other villages are going to speak. They're recruiting for the Resistance, ready for the invasion."

"Believe me, they won't need much persuasion." Sybilia shrugged.

Maria sighed. "Then they're fools. We're cannon fodder for the French, always have been. Thirty thousand of our young men were lost in the First Great War. How many this time? Our sons—"

Maria stopped talking abruptly. With her face so pale and her eyes so bleak, she looked her age suddenly.

"What is it, Mama? Tell me what's upset you so."

Maria looked away evasively. "War, of course. The war upsets me. If you had any sense, you'd be upset, too."

Sybilia's mouth hung open with astonishment. It was not like Maria to scold her.

"Forgive me, dear Sybilia," Maria said, struggling to smile at her daughter-in-law. "I forget how young you are sometimes. For the young the unimaginable can never happen, but it happens all the same. Yes, believe me, the impossible becomes reality with such speed that it leaves you breathless."

Her eyes wavered. Suddenly she was lost in her own world of strange omens and disconnected events as she sat hunched in the corner, wrapped in gloomy foreboding.

Sybilia made some tea and chattered about Bastia until Maria recovered her good humor. Then she said: "Mama, we're going to go to the meeting. Come on! Please don't say no. I need you for moral support. Please, Mama, come with me," she begged. "I won't allow the men to keep this war to themselves."

"You go. I'll look after Jules. You can't leave him by himself."

"Oh!" Sybilia gasped. For a moment she had forgotten Jules. What a careless woman she was. How could she forget her own baby? "Thank you, Mama," she said contritely.

Michel returned with Jules and hurried off again. The two women bathed the infant and put him to bed. He was sleeping soundly when Sybilia took a shawl and hurried into the square.

It was late October. After sunset, the mountain mists had drifted down and enveloped Taita with damp cold. The villagers stamped their feet and sent the children to fetch shawls and jackets. The lanterns flared and hissed, and the air was charged with tension. Everyone was longing for something to happen. The Corsicans had been chomping at the bit for the past year, ever since the Vichy administration, under Marshal Pétain, had become the legal government of the island.

Only one of the Corsican-elected representatives, Xavier Rocca, had refused to vote for the transfer of full power to Pétain; for the rest—two had abstained from voting, and three had voted in favor. But de Gaulle's Free French broadcasts, his promise that victory would be theirs eventually, struck a responsive chord in Corsica, and several groups of the Resistance were beginning to get organized. The most vigorous was the National Front, led by Xavier but containing many prominent communists.

That evening Xavier was in charge of the meeting, and he was sitting at the center of a long trestle table right under the church steps beside the fountain. Michel was there, too, Sybilia noticed, along with several men whom she had not seen before. Behind the table was a large printed poster with Xavier's face grinning down at the crowd. "Follow the Wolf to Freedom," read the slogan.

"All right. All right!" Xavier bellowed, hammering on the table with a mallet. "We haven't got all night. Let me introduce Pierre Landy on my right and Daniel Campinchi on my left. They've come from Ajaccio, where they are leading figures in the National Front. The others I think you all know. To put this matter in a nutshell, we've all got our own ideas on what's best for our beloved Corsica. Am I right?''

A slow chorus of assent flickered from the crowd.

''Landy here's a member of the Communist party, as some of you know. You probably know, too, that I oppose the communists, yet my own son, in his wisdom, has joined the Party.'' He turned and scowled at Michel, who remained gazing impassively into the darkness.''Guerrini, on the other hand, has been known to voice his heretical opinion that Corsica should be linked with Italy.''

There was a chorus of groans from the crowd, and Guerrini, red-faced and sweating at the end of the table, leaped to his feet. ''Not anymore, I assure you. I'm here to swear my wholehearted personal support. As the spokesman of the Veterans' Association I speak for many more. Let's not waste time with ancient feuds, Rocca. The present situation is entirely changed. There's nothing wrong with my patriotism, friends, believe you me. That's why I'm here tonight.''

''Exactly,'' Xavier cut in, impatiently signaling him to sit down. ''We're here to plan our strategy, and to sort out the men from the boys. If the Boche or the Italians—or both—are stupid enough to invade our island—well, my friends, we'll be ready for them—with our guns, our stilettos, our pitchforks, and our fists.'' There was a bellow of approval from the crowd. When it had quieted, he added: ''They'll find things a little hot for their taste.''

He wiped his forehead with a big red handkerchief and turned to smile at his supporters. ''Well, what I was trying to say to you, when our friend Guerrini here got all hot under the collar, was that we're still one family, and we've got something very important in common. We all love our island home, our beloved Corsica. When she's threatened, we put our differences aside, as we have always done. We all know the fascist press is calling for the assimilation of Corsica into Italy. Believe me, they'll use this war to get their way. The invasion is coming. That much I can promise you. Only I can't tell you exactly when. So we must be ready for them. It's up to us to show the world the stuff Corsicans are made of.

''One thing I'll promise you now. If we don't show the

Western world our total abhorrence to all land-grabbing powers . . ." His voice was shaking with passion. "I say to you, if we don't show them that we're tough . . . yes, tough and nasty . . ." Now he was moving toward a crescendo, and the crowd was roaring its approval. "If we don't show them we're tough and nasty and capable of fighting for what's ours, if we don't make a stand . . ."

There was a sudden pause. The crowd was hushed and expectant, hanging on every word as Xavier looked around. "Then . . . after the war . . . when the big powers get together . . . these victors . . . when they pat each other on the back and sit around a table handing out bits and pieces of other people's countries, like prizes at a party, as I promise you *they will,* we could end up as booty, tossed like a bone to a dog. To Italy . . . or America!" he roared, letting his imagination run away with him. "Or the Greeks, or the Algerians. One thing's sure, my friends. When you lie down like a doormat, people wipe their feet on you. Is that what we want?"

"No," the crowd roared in approval.

"Do we want the dirty Boche goose-stepping all over the island?"

"No!"

"Do we, hell! Or the Americans?"

"No!" The roar was louder now.

"Corsica for Corsicans! Corsica for Corsicans," the crowd chanted, and Sybilia, who was caught up in the heady feeling of mass elation, sang with them.

There was a great deal more rhetoric, oaths were sworn and resworn, strategy was mapped out. All the able-bodied men of the village were to take to the maquis, Corsicans' traditional strategy, and from there they would work in isolated guerrilla bands from a central control near Bastia. Fishermen would smuggle in arms and ammunition and maintain clandestine radio contact with Free French authorities. The villagers, who to a man preferred fighting to herding sheep, were clamoring to join the Resistance. Young and old, fit and infirm, lined up to sign their names and swear the oath: "Victory or death."

Xavier caught sight of Father Andrews and called out tauntingly: "Who's side are you on, Father Andrews?"

"On God's side," he answered glibly, neatly sidestepping the question.

"And I'm wondering which side God might seem to be on, in the eyes of an Irish priest, nursed on anti-British sentiments and schooled in Rome? Could we have your holy opinion as to the merits of the fascists? Just so that we know who we're dealing with."

He grinned wolfishly, and once again Sybilia noticed the uncanny resemblance and smiled inwardly at his nickname.

"When I go hunting I like to know the type of men I have behind my back," Xavier went on. "That way I know I'm safe. So let's hear you speak, priest. Which side are you on?"

"I am a representative of the Catholic church, which is above petty politics and uniquely concerned with the spiritual well-being of each individual."

"Petty politics is it? Well, I'll tell you this to your face. Climb off the fence to one side or the other, Father Andrews, or you'll find yourself impaled upon it with a stake up your arse."

The crowd was becoming angrier. Father Andrews watched them with misgiving as they yapped and bayed as one. Like Xavier's dog, he noted, and as cunning and obedient to his will.

"I'll not be threatened by you, Xavier Rocca," he roared. "You can come to church on Sunday and listen to my sermon, if you're so interested. I aim to define the Catholic duty in the event of an invasion, for the benefit of my congregation. You are a member, are you not, my son?"

For once Xavier was at a loss for words.

Oh, well done, Father, Sybilia wanted to call out.

After this the crowd quieted as they lined up to sign the pledge. Sybilia pushed her way into the long file and eventually found herself at the table, in front of Xavier.

Looking up, he scowled momentarily and then restored his public smile. "You can't sign, Sybilia, you're a woman," he gibed. "Go home and look after your baby."

She flushed and bit her lip. "If they come, I'll fight," she said. "And you won't stop me, even though you stop me from signing now."

"Next," he said, scowling as he waved her on.

So the men signed, toasts were drunk, oaths of allegiance were sworn, and Xavier and his colleagues retired to a cafe while the young men danced in the square. Only Sybilia sat alone on a bench, brooding over Jean Perrier's offer and nursing her indignation.

CHAPTER 25

As Sunday's sermon drew closer, Father Andrews needed help, but he was all alone. Cut off by the war from the Mother Church in Rome and his superiors in Ireland, he did not know how to cope with this delicate situation of Catholic against Catholic. For the first time the young priest was forced to shoulder full responsibility for his small community's spiritual needs, since Father Delon was now speechless and almost paralyzed following a second stroke.

What was he to do? He had been taught that the Church was above politics. Reconciliation was the traditional formula for keeping the allegiance of Christians on both sides. But what good was reconciliation in the face of an invasion?

His community was split into three distinct factions, pro–de Gaulle and the Free French; pro–Marshal Pétain and the Vichy administration; and the pro-communists. Xavier Rocca and his supporters identified completely with the Free French forces. He was already organizing and coordinating Resistance fighters in the villages, ready for the long-expected invasion. It would come soon, they all knew that, and the congregation were looking to their priest for guidance.

When Sunday came at last, Father Andrews was looking pale and gaunt after a week's fasting and meditating. He had delved into the Bible for inspiration, knowing all too well what weight his words would carry.

After ringing the main bells for the Sunday service, he dressed nervously in his green alb and cope and listened to the excited babble of voices in the square. He was amazed by the crowds of worshipers from neighboring villagers who were intent on squeezing themselves into Taita's small church. Obviously his promise to Xavier had spread far afield.

The first part of the service passed like a dream, and all too soon he found himself in the pulpit facing the congregation, which was overflowing into the aisles and the back corridor.

"Some of you have demanded that I state whose side I am on," he began rather nervously, unable to employ his usual sonorous intonation, which was reserved for God's holy words rather than his own arguments. "My answer to you is that I am on God's side."

He ignored the soft murmur of discontent that spread like a sigh through the congregation.

"But now, more than ever before, God's work needs some clarification. We are about to witness fratricide: brother fighting against brother, Catholics killing other Catholics. So we ask ourselves—what is our Christian duty?"

He paused to lend weight to his words and noticed that all eyes were fixed firmly upon him. There was no need for his notes. Each word was engraved on his heart, yet he found it hard to begin. The responsibility of what he was about to say seemed to stick in his gullet. But was there any alternative? No, he decided, and cleared his throat.

"When the occupying troops come, as they surely will, this island will become one of the many oppressed nations of the world," he began. "Civil liberties will be curtailed, life and limb and property will be at risk, and armed men will oppress an unarmed civilian population.

"I have heard the words 'reconciliation,' 'truce,' and 'neutrality' bandied around the village these past few days until I am sick of hearing them. I tell you now, to speak of reconciling the two sides is a mistaken application of the Christian idea of forgiveness and a total betrayal of all that Christian faith has ever meant."

Warming to his theme, he thumped his fist against the pulpit. "Our Christian duty is to do away with evil, injustice, oppression, and sin, not to come to terms with it.

"It's true that God wants peace, but not the peace the fascists want," he went on more forcibly. "The peace that God wants is based upon truth, repentance, justice, and love."

He paused and looked around. Xavier Rocca, in the front row, pale with patriotic fervor, was smiling softly, but there were many others who looked afraid.

"To give you the doctrine of nonviolence and turning the other cheek, in the face of this terrible war, with its cruelty, brutality, and callousness, would be to hamstring you and to curb your natural longing for justice and freedom.

"I promise you that there is a long and consistent Christian tradition about the use of physical force to defend oneself, or others, against aggressors and tyrants. Oppression as a theme runs right through the Bible in both the Old and New Testaments—there's no shortage of examples.

"This morning you have come to church looking for guidance. I say to you—there must be no misunderstanding about the moral duty of all who are oppressed.

"To try to live in peace with the fascists would mean becoming accomplices to our own oppression. No reconciliation is possible.

"As our fears of invasion increase daily, I want to assure you that you are not alone. Christians the world over are engaged in the conflict. We must all participate in the cross of Christ—that is, if we wish to participate in Christ's resurrection. It is time for Christians to unite in a struggle for liberation and a just society. Moreover, it is the duty of the Church to participate in this struggle. The Church should never do anything that gives legitimacy to a morally illegitimate regime. The Church must help to mobilize its members in every parish and support them in their plans for overthrowing the fascist invaders.

"It's up to us to adopt a biblical theology of direct confrontation with the forces of evil. I give you a message of hope: Wake up and act with confidence. Let us pray together for courage to do what we have to do in the difficult period ahead of us."

In the silence that followed, you could hear the congregation let out their breaths in a long sigh. There were so many frightened faces, especially among the women, so he added one more sentence that he had not planned. "Each of you will give according to your capability," he went on more gently. "Some will give their lives, some their bread, some their prayers. We will all give what we can."

Looking around the pews, he was caught by the sight of Sybilia's shining eyes. He could see she was fired with courage and determination. She would always be there to do her duty and never count the cost. His heart went out to her as he made the blessing. "Let us pray."

As he finished the sermon, Father Andrews found his hands were shaking and his clothes were soaked with sweat.

CHAPTER 26

The voices were coming. They had been crowding in on her all afternoon. Maria groaned quietly and hid her head under the blankets. Foolish to think she could evade them, for they were in the very air she breathed: high-pitched, gabbling voices, but too many and too far away to understand their message. Perhaps they would go, but she did not hold out much hope.

After Father Andrews's sermon she had felt unaccountably depressed, and her dreaded headache had begun. She had left Sybilia to cope with the supper party while she hid in bed. Now it was late, and she was lying sleepless.

How could that young priest talk so bravely of death? Was it because he was so young? What was death to him—to walk with angels? To her, death meant the cold stone of graveyards, the dank, dark smell of the Rocca mausoleum, of hideous, unimaginable decay, of the capricious, jealous spirits that nightly haunted the maquis to plot the destruction of the living. Yes, even now they were waiting for Michel, and they had warned her. Today the young priest's sermon had brought a sudden and vivid recall of her vision the day of Michel's wedding, and he had shown her how her son's death would be accomplished. For the first time she understood the guns the mourners carried and the coffin draped with the French flag. "Oh, God," she wept. She could not bear another vision.

She reached out for a bottle of sleeping pills and took two, washing them down with a full glass of water. After a while the babble was stilled. She could hear Xavier snoring gently beside her. He always fell asleep the moment his head touched the pillow.

She wanted to sleep on pleasant thoughts, so she willed herself to think of Michel as he had been when a child. So much happiness. Gradually the pills took effect, and she felt herself sinking . . . sinking . . . as if washed by a wave into the black sea, down and down.

Was it later? How much later? She did not know. She felt confused, for she was standing on the first mountain crest above Taita. Her boots were soaked with dew, her clothes torn by thorns and brambles. The voices were chiding her. She had stayed too long hiding under the blankets. She shuddered. It was so dark. There was no moon, and the maquis stretched out like a gigantic dark stain over the flanks of the menacing cliffs towering above her. She felt stiff and tired. Her hands were stinging, and when she pushed her fingers into her mouth she tasted blood. Oh, God, where was she?

It's a bad dream. It's always a bad dream, she decided. But still she walked on, and in spite of the stygian blackness of the night, for there was no moon, she recognized the path. It was the old goat track that led to the ruins where gigantic statues lay half-buried in the maquis.

She must turn back. She must. But when she tried, she saw that the track down the mountain was quite obscured with a thick rolling mist, and she knew that she must go on. It was then that the drum began, a muted, sullen beat that hammered against her heart. Death! The drum signified death. She caught her breath with terror at what was about to be revealed to her.

The drumbeats went on and on, knocking reason out of her head, beating in panic. Soon she was running, running for her life. Who was she? A younger, fitter, stronger body carried her panic-stricken mind through the maquis, twisting and turning, doubling up the mountainside and sliding down again, *desperate to escape*. She could have told him there was no escape. Not from Corsican hunters. Why he? Why was she so sure it was a he? Then she heard a gunshot crack beside her. Another shortly afterward brought red-hot stinging pain to her thigh and then to her shoulder. She felt the panic of the hunted as she dragged her leg up the narrow goat track toward the ruins. Yes, irresistibly she was drawn toward those ancient rocks.

She arrived panting and terrified and gazed at the awesome sight of the ruins bathed in the light of the full moon. Yet there was no moon tonight. The rock shone as if with an incandescence of its own, a glow that seemed to signify the end. She staggered to the cave and hid herself in the inky blackness, trying to hold her panting, sobbing breath, trying not to reveal her position to . . . *to whom? Who were the hunters?* She had no way of telling.

Then she sensed approaching evil. There was nothing to be seen, nothing at all, yet she felt the presence of something so evil that she cowered back in terror. It came up over the hill like an invisible presence, and it was coming for her. Surely it was Satan himself. She could feel its eyes upon her and its whole being centered with hatred upon her. She was defenseless, as vulnerable as a shocked rabbit as the snake slowly approaches. There was nothing she could see, but if she reached out, she would feel it, she was so sure of this presence. Then she saw a darkness, like a dark ball rolling —or, rather, an absence of light, for there should have been light in the brilliance of the full moon.

She cowered back and gazed up. This was the end. The knowledge seemed to lessen her fear, but her sadness was increased. She opened her mouth and said in a man's voice: "Help Sybilia—for the love of God, help Sybilia."

Then she distinctly saw a wolf as if through a haze in the dark patch around her, and on the wolf sat a small boy with a pistol. There was something oddly familiar about the boy, yet she had never seen him in her life before. He lifted the pistol, pointed it at her head, and she saw his finger tightening on the trigger. Then consciousness exploded. She was falling, falling, through stygian shadows. Dimly she heard the shot.

When she came to her senses, she was standing alone on the mountainside. She could not feel her feet as she hurried down the track toward her home. She felt deadly afraid, but she did not know why. Then she saw the wolf running ahead in the mist. However hard she tried, she could not catch up with it. She would kill it, if she could. The wolf raced down the hillside and passed through the door of her house as if it were as insubstantial as the mist. She had to warn Sybilia.

"Sybilia," she sobbed. "Sybilia." She fell headlong down the slope, and that was the last thing she remembered.

When she awoke she was in bed, and Sybilia was holding her hand. She felt so cold. The dear girl had surrounded her with hot-water bottles. She felt surprised, but she tried to smile.

"All this fuss for a nightmare?" she queried weakly.

"I found you in the maquis," Sybilia whispered. Her eyes implored Maria to tell the truth.

Maria clasped her hands together and began to recite in the high-pitched chanting voice of a child. "They called me and they showed me a place of evil and I stood face-to-face with the devil." Suddenly her eyes fixed on a point over Sybilia's head, and she began to tremble. "I felt a man die, I knew his anguish and his fear," she chanted. "I felt the shots that killed him. I know the place, but I do not know when it will happen. He said . . ."

She shuddered, broke off, and pressed her lips together.

"Who was it?" The question burst out of Sybilia although she really wanted to run away from this other side of Maria that frightened and repelled her.

"I don't know," the old woman replied. "Perhaps it was just a bad dream."

By way of an answer, Sybilia held up Maria's dress, torn to rags, and her boots, wet and muddy; all irrevocably ruined.

"I was called," she whispered. "To be a witness. I do not know how I got there. Perhaps I was sleepwalking. It has happened to me before, my dear. Things are revealed in this way. But why me? Why me?

"Sybilia," she whispered. "I am afraid—I was never so afraid. The evil—no, the devil—entered this house. I saw it push the door open and walk in."

"I will go and see the priest," Sybilia said. "He will help us . . . help you. Perhaps you were sleepwalking."

"Perhaps," the old woman muttered sleepily. "I seem to be forgetting it all. It's fading away, as dreams do. Yes, you do that, dear. I'm sorry I alarmed you."

"She's a *mazzeri*," Sybilia whispered. She was sitting nervously in the sacristy, telling the priest of Maria's experience. "I never believed it. How is it possible—I mean—so gentle a person?"

"Maria's gift, or curse, is not magic, or witchcraft, it's a degree of second sight. It's not unknown in other countries, soothsayers, fortune-tellers, Nostradamus. You've heard of him, I know. In Corsica we have this peculiar twist in that the *mazzeri* can only foretell death, so the superstitious villagers sometimes hold her responsible, rather like the old days when the king would punish the bearer of bad news."

"So you believe in Maria's second sight," Sybilia said nervously.

"I neither believe nor disbelieve, because I don't know. I have heard that she foretold the death of many people in this village, and they are all dead," he said. "There are certain things that primitive man knew by instinct, things that science has not yet discovered. The mountain Corsicans are . . . well . . . 'primitive' is an unkind word, let's say isolated and still full of their old ancient ways. This much I know: if Maria believes that Satan has entered her home, then we must exorcise this evil spirit in God's name."

When Father Andrews had performed the traditional ceremony with prayers and holy water, Maria seemed to be relieved. She fell into a deep sleep and awoke the next day. By then she had almost forgotten her experience.

CHAPTER 27

As the time to leave drew closer, Sybilia had deep misgivings about leaving Maria alone. There was no doubt that the loneliness caused by living without her children had brought a resurgence of her psychic experiences, which Sybilia considered unhealthy.

Sybilia had promised to give her answer to Jean Perrier on her return, but how could she when she changed her mind from one day to the next? After listening to Father Andrews's sermon, she had felt inspired, but later in the house the war seemed far away when family problems were far more pressing. How could she leave Maria alone? Worse still, how could she trust her baby to Maria? Then there was Michel to worry about. He was pale and drawn and losing weight. She had only a vague idea of what he was suffering, but she knew the only way she could help him was by being around when he needed her.

Was she to abandon her family for patriotic reasons? Yes, a part of her said firmly, but the womanly part said no. Sybilia returned to Bastia feeling heavyhearted and confused. She lay awake night after night wondering what to do, longing to have someone to talk to but not wanting to burden Michel again.

Nevertheless, when Jean arrived for his lessons, unexpectedly she found that she had made up her mind. The answer was yes, irrevocably but sadly.

From then on she was caught up in a whirlwind of activity. Her training took place in a bare apartment in Bastia. There was only one other man there, and he was a foreigner. She never discovered his name or his nationality, but from his demeanor, she assumed that he was a serviceman. She was issued a camera, and she was taught how to photograph documents, or people, surreptitiously. It was a Leica IIA, the latest version of the new miniature cameras, she was told. It was small enough to slip into her largest handbag, but it was bulky and uncomfortable, weighing almost a pound.

To her horror, she discovered on her first evening that she would have to learn to ride a bicycle. After overcoming her embarrassment at showing most of her legs, she soon came to love her bike. Night after night she cycled around Bastia's streets with Jules tied in a basket on the back.

The following week was devoted to communications. Learning the Morse code was simple for Sybilia. She could rely on her excellent memory. The radio transmitter proved more difficult to master, but by the end of the month she was adept at everything she had to know.

One of her duties was a nightly radio communication with Free French forces in Algeria. "No invasion as yet," she would tap out at fifteen words a minute. "Resistance forces have been set up in each mountain village. Approximately ten thousand able-bodied men are available to fight, but we are untrained and badly equipped. Send us arms."

Two weeks later she received a message that a small consignment of arms was available, to be collected from Algiers.

Smuggling was a traditional Corsican passion. It was not long before Uncle Pierre and his colleagues were gunrunning on a nightly basis, using their fishing as a cover and delivering precious supplies of arms and explosives from the Free French.

On the first day of November Sybilia began work at the Bastia International Hotel, an old but impressive institution known for its excellent seafood cuisine and good service. Because it was the best hotel in Bastia, it was assumed that it would be requisitioned for middle- and senior-ranking German officers. Sybilia was to work three hours a day while Granny Gaffori minded Jules. She was to play the role of an ignorant, part-time charwoman, keeping her eyes open for discarded information in the bins and using her knowledge of German to eavesdrop.

On her third morning she had to help at the breakfast table, and she received five francs in tips. Sometimes she lingered after lunch and watched *thé dansant*—afternoon dancing that was the craze all over Europe. One morning a group of German officers arrived on the ferry from Marseilles and spent half an hour inspecting the rooms, the menus, and the service, all of which she reported in her nightly transmission.

Was this war? she asked herself daily. Her days were varied and stimulating, but at night she tossed restlessly beside Michel. Like everyone else, she was living in a state of nervous tension. Everyone knew that it was only a matter of time before Axis troops overran southern France and with it Corsica. But when would they come?

CHAPTER 28

November 11, 1942

It was a sunny morning on the balcony of the apartment house.

The baby, Jules, now nearly one year old, played happily in his cradle, while Sybilia sat at her sewing machine, humming an old Corsican ballad as she stitched a floral dress.

The reflection of the sun first caught her attention. She paused in her work and peered out to sea toward the fishing fleet. Far above, tiny pinpoints of light in the luminous blue turned and hovered, dived and soared. Quite odd, really. She put down her work, wrinkled her forehead, and screwed up her eyes to see better.

There was a faint humming noise in the air. The sea around the tiny boats was suddenly white instead of blue.

Shiny, malevolent bees were diving at the fishing boats. Then they came on, growing in size and stature. At the precise moment when they became visibly man-made, the air was filled with the sound of church bells and sirens.

"Uncle Pierre," she gasped. "Oh, Lucilia. Does she know? Was it the Boche? Or the Macaronis? Oh, God—it's come!

"Dear God, save Uncle Pierre," she whispered, remembering how often she had begged him to learn to swim.

Why are they bombing us? This can't be happening. Insane! She remained at her sewing machine, rooted to the chair with shock.

It happened so quickly. By the time she had risen to her feet the first bombers were approaching Bastia in formation. Then the bombs were falling in lines, like skittles flung from a gigantic crate in the sky. Planes were screaming overhead, and the bombs kept falling—on the harbor, the central city, and the houses.

The sound of the explosions was like nothing she had heard in her life before. It felt like a simultaneous blow to her head and kick in her stomach. She reeled from the shock of the noise but stood there still, feeling overcome with bewilderment and fear.

Jules was wailing. That noise, more than anything else, brought sanity surging back. With a cry she grabbed her baby and fled through the living room to the staircase. By now the old house was vibrating with the shock of falling bombs. There was one earsplitting crash. Surely the house had been hit. Plaster fell around her, and glass crashed from every window.

The cellar. I've got to get Jules to the cellar.

Somehow she managed to cushion Jules in her arms and keep on her feet as she raced down. She was dimly aware of people ahead of her, but she could not see through the fog of dust and plaster. She almost knocked Madame Gaffori down as the old lady hobbled on her bad leg. Pausing for a moment to cough out the dust and regain her composure, she grasped the old lady's arm.

"Lean on me, Granny," she gasped, "but hurry. Faster! The roof—the plaster—I don't know how long . . ."

They reached the basement after what seemed an hour's struggle. It was filled with the screams of children and the moans of frantic praying.

"What is it? What's happening? Who is doing this thing? What does it mean?" The cries echoed around the cellar.

"It means we are being invaded," Sybilia called out. "The Italians are bombing Bastia."

"The fascists! Those bastards!"

"They want to frighten the shit out of us," an old man called out. He was the butcher's delivery man.

"What cowards we are to wail and cry and shiver in the cellar," Granny shouted. "We're behaving more like Italians ourselves."

There was feeble laughter. Mothers began to calm their children. "Stop sniveling. Be brave. You want something to cry for? Here's something to cry for! Not the Macaronis. Corsicans don't cry for Macaronis!

The children were soon quieted, but the bombing continued. Unbelievably, their house was still standing. Suddenly, Sybilia realized she shouldn't be shivering here with the women when she had work to do. Thrusting Jules into Granny's arms, she ran out of the basement and up the stairs.

The dust was settling; the floors, ledges, and furniture were white from a thick covering of plaster dust. It hung in the air like smog. After a fit of coughing she tied her scarf over her mouth. There was a strong smell of garbage, mixed with damp plaster and dust. The city sounded very silent.

Suddenly the church bells began ringing again, but whether they were signaling the end of the raid or the start of another one she did not know. Her heart was fluttering with fear as she rushed breathlessly up the stairs and out onto the balcony again.

A trolley bus was winding off into the residential area, but otherwise the streets were as deserted as an early Sunday morning. Searching the skies, she saw the planes disappearing into the haze toward Italy. They seemed to move so slowly across the sky. As she unfastened the straps of the suitcase containing her transmitter, groups of men came running down the street toward the bombed-out buildings. The sound of the ambulances and the fire brigade could be heard simultaneously. The shock was over. People began milling into the streets, waving their fists at the sky, cursing the fascists.

There were only two burning houses in their district. A crowd was milling around them. She saw a man in police uniform race out of the flames and smoke with an unconscious child in his arms.

"Oh, those swines," she gasped, forgetting her duties as she watched more limp figures being carried out by firemen.

Cold anger set in as she began to send her message in Morse code. *Ten-fifteen, Italian bombers raided Bastia. Two buildings burning in the old city. Raid lasted approximately ten minutes.* There must be more damage. She would have to go out and see. She added: *Further bomb damage estimates follow shortly.* She stopped and looked up in surprise. On the horizon she saw a massive fleet of boats materializing out of the haze. So did the crowds. They gathered on wharfs and jetties, squares and corners, and cursed the incoming flotilla. Then they went back to work, reluctant to appear overtly interested in the invaders.

Sybilia was watching anxiously for the fishing fleet to return, counting the boats as they docked one by one. They had thrown their fish overboard for extra speed. Uncle Pierre was safe, and Sybilia thanked God, but two of their neighbors' boats were missing.

At noon the first troops came ashore in their landing craft and found the city back to business as usual. The Italians were largely ignored by the population except for rude comments by cheeky children, who threw a few stones. They marched smartly to police headquarters and took control. By nightfall they had commandeered the best buildings and houses, imposed a curfew, banned fishing, and taken over the principal services and roads.

All day Sybilia reported the news to headquarters. Later she was joined by Jean, who brought her more statistics. The bombers had been two squadrons of Caproni CA-135 bombers. "Naturally they will use their obsolete craft since they know we are undefended," he told her bitterly. They had dropped approximately fifty bombs. He had exact details of the damage. They had avoided hitting the harbor. It was merely a punitive raid to set the tone of the invasion.

By evening Sybilia was packed to leave. She knew that by now Michel would have joined his guerrilla band in the mountains, as had most other able-bodied men in Corsica. She, too, had a job to do, but first she must take Jules back to Maria.

She felt no regret as she glanced around her apartment. A home without love is not much of a home, she reasoned. Her sadness over Michel now seemed trivial compared to the threat to her country.

She bolted her shutters, but she could not drown out the sounds of the invaders: marching feet, shouts, and whistles, an occasional gunshot, and the distant strains of a brass band coming from the harbor—all this served to intensify her feeling of humiliation and despair. The rape of her island would be avenged, as would the deaths of her neighbors. The brutality of bombing the defenseless population of Bastia heightened her determination. To a Corsican, life without freedom or dignity was not worth living.

PART III

CHAPTER 29

December 11, 1942

The flight from Yeoville aerodrome was short and uneventful. The Lancaster flew smoothly at fifteen thousand feet, until they reached the French coast. Then the flak began, and they pitched and rolled, rose and fell.

Captain Robin Moore curled up in the corner among the containers and tried to ignore the gaping hole through which he would have to jump soon. He was a tall man, twenty-five years old but looking older, with bright red hair, a muscular physique, and suntanned, freckled skin. He was not handsome: his face was too square, his chin too blunt, his nose, which had been broken twice, was slightly askew. But his blue eyes were extraordinarily expressive. They normally glowed with good humor and warmth. Consequently women thought of him as good-looking. Right now his eyes were shut, and his body swayed like a sack to the pitch of the plane. It was midnight. He had eaten a huge farewell dinner at the American mess, and he was tired. For his entire twenty-four-hour leave, he had been holed up with a Parisian typist attached to American headquarters in London. He knew he would never see her again. It was just one of those wartime interludes. Right now he was hoping he would be able to get a good sleep when he reached whatever accommodations the Corsicans had planned for him.

Corsica! Christ! He would laugh if it weren't so damned annoying. He relived the briefing with his immediate superior in London forty-eight hours ago. "You're going to a holiday camp," Major Ronald Hartman had told him. "It's called Corsica. An idyllic island in the Mediterranean, renowned for the beauty of its scenery and its women. You deserve a rest."

He hadn't joined up for a rest. He wanted to fight the Nazis. He'd done this successfully with the Yugoslav patriots in June 1942. On both occasions they had needed his particular skills in demolition and operations behind enemy lines. Other than a couple of skirmishes with fellow officers in various schools, his record was exemplary. So why this assignment so far from the front line?

"Because you have no equal in demolition, because your French is good, and because we have no one else available here and now," the major had explained. He had gone to some trouble to explain why it was necessary to send an agent into Corsica at all:

"Eighty thousand Italian and ten thousand German occupying troops haven't been able to penetrate the interior of this island. The Corsicans are ferocious fighters. All able-bodied men took to the maquis as soon as the enemy invaded."

"Maquis?" Robin had queried.

"That's what they call the junglelike scrub that covers half their island. Hence the term 'Maquisards,' which the French adopted from the Corsicans. The partisans appear without warning, inflict as much damage as they can, and disappear. Once in the maquis, no one can find them.

"The only decent roads in Corsica are around the coast, linking the main coastal cities. Roads into the interior are few and far between. Most Corsicans keep donkeys to travel the narrow, winding tracks up precipitous slopes. High, inhospitable mountains, dense scrub, good visibility to see approaching enemies—all that has made the island well-nigh impregnable.

"So while the interior has remained free, civilians in the coastal cities have to live with the restrictions and humiliations of the Axis occupation: curfew, rationing, and the brutality of the hated OVRA—Opera Vigilanza Repressione

Antifascismo. That's the fancy title of the Italian secret police. They are every bit as ruthless as the Gestapo.

"There are several Resistance groups, chief of which is the National Front, led by Xavier Rocca.

"The Resistance has established several first-class supply routes between themselves and Algiers, as well as a clandestine radio link. This is reportedly operated by a woman. I don't know why they couldn't find a man for this job. I've heard she's a relative of Rocca's.

"It's only a month since Corsica was occupied, but General de Gaulle and General Giraud are finding it increasingly difficult to hold back these guys from a major commitment against the occupying forces. Uprisings, battles, and partisan raids are taking place without planning or permission. This is sparking off a hell of a row at headquarters. The Corsicans couldn't give a damn about Allied strategy. They just want the fascists out of their island. Strange people. You'll find that once they set their minds on a target, they have no concept of self-preservation. They just go for it.

"The Corsican Resistance numbers about ten thousand untrained and badly equipped men, all of whom are determined to evict the invaders at once, by any means. The different groups are at loggerheads. Some are even communists. There's no discipline, no order. Just about every shepherd who can pick up a gun is determined to do his bit.

"Essentially the Corsicans should understand that the Resistance is small business: damage the enemy's equipment, steal their arms, and harass their men. Their job is to goad the Germans beyond endurance. Any attempt to make it more than that is doomed to failure. Just remember, Moore, keep the Jerries guessing, keep them worrying, *but above all, keep them there*. . . . You hear me?"

"Sure I hear you. Can't say I like what I'm hearing."

"Right. Now a word of warning, my friend." Hartman had grinned to take the sting out of his words, but he hadn't been able to disguise the anxiety in his voice. "Touch one woman and you're dead. I guarantee it. They're worse than Arabs about things like that."

"Christ! No women, no action. Just boring months of acting wet nurse to a bunch of unruly shepherds. This isn't why I volunteered."

"It's no good beefing, Moore," the major, who was also his friend, had said. "You're going to an area with a dangerous history. This time your allies are likely to be more dangerous than the enemy. They don't like foreigners, particularly if you throw your weight around. You did well with the Slavs, so maybe you'll be lucky again. Just guard your back and use some tact.

"The truth is, that's why you were brought back from North Africa. You're known as a sweet-talking Yankee, so get out there and use your charm."

Robin had felt offended. He still felt sore, remembering Hartman's gibe. He was not a phony. He just liked people. At one stage he had thought of entering the Church, but in his teens sex had entered his life, and he'd decided there were other ways of interacting with humanity.

Robin was brought back to the present by the dispatcher, who was shaking his arm.

"Hey, you! This is where you get off. Unoccupied territory, and the hunting's superb. I was there on holiday once. Have a good war, pal."

Through the hole, Robin saw the ground shimmering white in the moonlight. The twelve canisters were being thrown down. One of them contained his radio transmitter. Robin saw the parachutes floating past beneath his feet. He was next! Suddenly the dispatcher's hand dropped. The word "Go!" was like a blast in his eardrums.

The next second he shot through the hole. For a moment there was nothing to see but the aircraft passing above him. Then his parachute opened.

Shortly afterward he was swinging from nylon ropes that gleamed in the moonlight. All he could see below him were snowy peaks like giant's teeth. He was miles off course, but that didn't matter, since the enemy was nowhere around. As he floated down he felt relaxed enough to notice and enjoy the scenery. He was passing over a frozen mountain lake ringed by snowy crests on the roof of the world. There was a wooden chalet, surrounded by clumps of pine trees. It looked incredibly beautiful in the moonlight, like a backdrop to *Swan Lake*. He'd come back here, he promised himself . . . one day.

He landed just past the lake. By instinct, he rolled to the

nearest concealing rock and dragged in his parachute. As he set off down the hill in deep snow, he remembered the dispatcher's gibe. By the time the Corsican patriots found him, Robin was floundering in a snowdrift.

As they approached he heard the click of a gun being changed from "safe" to "fire" position. He flung himself back behind a rock.

"Hey there," he yelled in French. "I'm American."

"Come out and put your hands on your head."

"Hey, what is it with you guys? Rocca knows about me."

"Never heard of him." They sounded a little more doubtful this time.

Robin scrambled out with his hands on his head.

There were three rough-looking men, unshaven and shabbily dressed in black corduroy with very old rifles slung over their shoulders. On closer examination he confirmed that one held a French 1892 M16 service rifle and the other an old English Lee-Enfield. He couldn't believe it. "You guys been raiding a museum?" he asked.

He was grabbed by one of them and pushed aside with unnecessary force. No sense of humor, he thought. He could make short work of the three of them, armed or not, but what was the point? He was here to make friends, wasn't he?

There was a good deal of arguing in the local dialect. Robin couldn't understand a word, so instead he looked around at the endless snowy peaks stretching out into the cold, moonlit sky. Below was a black void. Far away a tiny cluster of lights bravely flickered in the darkness.

Eventually they turned to him. "They say you are a Boche pretending to be American," the leader said triumphantly. "Can you prove who you are?"

"Not right now . . . unless you call Xavier Rocca."

They tied his hands behind his back and shoved him roughly down the mountainside.

"Hey now! Wait a minute! There's twelve canisters of armaments lying—" He decided not to tell them where they were lying. After all, they might not be the Resistance.

"Shut up!" Their leader, Leca, a short, stooped man with arms as long as a baboon's, shoved him forward with the butt of his rifle. Robin struggled down an icy slope, cursing all the way.

Shortly afterward another group came straggling up in

the snow. They were led by an imposing figure of a man, who towered head and shoulders above the rest. Robin had been shown a photograph of Xavier Rocca, but with the scarf around his head and a heavy coat muffling his figure, it was impossible to figure out if this was the right person.

"Are you Captain Moore?" he asked.

"Yes," Robin said. "And it's goddamn difficult to walk through snow with your hands tied behind your back."

"So what is the password?"

"I don't know. What d'you think this is? Boy Scout's Day? Fuck the password and go fuck yourselves."

"Yes, he is American," their leader said genially. "I know an American when I see one. I was there before the war. Permit me to introduce myself. I am Xavier Rocca. Untie him at once. Welcome to Corsica, Captain Moore."

CHAPTER 30

An hour later Robin was sitting in Rocca's front room. He was in a village called Taita, which was not on any of the maps he had been given. He was drinking a rough, homemade brandy with the toughest-looking bunch of thugs he'd ever seen assembled together. Mean! he thought. Real mean! Best keep on the right side of these bastards.

Xavier Rocca was dressed in a black corduroy suit, with a wide red cummerbund around his waist, and a red cravat. In the dim lamplight he seemed larger than life. Robin reckoned he weighed two hundred and forty pounds, all solid muscle. Robin had surreptitiously compared him to the photograph he'd been given, but the black-and-white likeness gave no indication of the startling color in his face: the jet-black curly hair, the glacial blue eyes, and bushy black mustache, which was carefully groomed. His mouth was unusually wide, his teeth large and white. When he smiled he looked kindly, but at other times his face revealed an animallike ferocity that was disconcerting. He would make a formidable enemy, Robin thought.

Among his clan, Xavier's word was obviously law. He was a born leader, too, Robin could see, but not one who would suffer discipline easily, unless it was self-imposed. If Corsica was full of men like Rocca, he could well understand the Allies' problem.

In spite of Robin's friendly grin and flamboyant good humor, he was sensitive to the point of clairvoyance. He could almost smell the Corsicans' distrust and resentment. Bad enough that the Allies had sent one of their own men—but to send an American was tantamount to an insult.

That night Rocca's living room was full to overflowing with his comrades. The drinking went on for hours. Robin was introduced to the Rocca-led partisans. He tried to memorize their names while making his own private assessment, searching for their strengths and their weaknesses. He was especially impressed with Paul Barnard, a shepherd; Pierre Castelli, son of the local shoemaker; Angelo Serra, a stonemason from Bastia; and Michel Rocca, Xavier's son.

Robin was surprised at the contrast between Rocca and his son. In spite of Michel's effeminate looks and his obvious liaison with Angelo, Robin sensed an underlying steellike resolve. Angelo Serra was a tough and dangerous man who could be trusted only because he hated the invaders to the exclusion of any other emotion. Barnard was the quiet stoic whose word would be honored. Pierre was quick and clever and a close friend of Michel's.

Shortly afterward, Antoine Romanetti came in and introduced himself. He was a tall, blond, blue-eyed shepherd. Despite his vocation, he was extraordinarily well read, Robin soon discovered. He wanted to discuss the war news and the political wrangling behind the scenes. Robin sensed that Romanetti was an independent thinker who would go his own way and accept discipline with difficulty. There was no doubting his intelligence or his integrity. He seemed to have no great loyalty to Rocca, either. Robin singled him out as a man he could trust.

When the Corsicans had put away enough liquor to down an army, the Rocca women and neighbors brought in bowls of mutton soup, thick with meat and dumplings, plates of cheeses and olives, and mountains of vegetables.

Robin groaned inwardly at the prospect of another large meal. He was doing his best to look enthusiastic when he almost dropped his plate with astonishment. The woman who was approaching him, carrying a bowl of olives, was so voluptuous it hurt. He jumped to his feet and tried to conceal his reaction to her, but he could only stare silently, totally absorbed by her presence. She was an incredible beauty. Her appeal, however, lay in her underlying sensuality. Here was the ripe fruit of womanhood left too long on the tree, pleading to be picked.

Who was she? She was so young. Too young a custodian for all this incredible loveliness. Robin seemed to be standing at the mouth of a long tunnel and she alone was at the other end. For a few moments nothing else existed for him. He knew at once that this was the woman he wanted. To hell with the Corsicans and their taboos. His eyes said as much as he took the bowl of olives from her hand.

She flushed. For a moment her eyes wavered. Then she regained her courage and smiled straight at him. "Captain Moore, my name is Sybilia Rocca. I am also a member of the Resistance. I operate a radio transmitter. I'm sorry I was not there to welcome you when you arrived. To tell the truth, I was waiting at the right place, but you were not. Papa and Michel went to fetch you, but I decided not to brave those snowdrifts. Hardly a hero's welcome. I'm sorry."

Her voice was low and cultured; her French was flawless. So this was the relative Major Hartman had mentioned; not just a relative, but Xavier's daughter. How did that old bastard spawn a lovely girl like this?

She switched to precise English: "We're so grateful for your help, Captain Moore." Robin's astonishment was too obvious for good manners. He tried to pull himself together. Suddenly he became aware of Rocca's angry gaze, so he turned away with murmured thanks.

Sybilia rushed back to the kitchen and tried to compose herself. She had never seen anyone quite as appealing as Captain Robin Moore. But was he handsome? No, not really; his nose was too broad and looked as if it had been broken. A lovely nose just the same, she thought. His eyes were deep blue. They seemed to hold a special message just for her.

"Tough-looking man," she heard a neighbor whisper to Maria distastefully.

How wrong she was. He wasn't like that at all. He was the most sympathetic man she had ever seen. Someone you could trust, she was sure, someone who cared. There was humor there, too, and compassion. She did not know what prompted her to run up to her room and burst into tears. "Why?" she kept murmuring. "Why? Why did you have to come here? Of all places?"

Captain Moore obviously thought she was Xavier's daughter. Well, she would have to show him that she was not. And quickly, too. Everyone had noticed his interest in her.

To Robin, the sight of Sybilia bringing her baby to say good night to his father was like a dagger in his gut. So she was married to Michel. What a waste! An arranged marriage, no doubt. He grieved for that sad, lovely girl. When she left shortly afterward, the room seemed strangely empty.

That night Robin slept on a comfortable goose-down mattress in Xavier's home. It was the last comfortable night for many weeks. At dawn he left with Rocca to tour the various Resistance groups. He wanted to improve communications and cooperation between the leaders. He found fierce, rough squads of men who only had one common aim, and that was killing the invaders. They were short of weapons and training, but there was no lack of determination.

It was strangely archaic traveling around the island on foot and by mule. There were few roads, but dropping in several dozen motorbikes might ease communications somewhat. This would be his first request to headquarters, he decided. Ideally they should operate under one leader with mutually planned strategy. Xavier Rocca was their man, but listening to him, Robin realized that he had no strategy. He lacked soldiering or any technical training. He was, plain and simply, a politician. It was totally impracticable to expect Rocca to control more than his Taitan squad. Robin wondered if he could control the men through Rocca. Ostensibly he would be maintaining liaison between the groups, but in fact he would be leading them, using Rocca's name. He reckoned it was worth a try. At least he must instill some sense of discipline. Perhaps with Rocca's help, he could get their wholehearted cooperation. As for holding them back, you could as well tell the wind to stop blowing or the tides to hold off for the duration of the war.

CHAPTER 31

April, 1943

Armed with a master key, Sybilia wheeled her trolley from one hotel bedroom to the next. Her daily task of scanning the wastebaskets had not yet yielded any information, but she had overheard a number of plans, which she had relayed to Captain Robin Moore.

It was three months since Robin had taken charge of liaison of the Resistance groups. In the face of Rocca's antagonism, he was winning their grudging respect. He never sent men on a dangerous mission without leading them himself. He slept out in the bush in all weathers. He was even polite and grateful when the villagers invited him for a meal. Yet in spite of his gentle manners and warmth, he was expert in unarmed combat and sabotage, which he taught with great enthusiasm. He was a superb shot, too, and he had shown that he could match the Corsicans at horseback riding and hunting.

Sybilia knew what a difficult position Robin was in. She would have liked to warn him of the pitfalls of Corsican infighting, but he seemed to avoid her as much as he could, even when they were both in Taita.

With his rugged good looks and warm, humorous eyes, he was becoming every woman's hero as well. Sybilia adored him and worked all hours to demonstrate her usefulness. She did not succeed. Did he dislike her? she wondered. Or was it just that he did not trust her? Surely he could see how necessary she was. She could not understand why he badgered Xavier and Michel to send her back to Taita, forcibly if necessary. It was out of the question, of course. The Maquisards needed her. No one else had her grasp of languages.

Well, what did it matter? she told herself daily. She had been recruited by the Free French, and she had a job to do. All the same, she was surprised and then hurt by his attitude.

Major Ernst Krag, commander of the German garrison in Corsica, had taken over half of the Hotel Bastia. Ostensibly his reason was that it afforded a superb clifftop view over the harbor and parts of the main city center. Members of the Resistance had gone to considerable lengths to research Major Krag's background. They had noted that Krag's rapid rise to his present position had more to do with his Nazi affiliations and relatives than with his skill as a soldier. He was both flamboyant and selfish, despised by his fellow officers, feared by his subordinates. His looks were exemplary in his Teutonic world: blue eyes, ash-blond hair, pink complexion. But behind the groomed exterior lurked an emotional cripple. Krag was a casualty of the eastern front. This post in Corsica was his compensation for three toes lost from frostbite and a long spell in the hospital after a nervous breakdown.

Krag was a gourmet. Knowing his tastes, the Resistance had acquired a three-star chef—a man who in peacetime ran a superb restaurant in Cannes—and they had ensconced him in the hotel's kitchen. It was only a matter of days before the major and his staff operated exclusively from the hotel. Already Krag paid only cursory visits to the old building in the main square originally commandeered for his headquarters.

In prewar days the hotel had prided itself on its first-class recitals of chamber music. The concert room, which took up the entire northern wing of the first floor, had been converted into operational headquarters. Here Krag had his desk and his maps of North Africa and Europe, covered with flags and arrows, all of which were superfluous. He had nothing more important to do than supervise the occupation of a relatively unimportant island.

The Resistance had converted a small room above the concert hall into an additional linen cupboard. Behind the shelves, piled high with sheets, towels, and tablecloths, was a concealed space just large enough for Sybilia to sit at a table. With the help of an amplifier laid into the ceiling of the room below, connected to headphones, she listened in on Krag's conversations.

She was leaning over a bed smoothing the bedspread when Jean Martoli, headwaiter and Resistance member, hurried in.

He jerked his thumb toward the floor below. Sybilia wheeled her trolley out and hurried to the cupboard.

She had only seen Major Ernst Krag in passing, but she knew his voice well, along with those of every one of his staff. She had not yet caught a glimpse of Captain Dino Renucci, head of the Italian secret police, but he, too, called on Major Krag daily. Sybilia could recognize his soft, insidious voice.

She hurried to the cupboard, locked the door behind her, and grabbed her earphones. Renucci was annoyed. She could tell that from his tone of voice, which had become a hiss that whined into the headphones. Krag was lecturing him because Louis Poli, a Resistance leader from the southern part of the island, had managed to hang himself in his cell, thereby cheating his interrogators. Krag was furious.

After this they discussed the strengths of the various coastal garrison towns. Krag spent a great deal of time discussing the necessity of rationing supplies until their next supply ship arrived. The inability of his troops to conquer the interior, so that they could live off the island's farm produce, was a constant annoyance to Krag.

After an hour Sybilia thought she would faint from lack of air. The Resistance had given no thought to ventilation when they'd constructed her small space. Now it was too late. She dreaded the coming summer months.

Shortly afterward she heard Krag's chief of staff, Captain Otto Weinrauch, come into the room. Suddenly she forgot her cramped conditions in her eagerness to hear their conversation.

An hour later, clad in her peasant black, a scarf pulled tightly over her face, Sybilia hurried out of the servants' entrance of the hotel. Taking her bicycle, she pedaled hurriedly to her flat, which was only ten minutes away. It was a lovely April evening. Fluffy clouds, tinged with red hung over the misty horizon. The sea was covered with a pearl-gray mist that had crept into the streets, blurring the outlines of boats and houses. Sybilia had no time to waste gazing at scenery. She flung her bicycle against the wall and raced upstairs to her apartment.

Her radio transmitter was concealed behind the false back

of the wardrobe. Captain Moore had warned her of the danger of keeping it in her home, but she had not yet been able to find another suitable hiding place. Five minutes later she was sending out her message in Morse code.

A shipload of armaments will arrive in Bastia on the steamer Dunkerque, *at noon on Wednesday, April 7. Apart from the standard Mauser rifles, there will be Schmeisser MP-40 submachine guns, MG-34 belt-fed heavy machine guns, and several dozen mortars. The cargo will be transferred to waiting trucks for transportation across the island to Saint Florent and other west coast garrisons where resupply is urgently needed.*

Then Sybilia stowed away her radio transmitter and hurried back to the hotel. She spent the next few hours scrubbing bathrooms and making beds. She hummed to herself as she worked. Now Captain Robin Moore would see how useful she was.

CHAPTER 32

From bitter experience, Robin had learned to distrust much of the intelligence he received. If an armored car and a truck moved into a town, invariably he was told it was a battalion. Two half-tracks made a Panzer regiment. But Sybilia had a habit of being accurate, he'd learned. So he thanked God he'd taken the necessary steps to cope with the manpower he would need. He had Rocca and his squad of twenty men, to which he had added Castelli's communist buddies, numbering fifty in all. Rocca had exploded when he heard about the communists being included in the raid. They'd had a bitter fight in the mountain chalet that served as their headquarters, and Robin had eventually pulled rank on Rocca, overruling his objections.

Rocca's anger was not just a matter of self-vindication, Romanetti pointed out to Robin as they made their way toward

Poggio. By pushing Castelli's squad into the limelight, Moore was striking at the foundation of the island's clan loyalties, on which the delicate balance of Corsican democracy rested.

"Oh, spare me the lecture," Robin said impatiently. "My job is to help you guys win the war. The best-trained fighters are the communists. They're experts in sabotage and guerrilla warfare, and I need their skills."

The mountain pass that cut through the island was a winding, uneven ledge, chipped out of sheer granite slopes, falling to a swiftly flowing river in a chasm fifty yards below. The road crossed several rivers, chief of which were at Mori and at Poggio. Set about five miles apart, each river could only be crossed over ancient stone bridges. Robin had chosen the curving treacherous road between the bridges for his ambush.

In the past three months, the Resistance had used most of their explosives blowing bridges around Bastia. They had no bazookas or mortars, but Robin still thought that they had enough dynamite to make the bridges impassable, thus trapping the German troops in a narrow gorge.

At noon, he placed himself, with ten of his men, around the Poggio bridge. The others were hidden among trees and rocks on either side of the road. Castelli's squad had stayed at the Mori bridge to blow it when the convoy had passed. Then they would move along the forest, on the north side of the road, to attack through the trees. The success of the mission depended upon split-second timing.

There was a charcoal burner's cottage near the base of the forests. Michel had hurried down earlier to warn the old man who lived there to get lost rapidly. Robin was always surprised by his contradictions. On the one hand, Michel did not like any living creature to be hurt. Yet when it came to killing the enemy, he was ruthless and exacting.

"Almost here," Romanetti called, his voice unnaturally calm. A minute later the convoy could be heard nearing the second bridge. The shepherd took his position behind a nearby rock.

Within minutes the enemy trucks rounded the last curve. At the sight of three motorcyclists in the lead, Robin's stomach lurched with excitement. He needed those bikes badly. He sent three good riflemen to a vantage point beyond the bridge. Then he yelled to Romanetti to let the bikes through before he blew the charge. After that there was nothing left but the agonizing wait.

Minutes later an ear-shattering explosion rocked the ground. The first bridge at Mori had buckled. Simultaneously the convoy came round the last bend below them.

Goddammit, it was too early! The leading bikes and half-tracks were not yet on the second bridge. The enemy driver braked sharply when he heard the explosion. Behind him, the convoy slowly ground to a halt. The silence was eerie. Then two infantrymen climbed down from the half-track and began to inspect the bridge.

Blow it, Robin prayed. Do it now, for God's sake. Blow the goddamn bridge and get the hell out of there.

Romanetti hesitated. Robin knew why. If he took the bridge now, they would miss the chance to destroy the half-track and a dozen Boche. It was all or nothing. That was Corsicans for you. Robin sweated it out as the soldiers leaned over the rails and stared toward the shepherd. Too late! They must have seen him, for he was only half-hidden in the shadow of the bridge.

Miraculously, they signaled to the drivers of the convoy to proceed, and the vehicles advanced toward the bridge. The half-track moved onto it. Then a cloud of dust rose in the air as the charges ignited, followed shortly afterward by the rumble of the explosion. In slow motion Robin watched stones flying through the air. The half-track tumbled into the river and burst into flames. On the other side, the motorcyclists braked and scrambled toward the ditch.

The smoke was choking as the Maquisards let rip with their Schmeisser submachine guns. The enemy troops scattered for cover among the boulders and trees and returned the fire. Everything seemed to be in confusion now. The air was shattered with smoke and dust; visibility was down to a few yards, and the noise was intense.

Impossible to see which of us is winning. And where the hell is Castelli's team?

German drivers farther down the convoy were trying to turn their cumbersome vehicles in the narrow road. They seemed to be unaware that they were trapped between two blown bridges. In the confusion, several more Germans were shot. Others took cover among the trees along the mountainside and fired from relative safety.

Seeing that some of the Germans might escape, Rocca gave a yell and climbed up the bank into the road.

"Get back. Take cover," Robin yelled, but no one listened.

The Maquisards raced after him. Completely disregarding orders, they swarmed up the rocky slopes, following Rocca's lead. Some dived behind the trucks. Others simply stood in the road firing into the ditches. Robin saw one man clamber onto a truck and fire down from his vantage position until he was shot.

At last Castelli's squad put in an appearance, racing down through the trees from the opposite side of the road.

"What the hell kept those bastards?" Robin yelled to Romanetti.

Robin had chosen this spot in the hope that the trees and the high peaks on either side would conceal most of the smoke from Bastia. Nevertheless, time was short. Half an hour at the outside, he reckoned. The Germans would race reinforcements to the scene. The blown bridge would not hold them up for long. He swore as the first ammunition truck in the convoy exploded with an earsplitting din. Miraculously, it was the only one to blow.

Peering toward the mountain crest, Robin saw a long line of mules coming toward the river. To his dismay, he realized that most of them were led by women. Clad in black, scarves over their heads, they came on, ignoring the battle. Was it fifty? Or a hundred? They collected their dead and wounded, loaded the ammunition onto the pack mules, and disappeared.

Twenty minutes later it was over. The last of the mules were disappearing into the forest. Only the Germans were left, and most of them were dead or wounded.

Robin and Romanetti went from truck to truck, laying their charges. Without roads the trucks were of no use to the Resistance. Eventually Robin took the remaining motorbike. With the shepherd riding pillion, they returned to their camp.

Rocca was looking pleased when they reached headquarters. This made Robin furious.

"An excellent maneuver," Rocca said, handing Robin a glass of brandy. "We can congratulate ourselves."

"Do you think so?" Robin said cuttingly, pushing the glass aside. "To my mind it was a disaster. Your men don't understand the simplest principles of crossing ground under fire. Nor do they care. What's more, neither do you. What's so fantastic about three good men dead and twenty-four wounded?"

Rocca's eyes narrowed, his lips drew back in an ugly grimace. Robin was too angry to notice.

"It's back to school for everyone, and that includes you, Rocca. I saw you standing in the middle of the road mowing down the Boche in the ditches. What did you think they were firing at you . . . dummy bullets? You looked like a fucking cowboy."

"Corsicans don't count the cost when there's a battle to be won," Rocca said stiffly. "My men are not cowards."

"Sure they're not. They're brave and loyal boys. As such, they're valuable. Too valuable to be sacrificed for nine trucks of small arms."

"We needed the arms."

"We needed those men."

Now they were both shouting. Romanetti came in and stood by the doorway, watching curiously. They ignored him.

"What inspired those crazy idiots to leap into the road and stand on trucks while they're being shot at? Some sort of death wish? What's wrong with you guys?"

"My men were following my example. That's natural."

"You won't be setting any more examples. Not until you learn to look after your squad. I'm taking charge from now on. At least until I've drilled some common sense into you. You may be one hell of a politician, but you know very little about fighting. Bravery is only a part of the qualities needed."

Robin refused to join in the celebrations. He went to visit the wounded in Taita. To his surprise, Michel was there helping with first aid. The village doctor was doing his best under trying conditions, but he was short of drugs. Besides Michel, he only had the midwife to help him. Before midnight another man had died.

Those goddamn crazy Corsicans! Robin sighed. There was only one thing that counted to them—their honor. Honor caused them to advance in a hail of machine-gun bullets; honor prompted the women to bring out their month's food supply to give the Maquisards one good supper. Sadly, Sybilia's honor would keep her at her post long after her cover was blown. Her crazy code would cause her death, and that was something Robin wanted to avoid at all costs. He was still thinking about her when he fell asleep.

CHAPTER 33

Major Ernst Krag's first knowledge of the destruction of the convoy came with the arrival of the grim-faced Italian police chief, Dino Renucci. He could only report that he had found tire tracks beyond the bridge. It was assumed that the three riders had been killed and their bikes captured.

There was a leak, Krag insisted angrily to Renucci, and not from the German side. Only five men had had advance knowledge of the arms convoy: Captain Otto Weinrauch was dead; one was his assistant, Lieutenant Hans Bleicher; and the other was Krag's immediate superior in the German High Command on the mainland; the fourth was Renucci. It was well known that some Italians were fraternizing with the Corsicans. No doubt there were spies. The Germans had no intelligence forces on the island, Krag reminded Renucci. It was up to him to find those responsible for the leak. Renucci insisted he must interrogate the entire staff of the Hotel Bastia. Krag agreed, on condition the hotel's services would not be interrupted.

Major Krag was not satisfied. He ordered reprisals on local peasants and landowners within a ten-mile radius of the attack.

This was all carefully recorded by Sybilia, who felt sick with fright. She hurried home to broadcast the news.

All night local peasants heard the roar of vehicles searching for tracks through the woods and saw the river lit up by flares. Later the cyclists' bodies were discovered in a ditch, minus their uniforms.

By now most of the locals had been evacuated, but two farmers who had refused to leave their farms were shot in full view of their families. The charcoal burner did not return to his cottage. The Germans had to content themselves with burning it down. As a reprisal for the ambush, five citizens of Poggio were shot in the square. This, too, was relayed to Robin by Sybilia the following evening.

Another broadcast finished. Sybilia pushed her radio receiver into its suitcase, fitted it into the false back of her wardrobe, replaced the wallpaper, and waited for the dreaded footsteps.

It was her turn to be interrogated by Renucci. She knew because she had listened in on his daily reports to Krag.

It was a long, exhausting wait. Every instinct urged her to flee, but she could not do that. Not if she wanted to continue working at the hotel. She must sit and act out the role of the ignorant peasant girl. Sybilia forced herself to undress and put on her nightgown. She had to appear as if this were a normal night, or they would suspect her. But she did not sleep. Instead she gazed at the black rectangle of night through the window and longed for morning. Eventually, when the sky turned a pale, translucent rose, she heard them coming.

There were four men, and they were obviously secret police with their well-cut civilian suits and arrogant manners. They poked around her flat in a desultory fashion, opened a few drawers, rifled through the wardrobe. They allowed her to dress. Then they walked her to the car. She sat in stony silence during the ride to headquarters in the central square, where she waited for over an hour in a drafty, gloomy passage, fearing the worst.

I'm like a bird glued to a branch here. I can't get away. If anyone betrays me to save themselves, I'm trapped. What a fool I've been. If I ever get out of here, I'll go straight back to Taita.

When she was pushed into the office, a stranger confronted her. The moment he began to speak she recognized Dino Renucci's voice. Her feeling of dread grew stronger.

Renucci was tall for an Italian—over six feet, weighing well over two hundred pounds. He had quick, restless movements, even when he was sitting behind his desk. His massive head was thrust forward while his hard brown eyes flickered alternately over her face and her body. He had a high forehead, and he was bald, giving his skull a curiously naked appearance in contrast with his thick black eyebrows. There was a suggestion of coarseness in his nose and a touch of cruelty in his grim, fleshy lips. Sybilia did not have to act intimidated. That was exactly how she felt.

He turned to the file, reading with concentration, frowning now and then, tapping his fingers. Sybilia gazed at his face, unable to tear her eyes away.

"You are Sybilia Rocca?" He asked the question in German and then Italian.

What am I supposed to do? After all, I can recognize my own name, can't I?

"Yes. I understand. You were asking my name? Yes? It is Madame Sybilia Rocca," she replied loudly in the dialect, nodding her head as if anxious to make him understand.

"My men noticed that your apartment is exceptionally clean and well furnished for a humble chambermaid," he said in Italian.

"Please, could you speak my language? If not, I speak only a little French. If you speak slowly, I will understand you," she whispered. Her fear and dread were now terrible. She struggled to control her expression.

Why did I try to bluff this man? I should have fled into the maquis. Those terrible eyes. They seem to look right through you.

He repeated his sentence in French, and on impulse Sybilia decided that a show of rebellion might stand her in good stead.

"There is nothing humble about my job," she said sourly. "Jobs are hard to come by, and I earn an honest living. As for the sculpture and the decor in my flat, it was done by my husband, Michel, who was a stonemason before you invaded our island. He is serving with the Free French in Algeria." She could not meet his eyes; instead she looked at her hands.

Oh, God, what have I said? Now he'll go back and search my rooms more carefully, and he'll find the radio. I'm lost. Any minute now they're going to drag me down to their terrible interrogation cells in the basement. I won't escape. I'll die there.

There was a very long silence while he studied her. "Exquisite," he said quickly in Italian. "Quite exquisite, and courageous, too. I shall continue this interrogation personally from time to time. In the meantime, let her go."

She was so relieved she almost stood up.

God protect me! I nearly gave myself away.

"You may go," his assistant said in the dialect.

From his accent Sybilia knew he was Corsican and that he came from the south, near Ajaccio. "Traitor," she said. She spat at him as she hurried out, knowing that this was in keeping with the image she had tried to project. It would be only a matter of time before Renucci came knocking on her door, but she would deal with that problem when it occurred.

Outside, a car was waiting to take her and two other maids to the hotel. Evidently Krag was not keen to suffer too much inconvenience over the interrogation. She was not even late. As for returning to Taita, what nonsense! She'd been a momentary coward. She would forget all about that now, and work all the harder.

If you discounted the dead and wounded and those killed in the German reprisals, the capture of nine trucks full of small arms and ammunition was still significant, or so Robin thought at first.

Then Rocca waylaid him at headquarters. "This is what happens when they send boys to do a man's job," he said contemptuously to Romanetti.

He turned to Robin. "My men gave their lives for something they believed in. We needed those armaments desperately. Now, because of you, they lost their lives for nothing. Less than nothing. After the war those guns will be turned on us. Castelli and his communist friends have stolen over half of the arms. You let them walk off with it all—right under your nose. What sort of a fool are you? Why don't you piss off back to America?"

Robin watched Rocca sit down and light his pipe. His face was paler than usual. He'd lost weight in the mountains. His eyes seemed more slanting, his smile more sinister. He looked pleased with himself rather than distressed. That annoyed Robin.

"You fucking Boy Scout," Xavier went on. "We got less than half of what we fought for. You should have put guards on the mules."

"No. You should have seen to that," Robin retorted. "You know the people here. You knew what to expect. Now get off your backside. Take your squad and retrieve every box of it."

"Captain Moore, you're making a mistake in speaking to me like this." Rocca fingered his knife.

Robin stepped forward and leaned over him. "I've got you sized up, Rocca. You won't knife me in full view of all your men. That wouldn't be a politically viable act, would it? A dark night is more your style. Well, I'm telling you now, I'll be waiting for you."

Robin made an effort to pull himself together. "Now listen to me, Rocca. Those men dying didn't win the battle. We'd have won anyway, even if they'd stayed under cover. Why don't you start getting smart? Think up some strategy to recover those armaments."

"You're mad," Rocca said. "By now they've got the arms so well hidden we'd never find them. They could be anywhere in Corsica."

"Then guard what's left," Robin snarled.

Rocca was right, of course. There was little point in stirring up strife between the Resistance groups. They'd never recover the arms anyway.

Robin felt vaguely uneasy as he stormed out of the chalet. He was destroying Rocca. He didn't want to. It was not an intentional act on his part, but like all very proud men, Rocca was vulnerable.

"To hell with him and his crazy pride," he muttered, and tried to dismiss the matter from his mind.

Robin settled down to a boring period of trying to train and control the Maquisards. The best way, he discovered, was to keep them busy and active. This prevented them from turning on each other. He worked out an ambitious and ruthless campaign against all the coastal garrisons. He sold this plan to Rocca, who accepted it reluctantly. It involved attacking trains and convoys, rail links and roads. Hardly a day went past without some Axis casualty for the invaders somewhere.

Robin had already discovered that hit-and-run tactics were ideally suited to the island, at least until the men were more disciplined. Soon he was able to make use of the younger men hiding in the maquis: those who had been at school prior to the invasion. These boys were often slovenly, they were bored, and they were pathetically grateful for even a small job in a man's world. He put them together in twos and threes and sent them to steal camping equipment as well as supplies of tobacco from German stocks. They were also useful for helping the villagers to supply food for the Resistance. Keeping up morale was his biggest problem. The men needed constant successes, however minor, which he took care to publicize well.

Slowly Rocca began to take a backseat as Robin emerged as the acknowledged leader of the Corsican Resistance.

CHAPTER 34

Why don't you brand me? Yes, go on, why don't you? Just burn the word into my skull—disonorata. *You might as well. Everyone can see it as plain as the nose on my face.*

Or so Xavier thought as he forced a glimmer of his mirthless smile, gritted his teeth, and settled down to guard duty on Moore's instructions, while the younger men went off for a lightning raid on a supply truck that their lookout had spotted laboring up the mountain road.

Soon he was alone with his humiliation. He lit his pipe slowly and contemplated his problems. By far his greatest resentment was reserved for Captain Robin Moore.

God save me from Americans! They have no subtlety. Naive like children, always believing in goodness, justice, mercy, and truth, together with fairies at the bottom of their gardens—I shouldn't be surprised. Evangelists—each one of them—touting the American dream and American morals. What makes them think that what they have is better than what we have?

Xavier sat on a rock and puffed moodily at his pipe. He contemplated the cave filled with Allied largesse that they periodically tossed out of their aircraft. It was little better than charity, to Xavier's mind. The Allies thought it gave them the right to dictate to Corsicans how and when they would liberate their island. Now they had their representative, namely Captain Robin Moore, pushing them all around.

If I hadn't insisted on a guard here, Leca and Castelli would have most of this lot salted away, ready for a postwar revolution. If Moore had his way, they'd succeed, too. He's pushing the commies into the limelight, and personally challenging me, the Wolf, for leadership. But how to beat him? He controls communications with the outside world and therefore the supply of arms, explosives, and ammunition. He's been sent here to take charge, hasn't he?

In the brief five months since the invasion, Xavier's swagger had crumpled. Even Gus sensed it. Nowadays the dog spent most of his time head hanging, slinking around the camp. Yet another of Rocca's humiliations was the behavior of Michel, who no longer tried to keep his private life secret.

It doesn't seem to worry Michel, or Angelo, when they're seen holding hands in the woods or when they make their frequent disappearances. The men try not to comment for fear of raising my wrath.

As for Angelo. I'll settle his hash one of these days. He and his cherubic face and his wriggling, plump, woman's buttocks. He's like a fetid bog, and Michel's fallen into it. Well, more fool he, but one of these days I'll have to haul him out. Michel is, after all, my only son, and I can whistle for more grandchildren while Angelo's around. Maria's fault. She brought the boy up too soft.

His thoughts veered back to Robin like fingers to a scab. He could never relax, not for an instant. It would never do to show his men the slightest glimpse of his distress. So he sat back and kept smiling his famous, mirthless, wolflike smile while he seethed inside.

CHAPTER 35

Easter came at last. The villagers errupted with an unprecedented show of joy, which was not altogether due to religious fervor, Father Andrews realized. It had much more to do with the improved war news and the return of their sons and husbands from their camps in the maquis to spend a quiet holiday at home. The women greeted the priest with smiles, the first he had seen for a long time. "Christ is risen," they called to him happily. "Yes, indeed, Christ is truly risen." Even Maria decided to shed her mourning for Carlotta's death and enjoy having her family back at home for once.

Sybilia, too, returned to Taita to see her son. On Thursday evening, veiled and trembling, she went to confession. When her turn came at last, she hurried into the familiar cell, but the heady scent of incense, the feel of the polished wood under her nervous fingers, even the sight of Father Andrews's profile in the dim candlelight, did nothing to calm her anxiety. If anything, her agitation increased.

"Forgive me, Father, for I have sinned."

As he said the blessing, the priest's heart leaped with pleasure to hear her voice.

"It is two months since my last confession. These are my sins."

She listed them to the best of her ability, not forgetting her anger at her parents for marrying her to Michel. "I can't find it in my heart to forgive them," she murmured. "Never! Never. How can I?"

He listened while she vividly described her anger at Michel and Angelo for their shameless public displays of affection. "All yesterday they were in the bistro together. People are talking. This morning I heard the women at the washing troughs. They could scarcely talk about anything else. Why are they doing this to me?"

"But listen to me, lassie. We're here to discuss your sins, not Michel's sins. You must try to forgive and be patient. Perhaps with time Michel will see the error of his ways and come back to you."

"I don't want him," she said contemptuously. "How could I take him back, knowing what he is?"

Sybilia had intended to confess her growing obsession with Captain Robin Moore. Now she realized that she was not ready to talk about it. Besides, Father Andrews would never understand. How could he? He was a priest. He had never experienced nights of torment. He'd never known what it was like to physically need someone to the point of agony.

She accepted her penance and hurried away, entirely missing the joy she usually felt after confession.

To Robin, this brief interlude in homely surroundings was paradise. Good manners and the need to keep up appearances had forced Rocca to invite Robin to make use of his spare room, and Robin had joyfully accepted. He needed a rest badly and hoped to find the opportunity to talk to Sybilia.

After sleeping for forty-eight hours, he surfaced on Saturday evening and went to look for a familiar face. As he thought, the men were in the bistro. To his astonishment, Angelo was there, too. Robin deduced that Michel had found his friend accommodations elsewhere in the village. Rocca seemed civil enough, but Robin could sense his suppressed rage.

Robin stayed to buy a round of drinks and listen to Antoine Romanetti singing his heart out, and then he returned to the house, where he found the women slaving in the kitchen as usual.

"It's not right. Why should you two work all night? It's Easter for you too, isn't it? I'll help you."

They looked astonished.

"Well, don't just stare at me, Madame Rocca. Give me a job. I'm a pretty good cook," he said. "I can even bake bread. Want me to make a few hamburgers? You can bet those boys'll be back from the bistro good and hungry pretty soon."

Maria complained a great deal but finally agreed. She brought him an apron, which he put on, but Sybilia seemed offended. Robin was making a fool of himself. She must tell him so.

"You're being foolish," she whispered in English. "You'll never be able to command these men if you hang around the kitchen like a woman."

"Watch me," he said. "Now, where's the mincemeat?"

The men who had homes in Taita went back to eat. Some took their friends with them. About two dozen Maquisards trooped into Rocca's living room. Soon Rocca was demanding supper in a loud voice.

When their commanding officer appeared, carrying a large tray of hamburgers, followed by the women with salads, olives, and cheeses, there was a long, embarrassed silence.

"Don't be shy," Robin said, grinning oafishly. He had drunk a fair amount of Rocca's homemade brandy, and he was feeling overconfident. "Tonight we're making like Americans."

"This is one of those droll habits we'd hoped you'd keep to yourself," Rocca said dryly.

"Well, let's go the whole hog. Tonight it's a buffet. Grab a plate, help yourselves, and find a chair somewhere. We'll help with the cleaning up afterward."

Sybilia gasped. He was going too far. She pulled Robin's sleeve and gestured for him to come into the kitchen.

"Xavier cannot insult his guests with such a humiliating task—" She broke off as they heard a loud voice laughing contemptuously.

It was Ambrosini, a shepherd from Chiornia. "This is the American's secret weapon. Do we eat them or throw them at the Boche?"

Robin and Sybilia walked back into the living room. "Hey there, you lousy bastard. Why don't you taste one before you start throwing insults around?" Robin was only half-serious.

"Hush," Sybilia whispered. "Don't tangle with Ambrosini. He's a mean man. I don't like him. Besides, he's the champion wrestler around these parts, and he fights dirty."

Her words were a challenge to Robin.

"They taste like shit." Ambrosini spat a mouthful on the floor.

"Why, you dirty son of a bitch," Robin said, ignoring the insult. "This house is spotless. You're gonna clean up that mess you made there."

"Who says so?" Ambrosini turned away contemptuously.

"I do," Robin lunged out and kicked Ambrosini in the

backside. He watched the man lurch forward, then spin round, a stiletto in his hand. His face was taut with anger.

Suddenly the room was quiet.

As Ambrosini lunged at him, Robin sidestepped, took his arm, and pulled him over his shoulder. He staggered through the door, running half-crouched with Ambrosini's massive weight. They collapsed in a heap in the darkness.

Sybilia grabbed a knife and ran to the door, but Rocca caught hold of her. She heard the dull smack of fists pounding flesh. Then a groan and a thump. She clapped a hand over her mouth, but the next moment Robin returned, trying to grin. She could see it was an effort.

"I guess it's my night for cleaning up stinking messes," he said, and fetched a cloth from the kitchen.

"Please let me—"

"Sybilia, you're not going to do it. Hey, Leca," Robin called out as he went to the kitchen. "Ambrosini's out cold. You'd better see he gets to his home."

"Well now . . ." Rocca tried to hide his disappointment at Moore's reappearance. "Personally I like American food. Did I tell you that I toured California? Let me see now, that was about thirty years ago. . . ."

When they had finished eating and were sitting around smoking, Xavier said, "Captain Moore, I respect your ways, but you must respect ours. No Corsican would ever wash dishes. That's women's work."

"How about spying on the German High Command; risking her life every minute of the day. Is that women's work, too?"

"Not in my opinion," Rocca said gravely. "I told her to stay in Taita. Jules needs her."

"That's my viewpoint exactly. She's a liability in Bastia."

Sybilia reacted angrily. "Oh, how could you? How dare you! I was the one who told you about the convoy of arms. Good heavens . . . I thought—" Sybilia broke off and bit her lip.

Michel rushed to support her. "She's doing a good job, Robin. She can look after herself."

"No, she can't," Robin snarled. "It's just a matter of time before they catch on to her."

"Someone has to do it," Leca said. "She's a good linguist."

"If she were just any dame, with a face like any other dame, I'd say okay. But look at her. She sticks out like a lily in a turnip patch. She doesn't match the ignorant peasant woman she's supposed to be. The whole idea is crazy. Whoever thought of it must be blind as well as stupid. Believe you me, now Dino Renucci's seen her, he won't rest until he gets his hands on her. He'll be sniffing around, prodding and prying, and something will give her away. Goddammit, what's the matter with you all? She's lovely," Robin said. "Or hasn't anyone noticed? Rocca, you've got eyes to see, haven't you—even if your son hasn't."

Rocca jumped to his feet, sending a chair crashing to the floor.

"I guess that was uncalled for," Robin said uneasily, realizing he had overstepped the bounds of good manners. He was, after all, a guest in Rocca's house. "I apologize. It's just that I'm scared for her, as you should all be."

My God, look at their faces. You'd think I'd pissed on the carpet. I must be drunk as well as stupid. Why did I open my big mouth? But someone had to say it, and I can't quit now.

He turned to Sybilia. "If only you would believe me. You are in terrible danger."

Michel crossed the room and switched on the radio. It was tuned in to the BBC.

Hell. She's as stubborn as the rest of them. Look at her, with her bottom lip stuck out like an obstinate child. What does she know about war? It's just a game to her.

"Hey," Michel called out, "listen to this." In silence they heard that British and American troops were advancing on two fronts in the North African desert. The two forces were about to meet up. After two years of bitter fighting, the desert war was about to be won. The villagers drank another toast. In the celebrations that followed, everyone pretended to have forgotten Robin's indiscretion. Only Sybilia slipped off to bed feeling a warm glow inside her.

Robin cares. He really cares. And I've been worried sick because I thought he didn't trust me. How could I have been so wrong? Nevertheless, I won't give in. He has no right to tell me what to do.

CHAPTER 36

Dressed in her shabbiest black skirt and blouse, Sybilia strode through the dappled, dew-drenched forest, feeling thrilled by the profusion of spring flowers. Noisy birds were twittering in the trees, warmed by the April sun.

She was going to gather mushrooms, she had told Maria. The truth was she wanted to wander freely through the mountains, as an antidote to months of confinement in the stuffy cupboard.

Mushrooms were few and far between. They were scattered among leaves and grass, and it was difficult to find them. She had saddled Pierre with two large baskets, which she hoped to fill. Stooping frequently, she passed from one glade to the next. Sybilia began to think about Michel as she hurried along. Last night she had begged him to stay with her. Why had she been such a fool? she wondered. She should have had more pride. Was it because they were home? She was reminded of their first stumbling attempts to build a relationship. They had been happy for a while. So she had longed to hold him and to be loved, but he had been anxious to leave. He was going to Angelo. Shame and sadness had kept her awake for most of the night.

Maria had noticed. She had not said anything, but her blue eyes had been full of compassion and disappointment.

Sybilia made an effort to pull herself together. How stupid to be gloomy on such a lovely morning. She had a great deal to be thankful for, she reminded herself. Jules was an adorable and healthy baby. Maria was coping with him. She seemed to be saner lately, perhaps because she had someone to love.

She passed a flat boulder and sat down to munch her sour bread, while Pierre grazed on grass growing in the ditch. Her thoughts turned to Robin. Now there was a real man. . . . She went over the previous evening in her mind, remembering what Robin had said about her. He had made her feel warm and loved and more sure of herself as a woman. Was that why she had wanted Michel to love her? Forbidden thoughts!

She stood up abruptly, smoothed the pine needles from her skirt, and tugged at Pierre's reins. Eventually he plodded after her. When she came to the river she picked her way over stepping-stones and continued uphill until she came to prairielike grasslands, where their flock grazed in summer. As she had hoped, the field was full of large mushrooms.

She had been picking them for a few minutes when she heard a shout from the trees.

"Sybilia." The voice echoed around the mountains. Robin's voice.

"I'm here," she called. Her heart lurched. Suddenly she felt happy.

Robin emerged from the trees and looked around. Then he hurried toward her. "I followed you, but then I lost you. Can you believe it?"

For once Sybilia allowed herself the luxury of looking at him, taking in his size and strength. She had never been able to do that in public.

He was wearing army trousers, a thick homespun checked shirt, and a leather windbreaker. He was a big man, with wide bony shoulders and a long, lean body. His dark red hair was cut short and brushed back vigorously. For the first time she saw that he had high, pronounced cheekbones and a strong square chin. It was a belligerent face. Only his sensuous lips and deep blue eyes gave an impression of caring.

Right now his face was twisted into a shy grin. She had a sudden recall of last night. He had looked ferocious when he'd tackled Ambrosini. Yet, on the whole, he was a gentle man, she felt.

"I followed you because I want to talk to you."

He stood looking down at her so seriously. What was she supposed to gauge from that long, meaningful glance?

She turned away and groped for a few more mushrooms. "Talk away, Captain Moore," she said, making an effort to sound light-hearted.

Robin gazed at her. She was quite exquisite. Everything about her was lovely. Yet the real essence of her attraction lay elsewhere. It had something to do with the truth and goodness that shone from her eyes.

He realized he was staring. "Can't we sit down?" He saw a fallen tree trunk at the edge of the forest and pointed to it. "Let's sit over there."

Sybilia hesitated, scanning the mountainside guiltily. They seemed to be quite alone. Robin took her hand and led her toward the tree. The touch of his hand on hers sent the most unusual sensations thrilling through her whole being. She could hardly breathe. She moistened her lips with her tongue and stared away, hoping Robin would not notice her flushed cheeks and burning eyes.

When they were sitting down awkwardly, side by side, he put his thumb and finger under her chin and tilted her face toward him. Then he smiled. It was a slow smile that began with the crinkling of his eyes and spread slowly to his cheeks: an intimate smile that enfolded her like a warm blanket. Then he reached out and touched her hair, smoothing it back from her face.

"Last night I made a fool of myself," he said. "I drank too much. Foolish! I hardly ever do, but I felt relaxed in your kitchen. It reminded me of home. Hope I didn't make trouble for you—I mean with Michel."

Michel couldn't care less. He spent the night in Angelo's arms. How she longed to say those words, but that would be disloyal. Instead she shook her head, feeling tongue-tied.

"Sybilia, listen to me. I need a radio operator at headquarters. I have to keep in touch with the leaders of the Resistance. I don't speak the dialect."

"There are plenty of men who do. Besides, who would listen to Major Krag's conversations?"

She was teasing him. "Anyone but you," he said sulkily.

Her eyes veered away from him. She was not able to look him straight in the eyes for long. It was too intimate. Glancing anywhere but at Robin, she noticed that the sun was gone. How quickly the weather could change in the mountains in April. The mist was rolling down the mountain flanks like spirals of smoke.

"I like my job," she lied.

"You're so obstinate," he said, almost losing his temper. "Do you know what they do to women spies? Sybilia, you're not going back."

She shuddered.

"You're cold."

"It's just because the sun's gone."

What a nerve. Why is he so sure of himself? Does he always get his own way with women? Do they sink into his arms and agree to anything he says?

"Captain Moore, you cannot tell me what to do. You have no right to try. If my husband and father-in-law feel that the risks are justified, then it is my duty to go."

"Don't you have any rights or feelings?"

"I want to help win the war."

"The war will be won with or without you," he said. Suddenly, unbelievably, his arm moved around her shoulders.

"You're cold. I want to warm you," he explained.

"There's a raincoat in Pierre's basket," she said stiffly.

Why don't I stand up and walk home? What's wrong with me? I should feel insulted, but I don't, and I can't bear to go.

He fetched the raincoat and put it around both of them.

At that moment nothing else existed for Sybilia but her immediate sensations: the smell of Robin's skin, his breath on her cheeks, and the delicious warmth of his thigh pressed against hers. She longed to reach out and touch him. The intimacy of the shared raincoat was the most exciting experience of her life.

"Must I spell it out for you?" he murmured in her ear. "You're a liability, because you're too lovely. The Boche and the Macaronis will be after you just because of your looks. They'll be like wasps around a honey jar. You won't be able to get rid of them. Eventually you'll drop your cover."

"I can look after myself. Believe me, Captain Moore, you underestimate me."

"Robin," he said.

"All right. Robin!" Just saying his name lowered her defenses. "I want to be needed. I have to do something worthwhile. My work is all I have." She smiled sadly. "You'll never understand my situation."

She looked so wretched. All his resolve melted. "I need you," he muttered. "And I do understand. Really I do. I care for you more than I should, Sybilia. The moment I saw you, I realized that you were my sort of girl. When I found out that you were married to Michel, I, well . . . I can't explain how I felt. Sort of cheated.

"My feelings for you are not going to cause you any trouble. I just want you to know, that's all." He pressed his fingers into her shoulder. "The last thing I want to do is be a pest. So, in the future, if I seem to be avoiding you, you'll know why."

"Oh, Robin," she gasped. "Well, the truth is I feel just as you do. But it's too late. Oh, Robin, I want to explain how it is with Michel and me."

"There's nothing to explain. I've watched Michel with Angelo, and with you."

They sensed that there was nothing else to say. Silence was enough. Words would only get in the way. They sat close together, her hand in his.

Eventually they had to leave. Side by side they walked through the trees and parted at the edge of the forest.

"We'll never be able to be together like this again," she said.

He caught hold of her and kissed her. They clung to each other for a long time.

"We both know how we feel," Robin said. "We care for each other. That's enough."

As he watched her hurry away, he wondered if she would return to Bastia or stay in the mountains with his partisans. Sybilia had a mind of her own. Nothing he could say or do would influence her in the least. He knew that.

CHAPTER 37

Sybilia was spending most of her life in the dark, airless cupboard. No one else spoke German well enough to share the work with her. Her face grew pale and haggard, her eyes seemed larger and more luminous, she was draining away her youth. Sometimes at night she would dream of being normal: of sunlight and laughter, a family who loved her and who stayed with her, a man to hug her. In the morning she would experience a physical pang of fear in her guts as reality dawned. It was not so much a fear of the war or of being caught. It was a dread of the cupboard, of living and growing old there. It was as if she had been deprived of life.

She would dress and leave earlier than necessary in order to cycle around the hedgerows, admire the trees and the sky. Then off to that miserable cupboard for the day. Today, as she crouched in the dark, she could picture them exactly: Major Ernst Krag, a man of curious contrasts with his fanatic's eyes, his red gourmet's face, and his butcher's hands. Then there was his assistant: Lieutenant Hans Bleicher, a paler, slighter version of Krag, but perhaps more deadly.

As she listened to a low mumble of voices, the slurp of swallowed coffee, the crunch of buttered scones, she felt nauseated. She had a headache, and her back was breaking. They should have remembered her need for fresh air when they'd created this miserable cupboard, she thought. But she would never complain. No, not for anything. She wanted to play her part in winning this war.

Krag was in unusually high spirits, she noticed. He was teasing Bleicher about his latest conquest. Bleicher did not like being teased, she knew from his mumbled replies. Sybilia felt vaguely uneasy.

Why is Krag in such a good mood? He should be tense, shouldn't he? The scheduled arms convoy is due to leave this afternoon. At this moment the ship is being unloaded. So why is he laughing?

The sergeant on guard announced the arrival of Captain Dino Renucci. As she listened to a long preamble of area reports and Krag's instructions concerning the arms shipment, she was more conscious of her headache and her urge to stretch her legs than anything else.

Renucci left at last. After a short silence Krag laughed heartily. "This time, Hans . . . this time we've got them. Only you and I will know. Even you don't know yet. More to the point: Renucci doesn't know.

"Now, listen. The men are on standby for a special exercise. I'm putting you in charge. Don't fail me, Hans. Here's the plan. . . ."

Sybilia listened for a long time. She felt limp with shock. She must go, at once, without making a sound. What time was it? Ten A.M. Somehow she must leave early and warn Robin. At that moment all was forgotten—the war, the arms, the Resistance. She was only aware of her fear for the safety of Captain Robin Moore.

Half an hour later she was pedaling slowly through cobbled streets. "Mustn't look anxious. Mustn't hurry," she whispered to herself.

It seemed hours before she reached home, locked the door, and dragged out her heavy suitcase.

She could not raise Robin. The station was closed down.

Oh, God. What am I going to do?

She burst into tears of frustration. Crying won't help anyone, she lectured herself. She began again. An hour later she heard an answering signal and almost burst into tears of relief. It was Rocca, she deciphered. Robin was already at the Poggio bridge planning the attack, but he'd probably return later. The rest were putting the gear together. If it was urgent, he could send a messenger by motorbike.

She tapped out her message: *Advise Captain Moore that the convoy to Saint Florent via Poggio bridge is a trap. Two hundred infantry will be concealed in trucks. It is an ambush intended to wipe out the Resistance. The real shipment will be sent to Saint Florent via Cap Corse. Confirm that you understand and will inform Moore immediately.*

The reply was in the affirmative.

Sybilia leaned back. After a while she allowed herself a small smile. When she tried to stand up, she found she was shaking from delayed shock. Her legs had turned to rubber, but after a cup of coffee she felt sufficiently recovered to return to the hotel.

Fate had shown him exactly how to deal with his two bête noires, but there were complications, chiefly Michel. Nevertheless, Rocca grinned at this sudden stroke of luck. It was so perfect. Just perfect! He would wipe out Moore and Angelo in one lucky move. But what to do about Michel? His son must be prevented from going to Poggio. At the same time, he must never suspect that anything was wrong.

A number of possibilities flashed through Rocca's mind as he stood outside the camp, staring over the valley toward Bastia and the coast. As if on cue, his son called from the trees. Rocca saw Moore leading his squad back to camp.

Yes, he decided. Robin Moore was his enemy. He had proved that several times, and now he would be dealt with like an enemy. Once Rocca had made up his mind, there was no point in wasting more time.

Michel looked ferociously healthy. The war suited him. He collapsed on the ground and began to open tins of corned beef. Inspiration struck Rocca in a flash. It was so easy. Fate was dealing him all the aces.

"London called," Rocca said loudly to no one in particular. "There's to be a parachute drop tonight: explosives, they said. Usual place. They want flares lit at eighteen hundred hours. After that Sybilia called. A small part of the expected arms shipment—one truckload of ammunition, she thinks—is being sent to the German garrison at Macinaggio. That's in the north," he added for Robin's benefit.

Robin frowned. Rocca was flashing that particular, wolflike smile that he did not trust. It made him feel uneasy. Why should there be a drop now, after all these months of waiting? The Corsican Resistance was not one of the Allies' priorities, he knew. Would Sybilia break her routine of evening calls in order to tell him of one diverted truck? Yes, he decided. Knowing how short of arms they were, she would. All the same, something was wrong.

Rocca sat back and enjoyed his lunch while Robin began to fall into the trap. There was no other choice for him. Michel would supervise the parachute drop. Romanetti would assist him. Rocca would take some of the men to raid the Cap Corse supply truck. Robin would take the rest to Poggio and ambush the supply convoy as planned.

"We'd better get organized fast," Moore said.

Sitting on the tree trunk, Rocca smoked his pipe and sipped his coffee. The mist was gathering around the mountain crests and drifting down toward them. Soon the damp air crystallized into dewdrops on his hair and mustache. It was going to get thicker. Luck was on his side today, there was no denying it. By midnight he'd be back in control of the Resistance, and Michel would be burying Angelo.

He leaned back and contemplated Corsica. He saw its destiny stretching through time, past and future. Corsica was threatened. Not only its island beauty, but a whole way of life was on the very lip of destruction. It would take strong, determined men to fend off the degenerate cultures that had taken hold of the world. The West with their commercialism and easy morals; the East with their contempt of man and his ultimate freedom and dignity. Well, let them go their own ways, but God protect Corsica from both sides.

In a heavily armed, armored car and gun-mounted half-track, Lieutenant Bleicher's reconnaissance group ate cherries and sausages sent over from Marseilles. They were parked in a concealed forest path, some hundred yards west of the Poggio bridge. Bleicher sat beside his driver with a Sten gun between his knees, souvenir of an Allied container drop captured by his men. It was a tradition that on antiterrorist sweeps they kept what they found. While any Allied officer would have willingly thrown away his Sten in exchange for the much superior German Schmeisser, it pleased Bleicher to carry a captured weapon.

Far behind, along the route from Bastia, winding at ten kilometers an hour, came the trucks filled with infantrymen armed with mortars, machine guns, and grenades. Behind them came the engineer squads. They would repair the bridges destroyed by the terrorists. Bleicher had orders to annihilate the Resistance but to bring at least one of them back alive for questioning.

The first trucks breasted the crest of the mountain pass near San Sarsorio and saw the road wind away until it reached the Corbaia River. It was a perilous route, bordered on one side by steep rocky mountains and on the other by a precipitous cliff falling to the river. Here and there lay rusted wrecks of civilian vehicles from prewar days. The convoy moved up the winding road into the mountains. It was dense country, ideal for ambushes or sniping. The men were tense and silent as they clung to the supports in their trucks.

CHAPTER 38

Unaware of Major Krag's ambush or Sybilia's warning, Robin lay in tall grass less than thirty feet from the bridge that spanned the swiftly flowing river. After a pleasantly warm spring day, the evening was remarkably cool and damp. It was so lovely, he thought. The sun had set, the midges were swarming over the riverbanks, birds were singing in the forest above them. The Maquisards were out of sight behind rocks on either side of the road, and Robin was thankful for these few moments of peace. Then he heard a faint rumbling in the distance. Ominous and unmistakable, it shattered his reverie. Enemy trucks were approaching. They would soon be here.

Robin could not ignore his sense of unease. Major Krag was not a careless soldier. It seemed out of character for him to send the armaments along the same road where his last convoy had been destroyed. This route was ideal for guerrilla ambushes. With the many curves and bends between precipitous cliffs, visibility was minimal. There was ample cover for Resistance fighters behind the large boulders that littered both sides of the river. A hundred yards above the river were thick forests that covered the mountainside almost to the peaks, providing ideal protection for a quick getaway.

Robin checked his watch again. In precisely ten minutes, if all went well, the first shots would be fired, and the bridge would be blown. His men had the road covered from both sides. The enemy would be below, visible and at a distinct disadvantage in this narrow gorge. Nevertheless Robin tightened his lips, feeling tense and impatient. Was it a trap?

Turning to Angelo, he said: "Jerry is going to come looking for us. We don't have the element of surprise this time, and they aren't going to give up so easily, either."

"We'll take care of them." If he felt scared or apprehensive, Angelo gave no sign of it. "She's all set to blow," he said, indicating the bridge. Angelo was a superb saboteur. He knew explosives expertly, and he employed a certain creativity in his tactics that Robin admired.

An hour earlier he and Robin had been up to their waists in swiftly flowing icy water, clinging to the stones to prevent themselves from slipping on the smooth, treacherous river bottom. They had taped the sticks of gelignite beneath the stone supports of the bridge, and the detonators had been thrust inside the explosives. Now there was nothing to do but wait.

I wonder if these hotheads will remember my lessons and retreat if I give the signal? I'm becoming increasingly uneasy.

I'm almost certain this is some kind of trap. At the same time, Sybilia's never been wrong yet.

Thinking about Sybilia gave Robin a sick feeling in the pit of his stomach. What if they'd caught her? What if they'd forced her to set a trap for the Resistance? What wouldn't they have done to her to make her do that? She was a brave girl.

I've no reason to think these things. It's just a hunch that something's wrong. I normally back my hunches, but in this case I have to consider the men. They need the arms. They wouldn't think well of a leader who pulled them out for no good reason.

In the distance the rumbling approached, not more than a quarter of a mile away now. Robin felt the normally reassuring weight of the pistol in his pocket, touched the cold, hard steel and found that it brought little comfort. His mouth was dry, his stomach churning. *But why am I like this tonight? I've never been this scared.*

He turned to Pinelli. "Something stinks here. Pass the word. Tell the men to be ready for the signal for instant retreat."

Michel hung around camp, worrying. He tried to convince himself that he was being a fool. He had been on the point of confiding in Romanetti a dozen times. What was it that had been so strange about his father's attitude? His glibness? Why had he been content to chase after an unimportant truck and miss the main battle? There were too many inconsistencies.

Oh, shit! I'm being ridiculous. Can't I stop worrying?

As the evening wore on, Michel's doubts became unbearable. He fidgeted and paced up and down. Then he frowned and rubbed a hand through his hair. Was he being a fool?

Romanetti watched him with a strange expression on his face. Finally the shepherd said: "Why don't you face the truth, Michel? Your father's up to something. You know it, and I know it. He was too pleased with himself. He always grumbles when Moore takes control. He's never accepted an order so meekly."

Romanetti was right, of course. Leaving him to supervise the parachute drop . . . although Michel doubted there was any drop planned for a night like this . . . he raced for his motorbike.

The quickest route down to Poggio was an old goats' track that the Maquisards used in emergencies. Though far from ideal, it was viable. Michel set off.

For Robin, the last few minutes of waiting seemed to take forever. Above the thunder of wheels on the bumpy road, he thought he heard a motorbike approaching from Poggio. He felt regretful, hoping that whoever it was would have the sense to turn back. It was almost dark, but light enough to see the first two trucks of the awesome convoy swing round the bend.

An ambush!

The trucks were bristling with heavily armed troops. They were springing over the sides, taking up positions. The first truck swung round to straddle the road, revealing the Schwerfer mortars pointing straight at the mountain.

Robin whistled. Three shrill blasts in quick succession for rapid retreat.

"Back! Get back! It's an ambush. Fast retreat," he called. There was no possibility of any armaments and, therefore, no point in fighting. Angelo hung back, determined to blow the bridge. Robin saw him fling himself on the exploder.

The Germans screeched to a halt. Helmeted infantrymen spilled out, racing for the cover of trees and rocks, working swiftly around to outflank the Resistance. They were trying to cut off their retreat. They would not cross the river easily. As the first men raced toward the bridge, Robin yelled at Angelo to get back.

At that moment Michel careened around the curve of the road. Even in the dim twilight, Robin recognized his uniform and bike. He watched in anguish as the bike was thrown back by the blast. The bridge flew apart. The first German infantrymen were tossed into the air and fell slowly into the river with the debris. Robin saw Michel fall against the side of the road, hitting his head. The numbing explosion followed a split second later.

By now the entire convoy was rolling into view. Six trucks of infantrymen; several MG-34 machine guns; two panzers armed with 20-mm cannon. For the next few seconds there was complete confusion everywhere. Men were running in all directions. Guns were stuttering from the trucks and armored cars. The first two Germans were crossing the river, holding their guns above their heads. The pistol in Robin's hand barked twice as he raced to the shore. Both men threw up their arms and tumbled into the water. The others pulled back.

The Maquisards took cover and began creeping toward the relative safety of the trees. They were almost there when the first mortar shells exploded in the forest. Robin ran along the bank, searching for cover. At last, among the debris of the bridge, he crawled across the river and up the slope toward Michel. Then a burst of machine-gun fire lashed from the right. A squad of Germans moved up from the forest on the Poggio side of the bridge. They must have been hiding there all day, Robin realized ruefully. He saw two of them pick up Michel and carry him away carefully. So Michel was alive, and they wanted him for questioning.

Robin threw himself down, cushioning his fall with his left arm. Pain throbbed from his elbow as he lay winded. The machine-gun fire scissored back and forth through the darkness, only inches above his prone body. He decided to stay where he was for the time being.

It was soon dark. Still he waited, hoping for a chance to rescue Michel. Looking across the bank, he saw a slight movement and swore as he realized that not all his men had obeyed his order to retreat. Suddenly brilliant light focused on the ground where they lay. He saw Angelo and Cesari leap up and run, saw them throw up their arms, and heard the soggy thuds as they hit the ground and lay still. He felt guilty and angry. He should have followed his hunch. Then they wouldn't have died. Guilt brought the taste of bile into his mouth. He saw Barnard crawling forward on his hands and knees, desperate to reach the darkness of the trees. How many more were left behind?

Moistening his lips, Robin yelled at Barnard not to be such a bloody fool—that he'd never make it. But the warning shout was too late, for the orange glare of an exploding grenade erupted, and Barnard's body was flung into the air. At the same time, the truck where Michel lay took off toward Poggio. There was no chance to rescue him now.

Breathing jerkily, Robin slithered along the riverbank,

clambered onto a rock, and took aim at the searchlight with his submachine gun. He seemed to be standing in a hail of bullets. A moment later darkness flooded the hillside. Robin plunged into the river, raking the Germans with his Sten gun to draw their fire.

Miraculously he reached the other side, but the forest was ablaze from the mortars, which had ignited the bracken. As he charged into the smoke an explosion rocked the earth under his feet, and Robin blacked out.

CHAPTER 39

The forest was burning. Robin lay on the ground and watched the flames flickering around the trees. Amazing how the fire had spread so quickly. Or was it? He felt confused. It had been pitch dark a short while ago, but now the moon was overhead. Then he remembered the earsplitting crash next to him.

I've been lying here . . . unconscious . . . maybe for hours. . . . Where are the others? . . . Why the hell did they leave me here? I was about to be roasted . . . maybe that's what brought me around. Or am I in hell?

He didn't really believe that, but God knew, it was hot enough. The pines were crackling, their sap boiling and spitting, the smoke was choking him. He stifled a cough. As his mind cleared, he became aware of the need to get out fast and keep quiet.

How long? Dear God, how long?

He pushed himself up and bumped his head against the rock. Soon he realized that he had fallen down the hillside and landed in a cleft in the rocks. That had saved his life.

He crawled out. "Must hurry, must hurry," he muttered as he forced himself to keep moving uphill. He had lost three men—Angelo, Barnard, Cesari—maybe more. He hoped the rest had escaped in the dark.

It took Robin an hour to reach the top of the mountain.

By then his hands and feet were burning from pushing his way through smoldering bracken. His lungs were so full of smoke, he could hardly breathe. All he could smell was burning skin and hair; he wondered how badly hurt he was. He passed out once, but not for long. Halfway up he remembered Michel being taken alive. Then he remembered the reason for his frantic hurry.

Sybilia!

The Boche would have thrown Michel straight into shock treatment. That was their normal procedure. They knew they had to extract information out of him before the Resistance could move their positions or their supplies. They had to know who was spying on them. They knew there was a leak. Why else had they set the trap? Robin knew that it was only a matter of time before they uncovered Sybilia's role. When they did, she was as good as dead. Worse than dead, he decided. Thinking about Sybilia made him ill again.

It was a long, agonizing climb to the bushes where his motorbike was hidden. He passed a mountain stream and blundered into it, pausing to plunge his head into the cool water. He seemed to have no hair or eyebrows left, he noticed, running his hands over his skull. But he could see. That was the main thing, although he still felt strangely divorced from reality, as if encased in a cocoon of thick glass.

He reached the mountain crest and, looking back, saw that the road was deserted. The Germans had returned to Bastia. God, what time was it? How long had he been lying there? His watch had been smashed when he was knocked out. He began to pray that he would be in time.

Two hours later the throbbing in his head was like hammer blows from the vibration of the motorbike. When he moved his neck he felt pain all the way down his back. He had no idea whether or not he had been burned, but now was not the time to worry about it.

At last he reached the outskirts of Bastia. He hid the motorbike in the shrubs behind the wall of a scrap-iron yard. He had to creep through Bastia by foot because of the curfew. He began jogging, keeping to the shadows. The streets were deserted, except for Italian guards who had orders to shoot on sight. They stood around in groups for safety.

Robin had made a point of knowing Sybilia's address and

roughly where she lived. He had never been to Bastia before. Several times he took the wrong road. When at last he reached the old fishermen's quarter, he half expected to find the police out in force; but it was quiet. Everyone was sleeping. Presumably Michel was still holding out, and Robin blessed him for that.

There was a guard at the end of the road. He could see the glow of his cigarette. It was too risky to try knocking at the door, but he could break into the ground-floor window without much trouble.

A few seconds later he was standing in the front parlor, gagging at the smell of garbage and fish. Was this how she lived? No one heard him creeping up the stairs. He reached the top floor and knocked. Was it a trap? Had they taken Sybilia? Were they waiting inside for the Resistance to come for her? His hand tightened on his pistol.

Then he heard Sybilia's voice calling. He felt faint with gratitude.

Thank God! Thank God! he prayed. "Quiet," he whispered. "It's Robin. Let me in quickly."

When she saw him, she started to scream but clamped her hand hard over her mouth. "Oh, dear God. Your face, what's happened to you?" she murmured.

"Come," he said, trying to ignore her breasts thrusting against the thin fabric of her nightdress. "Get moving. At once," he said roughly. "Grab a coat if you must, but come now. Your cover's blown. There's no time."

"You're burned," she stammered.

"For Christ's sake!" he snarled.

"The radio?"

"It makes no difference. Not anymore. Come on."

"And them?" She gestured toward the Gafforis downstairs.

"Warn them if you must. You've got half a minute. Then we're leaving—if I have to knock you out, I will."

He waited impatiently while she took a coat. She hurried downstairs and tapped at the door of the Gafforis. The whispering went on until he pushed her out the door and down the steps.

They stood on the porch, listening. There was no sign or sound of the enemy approaching. The guards were still lounging against a lamppost, smoking and cracking jokes, as they crept around the corner. At last they reached the motorbike on the outskirts of Bastia,

"Hang on tightly," he muttered. The worst was kicking the engine to life. The noise was enough to wake the district. If the bike didn't start, they were lost, Robin knew. It did, on the second kick, and they roared northward into the country, bypassing the main mountain road out of Bastia.

With Sybilia directing him, they twisted up old gravel tracks, hardly wide enough for mules, into the maquis, until they reached the ruins of a Genoese tower and an old church nearby. They were far beyond occupied territory, according to Sybilia.

Robin braked. He could hardly drag himself off the motorbike. He was shaking and sweating, and he felt dizzy. He ducked his head into a fountain several times. Then he sat beside Sybilia on a nearby bench. For a while he tried to pull himself together. Then he gave in to the nausea that had been surging up for hours. He heaved into the bushes, choking and swearing at his own weakness. After a while he realized that Sybilia was supporting his shoulders. He felt as weak as a baby.

"I'll be all right," he said, pushing her away.

"Let's sit on the steps until you feel better." She half led, half supported him across the courtyard.

For a while neither spoke as they watched the sky turn pearl gray. The morning mists rose up from nowhere like phantoms, forming a landscape of conical shapes over the sea and the mountain slopes below.

Suddenly Robin pulled Sybilia against him. He nestled his face in her hair. "I was so afraid. . . ."

His hand moved around the back of her neck. His fingers tightened as his mouth moved softly over hers.

Then he remembered Michel and drew back.

She was unwilling to let him go. She twined her fingers around his neck and pulled him toward her.

"Sybilia," he said softly, pushing her away. "Not now. We have to talk. I have bad news. It's about Michel."

She looked horrified. "What is it? What's happened?"

"Angelo's dead. Michel's been captured. That's why you had to get out. Michel must have come to warn us about the ambush. He arrived just as we blew the bridge." He explained to her exactly how it had happened.

"No, please . . . don't cry, Sybilia," he said. He put his arm around her shoulders. "The darnedest thing was, I liked Michel. I thought he was a great guy. A hell of a good guy to work with, even though he's your husband."

"Stop it. It's your fault," she said bitterly. "You should never have gone to Poggio after I warned you about the trap. What for? You had no right to risk the men's lives."

"You warned me?" He looked at her strangely. "Who took the message?"

"Rocca—" She broke off. Then she shuddered. "Poor, poor Michel. And Maria . . ." She began to cry again. "What will they do to Michel?" she wanted to know.

"They'll persuade him to talk by any means. They want to know how we got the information about their shipments and all the other details you've been giving us. They want to know where our headquarters are, that sort of thing."

"Yes, but what will they do to him?" she persisted.

He shrugged, evading her question.

"Michel won't tell them anything. I promise you that," she said fiercely.

"With this type of torture," Robin began painfully, "no one expects a man to keep quiet indefinitely. That would be impossible. One merely asks for time. A night or, better still, twenty-four hours. That's enough. Just time to save the rest. If Michel holds out that long, he'll be a hero. . . .

"Hell! We must get back. Taita must be evacuated. The Germans might bomb the village. Our supplies must be moved, particularly the arms depot. There's too much to do and not enough time."

"It's unnecessary to worry," she said calmly.

"Syb, Syb . . . you don't know what you're talking about. You can't know. I don't want you to know."

"He won't tell them anything." There was a touch of pride in her voice.

"You love him?"

"I trust him. He's too proud to give in."

"Let's hope so, Syb. Let's hope so. Now let's go. We're running out of time."

What the hell got into me—sitting here for so long? I must have had a concussion, but now I'm feeling a bit better. Jesus! I should be court-martialed for this. We must get back and shift those armaments. Syb, I can't tell you this now, because it's all wrong—wrong time, wrong place—but I'm going to marry you. Whatever obstacles you and your family throw in my path, I'm going to overcome them. One of these days I'll tell you that. Later, perhaps, when this is all over.

Within eight hours Robin had Sybilia and the Taitan women and children evacuated into the mountains. The arms were transferred to a new hiding place. His headquarters and radio transmitter were moved to another summer hut, higher in the mountains.

One week passed, then another. They heard from an informer inside the Italian headquarters that Michel was still alive.

Days later Robin went looking for Sybilia to tell her this. He found her with the villagers in their temporary camp in the mountains. For a few brief minutes they forgot the war as they walked along the mountainside holding hands. It did not take them long to piece together the story of Rocca's treachery. His attempt to keep his son out of danger had backfired.

"He will never forgive himself," Sybilia said.

"Why did he do it?" Robin asked. "I can understand his motives in wanting to wipe out Angelo, but to destroy a squad of good men, just for a personal vendetta . . ."

"You don't understand us," she said. "You undermined his position. You humiliated Rocca by taking over. You condoned Angelo's behavior by making him your friend. You were wrong. You ran the Resistance as only a foreigner could. You had no idea of the politics or the undercurrents, the rivalry and the clan hierarchies."

Robin left shortly afterward and raced back to headquarters. He mused over Sybilia's lecture all the way. *Perhaps I've been at fault. Xavier Rocca is a murderous bastard, but he is the head of the most powerful clan in the district. Perhaps I should have tried harder to control the Resistance by proxy. Yes. In future, Rocca shall have all the glory. I'll work through him again. Just so long as that arrogant bastard doesn't try to interfere with my strategy.*

After two weeks Michel was transferred to German headquarters so that Major Krag could take charge of the interrogation. Robin became obsessed with Michel's extraordinary heroism in keeping silent for so long.

CHAPTER 40

May, 1943

It was pitch dark. Michel lay somewhere in the bowels of the earth, a place so deep that not even a glimmer of light showed. He could hear water dripping and smell the dank stench of mildewed walls and his own excrement. There was nothing else except his pain. Existence had become a torment, but in spite of his agony and his total degradation, he was still alive. He clung to that desperately. Each additional second that he lived was a triumph.

At first he had hoped they would release him eventually. Now that he knew them better, he realized it was a vain hope. Then he had prayed to be rescued, although without much conviction. Michel was an atheist. To him the dogma of his parents' faith was indivisible from the other mores and traditions he had always been intent on discarding.

Sybilia would be praying. He knew that. Father Andrews would be holding prayer meetings and lighting candles for him. Probably all Taita was praying, so his own insincere mumbles were unlikely to make much difference either way.

Eventually he must have dozed or lapsed into unconsciousness, although it seemed that he was still awake.

He was a white bird, larger than a dove. More translucent than white, shining as if in sunlight. He simply flew out of his battered body, through the cell walls to the prison yard. Then he thought to himself: How simple. How gloriously, marvelously, miraculously simple! Why didn't I do that before? I could have done that long ago. Looking round, he saw a crowd of people, mainly women in black. They were kneeling on the cobbles around a large notice pinned to the wall. Without reading it, he knew that it had to do with his execution. He thought: Who cares? They can only execute a corpse. I'm here, not there.

He awoke smiling. Even the approaching footsteps of the guards could not entirely obviate the happiness of his dream. He remembered Angelo and Jules, and his parents with Sybilia. They were all safe. I didn't reveal a damn thing, he thought.

It was the only triumph of his life.

The guards took him under each armpit and propelled him through the door, along the passage, up the wide stone steps, on a journey that used to send him into a fever of despair, but which filled him with relief this morning.

The sunlight seared his eyeballs and burst into his mind like an explosion. He saw the blue sky, the sea gulls circling overhead, leafy trees bursting through cobbles around the perimeter of the wall; he heard a bird sing. The abundance of life and beauty crowded in on him. He felt a wave of gratitude for having experienced the privilege of existence. If there's a God, he thought, He's an artist, like me. More than anything else, He loves beauty. It seemed that they had something in common after all.

A wave of hot love burst through him and out of him. A part of Michel went with it. He saw his body being dragged across the yard, and he had no regrets. It was over and done with. Michel Rocca was about to come to an end, and he, who was not really Michel Rocca but a part of everything, was free.

He watched as they stood his shell against the wall. It was just like his dream, only this time the women were singing. In the split second before they fired, he knew without a shadow of doubt that he was indestructible. He smiled.

Michel's corpse was dumped outside the main gate of the Nazi headquarters.

"He had not talked," said the prison chaplain, who had tried to ease the boy's suffering. The local undertaker collected the body and made a coffin out of pine. That night the Maquisards rendezvoused with the hearse in a back street near the outskirts of town. They had come to carry Michel home.

Maria marveled at the moon. It hung like a luminous lemon globe as if resting on the mountaintops. She was tired. Am I dreaming? she asked herself as she pushed the bushes aside and climbed up, ever upward, toward the summit. She had her crook in her hand, and that frightened her. "I want to go home," she muttered, but her feet seemed to be willing her upward. It was almost like being a pin drawn by some huge, demonic magnet. She could not turn away. She had to keep climbing. Much later she saw a wildcat lurking by a rock, mouth spitting, eyes glittering. Her arms struck out savagely, catching the cat with a deadly blow on its skull. Turning it over, she saw Pierre's face. Pierre Gaffori, her cousin. She had not seen him since before the war. He looked much older and terrified. He was staring at her with his eyes bolt open. She screamed.

It was a long, anguished scream that woke Rocca. He fumbled for the matches and lit the lantern.

"I'm sorry. Just a nightmare," Maria apologized. "Terrible . . . terrible . . ."

"Don't tell me who died," he muttered. "I don't want to know. The wrong ones die."

To Maria's amazement, Rocca's cheeks were wet with tears. She put her arms around him, but he swore at her, so she went to make coffee.

When she returned carrying two mugs, he was crumpled on the bed, his knees under his chin.

Maria looked at him oddly. "What is it, Xavier? What's the matter with you?" she asked. Even after Michel's capture he had not shown his distress.

He ignored her. He reached for his coffee. Then he fumbled for his pipe and spent a long time drawing on it.

He got up and sat by the window. He had to think. Too many conflicting ideas had been jumbled around inside his head lately. Too much had happened. Worst of all had been the sorrow of Michel's torture and death.

Almost simultaneously, and inexplicably, he had found himself thrust back into a position of leadership by Captain Moore. That sod was playing backroom boy once again. Why?

It was odd that Moore had suddenly changed his strategy, he thought. Was that how Americans reacted to treachery: by backing down? Giving in? Somehow he did not think so.

Moore was deliberately pushing him back as the leader of the Resistance. As if he needed pushing . . . it was his rightful place.

Someone had told Moore of his treachery. It stood to reason

it was Sybilia, since she was the only one who knew. He wondered when the two of them had had the chance to talk together. Perhaps when Moore had fetched her back to Taita.

Rocca shuddered. Then he grabbed his coffee. In the back of his mind was a thought so horrible that he was unable to look at it fair and square: it was that his plotting to kill Robin might have had something to do with Michel's capture.

But no! No! Impossible. His mind could not play host to such an idea. It searched around for a suitable alternative: new motives, another culprit.

A sudden thought struck him. What if Sybilia had called again? Yes, that was it. Captain Moore, knowing about the ambush, had deliberately lured Michel to his death. Strange that the bridge had blown at the precise time Michel had driven up. Yes, that was indeed suspicious. Now the debacle was beginning to make sense. What other reason could there be for Captain Moore's miraculous escape or his haste in rescuing Sybilia? It explained Michel's sudden flight down to Poggio. They'd deliberately sent him to his death.

Oh, God! The pain of it.

"Moore killed our boy," he exploded into the silence. "Did you know that? He killed Michel. He called him down there to be ambushed. He's after Sybilia. You must have noticed."

Maria did not answer. She gave a soft moan, obsessed with her dream. Horrible pictures in her mind's eye, tumbling through without time, sequence, or logic. There was blood. There was a man hunted through the maquis. There was a wolf running through the mist. There was a child with a gun. Blood! Blood! She moaned and prayed aloud.

There was no sense in any of these things: images, memories, dreams, what were they? It was hard to tell, for they were muddled in her head. There was no end to this nightmare, and she lived within it.

"I'm telling you, Maria, Moore sent Michel to his death. I know it. I know here." He pressed his hand against his heart.

Rocca made an effort to pull himself together. He would have to learn to live with his anger and bide his time.

Of course Robin had his version of the debacle, but he was clever enough to keep quiet. Sybilia, too. A silence born of their guilty conscience. He knew. He knew.

CHAPTER 41

When news came of Michel's death, the Taitans, who had been hiding in the mountains, returned to their homes. But Sybilia remained in the hills. She was waiting for the Resistance to bring back Michel's coffin.

Maria saw them first. The scene was so familiar . . . just as it had been on the day of her son's marriage. A long straggle of tired, unshaven men, shouldering Michel's coffin, their faces set into lines of anger. Behind came Sybilia, in men's camouflage, shouldering a rifle, tears streaming down her muddy face. There were no drums and no mist, but otherwise all was as it had been. When the villagers heard the women's cries they crowded into the square, hammering their rifle butts on the cobbles.

Maria stood in her doorway trying to come to terms with past, present, and future. "It is all one," she mumbled to herself. "Time is our illusion. There's no time for the spirits in the mountains. If there's no beginning and no end, no birth and no death, can there be time?" She was still mumbling to herself and peering anxiously at the mountains when her friend Germaine took her arm and led her home. Michel's death had hit her badly, in spite of her brave front. She had retreated into her shadow world of spirits and emerged only briefly for periods of sanity.

Black, black, everything was black. Even her face was concealed behind a thick veil. Only her white hands stuck out, looking naked and defenseless. My thoughts are black, Sybilia thought guiltily. And so is my soul. If only the funeral were over and done with.

She and Maria had been up since dawn, making the traditional food for their guests: anchovies in vinegar, bread, wine, cheese, and a special sweet cheese called *broccia* made from goats' milk.

Most of the villagers and the Maquisards were coming for the wake. At that moment they were taking turns entering the house to pay their last respects to Michel in his coffin, prior to the memorial service. Robin had come earlier, but he had not stayed for long. He'd told her he was organizing a raid on a garrison later that day. A reprisal!

Outside, the men were still pounding their rifles on the cobblestones, vowing revenge on Major Krag together with all occupying forces. The *voceri* were in the square shrieking and tearing their clothes as they composed their laments.

Sybilia shrugged helplessly. How contemptuous Michel would have been. How he hated these primitive Corsican traditions.

There had been a great deal of good in Michel. Today she would try her best to remember this and grieve for him. She had lost him to Angelo, and now they were both dead. She was genuinely grief-stricken and horrified at the wounds on Michel's body. But there was no point in lying to herself. She was not totally sorry that Michel was dead, and she had no tears for Angelo either. Instead she would grieve for Maria.

She hurried downstairs. Maria was sitting on the balcony, gazing out over the valley. Sybilia knelt beside Maria and wrapped her arms around her. Suddenly the tears rolled down her cheeks. She sniffed and fumbled for her handkerchief.

"Don't cry for my benefit, Sybilia," Maria said sharply. "We've always been honest with each other. These past two years, he was no husband to you. He caused you too much suffering. You put up with it, and I didn't hear you complaining, *but your love for another man killed my son*. Now he's gone, and you don't have to pretend."

"No! That's a lie." Sybilia pressed her lips together. She could never say the words: Your husband, Xavier Rocca, killed your son because of his jealousy and spite. No, she would rather die than let Maria find out. Instead she stood up, stumbled to the table, and crumpled on a chair.

"I wasn't being insincere. I was crying for you," Sybilia said. "He was your only son. And for Michel, too. Surely a stranger could cry for him after the way he's suffered. I came down because I felt you'd need someone . . . I thought you wouldn't want to be alone. . . ."

For a while the two women sat in silence. Then Sybilia plucked up the courage to begin again. "You are very wrong to think that Captain Moore was in any way involved with Michel's death. That's not true. He tried to save him."

"Is there something you are keeping from me, Sybilia? I get that impression quite strongly."

Sybilia turned away Better to leave things unsaid. It would be too cruel to tell her. Maria would survive Michel's death. They all underestimated her strength. "You should cry. You'd feel better if you broke down and cried," Sybilia went on.

"I saw his funeral on the day of your wedding. He's been a long time dying, and I've had long enough for grieving. Sybilia," she went on, "I've always loved you for yourself, not because you were my son's wife. You tried to be good to Michel, I'll not forget that."

"Mama." Sybilia twisted her hands. She felt the need to say something, but what could she say in the face of Rocca's lies? "You've made this house seem like home to me. You are much closer to me than my own mother ever was."

Suddenly the grief for her wasted love, and her wasted youth, the crumbling of her hopes and dreams, the tragedy of her arranged marriage . . . all the tears that she had stoically held back came pouring out in a torrent. She let herself go. She could cry now without shame. It was allowed. After all, she was burying her husband.

Father Andrews held the memorial service for Michel at the graveside the following day. There had been a storm during the night, but now it had passed. The earth was newly washed and flauntingly lovely. The priest looked down at the battered features of Michel for the last time and sighed.

Michel had proved to be a hero. How had this oversensitive, stubborn boy withstood the cruelest torture? Now his poor, battered body was to be returned to the earth. It would be reprocessed into this endless resurrection, along with his soul. Not death, but rebirth. Surely a cause for joy?

Father Andrews crossed himself. Was this foundling thought heretical? He should banish it, but he could not.

He looked around at the mourners. He saw Sybilia crying behind her veil and clinging to the arm of Maria. Captain Moore was waiting with a group of Maquisards. Xavier Rocca stood apart from them all. His face was distorted into a scowl. Consumed with grief and anger, he had been vowing vengeance for the past twelve hours.

Father Andrews could find no mention of bravery or heroism as a virtue in the Bible. Even as he began, he had no clear idea of what he would say. Then a sudden inspiration struck him:

"What is heroism?" he began. "In this island, it's a virtue which is held dear to every man's heart. Everyone here longs to do great deeds. Yes indeed, Corsicans are unique in their pursuit of individual worth and their passion for bravery and honor.

"Nevertheless, to my way of thinking, and I think to God's way of thinking, a lot of feats which pass for bravery are really only showing off. Michel never showed off. He was never to be found wrestling in the village square, hunting boar, or getting involved in brawls. He was a sensitive boy. Yet when it came to the test, Michel outshone us all.

"Why was that? I'm asking myself. I think the answer is quite simple. It's because he loved us too much to betray us to the Boche. He never told his torturers where he came from; nor where the arms were stored; nor where the Resistance headquarters were; nor who was the person passing information to the Resistance. He saved many of our lives.

"His silence cost him dearly. We will none of us ever be able to imagine the agony Michel went through, second by second of every night and day for over a month. He knew he would be shot eventually, whether he talked or not. There was no one to see how brave he was being, no reward coming his way, no applause. Only suffering.

"So why did he do it?" He paused and looked around. "Because of love. He loved us, jointly and severally. So we must remember him with love, too. While thinking about Michel's incredible fortitude, I've come to the conclusion that true bravery is love."

By the time Father Andrews finished his sermon, most of the women were crying openly into their handkerchiefs, while the men looked solemn and sad.

It was two days after Michel's burial. Sybilia was packing to return to her work in Bastia when Father Andrews arrived unexpectedly at the Roccas' house. He had to speak to Sybilia, he said. Maria sent him up as usual.

He was always amazed at the charming apartment Sybilia had created in the eaves. The decor was white, but she had one large, yellow wood table, four chairs upholstered with bright chintz, and several bookcases with volumes in French, Italian, German, and English. Michel's sculpture stood around the walls and on corner shelves. There was a sensuous statue of the Virgin Mary on a mantelpiece. Something about it caught his fancy.

"Why, it's you," he said.

She flushed and nodded. "I always told Michel it was wrong to do that."

"No! Not wrong. It's lovely. Most artists use models for statues. Most of the models are a lot less saintly than this one," he said as he gently replaced the piece.

She glanced at him with a confused expression. Was that supposed to be a joke? Father Andrews was gazing at her compassionately.

"You're an asset to your country, Sybilia," he said. "Captain Moore tells me he'll recommend to the Free French authorities that you and Michel receive rewards for bravery. That would be after the war, of course."

She shrugged. "You can tell Captain Moore it is of very little interest to me," she said.

"It would mean a lot to Rocca."

"Yes," she said. "You're right. Forgive me."

"I see you're packed and ready to go."

"I should have left an hour ago, but I can't tear myself away from Jules. Have you ever seen such a lovely baby? No, really. Not because he's mine. It's just that he's so beautiful. Quite perfect, really, and so clever. You wouldn't believe the things he can do, and he's only a year and a half."

Jules was crawling over the rug, surrounded with the toys she had sent from Bastia. He was dressed in diapers only, because it was so warm. As she leaned over him, her face softened with tenderness. "Poor darling Jules. He misses me, Maria says. He cries for me at night. He always calls for Mama. I miss him desperately. . . .

"Oh, forgive me, I should have thanked you before. Maria says you often play with him. I'm grateful."

"I love him like my own," Father Andrews said softly. "He's a fine boy."

The child, who was big for his age, pulled himself to his feet, grabbed Tim-Tim's tail, and hung on. The cat snarled and spat but did not scratch him.

"Oh, Jules. What a little ruffian you are." She swung him into the air, and he laughed happily. He looked angelic, but Father Andrews knew all about his temper tantrums. Jules was the spitting image of his grandfather, but the priest never said this to Sybilia for fear of offending her.

"He needs you, Sybilia. Every baby needs its mother, far more than anyone else in the world. Maria loves him, but she can never replace you. Please don't go back to Bastia."

"If I don't go back, who will listen to Major Krag's conversations?" she said briskly. She hugged Jules close to her, as if she could not bear to let him go, but the child struggled out of her arms. He wanted to chase the cat.

"A replacement can be found. Your place is at home. Besides, there's a job in the Resistance for you here. Captain Moore needs someone to replace Michel."

"Ah ha! So that's it. Robin told you to come and persuade me not to go."

"He has impressed me with his concern for you. He feels that it's only a matter of time before you are discovered. Please, lassie. Stay here."

"Did he tell you that he loves me? And that I love him?"

The priest's face registered shock. "That would be playing with fire, Sybilia. You know the customs here. You're in mourning."

"After the war, we'll see. Perhaps I'll go away. Meantime, I'm going back to Bastia. I have a job to do, and no one else can do it as well as I."

Suddenly her stern resolve melted. She crumpled onto the bed. "Oh, Father Andrews, help me. How could this happen? I love him, so help me God."

"I will pray for a happy ending for you," Father Andrews said kindly, "but right now it would be wrong. I know that you never loved Michel, but he's hardly in his grave. . . ."

"Oh, I know, I know. D'you suppose I haven't told myself that day after day? So I'm going back to Bastia. Today. Now!"

As she picked up Jules, hugging him tightly, the tears were rolling down her cheeks. "Stay with him," she begged. "Just a little while, and then hand him over to Maria. If you play with him, he won't even notice me leaving."

CHAPTER 42

It was late in May. Sybilia emerged each afternoon with a splitting headache and a glint of triumph in her eyes. Krag's bitterness over the war news was a matter of intense satisfaction to her. The Allies were winning on all fronts. It was only a matter of time before they invaded Italy. When they did, the Italians would try to oust Mussolini and capitulate. That was the gist of the conversations Sybilia recorded. The comings and goings of troops, arms, and supplies were reported faithfully each evening. Sometimes the Resistance was successful in ambushing them. Krag blamed the Italians, and specifically Dino Renucci, for the information leaks.

Once outside her cupboard, Sybilia felt exposed and vulnerable. The cupboard was growing on her, like a shell on a tortoise. She felt safe only when she was walled up in her stuffy cocoon.

Nevertheless, she found less opportunity to eavesdrop now that she had to account for her time. Renucci was convinced that someone in the hotel was an informer. He spent most of his time noting the activities and whereabouts of several staff members, notably Sybilia, who appeared to be his prime suspect.

The sight of Dino Renucci's snakelike eyes, watching her work while his hands flicked the pencil over his notebook, sent her into panic. Sometimes she felt too scared to move. She would pause in her scrubbing or bedmaking to stare as if hypnotized. Oh, how she despised herself. Never again; never again! But next time she would be transfixed with shock and simply stare, vacant and trembling.

It's probably lucky for me I'm such a coward. I'm acting like a stupid peasant. Quite in character, really. Yes, it's a good thing.

After a few days of this, Renucci seemed to lose interest in his amusing game of watching Sybilia. She began to take chances and spend more time in the cupboard.

On Friday, when she returned from work, the house was strangely empty. She called out to Lucilia, but there was no answer. Even Granny was missing. How odd! Strange quivers of misgiving were fluttering in her stomach. All her woman's intuition was screaming: Go! Get out! You're blown! Run for it! Yet she forced herself to keep calm. She would not listen to her sixth sense as she climbed the three flights to her apartment. It was nerves. She could not allow herself to give way to nerves.

Why? Why was she so stubborn? she asked herself as she walked into her flat. She gazed hopelessly at Dino Renucci. He had ripped open the false back of the wardrobe and was studying the radio intently.

Gazing over her shoulder, she saw two armed, uniformed men on the stairs and two in the room behind the door. Could she possibly race to the balcony and throw herself off? No, she realized dismally. Another guard was stationed there. They had thought of everything. Strange how her mind was calm, but her body had reared into panic stations. Her breath was coming in short, sharp gasps, her palms were damp, her insides felt like molten lead, her legs had turned to jelly. She sank onto the settee and buried her face in her hands.

"You're too late," she said in the dialect with a low, moaning sob. "Krag took Michel and shot him a month ago. He didn't talk. He didn't even tell you where his radio was. You're too late."

Renucci's eyebrows shot up with surprise. His mouth slackened with disappointment. She could see that he half believed her story. Good, she would stick to it.

"Come now, my pretty Sybilia. Are you trying to say that you don't know how to operate this?"

Why was he still speaking in Italian? Why didn't he believe her?

Sybilia burst into tears, which was not difficult. "I begged him to give up his work. He could have fled to the maquis. Now he's dead," she moaned.

"Do you speak French?"

"A little."

"Why a little? It's compulsory here, isn't it?"

"In school. I didn't go to school."

"And these books?"

"My husband's."

"My, my. For an illiterate Corsican scrubber you certainly married a well-read man. Look at these books: *The Oxford Companion to English Literature*, Samuel Butler, Hermann Hesse, Mark Twain. Ah ha! Zola. My favorite, too. I can see we have much in common. Where did your husband go to school, my dear?"

"You tortured him for a month. Whatever he wants you to know he's told you himself. Don't ask me these questions. I'm not going to answer them."

"You will, Sybilia. I promise you that. I have no doubt you'll soon be talking in as many languages as you have in your books. Rebecca West! Now I ask you, what would a man want with Rebecca West?"

He turned to one of the guards. "Handcuff her. We'll take her to headquarters."

Why can't I walk? What's gone wrong with my body?

Sybilia tried to talk, but her mouth was too dry. Eventually she managed a whisper: "Can I go to the toilet?"

"You can, but with handcuffs on you're going to need some help. Allow me to assist you."

"I'll wait," she said.

He laughed. It was a cruel laugh.

In the Fiat, his fumbling hand explored her body.

Oh, God, what can I do? I can scream, try to fight, moan, curse him, all of which will be so useless. All resistance will be utterly useless against this man. I know.

She took refuge in stony silence while his fingers alternately prodded, caressed, and pinched. Her feet were wedged between two men's legs. Her hands were handcuffed behind her back. Robin was right, she thought, feeling half-crazy with fright. This is the reality. It's so much more terrible than I could have imagined.

She was taken to a cell, stripped, and searched by a female warden while Dino Renucci watched. Then her clothes were returned, minus her handbag and belt. At last she was left alone.

The cell was whitewashed and freshly scrubbed with ammonia, but the walls seemed to be impregnated with vomit, urine, and misery. She sat on a bed and waited for them to send for her, but no one came.

After an hour or two she looked around her cell. There was nothing much to see: a bucket in a corner, a barred window set into the wall adjoining the ceiling. Even if she stood on the bucket, she would not be able to see out. There was no light fixture, which seemed odd, no table or chairs, only the bed, which was bolted to the floor. The mattress was of straw, and there was no blanket.

Nothing! There was nothing to help her kill herself, but at the same time she did not want to die. Far from it. She emphatically wanted to live and to get out of that cell. If only she could see out of the window.

The silence seemed to burst in on her ears. After a while she scuffed her feet on the ground and hummed to herself. Anything rather than endure the silence. She was hungry, but no one brought her food or water. Her thirst began to cause her physical discomfort. She knocked on the door, then kicked it and called out, but no one came. It was part of the softening-up process, she knew that.

It grew dark, and Sybilia became increasingly dejected. She felt lost. Hopelessly, utterly lost and forgotten. Who cared if she was alive or dead? If she slept or stayed awake? If she died of thirst or not?

Eventually she cried herself to sleep.

Nothing changed the next day. In the middle of the second night, she heard footsteps. Her cell door was opened quietly. Dino Renucci came in with a jug of water, a bottle of wine, and a large pile of sandwiches.

"I could lose my job for this," he whispered in Italian. "Come on, eat up and drink as much as you can. It will help you last out tomorrow."

A surge of gratitude swept through her. "Thank God, I'm so thirsty," she croaked.

"I've spent the last two days trying to keep Krag away from you. He wants to tear you apart, literally. Just as he did to the hotel's carpenter. I suppose you know it's he who informed against you. It didn't help him. He died today."

"How terrible!" she said. "He was a kind man."

For a while she sat shivering against the wall, but she was hungry. She could not resist finishing the sandwiches with Renucci, who complained that he hadn't had a meal all day. Suddenly his arm was around her.

"I'm doing my best to help you," he said.

As his hand fumbled to her breasts, she pushed him away.

"You're not making it very easy for me."

She began trembling. Then she screamed, a long, loud, dismal wail for help. But who was there to help her? Pointless to waste her breath.

She crouched in the corner of the bed, but he caught her by the ankles. She felt his loathsome hands running up her legs to her thighs. It was the most revolting feeling she had ever experienced. She lunged out toward his eyes, but he was so strong. She felt herself being hauled down the bed. She hung on, kicking. Then she began beating his face with her hands, but he caught both wrists and held them above her head with one hand.

Oh, God! How could anyone be so strong? She waited her chance and brought her knee up, slamming it into his testicles. He winced. Then he laughed and slapped her face hard.

For a moment she was stunned. He had hurt her eyes. She could see nothing but purple blotches. After blinking several times she could see dimly. Orange-and-yellow bicycle wheels were spinning madly around the edge of her vision.

Now she was terribly frightened. She screamed again, but he flung his full weight on top of her.

"Get off me. Get off," she gasped.

He smirked down at her. She saw his face as if through a magnifying glass, distorted and grotesque, with the spittle on his lips and a wart on his cheek.

Time seemed to stand still. She could hear her own sobbing breath. Gasping a lungful of air seemed to be all that she could do. She bellowed like a heifer when she felt his hand fumbling at her waist, tearing her clothes away. Horrible! Terrible! This couldn't be happening. She would kill him . . . if only she could.

He was crushing the life out of her. She could not breathe at all, only in small, short gasps. When the inevitable thrust came, she was almost choking to death and obsessed with trying to survive.

Afterward she pulled her clothes together and sat up staring at the wall. She could not look at him.

"That wasn't much fun," he said. "You're not much good."

"You had no right," she whispered.

"Sybilia," he said, smiling at her, "this place transcends the barriers of right and wrong. You have no rights here at all. Not even the right to drink water, or use the bucket. It can be taken away. Everything can be taken away, even your life. Help me to want to help you."

"No never. Never." She waited until he left before crumpling into the corner of the bed and sobbing out her grief.

CHAPTER 43

June, 1943

Her food was a bowl of thin soup with little nourishment and a slice of gray, stale bread once each day. Worse than the hunger, the boredom, and the solitude was her fear of what was to happen. She had never been brave. Besides, she had an extraordinarily low pain threshold. Michel had always chided her for that. She would share Michel's fate, she knew, but she doubted she would acquit herself as well as he had.

Was it morning? She glanced up at the barred window, but there was no glimmer of light. She had no idea how long she had been there, but now she could hear footsteps approaching.

Two guards explained that they had come to fetch her for interrogation.

She was taken upstairs to a room on the third floor. This time she could see out the window. It was almost dawn. There was a wonderful view of the mountains in the distance. Robin was there somewhere. She hoped he wouldn't be wasting his time thinking of her. She did not think of him anymore, either. She felt too guilty. Nevertheless, she could not tear her gaze away from the mountains. Eventually the guards forced her onto the chair.

Dino looked very healthy and fresh. He smelled of soap and after-shave, and he was wrinkling his nose in disgust at her. They had given her no facilities for bathing or washing or any way of cleaning herself.

His assistant, a blond, blue-eyed Italian, smelled strongly of perfume, and he kept moistening his lips as he studied her.

Dino said in a brisk, businesslike voice, "Sybilia, you've been lying to me, but this must stop now. Here are four questions, and you must answer them. They are: What is your frequency and code number to radio headquarters? Where are your headquarters? Where have you stored the arms you stole from us? And lastly, who is your leader?"

"I will tell you nothing."

"We'll hear a different story quite soon, I have no doubt. I also want the names of your colleagues in the Resistance, and particularly those who are working at the hotel.

"You see all these matters are of great importance to our war effort. If you won't tell me, I shall have to hand you over to Major Krag."

"I won't tell you anything."

"Sybilia, you are irritating me. I have the means of making you talk."

"No. You don't," she whispered. "Everyone knows what butchers you are. We saw what you did to Michel. You couldn't make him talk."

"We? . . . Ha! Now we're getting somewhere. Define 'we,' Sybilia."

"I will not." She choked back a sob and saw him smile.

Oh, God, help me. Mary, mother of Jesus, help me.

Someone was removing her shoes and her stockings. "I will do it," she gasped, but she could not. She was shaking too violently. Finally she leaned back and closed her eyes as she acknowledged defeat. It didn't matter. She was an impersonal body to this man, which made him all the more terrifying.

He pressed the metal jaws of his pincers over her nail and pulled. The pain was excruciating, and she began to cry. Not because of the pain, but because human beings could do this to one another; because a man could do this to a woman.

As the blood started to drip on the floor, she passed out. She revived a few moments later when they threw a bucket of water in her face.

"Would you like to tell us where your leader's camp is?"

She tried to speak but could not. Instead she shook her head.

Dino Renucci nodded to the man, who grasped her next nail. It was dragged out slowly and dropped on the floor.

He moved to the next toe and, hours later, it seemed, to the next foot.

Could it be hours? The sun had not yet risen. She gazed horrified at her bloodied, mangled feet, but there was worse to come.

Dino lit a small gas stove in the hearth and put a poker onto the flame. When it was red hot, he picked it up and held it in front of her eyes.

"Last chance, Sybilia," he said, smiling happily.

When the young Italian held the poker against the sole of her foot, she screamed in agony. Mercifully she passed out again, but once again they revived her with a bucket of cold water.

"Back to your cell, Sybilia. Next time we'll try our pincers on more intimate places. We have another treat for you later this morning. You can't walk? Well, you must. Try your heels, my dear. If you hang around here, we'll think you want some more. . . .

"Just remember one thing, Sybilla," he called down the passage after her. "If you won't talk for me, you'll talk for Krag. I promise you that."

They came for her again at eleven. She had torn her petticoat into strips and bandaged her feet. She could no longer push them into shoes, they were too swollen. Now she had two bloodstained, dirty lumps to shuffle along on.

The "treat" was to be driven in a convoy of six official Fiats to the Gafforis' home. Renucci wanted her to see Uncle Pierre being hung from a lamppost for his involvement with the Resistance, and more specifically because of the radio transmitter, which had been hidden in their house. They hadn't even known about it, Sybilia reminded herself.

Because the road was a series of cobbled steps, the cars had to be parked at the bottom. They proceeded on foot.

Sybilia was half pulled and half pushed behind Dino. By now her feet were hideously swollen and every movement was agonizing.

Uncle Pierre looked shocked and terrified, but he smiled. He was trying to show her that he did not blame her. Lucilia was screaming, and the children were crying.

"Get on with it quickly," Dino said. He seemed worried.

They put a rope around Pierre's neck and strung him up. As he began kicking, a shot rang out from a second-floor window, severing the rope. His body fell with a dull thud on the pavement.

The world had turned to slow motion for Sybilia. She saw Dino frown and then lurch toward her. She dropped down on her knees and tried to climb under a car. Suddenly Dino was propelled forward and upward. His hands were flung out, his head shot back. A crimson stain burst out on his chest. He fell, spattering her with blood.

Sirens, shots, yells, whistles—pandemonium broke out as Robin's squad came roaring down the cobbled steps on motorbikes, armed with submachine guns. Someone grabbed her—she did not know who—and thrust her behind Robin. She hung on as they raced back up the steps, through the old town, toward the maquis and freedom. A waste of lives, she thought. He should have left me there. I'm not Sybilia anymore. He's been cheated.

CHAPTER 44

He took her to Maria and left her there. A day later he came back with bandages, disinfectants, ointments for burns and wounds—all that he thought she would need. He looked haggard and exhausted. Maria heard later that he had broken into the German army hospital and fought his way out again. After that he hung around the bistro for days and slept in the presbytery, since no one invited him to sleep in their homes.

He was waiting for Sybilia to snap out of the depression

she was in. He needed her to replace Michel. And there was something else besides—he loved her. Sybilia sat in her room for days, but if anyone approached her, she hid her face against the wall. She could not hold her baby. Any type of physical contact seemed anathema to her, and Jules suffered. After two or three tantrums, Maria kept him downstairs.

"Sybilia needs hospital treatment," she confided in Robin. "We must do something."

But what? All the hospitals were in the occupied zone.

"It's as if . . ." Sybilia could not explain. Not even to Maria. She hated herself. She studied herself in the mirror and planned how to do away with the image she saw there. She appraised her body: long, supple, sinuous legs; hips that could writhe and sway and tempt; breasts like goblets.

"When you're crawling with ants and maggots, you won't look so good," she told the image. "When your bones are picked clean of flesh, perhaps you'll be clean." She was contaminated, a filthy receptacle into which Dino had squirted his pus. All the cruelty of the war seemed to have been pumped into her womb. Her wounds festered, her feet became more swollen, poisoning her body, which reacted with pimples and boils. Her hair hung limp like rope, her eyes were dead, her mouth slack and downturned. She would not eat and seldom spoke.

"I know a place where she can be looked after; where she will get better," Robin told Maria one morning. "It's a convent in the mountains of Cap Corse," he lied.

He carried her down, placed her on Father Andrews's donkey, which he had borrowed, and led her away. The villagers came out to cheer her. They sang and waved flags because she was a heroine, but she did not look around. Father Andrews held a prayer meeting for her recovery, which everyone in the village attended.

Robin took her up into the mountains, to that magical place he had first seen by parachute. It was a summer grazing hut owned by Romanetti, who had lent it to Robin for the duration of the war. It had become Robin's private den, a place to go to when he had to be alone. He had a few books, some odd bits of furniture, a reconditioned wood stove, pots and pans. All begged and borrowed, but enough to get by. It was not just a case of indulging himself, he had often rationalized. There might come a time when he needed a hideout that no one knew about, except Romanetti, whom he trusted implicitly.

Subtly sensing Sybilia's degradation and self-loathing, he thought his camp might act like a purification bath for her. It was the closest place to purity he had ever seen, a place of snow and ice even in summer, unadulterated by man. A lake of crystal-clear and deepest blue, ringed by a circle of icy mountain peaks. There was a hut among the pines, a glade where hares and chamois grazed, a place where the songs of birds shattered the silence.

It was dark when they arrived. He went to unlock the door and light the lantern. Then he returned and carried her into the hut. He laid her on the bed with a straw mattress and heaped hand-woven blankets around her with a box over her feet. He forgot nothing, but he wished he had something better for her.

He said: "Funny how the donkey senses that you're ill. She's really behaved herself today. The priest says she'll find her way home eventually, so I guess I'll just smack her on the rump and say, 'Thanks, pal. Be seeing you!' "

He kept up a stream of inconsequential chatter as he unloaded the donkey. Then he fiddled with the radio to find some music, lit the stove and another lamp, chopped more wood for the morning, and made some coffee laced with brandy.

"You know what I miss more than anything else here? It's a straight bourbon on the rocks. When I get back to the States that's the first thing I'm gonna have."

She never bothered to answer. Perhaps she didn't hear, but Robin talked for two of them, bombarding the silence with his chatter, whistling, and singing. He liked country and western. He sang as he chopped wood, peeled the potatoes, made the soup.

"Bet you're gonna love this soup, Syb," he told her. "You're gonna wonder where I got this recipe. Well, I'll tell you a secret. It's Russian. Called borscht. My granny used to make it. She came out from Russia with my grandfather, but Mama ran away from home and married a gentile, my pa."

Robin had been the cherished son of an all-American deputy sheriff and a typical Jewish mother, he told her. He wore his mother's Star of David always, although he himself was a Catholic. He showed it to her. His face lit up when he talked about his home. He and his family had lived in a clapboard house in a high village in Silverton, Colorado.

"Best guy in the world, my dad. And Mom loved him. The old-'uns forgave her eventually and invited us every Sunday. That's when I learned about borscht, and many other things. Quite honestly, Syb, I think I'm more of a Jew than anything else. I used to listen to my granny, and I liked what she told me. They had some fine old ways in those days, although their lives were grim. Boy, I can tell you some stories . . ."

And he did. Day after day, night after night. After a week she knew him better than any person she had ever known in her life. She tried to resist the knowledge but failed. His earnest, happy, easygoing voice kept seeping into her psyche. While he talked he dressed her wounds, fed her, brought her warm water to wash with, carried her out into the sun. Sometimes he left her.

The first time, he was gone for most of the day. He went to fetch his motorbike and check that the donkey had returned to the priest. Afterward, with his bike, he could whiz up and down the goat track at high speed. When he fetched provisions or saw Rocca, he was always back within a few hours. He ran the Resistance by proxy. This wasn't too difficult since he had pushed Rocca firmly back into the leadership . . . at least as far as the men were concerned.

Robin cleaned their hut, cooked their food, washed her clothes, and she said very little. Sometimes she read to him while he cleaned his guns, put together explosive devices, or peeled the potatoes. To Robin, all work, however lowly or complicated, was just another job to be done. He got on with it cheerfully. Sybilia was watching, learning, soaking up his warmth and humor. She was like a poor half-drowned kitten, drying out in the sun. He understood.

He spent hours describing his school, which he had loved. Sometimes he talked about his passion for zoology and biology. At home he'd always been out in the woods and the hills. In winter he skied during much of his leisure time.

He used to go hunting with his father, but when he reached his teens he'd lost his taste for it. Conservation was his passion. He spent his summer holidays camping in the Rockies, taking photographs and studying wildlife. The Corsican scenery was much like this camp, he told her. "Although we have chipmunks and bears and hummingbirds."

"I would like to see a chipmunk," she surprised him by saying. So he drew her one, and she discovered yet another part of Robin. He was a naturally gifted artist with a passion for wildlife.

When he was fifteen both his parents had been killed in a car crash. "That's when I got this bent nose." It had destroyed his faith for a while, he told her. He couldn't believe in a divine providence somewhere up there looking after him, after such a tragedy. He'd gone to live with Gran, who was a widow by that time, and she'd replaced his church schooling with her religion. She'd enabled him to live with himself and with God. After that he became a loner. He felt he didn't fit in with others his age.

A year later he studied forestry at Denver University and went to work for the Forest Service in Colorado. That gave him an excuse to be alone, which he needed at the time. He loved riding, and skiing was his second love. He'd had to give them both up, along with his solitude, when he joined the service. He'd been one of the first to volunteer. Defeating the Nazis had overridden all other ambitions. Right now he couldn't think further than the end of the war.

Day after day he wrote up his reports. He was meticulous and painstaking, and everything had to be described in detail: how they had hijacked the armaments, the failure of Major Krag's ambush, the atrocities perpetrated on Corsican civilians.

As the weeks passed, Robin became depressed by the war, which dragged on and on. He complained at the lack of backup from the British or the Free French. He hardly ever received a parachute drop, and it was never what he'd requested. "We're running our own private war here," he told her. "If we need arms or medicines, we have to raid the Macaronis. They're an easier touch than the Boche."

Days merged into weeks. With Robin running the Resistance by proxy only, through Xavier Rocca, he was able to spend much of his time with Sybilia.

He wanted to love her physically, touch her, kiss her, feel her in his arms. He watched her all day long, hoping to glimpse that veiled, sensual, provocative smile that used to tempt him so. Her expression remained mute and secretive, like a bird that would not be tamed.

"Is your gran still alive?" she asked one day out of the blue. It was the first time he realized she'd been paying attention to his monologues. His heart lurched with happiness.

"She died of old age during the war. I felt it worse than the death of my parents. Perhaps because she was all I had. I felt bad that I couldn't be there with her at the time. She died alone, and that's tough."

"Now you have me," Sybilia said.

He looked around—caught off guard. He'd longed to hear her say that, but lately there had been no indication of any bond between them. Not anymore.

"You mean that? You really mean that?"

"Be patient, please. I just need time to forget."

"We don't have much of that, Syb. Time's running out this time round. After the war it'll be different, but that's a long way away."

She didn't respond any further.

CHAPTER 45

The first time she offered herself to him, it was with such casualness that he felt hurt. For days afterward he went around looking humble and offended. Surely she realized that he loved her. Not just for her body or her looks, which, if the truth were to be told, had faded. No, he loved her for her brave, defiant, obstinate, endearing self. For her intellect, her subtle sense of humor, her wisdom, all these things and more. He tried to tell her, but those abused, dead eyes gazed sullenly back at him.

After that he refused to sleep in their bed at night but made a makeshift mattress of hay on the floor.

"Why do you torture yourself? What are you trying to

prove? You are a man, after all. Men need sex. I'm here, willing and available."

"Don't talk like a tramp," he grumbled. "You can't sell yourself as payment for services rendered. Syb, if you can't love me as much as I love you, then it's no go."

Love him? That was foreign. That was new. A new dimension! She worshiped him, but she had never expected a man to want her to love him. She was not sure that she believed in love between a man and a woman. There was comradeship, which came with time. Sometimes there was loyalty or trust; but love?

She came to him in the night. She said: "Help me. I want to love you, but maybe you won't want me to when I tell you what happened." It all came pouring out in pitch darkness: her loneliness; her failure in marriage; then Dino, who had turned her into a whore. He had defiled her, made her inhuman, until all that was left was her own self-loathing and disgust.

"Dino's dead. I wish he wasn't," Robin snarled angrily. "I'd like to kill the bastard again."

"Now you know, will you go away? Will you leave me?"

"I love you."

Suddenly she wanted him so much. She stripped off her clothes and snuggled down beside him on his bed of rugs on the floor. He pushed his coat over her and pulled her roughly against him. "I'm going to cherish you all my life," he said softly. "You're the greatest thing that ever happened to me, Syb. You've got no idea how much I love you."

He couldn't explain to her. There weren't any words, but he could show her. He had to show her with his body. He had to know each part of her, had to own and cherish each small particle of this soft, warm, clinging body melting into his. She lay quiet and close, trembling slightly, a mixture of fear and lust. It didn't matter. All that mattered was that they be joined as one. That was how fate had intended them to be—joined as one.

It was too dark. He fumbled beside him for his matches and lit a candle. Her eyes shone. He glanced round at the rough wooden beams, gleaming yellow in the golden light. This was what it was built for—for this moment. For this moment in time, the beams had mellowed and aged and reached this precise richness of texture. For this moment the fire had blazed and died and left the smoldering, scented pine embers. All this! All of it had been brought together with this lustrous, sensual woman to create this specific moment of perfection which was etched on his mind, never to be forgotten.

He was bursting with desire. He felt himself rearing up like a massive, selfish limb bent only on impaling itself into yielding flesh, but he wanted so much more. He took her hand and guided it gently, wrapped her fingers around him, felt their cool, soothing touch. He buried his face in her neck, ran his lips over the soft, moist skin, licked her musky, salty taste, sighed.

Was that his voice coming from so far away? A stranger talking. His consciousness was hovering somewhere between his thighs. He clutched her breasts. They were smooth and strangely cool to his touch. Then he ran his mouth over her nipples, felt the puckered skin, so rough against the tip of his tongue. He wanted to touch all of her, all at the same time, so he ripped off his shirt and lay over her, smoothed his hands down her sides, and cradled her buttocks in his hands. "Cold, so cold. Why are you cold?"

Her body gave a long shudder. Then her mouth was searching like a small bird impatient for food. It found his. Her arms coiled round his neck, strong as a python, and her legs clamped over his thighs. She was shifting and moving, her skin creating vibrations and feelings that sent his body into a fever of impatience. "Do it, do it!" A whispered voice in his ear.

He was so near, yet still he held back. Uncertain! He wanted her to want him.

She bit his shoulder, and the pain was excruciating. It merged with his desire and momentarily angered him. He lost all control, thrust hard and deep, heard her moan with passion. Then he eased up. Let his body ebb and flow with the rhythm of their shared passion. Faster! Until he lost all sense of himself and became part of a volcanic eruption, where every spurt was molten joy.

Later he gathered her into his arms and brushed his lips over her brow. "Next time," he promised. "Next time I'll wait longer. Was it all right for you?"

She turned her face toward him. She looked replete and

satisfied; her muscles were slack, her mouth slightly open; she was smiling, and her eyes were glowing with pride.

"Can't you tell?" she asked.

Sybilia felt reborn. The idyllic days that followed were links in a long chain of happiness. Seemingly there was no end to it. She was thrilled to feel a vibrant new vitality flooding through her. To Robin she was a living miracle, testament to the power of love. Together they milked their cow and collected eggs from the hens he had brought her. When the cow escaped into the mountains, they hunted for her and laughingly led her back. They loved the mornings, the squirrels that scampered down the pines, every flower in its turn, the sunsets, the starry night sky. It was a wonderful place for lazing around—broken only by the need to make love or to eat. There was only one sadness, and that was Robin's increasingly long absences, for it was August, and he was traveling over the island to see the various Resistance leaders.

Then, on the seventeenth, Allied armies reached Messina, and Sicilian resistance ended. Suddenly Robin was tense and excited. A different person. He had to get back in control, he explained.

"Rocca and I are at loggerheads. I can't stay here any longer. You must follow soon. I suppose we'd best not arrive together. Bring the cow, we'll fetch the rest later."

She was shaking her head obstinately.

"Syb, darling, I need you. There's no one I trust enough to replace Michel. I want you to run communications and the arms drops—at long last we're back in communication with the outside world. I've got to watch out before the whole lot gets spirited away by Castelli and his commie mob. . . ."

She didn't respond.

"Come on, Sybilia. You're better. No more shirking. There's work to be done."

"I'm not shirking," she said. She sat on the bench he had made, outside the door, and buried her face in her hands. "You've spoiled me. I don't want to go back to . . . all that." She waved her hand vaguely in the direction of Taita. "After what we've had here, I don't want to have to pretend, to hide around corners, to talk to each other like strangers. . . ."

"Then marry me now. Father Andrews will marry us. What difference does it make if we marry now or later?"

"Oh," she gasped. "We must think of Rocca and Maria. Michel has been dead for only three months. It would be like an insult to his memory."

"You know best."

After that they both felt awkward with each other. Their mood was strained and depressed. They ate their last meal in silence, and Sybilia snapped at Robin once or twice.

All too soon he was ready to leave. He stood at the door and looked at her. She sensed his hurt.

"It's just that I can't stand leaving all this . . ." she gasped, then choked and burst into tears.

Robin put down his haversack and his gun, came inside and shut the door, and wrapped his arms around her.

"And me? D'you think you're the only one who's grieving?"

Suddenly they were close again. They made love passionately, promising each other to be brave and loyal. When Robin left, Sybilia felt calm and sure of herself and ready to face the world again.

CHAPTER 46

It was dawn. The sky glowed red above the eastern mountain peaks, then golden streaks appeared. Sunbeams slid down the barren slopes, lending a rosy tint to granite rocks, penetrating the purple shadows of the valleys. Even at this hour of the morning it was hot and dry. The sirocco had blown without mercy for five days, bringing the heat and dryness of the African plains, baking the earth and shriveling the maquis, until the whole island was filled with the pungent scent of toasted herbs, heady as incense.

Robin was riding southward toward Corté. He had called a meeting for noon. The island's political and Resistance leaders would be there. He was expecting trouble.

When he first caught sight of Corté, he braked, pushed back his goggles, and stared in amazement. "Unreal! Like an illustration from a child's fairy book," he muttered. High among the island's central granite peaks was a hollowed-out plain, like a gigantic amphitheater, from the center of which rose a weird rock formation hundreds of feet high. On it stood a medieval fortress, complete with high walls, massive fortified gates, turrets, and lookout posts, silhouetted against the somber mountains. As he approached he discovered that the walls enclosed only little homes huddled together on the hillside. The fortress was only a ruin.

Robin was shown into the local school hall, where a number of Resistance leaders were already waiting. The air was thick with the stench of the pipe smoke and sweat. They had all ridden hard and fast to get there.

Xavier Rocca scowled from a chair on the platform, next to a vacant seat, presumably for him. Robin recognized the three others with Rocca, all National Front men from various parts of the island. Antoine Romanetti was there, too. Fiercely independent, he had never really given his allegiance to any party. Robin had thought he would find a friend in Romanetti, and in a way he had. But Romanetti was a strangely introverted man who kept his feelings to himself. Yet he was trustworthy and dependable in a fight.

Robin cleared his throat. "Gentlemen!" He glanced at his watch. "At precisely this moment, the Italians are capitulating. Right now!" He had to shout above the roars of approval and the stamping feet. "Right at this moment they are signing a peace treaty with the Allies." He could not get on with the meeting, and that annoyed him. Instead he had to shake hands all around the room, and there was a good deal of backslapping before he could continue.

"The peace treaty contains a clause which provides for the handing over to the Allies of Corsica, as well as Italian peninsular territory. This treaty is to be kept secret until September eighth. On that date the Italians will formally hand over key installations in Bastia and other coastal towns. Those of you here today who lead the National Front will be called upon to form some sort of temporary civic administration. Now is the time to decide who will take over, be it ever so briefly."

"Briefly!" Rocca bellowed, leaping to his feet. "Explain that point more clearly to the hall."

"In my opinion," Robin said, "the Germans will immediately move to retake Bastia and anything else the Italians care to hand over to us. They may take punitive action against those in temporary control. I feel I should warn you of this."

"You called this meeting to warn us of danger?" Xavier said with a roar of laughter.

"And other things," Robin told him. He sighed inwardly. As usual, matters of vital importance were to be twisted to create ammunition for Rocca's personal vendetta against him. "So what's new?" he muttered, and immediately felt better about it.

Robin continued. "I bring you a direct message from the Allies, and specifically from General Giraud and the Free French in Algiers. The message is: 'Cool it!' In other words, be patient. The battleground for the next year, at least, must be the Italian mainland. No troops can be spared to help Corsica.

"Lately you've been raising hell with the Boche with your own private wars. To tell the truth, this has sparked off a number of rows in Algiers. This is a direct appeal from the general to you. Hold back your commitment against the occupying forces. Otherwise . . ."

A loud chorus of disapproval drowned his words.

"Look! Hang on!" He held up his hands. "We're all used to plain speaking. I'm giving it to you straight. Just like they gave it to me. The truth is the Allies have only meager forces to assist you. They'd prefer to concentrate all their troops and weapons on a major thrust up through Italy. There's ninety thousand Axis troops here in Corsica. We don't need them on the mainland. Besides," he went on against catcalls, whistles, and shouts of disapproval, "the Free French can't spare troops for Corsica if you run into trouble. So cool it. Okay? That's the message I bring you today."

The hall was pandemonium. Rocca waited until they had cooled down, and then he stood up and yelled, "You might have saved yourself the time and trouble. Is that it?"

"More or less."

"Okay, so we've heard what the Allies say. And we've heard what our so-called commander, Captain Moore, wants us to do." He stepped forward, and Robin felt himself being thrust to one side. "Our reply to the Allies must be . . ." He paused significantly and suddenly roared: "They can go stuff themselves, and so can you, Captain Moore."

Rocca had their full agreement, judging by the applause. It was five minutes before anyone could hear themselves speak.

Those in command should do a little more research before they try pushing people around, Robin decided, but he kept his thoughts to himself. By this time Rocca was deeply into his rhetoric, but Robin hardly listened. He'd heard it all before.

"We'd all give our lives gladly for France, but our honor? Well, that's a matter between ourselves and God."

For once Robin agreed with him. Since the Corsicans were bent on fighting, as he'd known they would be, then they would have to start planning now. There wasn't much time left. He'd get back on the radio, report which way their inclinations lay, and beg for more men and equipment. In Robin's opinion the Germans would try to take the entire island. It was a strategic base, and they wouldn't want the Resistance firing into their backs.

For once Rocca's eloquence was matching his own thoughts, although he would never admit it.

"I say to you now, to hell with the Allies' plans. Must we sit around and wait to be given what's rightfully ours? No! We must move together and expel every last one of the enemy forces illegally occupying Corsica. So far we've had it easy," he went on. "They never penetrated the interior, so they never got their hands on our food, or our women. Our homes and farms have not been destroyed. We must make sure they never are."

By now the school hall was rocking with whistles, shouts, and rifles thumping on the floor. When at last there was a relative calm, Rocca shouted: "Perhaps Captain Moore would care to leave. He's obviously not on our side."

The Corsicans were quick to turn. Robin felt deeply disappointed as he listened to his former buddies shouting insults at him.

Romanetti stood up and elbowed Rocca aside. For a moment Robin thought that they might come to blows, but the shepherd stood his ground and insisted on speaking.

"We're wasting time," he yelled. "Time we don't have.

It's pointless to blame Captain Moore. He's carrying out his orders the best he can. Come on, Robin. It was a good try, but we're going to fight. You must have expected that. Are you with us or against us?"

"I'm with you," Robin said.

There was a mild cheer, but Romanetti persisted. "Will the Allies assist us when they hear our decision?"

"A direct appeal to General Charles de Gaulle might swing a few tricks our way. I'll do my darnedest."

"In your own opinion, Captain Moore, what will the Germans do now?"

"We've all heard more than enough from Captain Moore," Rocca interrupted.

It was Rocca's turn to be shouted down.

"Captain Moore, what are our chances without Allied help?"

"Depends how many reinforcements the Boche send over from Sardinia. My personal view is that the Germans will bring in their Ninetieth Panzer Division, comprising thirty thousand crack troops and a massive amount of equipment, which is now based in Sardinia, and try to take the interior. It stands to reason."

Suddenly he was speaking to an attentive audience: "Corsica will become increasingly important as a Mediterranean airbase, especially as the Germans lose territory on the mainland. They already control the coastal towns and roads, and they won't want us stabbing them in the back when this island becomes a vital supply depot. They'll try to push inland into the mountains in order to annihilate all resistance and secure their supplies of foodstuffs.

"If I'm right, there will be no possibility of matching them in the coastal plains. Our strength will be in the mountains, where the Germans' superior numbers and equipment won't count for much.

"If we were properly organized, we could defend the central areas long enough for the Boche to decide that this island isn't worth the effort. Then they'll pull right out and shift their forces to the Italian mainland."

Robin couldn't match Rocca's rhetoric, but he had sound common sense on his side. At first they could not agree on a plan of action. Rocca wanted an all-out attack on the German garrisons. Robin wanted to hold back most of their manpower for defense. The infighting between the two of them became bitter and personal. Finally it was agreed that a two-pronged plan—attack and defend—would be best. But their main strength was to be held in reserve to back Robin's strategy. Rocca left the meeting in a bitter temper.

At dawn the next morning, Robin sent in his report:

All over Corsica, every man of fighting age is mobilized and moving toward the coastal areas. Badly equipped, poorly trained, they are throwing down their lives in a spontaneous national revolt. There's no possibility of holding them back or deterring them from their determination to liberate their homeland. We need men, arms, explosives, and equipment.

The following morning General Charles de Gaulle broadcast to the world about Corsica's bravery: "In the towns and villages of Corsica, the French people are again to be seen as they really are—courageous, united, and determined to achieve their freedom. I await with joy the liberation of Corsica."

CHAPTER 47

September 4, 1943

At the same time as Robin was reporting to the Free French, Major Ernst Krag received an urgent communiqué from headquarters. He sat reading it with distaste. After several minutes of gloomy foreboding, he called in Lieutenant Bleicher.

"At ease, Lieutenant." Krag sighed, stood up, and peered out at the city. "I've received orders directly from Berlin. The situation is becoming . . . well, confusing, to say the least."

Bleicher nodded. He regarded Krag coldly. As a man, Krag disgusted him. He was a bully and a coward, as bullies always were. Bleicher considered Krag unfit for his position. He did his best to obey the major's orders, but Krag was always taking the easy way out. Bleicher, however, was zealously anxious to do his best for Germany. He was a soldier and only wanted to fight. With any luck he would be fighting on the mainland soon.

"Our orders are absurd," Krag went on.

Bleicher assumed a rigid stance, his eyes expressionless.

"Nevertheless, we shall do our best to carry them out. Listen while I fill you in on the details. It might be the last occasion I shall have time."

Bleicher leaned forward, trying to read the gist of the message from the report lying on the desk.

"Yesterday our former allies, the Italians, unexpectedly signed a peace treaty with the British and American forces. We had gathered that they might crumple, but hardly with this speed." He took out a handkerchief and mopped his face.

It was a hot day, but not that hot, Bleicher considered.

"So, we fight on alone, Lieutenant. At this moment, the peace treaty is supposed to be secret. It will be announced to the world on the eighth. German forces are moving in on Rome. All of Italy will fall under German occupation. At the end of the day, the Italians might wish they had stayed with the fight.

"As for Corsica . . ." He sighed. "Within an hour of the peace treaty being signed, the Italians intend to hand over key Corsican buildings and civil administration to leaders of the National Front. I know for a fact that these arrangements have already been made—clandestinely, of course. . . .

"Look at them out there. Strutting up and down in their showy uniforms. Soon they'll start scurrying home as fast as their ships will carry them. This is the fourth ship to arrive in Bastia this morning, ostensibly with supplies.

"We are to take Bastia at once. Reoccupy the key installations as soon as our former allies hand them to the Corsicans. That won't be difficult. However"—he glowered at Bleicher—"our orders go further than that. We must occupy the entire Corsican island, even the obscure mountain villages. Corsica is to replace Sicily in strategic importance. It's to become a staging post to the mainland, and it's vital that we are fully in control here. All resistance is to be firmly squashed."

Krag's eyes blinked rapidly, without a trace of their former zeal. "I'll tell you this, Lieutenant," he said, indicating the report on the desk. "Our superior numbers and equipment won't be of much use to us in those mountains."

He pulled himself together with an obvious effort. "Well, Bleicher, you must inform Captain Knopfmann that I'm calling a staff meeting at eleven hundred hours. Taking Bastia is his responsibility. He has a thousand men. More than adequate. We must plan how to overrun Corsica with the least-possible losses.

"Meantime, as you know, the remains of the Ninetieth Panzer Armoured Division, comprising thirty thousand troops stationed in Sardinia, are moving here to assist us to wipe out rebel resistance.

"Even then it won't be easy. We must expect that the Allies will also send troops in by some means or other. We must guard the coasts. Make sure they can't get a foothold on Corsican soil." The lieutenant was dismissed.

Major Krag picked up the communiqué and stared at it. Like Robin Moore, he was wishing that his superiors had a better understanding of the Corsican nature. " 'Destroy all persons who are actively engaged in hostile acts against the Third Reich,' " he read for the tenth time that morning. "My God," he murmured. "We'll have to kill every man, woman, and child on the island."

CHAPTER 48

It was two weeks after the Corté meeting. Robin was writing his nightly report. By now he had filled several box files with concise accounts of the day-to-day resistance in Corsica. He had not been able to send them to headquarters, so they were being stored at Romanetti's chalet. Today he was running out of paper, but he reckoned there wouldn't be many more to write. If all went well.

September 17, 1943.
Operation Vésuve began two days ago. It was spearheaded by a hundred members of the Bataillon de Choc, under General Gambiez from Algiers, who were put ashore by submarine without casualties. For some nights, Free French forces have been landing on Corsican shores. They now number about 6,500 men on the island. In addition, we have been sent a small force of four hundred American marines. Local Resistance numbers ten thousand poorly armed and trained men.

The Battle of Corsica began on September 9 when the National Front took over key installations from the Italians. Within hours the Germans moved in and retook Bastia. Shortly afterward they brought in thirty thousand troops, their Ninetieth Panzer Division from Sardinia.

Corsican Resistance has mounted a series of delaying actions in order to hold strategic towns and villages in the interior, such as Zonza, Quenza, and Levie. They hope to hold out for several days. They have blown up bridges and roads behind their positions.

German troops have advanced from all sides into the interior. They are suffering continual harassment from the various guerrilla groups.

He stopped and thought for a while. It was not often that he added a personal note. Robin was a soldier, not a writer, but he wanted to express his feelings of admiration and sadness. He wrote: *This account gives no indication of the tremendous heroism shown by almost every villager, young and old, who is fighting with anything and everything that comes to hand, from pitchforks to rockfalls. They hope to be able to hold out until the Germans give up.*

He concluded: *The Corsicans will never retreat.* It sounded melodramatic, but he knew it was true. He put down his pen and sighed. The Maquisards would die there if necessary, before they gave up an inch of road to the invaders. He hoped he would acquit himself as well as the Corsicans.

His responsibility was to organize the defense of the strategic road from Bastia into the interior, via Casamozza and Ponte Leccia, to Corté, the island's historic capital. If this route should fall into German hands, they would control the central railway, which was the nerve center of the island.

Robin had spent days studying this tortuous road, carved in diagonal lines from almost vertical cliff faces among the granite mountain ranges. The scenery was spectacular. Slopes of bare rock were interspersed with lush chestnut or pine forests and rich Mediterranean jungles. It was ideal for guerrilla warfare.

Robin was short on manpower. He had one hundred and twenty-four U.S. Marines, all engineers; three hundred Corsicans, including Leca's and Castelli's communist groups; a hundred Free French fighters; and the Taitan team, numbering twenty-five men. That was all, against a fully mobilized and technically advanced German division.

No, not all, he decided. He had the Corsican terrain, and that would count for a great deal, if it were used wisely.

He had determined that his main assault would be from the steep rocky slopes of Mount Castellare, and their last stand would be one kilometer before Ponte Nuovo. The Germans must never reach the crossroads and the valley at Ponte Leccia.

By the following afternoon, the Germans had not attempted to penetrate this route. Castelli, whose men were strung out along the first two miles of the road, was sending in regular reports to Sybilia by radio. However, the Germans had spread over vast stretches of the flat coastal plains, which were mainly uninhabited.

Later that evening, Sybilia hurried out of the communications chalet looking pale. Castelli had reported that an armored unit from the Ninetieth Panzer Division was moving out of the city toward the south: tanks, armored cars, mortars, mobile artillery, and five hundred crack infantrymen.

Robin summoned his men from their camps in the lonely hills. They took up their positions and waited. Within a few hours the sound of explosions farther back along the mountain road told them that the Germans had swung inland toward Ponte Leccia. Castelli had begun his lightning attacks on the Germans.

Would he obey orders? Robin could trust Castelli's men to fight to the death, but today their brief was to throw up inferior roadblocks along the route, engage the enemy halfheartedly, and retreat shortly afterward. The Maquisards were acting as decoys. They had to give the Germans the impression of inferior strength and halfhearted combat. It was hoped that the enemy would press on confidently, without too much care for their defensive positions.

Sybilia reported that the Boche were firing eight or ten rounds every half hour, just to keep the guerrillas off balance. Most of the time they had nothing concrete to attack, so their shells kept pounding along the entire mountain ridge, just above the treeline. Casualties were mounting, but the real battle had not yet begun.

At four A.M. Sybilia received a message from Leca: *The giraffe has a long neck.*

Good! The Germans were pressing on, diluting their strength as they stretched along the narrow track in places hardly wide enough for a tank to pass.

Robin and his men had dug their trenches two nights ago in a number of places. Now they moved into position for stage one of his plan.

As the sun rose, their lookout on the mountain crest reported that the enemy was in sight. First came the heavily armed armored cars and gun-mounted half-tracks of the reconnaissance group. Behind were towed artillery, the infantry, the assault gun battalion, and the flak units, followed by the tank battalion. Behind that were the engineers.

The tanks were moving far more slowly than the lighter elements, halting every two hours to rest and make running repairs. Consequently the farther the convoy progressed, the bigger the space between the different groups. As the sun rose the maintenance crews were kept busy, for the pins connecting the tracks kept snapping on the rough, rocky roads.

Having met only minor resistance from Castelli's and Leca's decoy squads, the enemy rolled westward toward Ponte Leccia. By the third day they were spread over ten kilometers of rough, winding mountain road.

For Robin the days and nights had been a tense, sleepless wait. His squad had dug down to four and a half feet, then tunneled under the ground for extra safety. They were spread out around a ridge that would give some cover when the firepower came.

At exactly eight A.M. on the morning of September 14, the entire mountainside began to tremble and rumble as the first armored trucks appeared round the bend in the road below. The French group let off a round of machine-gun fire into the first armored car. Its commander cartwheeled into the road and lay prone, while the truck skidded and went off the road, plunging into the gorge.

The barrage began. It lasted all day, the worst Robin had ever experienced. Shells were bursting everywhere. They were hitting the top of the ridge and powdering the forest below. Everything the Germans could muster was being hurled up at them, including rockets and mortars. Shells were landing with ear-shattering explosions, showering them all with earth and stones. Something jagged and heavy crashed into Robin's trench without hurting anyone, which seemed a miracle. When Robin crawled out to see if the Germans were advancing into the mountain slopes, a line of white-hot tracer whistled through the darkness over his head and smashed the trees to his right. The bark was being hammered off the trees as he staggered out of the trench.

The Germans had wasted no time in mounting an attack into the guerrillas' positions. A line of men with rifles was moving forward, with cover from mounted machine guns behind them. Robin aimed and shot one of the gunners, saw him slump over the side of the vehicles. The enemy kept moving up.

Where the hell was Leca's group? The plan was that they should move up along the ridge, parallel with the German advance but hidden behind the trees, followed by Castelli's men, so that both squads could attack the German positions from the other side of the gorge. Robin and his squad kept firing, but the Germans kept advancing. They'd be overrun shortly, he knew. Suddenly a series of short, sharp bursts came from the other side of the road. Leca had arrived. The gunner in the third truck lurched forward and hung grotesquely as the driver crashed over the edge of the chasm.

Everything was in confusion as the Germans raced for cover among boulders on either side of the road. Caught in a deadly hail of cross fire from both sides of the gorge, from men in well-prepared positions, their predicament was grim and becoming worse. Blazing trucks offered them no protection, for they were blocking the road and preventing the rest from passing or turning back. One of the trucks must have been carrying cans of gasoline, for it continued to explode.

Leca's team was firing steadily now. They were cutting

down the enemy as they ran and slid on slippery slopes. The Free French were shooting rapidly and with deadly accuracy. So was Castelli's group, farther back.

Nevertheless, the wave of infantry kept advancing. They were only two hundred meters below Robin's position now and racing up quickly in squad formation. The machine guns were cutting into their ranks, but they kept coming. Suddenly a tall figure leapt into the trees toward the first Maquisard. Robin catapulted himself forward without thinking. His shoulder hit the German in the thigh, and they went down together in a heap. The German threw up his hands and tried to lock them around Robin's throat, his fingers squeezing. Robin felt the pain in his neck and a pounding roar in his ears as he began to pass out. Then Susini's rifle butt smashed in the soldier's skull.

Suddenly they were fighting hand to hand with the first wave of infantrymen. Robin saw Ambrosini and Susini fighting back to back. He shot one of the Germans, but too late for Susini, who slumped to the ground.

At last the Maquisards' machine guns were getting the upper hand. The German lines were wavering. Their mortars were pounding the mountains from farther back in the convoy, but the shells were landing too high to do them any good, and eventually they ceased, perhaps fearing that they would catch their own men.

Unable to break through the machine-gun lines, the first wave of enemy infantry began retreating. Some soldiers carried the wounded as they moved toward the road, leaving a dozen dead German infantry lying among the trees.

Again and again that day they tried to wipe out the guerrilla positions, but each time the Corsicans managed to repel the attackers, although Robin had heavy casualties. Down on the road, the Germans had dug in on either side and were operating their guns from positions of relative safety behind boulders.

For the time being it was a stalemate. As Robin gave the signal to retreat, he caught sight of Father Andrews hurrying from bunker to bunker, organizing stretchers and medical supplies and saying prayers over the dead. Robin and his men were exhausted, but most of them had reached their second line of bunkers, farther along the road.

By now, the advance armored lookouts of the enemy division had discovered the next bridge over the swiftly flowing Golo River. An ancient, Genoese structure made of massive granite blocks, it had withstood the ravages of falling rocks and flood waters for five centuries. Just beyond it was a deserted village, which appeared to provide ideal cover for all the Germans' advance units. They were moving in.

By nightfall, more than three hundred German infantrymen had taken cover in the ruins of the village and in the rocky mountain ledges on either side of the gorge. Farther back, their division was camped along the road and well guarded. As their last tank slithered around a curve and parked by the hillside, Robin's mouth and throat felt oddly dry. Would his plan work?

During the night there was plenty of small-arms firing from the Maquisards. The guys were keyed up and feeling nervous. They had strict orders to hit and run—something no Corsican likes to do—they had to keep the Boche pinned down as long as possible, but be out of the area well before dawn.

Dawn came at last and it was glorious. Blackbirds were singing with joy as the first rays penetrated the forest. At exactly five A.M. the birds stopped singing. An earsplitting explosion ushered in stage two of Robin's plan.

One whole section of the cliff rose slowly into the air and toppled down. Then all hell broke loose. As the marines set off more of their charges in the mountains, hundreds of tons of debris fell down the mountainside, half-damming the gorge and destroying the bridge. The engineers were doing a fine job, Robin thought as the ground rocked under his feet. It felt as if an earthquake were hitting the area. The ground churned and vibrated. Explosion after explosion brought vast sections of the mountainside rolling down on the village and the armored column as far back as Casamozza. At the same time, four vital bridges were blown. Robin knew that the German division was now split into isolated, trapped pockets of men.

This was the signal for the Maquisards to attack. They no longer held back but gave the Boche all they were capable of giving. Soon their positions were throbbing to the pounding of shells as the Germans fought back desperately.

Robin's machine guns kept firing. Then the artillery began. Every gun Robin had at his disposal was plastering enemy positions.

By noon those Germans who were still alive were battened down in the cellars of the ruined houses, where they knew they could stay for days, if necessary, until reinforcements arrived.

Unbelievably, in spite of the chaos of the half-buried village, German infantry were spotted moving off the road and heading for the trees. Farther east along the road, Robin could hear machine guns firing and the dull thud of mortar shells being dispatched. The Germans were trapped and they knew it, but they were still fighting. In the long run they could only sit and wait to be picked off by the expert Corsican riflemen.

Castelli's group was catching hell with all the firing going on up the bend, Robin noticed. Machine guns and mortars were going full blast. Then rifles started to pop. It seemed that the Germans were trying to fight their way through the mountains right there. If so, they'd have a sad task ahead, he thought. Castelli's mob fought like demons. He decided to send up some of the Free French, who had been doing a good job of keeping the infantry bogged down in the cellars.

Just after noon the German planes moved in. Two formations of Junkers Ju-88's and Ju-87 Stukas flew just above the level of the highest ridge, like hawks looking for their prey. All they could see in the hell below them was their own division, trapped, half-buried and still fighting. The planes began to strafe the trees, but they could not see their targets. After a while they began on the village. Then, as if realizing their mistake, they turned and headed back to Bastia.

Fourteen hundred hours! It was time for stage three. Robin gave the signal, and his squad loaded up with grenades and went on foot into the village to await the bulldozers.

Five bulldozers, heavily guarded by Maquisards and driven by U.S. Marine engineers, should now be approaching along the undamaged road from Ponte Leccia. These were part of the loot left behind by the departing Italian forces. They were late. Robin cursed as he signaled for the attack on the village to be stepped up.

At last he heard them lumbering round the last bend. As they came into view he saw the drivers had put up the blades as shields in front of them. He saw Leca and his team walking beside them, guns ready for action. They crossed the road into the village without any trouble, although there was some shooting from the ridge and the trees, where a few Germans had managed to survive.

As they approached the village they headed for a wall that looked pretty stable, but after five repeated batterings it crumpled and became a ruin like the others.

Robin joined the groups around the bulldozers. Then they moved from cellar to cellar. As they passed, he pulled the pin on two grenades and dropped them in. The explosion was earsplitting, and shortly afterward the cellars were filled with rubble. Slowly the sniper fire and machine guns were stilled, and by dusk the village was merely a graveyard.

Just before nightfall the news came up the line that the Boche were in full-scale retreat wherever they could move. Their engineers were trying to clear the roads and mend the bridges.

For four more days Robin's guerrillas harassed the retreating enemy. The Germans retaliated with repeated sorties into the forests. Casualties mounted on both sides, but by the last day of September the road from Bastia into the interior was clear and there was no possibility that the enemy would try again. Robin dispersed his men, sending most of them to help other groups or to attack the west coast garrisons. Sybilia was receiving success stories from all areas of the Resistance. By the last day of September it was obvious that the German bid to penetrate and occupy the interior of the island had failed totally.

CHAPTER 49

October, 1943

Young Susini and the last few Maquisards to have fallen in battle were each to be given a hero's funeral in Bastia that morning. They would represent all those who had died in the

Resistance. Robin had agreed to go. Afterward there would be a speech by General Charles de Gaulle, followed by a formal celebration at the Hotel Bastia.

Robin resented this intrusion into his private time. The war in Corsica was over, and he wanted to be alone with Sybilia. But that was not to be.

He was wearing a suit donated by one of the Taitan widows. It was bright blue with exaggerated shoulder pads and a nipped-in waist. He felt conspicuous and silly in it. Rocca, however, was dressed in black. He was wearing a suit that looked both new and tailor-made. His hair was carefully cut, and his mustache was trimmed. He was an awesome figure of a man, and he made everyone else look seedy. Robin didn't mind being ragged by the marines, but he wanted to look good in Sybilia's eyes.

He emerged from the long, emotional funeral service into a glorious autumn morning of brilliant sunshine and deep shadows. Leaving the cemetery with Rocca, while Sybilia trailed behind, Robin saw a flashy German car parked along the road. It was gaudily painted with the Corsican emblem of the Moor's head on one side and an enormous tricolor on the other. His old team was jam-packed inside, all of them red-faced and yelling with delight. Now that they looked so clean, he noticed for the first time how dirty their teeth were.

Everywhere he went there were cries of "Long live the Wolf; long live Captain Robin!" The Wolf was grinning ferociously.

"We're a bit early for the speech," Robin pointed out. "Let's wait over there, out of sight. This fuss embarrasses the hell out of me."

There was a chestnut grove beside a small, formal park. Three benches were placed in the shade. They sat awkwardly together.

"What are you going to do now, Captain Moore?" Rocca asked, icily polite.

"First of all there's a war to be finished. They'll probably send me to the Far East. I reckon it will be another year at least. Maybe longer. Then I shouldn't be surprised if it takes me another year to get out of the army. I'll collect my back pay and use it to start farming—or maybe an engineering business. I'll see what turns up. As a matter of fact," he said, trying to sound casual, "I'm coming back here."

"That would be a mistake, Captain Moore. There's nothing here for you. One should never go back. Home is best for everyone."

Robin grimaced with annoyance. He saw Sybilia gesturing at him impatiently. She was trying to tell him to keep quiet. He understood her message. Their plans had nothing to do with Rocca.

He began to sneak glances at his watch. They only had this one day left together, and it was passing. Why couldn't they snatch a few minutes alone? Robin understood Rocca's polite but heavy-handed chaperoning. The wartime laxity of their traditional code was suddenly at an abrupt end. Sybilia was no longer his assistant, she was Rocca's daughter-in-law, a part of his household. Goddammit, he thought anxiously. I must get her alone. I have to talk to her. Yet what else was there to say? He had said it all one way or the other.

How sad she looked. She seemed to be settling into herself, as if he had already left. She looked vacant as she gazed off into the distance, a wistful expression on her face, her hands folded into her lap. She was shrinking into stillness, like a small, furry animal seeking to hide from the hazards of winter. He watched her surreptitiously. There were dark shadows under her eyes, and her lips were quivering. She looked very girlish in her powder-blue dress with its white collar and cuffs. Something from school days, she had told him that morning. Other than that and her wedding dress, she only had black. He'd send her something as soon as he could. All his male protectiveness was aroused. He shivered and longed to hold her. He felt his hackles rising, the blood hammering through his veins. He was so impatient to be back. He wanted to grab her and take her away, build a home, four stout walls erected fair and square around her—all of which was so impossible. Instead, he would leave his love clinging to her like a warm coat.

Rocca closed his eyes and began nodding in the hot sun. Robin leaned forward and poked his finger into the gravel. *Let's get out of here,* he wrote. *I'll meet you by the clock.* An idea was forming. A crazy idea. He'd do it.

"It's time for de Gaulle's speach," Rocca said, waking abruptly sometime later. He grimaced with annoyance when he saw he was alone.

He sauntered over to the main square and pushed his way

to the front of the crowd. General de Gaulle had flown in earlier that morning, less than twenty-four hours after the last German had left Corsican soil.

"Patriotic Corsica has displayed traditional courage in achieving her liberation; this is an example for the rest of the nation," the Corsicans' war hero told the crowd amid the cheers and clapping.

The afternoon passed too quickly. Robin had orders to embark with the marines at eighteen hundred hours that evening and return to England for further briefing. They had only half an hour left when he and Sybilia arrived at the airport.

Rocca found them at last. He looked furious because Robin had missed the speeches. At the airport there were two Thunderbolt fighters and the clumsier, twin-engined DC-3's bringing in hospital supplies. Robin was waiting for a Hudson that was to take him and some U.S. Marines back to England.

"Darling," he whispered, "we've had a taste of happiness, and it seems that it's over, but the truth is it's only just beginning. It's up to us, isn't it? We can build a life together any way we want—once we've won the war. It will be like this for always. Don't cry. I may be back sooner than you expect. I'll press for compassionate leave."

In spite of Rocca's presence, they stood in the waiting line holding hands, gripped by their shared misery.

"It's going to be hard for you," Robin whispered eventually.

"No, why? No harder for me than for you. At least I won't be fighting."

"It's harder to wait than to fight. Everyone knows that. It might be a year or two, maybe even longer. Of course I'll write. I'm not much of a letter writer, but I'll do my best."

"I will write to you often. Robin, my darling, promise me something. When you're faced with danger, don't be brave. Just remember Jules and I are waiting for you. Needing you."

There were shouts from behind: "Captain Robin. Where's Captain Robin?" Eventually he waved. Some of his squad had arrived to say good-bye. They had some bottles with them and were offering toasts, drinks, handshakes, singing. How different they looked in their best suits, faces bright red and sweating, necks bulging. Suddenly he was a foreigner. They were wishing him a safe journey home. They made him feel so alien. Where were the rest of his men? he wondered. He'd made a few enemies toward the end, he knew. The bond, if there had ever been one, was snapped. If only he could take Sybilia with him.

Odd that the war's over here while the rest of the world is up to its neck in it. I wonder where they'll send me next? Wherever it is, it won't be for long. Maybe a year, maybe two. When it's over I'll come back for Sybilia. Maybe we'll live here. She would like that. We'll have to see how it goes. I feel depressed. More than depressed, I feel empty, disoriented. Just like the major said, I've become dependent on the danger and the fighting. It's like a drug that's been keeping me on a high. Now it's over, and I've got withdrawal symptoms. That's all it is. A matter of adjustment. This is the beginning of our lives, not the end. Is she depressed, too, I wonder?

It was good last night. She loves me, and I'm lucky. This sort of thing doesn't happen often. A girl like her is one in a million. She walks like a chamois: strong but full of grace. She's so lovely it makes me feel good just to look at her. She'll wait for me. I know she will. Yes, maybe we'll settle down here in Corsica. We'll work hard, we'll have fun together, we'll prosper, and we'll have plenty of children. Eventually her family will accept me.

The night before he had awakened to find her leaning over him, her hair falling around his face, her eyes gazing at him. He'd thought he was still dreaming. He'd put his arms around her, and she had pressed forward, her breasts hard against him, her lips brushed softly on his. They had made love tenderly with their arms and legs entwined.

"I love you," she had told him afterward. "I'll be waiting when you come back."

"When I come home."

"Yes, home."

He had lain silently planning for a while. Then he'd bent and kissed the top of her head, moved her hair away from his mouth, and told her of his plans.

"I never mentioned this, but I have quite a sum saved up. Enough to get us started. A legacy from Gran, plus my savings. I've been looking around. There's some good places to start a ranch. You know that plateau underneath our camp? Well, I was thinking . . ."

At last he'd stopped talking to find that she had fallen asleep happily on his shoulder. He'd lain awake for the rest of the night, imagining exactly how it would be. He would not sleep. Not on their last night together.

The Hudson taxied up. It was time to embark. He picked up his gear and tried out a cheerful smile. "Come on. Cheer up."

She smiled sadly. "Promise! For always," she said.

"Of course. What else?"

Rocca was back. Leaning forward, he shook Robin's hand. He did not smile.

"Good-bye, Captain Moore," he said. Then he took Sybilia's arm and hung on as if he owned her. Robin joined the band of marines who were filing onto the plane.

PART IV

CHAPTER 50

April 15, 1955

A glimmer of gray in the east, the rise and fall of the steamer in the soft swell, the heady scent of the sea: evanescent streaks of fluorescence in breaking waves, a sense of belonging; all that and much more. I felt joined to the night by a mystical thread. I'd been waiting for the first glimpse of Corsica, which I knew so well from aerial photographs, geological maps, and travel books, but which I had never seen. As my hands tightened on the ship's rails, I knew my career hung in the balance of what I would find here.

Make or break . . . The cliché had sounded ominous when uttered by Professor Don Miller in the anthropological department of Boston University. We'd been facing each other across a worn desk, and Miller had looked angry.

"I don't know why you want it, Jock," he'd growled as he flipped through three hundred pages of detailed geological and archaeological evidence representing months of research.

I'd tried to explain, without treading on his toes. He was an anthropologist. He had little interest in archaeology. Now I wanted to ally the two social sciences in a major project.

"You and I have the same objectives," I began tentatively. "Trying to understand man and his institutions in order to improve them. We search for origins and order in our social groups, our taboos, and our beliefs. But what do we really know about prehistoric man in Europe? We try to understand him by transferring data from contemporary primitive societies: the Polynesians, Eskimos, Amazonians, aborigines, all of whom have vastly differing climatic conditions. My aim is to find an isolated European group, cut off for centuries by lack of communication and geographical barriers, and to study them side by side with an archaeological dig. A small village, perhaps, where certain life-styles, traditions—or merely legends or superstitions—reach back to the very dawn of time. In order to bridge the gap, I need an isolated place that has withstood the twentieth century. Corsica is my target."

"There's still time to call off the project," Miller said. "You're the up-and-coming star of this faculty, you know that. You can count on the chair when I retire, if you're still here, that is. I'd sure hate to see a promising career like yours knocked into a cocked hat by an expensive fiasco. Where's your logic, Walters?

"Look at it this way," he went on persuasively. "If you don't pick up that envelope, you'll certainly lead the Inca expedition next year."

"The Incas are played to death, but thanks anyway." I picked up the letter containing permission for the grant and thrust it in my pocket. It felt good there.

"You've five years," Miller said, scowling. "Minimal expenses, but generous allowances for the dig itself, if and when you find those ruins—and the village you're after. So meantime you'll starve a bit. I'll expect regular expense sheets and monthly reports." He stood up. He had seemed reluctant to shake hands.

Suddenly I became aware of a change in the steamer's direction. I looked up and shivered in the cool, predawn breeze. Around me, the sea and sky merged with the mist into one empty canvas, but slowly an outline of immense mountains was emerging. When the sky lightened I could see their summits shrouded in mist, their flanks dark with forests.

Corsica! At last!

It was then that I became aware of a curious scent, like a woman's perfume: exotic, heady, tantalizing, and all-pervasive. It brought with it an unwelcome feeling of unease. It was almost as if the island were reaching out to me, to lure me to her secret places, to woo and enchant me as a woman had once done. I braced myself and smiled confidently. Days of enchantment were firmly behind me. I would make short work of the wooing, notch up another success, and move on. That was my style.

Two years later I was beginning to regret my earlier, brash self-confidence. To tell the truth I was on the point of quitting. I'd been crabbing all over Corsica with nothing to show for it. I'd begun by moving south toward Filitosa. Not wishing to become involved in the French dig there, in spite of their friendly invitations, I'd moved north, cutting through the hinterland toward Bastia. The following year I'd succeeded in digging my way around the northern cape, known as Cap Corse, and down to Saint Florent. After that I'd spent a few months surveying and excavating the rocky mountain range of the northeast, extending up the center of the island and rising to five thousand feet or more. When spring came I had crossed the narrow depression running diagonally through the north center of the island, to explore the higher granitic peaks of the west coast rising to nine thousand feet.

For all this time I'd lived frugally, sleeping out like a hobo when weather permitted, catching fish and shellfish to offset my diet of bread when I was near the coast, and staying in the cheapest rooms. I'd endured the extremes of the Corsican climate, languorous and subtropical in the summer months around the coast, while alpine conditions prevailed in the high mountains. And then deluges of rain would come in autumn and spring.

In spite of my meager spending, it was clear that my academic grant was hopelessly inadequate. I'd have to find my site before the end of the year, or lack of funds would force me to quit. So I'd begun to work frenziedly, seven days a week, but I knew that hard work alone wouldn't be enough. Success required luck as well, and lately I'd not had much luck. I was feeling pretty low and sorry for myself as I ambled toward the sea, dragging my harpoon through the sand.

Taking off from the rocks at Girolata was like plunging into a psychedelic maze. The craggy passages and caves were choked with multicolored algae and anemones. Shoals of sargo, their silvery-green flanks striped with black, hung motionless around the rocks. Brown sea turtles galloped past. Fan-shaped shellfish quivered and opened, while a grotesque sunfish, which Corsicans perversely call "moonfish," was dogging me.

I didn't waste much time gaping at the view. I was too hungry. Rounding the lip of a deep cave, I saw a shoal of *corbes noir,* with dark, iridescent heads and large fins attached to their graceful olive bodies. They hung motionless until I approached and took aim; then they sped like arrows into the safety of a cave.

Swimming northward, I came across two man-size fish called dentis because of their formidable teeth for grinding crustacea. They stayed just out of reach, their eyes watching me mistrustfully. Time and again I homed in for the kill, but half an hour later, after an exhausting swim, they were still just out of my range.

At the top of a tall rock I came face-to-face with a superb bass. I was so desperate I was shaking. I steadied myself by gripping a rock, aimed, and fired, impaling the fish. Then, minutes later, I shot another, but by now the water was becoming cloudy. The mistral was whipping the bay into white caps overhead, so I surfaced and set out in a lazy crawl to the beach.

An hour later I'd cooked and eaten one of the bass, and I was feeling great. I decided to take the other back to my landlady, who as usual would offer a free supper in return, with some good local wine.

Thinking about my room in the tiny boardinghouse by the sea made me feel vaguely anxious. The rent was overdue, and cash was dwindling. I'd written to Professor Miller for more funds, but so far there'd been no reply. At the back of my mind was the nagging fear that my mail was not catching up with me. That was the main reason I'd hung around Girolata for two weeks in a state of enforced lethargy. I told myself that I needed the rest, but I had to admit I was tired and fed up and didn't know where to look next.

At dusk I ambled back to the small, rose-painted house by the wharf where I lodged. Madame Bartoli, my landlady, was in the kitchen. She was a buxom, apple-cheeked woman with bright green eyes that lit up when I presented the fish to her. She promptly kissed me on both cheeks and invited me to supper, as I'd planned.

"Oh, monsieur, wait a moment," she called as I went

upstairs. "This is your mail—yes? It came this morning, but you had left. You are a doctor, yes? Yet you did not register as a doctor." Her expression was a mixture of pride, annoyance, and curiosity.

I fumbled rapidly through the airmail envelopes, and my heart lurched as I recognized Miller's unique typeface. Fingers twitching with impatience, I explained, "I'm not a real doctor, ma'am, and I don't want to mislead people, particularly if there were an accident. I'm a doctor of archaeology, and I sure as hell can't think of anything more useless around here."

"Useless?" Madame Bartoli said with genuine amusement. "Around here? Well, really, what have you been doing with yourself all these weeks? Never mind. I can see you want to open your letters. You go ahead." She began to scale the fish in the sink.

It was no, I realized as I skimmed through the first two pages of excuses. I crumpled the letter and threw it into the bin. Miller had explained that I could expect further amounts only when I provided solid evidence of my theory, in the form of datable artifacts.

"Oh, heck!" I felt sick.

Thrusting the remaining letters into my pocket, I ambled off to take a hot shower. Only later, when I was sitting in the communal living room with a glass of wine, did I open the others. My mother had written the sort of letter widows always write to errant sons. My bank wrote to inform me I was low in funds. And lastly I opened the letter from my literary agent. A few seconds later I let out a roar of joy and rushed off to find someone to share my good news.

"My God! Just listen to this." I read the letter to my bemused landlady.

Dear Dr. Walters,

Regal Publishers have agreed to publish your manuscript, *Learning from the Past*. Publication of the hardback is scheduled for November this year. They have offered an advance of ten thousand dollars. Check to follow soon.

Regards.

It was a good excuse for a celebration. I stood several drinks for the clientele, mainly local fishermen who came for a chat and an inexpensive meal. Then I sat back in an alcoholic haze while they told me about the war. Much later, when they were still drinking, Madame Bartoli placed a shoebox full of crude hand axes into my lap and informed me that they had been left behind by a party of archaeology students from Oxford University.

"They said they were important, but they couldn't be bothered to take them back with them. What do you think?" she asked. "They said it wasn't their period. They were studying something else, a funny name. I don't remember anymore."

I was filled with a kind of wild hilarity, although I felt ridiculous. I'd chased around the island for two years, and a bunch of limey students had found precisely what I'd been looking for so painstakingly, but it wasn't their period. I began to laugh.

"Where did they find them?" I asked.

"Well, of course I don't know that," she replied anxiously.

"Someone must know."

"No. Why should we? We are not archaeologists."

It no longer seemed so funny. "But you must know where they spent their holidays?"

"No. Somewhere in the mountains, I suppose."

"Oh, God," I groaned. "I think I'm going to throw up."

"Over these stones?"

"Not stones. Stone Age weapons, axes, chisels, man's first survival tools, made possibly thirty thousand years ago or more. Makes you think, doesn't it?" I felt a tremor run through me as I gazed at the palm-size fragments of chipped flint. Undoubtedly they were late Magdalenian, and if they had truly been found in Corsica, then man had settled here during the final stages of the Pleistocene Ice Age, just as I had guessed.

"I'm sure they wouldn't have lied about them," she said. "They really were very pleasant young men. Perhaps my husband will remember where they'd been."

Her husband, a small, dark man with a ready smile marred by bad teeth, said he knew the route the students had taken. Sensing a captive audience, he was unwilling to relinquish his hold on me until he had talked about his experiences in the war. He had run afoul of the Italians, he explained. They had caught him and thrown him into prison and fed him on *singe,* the local equivalent of corned beef. They had shipped him to the mainland, but he had escaped.

The Italians and the Boche had left eventually and then an American division had been stationed in Corsica to drain the swamps of malaria. He shrugged significantly and then lapsed into silence as if to spare my feelings.

Much later, when we had finished eating and a visiting shepherd was singing doleful melodies to the throb of his guitar, Monsieur Bartoli suddenly remembered that the students had found the hand axes in Taita, a primitive village somewhere in the mountains.

Two weeks later I stood with concern at the bottom of the steep, zigzagging track that led to Taita. The village hung on a rock face over a sheer cliff in rugged terrain and looked as impregnable as any Gothic castle. I would never get my jeep up there, and all my equipment would have to be hand-carried with the help of donkeys. For the moment I decided to take a chance and leave most of the equipment in the jeep and continue on foot. I took my compass, notebook, pickaxe, and spade and began the long hot climb to Taita.

CHAPTER 51

July, 1957

Halfway to the summit, I detoured from the path and made for a nearby lake that curled moatlike, in the shape of a half-moon, around the base of the western cliff face. Coming closer, I could see that the slope above the lake had once been carved into a series of narrow strips of cultivated land, each one separated by high stone terraces. Most of them were overgrown now, but I saw an occasional row of olive trees or vegetables.

Earlier I had passed neatly stacked piles of wood where a charcoal burner was preparing his harvest, but the countryside seemed deserted now. I knew this was private property, but since there was no one around I decided to explore the terraces.

The morning yielded nothing as I tramped up and down the steep slopes looking for signs of the students' excavations. By midafternoon I was too hot to carry on. I longed to swim, but to reach the lake I had to trespass through strips of cultivated barley. This worried me slightly, but I was too hot to care much. Beyond the fields, dense maquis surrounded the shore. Eventually I found a narrow path tunneling through the undergrowth where honeysuckle and deeply scented lilies nestled among the scrub of myrtle and rosemary. The scent of the wild herbs was as heady as incense.

Suddenly I was sliding down slippery slopes to the water's edge. I landed ankle deep in the lake, stripped hurriedly, and plunged in. Icy bliss! From nearby came the thunder of a waterfall, but it was hidden by a promontory jutting into the lake. Climbing out, I lay behind a thick bush, suffused with a sense of physical well-being from the fragrant air and the hot sun.

While I sat lazily watching the water sparkling through tangled branches, I tried to imagine Corsica in the Stone Age. These scrub-covered slopes had been densely forested; reindeer and mammoths roamed the hills, while wolves and men preyed on them. If my theory was right, harassed Stone Age clans had been driven into these very mountains to find refuge from invading hordes of better-armed tribes. Did they come this way? Had they camped by the lake? And who had come first—perhaps the Neanderthal man of the middle Paleolithic period, carrying his primitive tools made of bone?

So long ago, I thought sleepily. I would be the first to find their fort, their weapons, and their burial sites and try to piece together what they were really like and who they were. The thought sent a thrill of anticipation through me.

Was I dreaming? The sun was setting in a blood-red sky, the lake was bathed in a mystical ruddy glow, and the trees stretched above deep violet pools. I could hear a slow beat of hooves approaching, and remembering that I was trespassing, I edged back into the shadow of the bush.

A peasant woman dressed in black pushed her way through the thicket, followed by a donkey loaded with firewood. They looked exhausted, but as the woman came closer I saw her face. I was staggered. She was that rare and cherished phenomenon, a perfectly beautiful woman. I gazed wistfully at her brown hair, shining with reddish glints in the sun, and her flawless golden skin. Yet her blue eyes gazed around dismally. She looked so sad that I longed to comfort her.

She led the donkey to the water's edge and tied his reins onto the halter. "There you are, Pierre. Have a rest." This was another shock, for she spoke in a cultured French accent.

Surely she would sense my presence, but it seemed that she was too exhausted. She sank to her knees beside the trickling stream, soaked her face, and then scooped up handfuls of water to drink.

Heck! I'm hallucinating! I couldn't force my eyes away from her as she began to take off her clothes, not provocatively but contemptuously, piece by piece, throwing each garment down as if she had waited a long time for this.

"Ursuline, where are you?" she called over her shoulder. There was an answering shout from a child some distance behind.

The woman was standing quite near, but on an incline. As I gazed up toward her, she looked statuesque, but her flesh was warm and glowed invitingly. Her hips were voluptuous, her waist slender, her breasts were globes of tender white, infinitely touchable, with wide brown circles around her nipples. When I could tear my eyes away from them, I noticed her square, brave shoulders and her long, unblemished neck.

With an impatient gesture she pulled the combs out of her brown hair, which fell in tresses over her shoulders. Slowly she looked down and ran her hands over her breasts and her smooth stomach, touching her thighs. She sighed, pushed her hands hard against herself, moving up and down. She gave a low, poignant cry, and her eyes filled with tears. Then she bent over swiftly and dabbed water onto her face.

By this time I was caught halfway between guilt and desire. I fought back an absurd, pristine urge to lurch out of the thicket and impale her with my own flesh. Insane! At the same time I wished to God I'd never come here in the first place. I'd never seen anyone so desirable or so unforgettable.

"Mama, Mama," a child was calling. A girl of about twelve years, with a tangle of thick red curls, burst out of the thicket. "Look at these flowers."

Her mother took the flowers and thrust them against her face. She turned abruptly and waded into the water while her daughter dragged off her clothes and followed her. Soon the two were splashing and laughing, nimble as two otters.

Who could they be? Corsican women never stripped, never swam, never spoke such perfect French. What if the husband followed them and discovered me peeping through the thicket? The thought of being sighted down the barrel of a Corsican shotgun was unnerving. Best shots in the world, I remembered gloomily. I crept out of the thicket, backed along the path, and hurried toward the road.

On the long climb to Taita, I could not banish the image of her face, although I tried. It wasn't just her loveliness that haunted me, but the sadness in her eyes and the underlying dejection I'd witnessed. How could anyone so desirable be so sad?

I knew that it wouldn't be difficult to trace a woman like her with a redheaded child called Ursuline. "But I'm not that big a fool," I said aloud. "I'll forget I ever saw her." It's not often I lie to myself, but at that moment I really believed what I said.

CHAPTER 52

Reaching the road at last, I climbed on toward Taita. On the very lip of the cliff, where the gravel road made its last tortuous twist up to the village square, stood a bistro. It was a ramshackle affair by modern standards: a converted cottage, open on one side, standing in the center of a large stone terrace overlooking the valley. In the shadowy interior I found a surprisingly well-stocked bar and a shelf filled with locally made produce.

This, I realized, was the villagers' watering hole. Several of them were sitting on benches on the terrace, smoking their pipes and gossiping noisily. Tough, middle-aged men, they wore somber black corduroy with checked shirts and red cummerbunds. I noticed their rifles were never out of reach.

The sullen barman was sitting with the villagers. I had to wait nearly ten minutes before he decided to take my order. He had only one good eye, but it looked pretty hostile to me.

I ordered Perrier with essence of citron and asked the barman if he knew of an inn or a boardinghouse where I could stay for a few nights.

"No."

"A place to eat supper?"

"No."

"Surely there must be someone who takes in lodgers?" I argued.

"Why should there be? No one comes here."

My friendly overtures to the neighboring tables also met with hostility. Conscious of angry eyes boring into my back, I reluctantly finished my drink and left.

As I climbed through twilight shadows toward the village, I heard footsteps gaining on me. Turning, I saw a tall blond man catching up fast. From his rifle, his corduroy trousers, and his thick boots and backpack, I guessed he was a shepherd.

"Hey there! Wait for me. Don't think that all Corsicans behave like these surly locals," he said in a loud voice as he hurried to catch up. I turned and shook hands ceremoniously, since he seemed to expect that.

His name was Antoine Romanetti, and he was lonely. Although he was from Taita, he, too, had suffered the insults of these inhospitable villagers, he explained. As I'd guessed, he was a shepherd. His sheep were grazing on common ground above the village. Later he would herd them down toward the coast.

Each year he spent two months at home and then went down to winter pastures. He liked to gamble, and there was a good deal of opportunity to do that around the coast; but the summers were boring, for there was nothing to do in the mountains—no gambling, no women. He would be delighted to take me home with him, but it would be more courteous if I called on the priest. Father Andrews liked to meet visitors, particularly English-speaking visitors, since he, too, was a lonely man. No doubt he would ask me to stay the night.

"You mustn't judge all Taitans by the ones in that cafe," he went on earnestly. "They fancy themselves all big landowners. The bistro is owned by Xavier Rocca, the biggest of them all, both in politics and in land. A right bastard!"

"And the man who served me was Xavier Rocca?"

"No, a brother-in-law, Pierre Bonnelli. One of Rocca's poor relations. He has enough of them. Rocca wasn't always rich, but he married well.

"Rocca's got everything except happiness. His wife's crazy, his son's dead, tortured to death by the Boche, and his daughter-in-law is a whore, a *putana*." He said the word contemptuously and spat on the ground. "It's enough to take the joy out of any man," he added philosophically. "No one knows why he keeps her in the house. Some say in memory of his son, some say because of his grandson. He adores that child, but he never speaks to the mother. It's over twelve years now, but not one word has he said to that *putana*, nor her redheaded bastard." He paused and then continued, "Well, I guess all folks have their burdens."

He stopped talking and sized me up for a moment.

"So what are you doing here?" Romanetti asked.

"I'm looking for prehistoric ruins. I'm an archaeologist."

"Take my advice. Don't trespass on private land. Ask first. It's safer around these parts. The priest will tell you which is common land and who owns what."

I shook hands and followed the shepherd's directions to the presbytery.

Father Andrews was in his cups. He looked embarrassed but pleased all the same as he wiped his grimy hands over his robe.

"My birthday," he said in a strong Irish accent giving me an apologetic grin. "I'm forty-one, though I can't believe it myself."

I could believe it. I'd guessed him to be pushing fifty.

"Will you have a glass of wine, then?" He ushered me to the best chair. "Sit here and tell me what brings a stranger to these parts. I don't often have the chance to speak my native tongue, although one member of my congregation speaks excellent English."

I couldn't resist staring at the priest's desk. It was the handwriting that snared my interest: neat, concise, and straight, it covered the numerous pages scattered over the desk. A large box file lay open. It seemed to contain some sort of thesis and, judging by the number of pages—I estimated close to a thousand—represented years of work.

"It's nothing but a foolish man's dream," the priest said quickly. Then he scooped up the pages and closed the box.

I explained about my grant and my reason for coming to Taita, and I was pleasantly surprised to find that the priest was quite knowledgeable about the history and prehistory of the island. When I showed him the hand axes my landlady had given me, the priest became enthusiastic. One of the villagers had given them to him, he explained. He could not remember who. Presumably they had been found in the maquis. He had kept them on his bookcase and given them to the students because they'd seemed so interested. He was quite sure that none of them had been found on a grave.

I tried not to show how let down I felt. I'd really hoped for something more positive. Early days! In my mind's eye I was exploring the mountain slopes, listing the possible places for excavation, discounting others, only vaguely aware of the priest's monologue. The poor guy had been sent to Taita for a year's stint to complete his thesis and been stranded there like a fish in a rock pool. Some dispute over a sermon during the war had thrust him out of favor with the Vatican.

"The Catholic doctrine of freedom," the priest explained as he filled my glass repeatedly, "was originally my theory, and I have my thesis to prove it." He hurried over to the cupboard and produced another heavy box file. "The germ of this idea was spawned in 1942," he said. "To be precise, October 1942. I had to advise the villagers on their Christian duty in the face of anticipated invasion. After the war I was severely criticized by my superiors, so I continued with my research. But, of course, my real work has been on pre-Catholic religious beliefs. All that," he said sadly, pointing toward his desk. "Good stuff, believe you me."

Was Father Andrews touched in the head, I wondered, or was his greatest crime being ahead of his time? Did it matter? For one reason or another the priest had been left to rot in Taita while his monumental research gathered dust on the shelves.

"Interesting," I said. But shortly afterward I regretted

having said that, for, overcoming his initial shyness, the priest explained his work at length.

Oh, God, I thought, half-asleep. I'll be sitting here all night. As I listened to the priest, my mind was occupied with the memory of that beautiful, poignant woman I'd watched furtively. I felt compelled to know her story, but I was not quite sure how to broach the subject. I was still lusting over her beautiful body when I dozed off.

When I woke shortly afterward, I was surprised at the change in the priest. His thick black brows met across his forehead, his mouth was set in a grim, straight line, and his chin jutted out ferociously. What a disturbing scowl! He must look fearful in the pulpit when his temper's roused, I thought.

"Well, let's hear about your work," Father Andrews snorted. "What exactly are you after here?"

Inwardly furious with myself for being so rude, I tried to recoup his friendship. It was vital to have the priest as my ally. Without his help it would be tough to enlist the support of the villagers. I would need food, supplies, and workers. I explained the background to my theory, the efforts I'd made to get the backing I needed, and my certainty that Taita was the right village.

"Let me see if I heard you correctly," the priest said. "Taita is to become a living laboratory, with you the scientist attempting to reach back, through superstitions, customs, and traditions, to some semblance of the life of prehistoric man."

"I couldn't have put it better," I said, smiling happily.

"And the villagers here will be your guinea pigs?"

"Well, something like that." I was beginning to feel uneasy.

"It's un-Christian, immoral, and a damned impertinence to treat people like rats in a cage. Worse than that, it's the biggest lot of baloney I've ever heard. Now I'll bid you good night because it's late and I'm tired. Good day to you, Dr. Walters."

I found myself ushered into his spare room with a speed that left me breathless. I wasn't sure what I'd done to offend him. If only I hadn't drunk so much wine, then I would not have fallen asleep or talked so much about myself.

I bathed in the old-fashioned bathroom next to my room. On the way back I almost collided with Father Andrews, who was bringing me a mug of tea.

"A peace offering," he said.

I drank it, although I hate tea.

"It would be a pity if the two of us can't get on with each other," he added. "Particularly since we share a common language."

"My work is sometimes hard to understand," I said, still feeling puzzled.

"Never mind that. A spell here with civilized men will do you no end of good," he went on.

I wasn't going to let him embroil me in an argument, although I could see he was spoiling for a fight. I went to bed, but I could not sleep. So many of the day's events kept flashing into my head in vivid detail.

Overwhelmingly, I could not banish the image of the *putana,* standing naked by the lake. Despite her incredible beauty, she had seemed defenseless, a tragic person. I longed to know more about her. Why was she so despised? She did not look like a whore. I tried to persuade myself that my interest in the woman was merely scientific curiosity, but I knew in my heart that I was suffering from a bad dose of old-fashioned lust.

CHAPTER 53

August, 1957

My curiosity about the lovely Corsican woman continued for the next few months as I dug my way around Taita. Although I found extensive evidence of Roman occupation, and one site containing ceramic beads and Iron Age artifacts, I could not locate the source of the Stone Age weapons Madame Bártoli had given me.

By the end of the first month I'd brought up most of my equipment and worked out a pretty good routine. I camped in the bush. Each morning I woke in the chill of the predawn. By the time the sun rose, I had made and drunk my coffee, eaten a stale roll, and was on site ready for some exploratory digging. By noon it was too hot to dig. That was the best time. I would go down to the lake and swim in the ice-cold mountain water. Afternoons were set aside for collecting anthropological data.

To me, Taita and its inhabitants had become a vital living organism. I had to document each facet of the villagers' lives, from their waking until they went to bed. No, even more than that. I wanted to know the thoughts, feelings, longings, and day-to-day actions of the village as a group. I thought of Taita as a termitary. The villagers were the termites. Together, by their actions, they kept the village alive.

This work was not new to me. My papers on the Eskimos and the Polynesians had brought me a good deal of scientific acclaim. But this time my concentration was being weakened by my excessive interest in Sybilia Rocca.

Instead of studying the Taitans, I would find myself studying the beautiful Corsican woman. Admittedly she was part of my investigation, wasn't she? She was the *putana*, the village whore, reviled, and therefore of interest. Or at least that was how I rationalized my curiosity about her daily activities.

In the days that followed I noted that Sybilia, being the daughter-in-law and therefore of lowly status, was always first to rise in the Rocca household. Dressed in an old skirt and blouse, her hair braided around her head, she raced from chore to chore. Apart from her hard work in the house and on the family terraces, she had also been given the task of writing up the books and checking the cash from the bistro once a week, which she did in a small dark room behind the counter.

From secret observation, I knew something about her, but I longed to know her better. I reasoned that knowing her routine, it would not be too difficult to engineer a "chance" meeting. The opportunity arose sooner than I expected and without my assistance.

On the last Friday in August, I was moving through the maquis, digging an occasional exploratory trench, when I decided to take a shortcut through the square to the presbytery. The priest had loaned me space in his garden shed to store my equipment. Passing near the Roccas' house, I came across

Sybilia in a rural scene of domesticity and paused to make notes.

Overlooking the river on a natural terrace below the house stood the four posts and tiled roof of the Roccas' baking oven. Beside the open door, Sybilia and her daughter, Ursuline, identically dressed in black calico, were shoveling long slivers of chestnut dough into the old stone oven. Charcoal embers leaped out at them in whirls and puffs. The gusty wind kept catching at the long, flat-ended pole with which the dough and then the crisp loaves were handled, and the girl struggled to hold it straight.

Above them, weird cliffs clawed the crimson sky. The few villagers who had been harvesting were toiling home, pulling their heavily laden donkeys up the winding track to Taita. Flashes of late-summer color could be seen in the maquis. Beyond, the cool lake glittered invitingly.

When I emerged so unexpectedly from the bushes, I startled them, and a loaf fell onto the ground. Ursuline dropped the pole with a cry.

I apologized and explained why I was trespassing on their land. I hoped my real reason was not too obvious: the truth was, I'd been passing this way for days hoping for the chance to talk to this beautiful Corsican woman. She was polite, but not talkative. She seemed uneasy as she introduced herself. I tried not to show that I knew both her name and her reputation. When I mentioned that I was on my way to the priest's house because I was thirsty, she remembered her manners sufficiently to produce a stone jug of lemonade. She asked me to sit down formally, as if we were sitting in her home. I squatted on a handy boulder. Ursuline, meanwhile, was dusting off the loaf with her hand.

"No one will know," she said, grinning mischievously. "I'll give it to Grandpa for his tea."

Sybilia's eyes glowed with affection. She had to control her smile. "Ursuline, that's a very mean thing to say." Her voice sounded stern, but her expression gave her away.

"I hate Grandpa," the child muttered, "and he will eat it for his tea, I promise you."

Sybilia sighed and took the pole from her daughter.

"Let me do it, Mama," Ursuline said, watching her anxiously.

"No, Ursuline. No, no, listen to me," she said as Ursuline grabbed for the shovel. "I only let you have one try because you wouldn't give in, but it's too heavy for you. Let go, I tell you."

She struggled to wrench it away, but her daughter was as strong as she was obstinate.

"Do as you're told, Ursuline, or I'll smack you."

"I'm too old to be smacked," Ursuline grumbled. She sulked off toward the stream.

Sybilia turned back to the oven.

"Can I give you a hand?" I suggested.

"No. Well, maybe you could. If you could hold the oven door open. This wind keeps slamming it just when I'm pushing the loaves in.

"Normally men don't help with this type of work." She smiled mysteriously to herself. "At the same time, they don't hide in the bushes making notes about women's chores. You might as well get some firsthand experience since you're obviously so interested."

I was shocked. For a confusing moment I thought she was referring to the afternoon I had spied on her swimming naked in the lake. My embarrassment must have shown, for she burst into peals of laughter.

"Your English is remarkable," I said huffily.

Noticing my flushed cheeks, she began talking confidentially, probably to help me regain my composure.

"You mustn't judge Ursuline by her bad behavior this morning," she said. "She has a hard life. She's learned to stand up for herself. She's very loyal, and she doesn't like to see me working so hard—"

Sybilia broke off in midsentence when she heard footsteps on the path above. For a moment she looked apprehensive.

Father Andrews pushed his way through the bushes. He hurried toward us, his head stuck out like a tortoise. It hadn't taken me long to discover that when the priest walked with that tread, it meant trouble for someone. He was covered in dust, and he looked tired.

"What a pleasure to see you, Father Andrews," Sybilia said, wiping her damp hair from her forehead with the back of her hand. She handed the priest a loaf and some chestnut pastries. He accepted the gifts absentmindedly and sat on a stone by the oven. He seemed to have difficulty knowing how to begin, for he commented on the heat wave and the quality of the crops this year.

Eventually he said softly in English: "Could you not go on up to the presbytery, Jock? I'll be there to split a bottle with you in next to no time."

That was that. My longing had finally come to fruition, only to be foiled by Father Andrews. Had he known I was there? I wondered guiltily. Was he going to warn her of me? I lingered behind a thick bush, eavesdropping and feeling guilty about it.

"Now look here, lassie," he said. "You know why I've come. I've been nagging you these past few years, but you've been turning a deaf ear to my pleas. Ursuline must go to school."

"Never!" That was Sybilia's voice. I could not see them through the thicket. "Don't ask again. It's no."

"I'm not asking you, lass," Father Andrews said. "I'm merely telling you the law. Ursuline *must* go to school. If you persist in this silly attitude, they could compel you to send her—d'you really want that to happen?"

"The police?" She gave a small, low moan.

Oh, God. Why don't I get the hell out of here?

The priest seemed to me to be pursuing too hard a line. "The school inspector will be round soon enough. I hardly managed to put him off the scent last year. Now she's recently turned thirteen. I know you've done your best. Let's hope it was good enough for primary school. Now it's time for the higher grades. She'll probably be behind the other girls."

"Not so," Sybilia argued. "She can read in English, French, and Italian. Her geography and history are superb. What can she learn at school that I can't teach her?"

"Mathematics?" Father Andrews suggested.

"She'll learn all about . . . Oh, God! You know what they'll tell her." She sounded agonized.

"Sybilia, you can't keep the truth from her forever. Next month the new school year starts. Ursuline must be there. But listen, Sybilia. I've been thinking . . . "

They had been walking slowly away from me, along the terrace. Now their voices had faded completely. I sat tight. So Ursuline was thirteen. It was a wartime liaison.

" . . . go to France. I can find the cash to start you off," I heard again as they walked back.

There was no answer from Sybilia.

"Robin will never come, Sybilia. I've been telling you that for years."

"Imagine hoping for thirteen years. That's crazy, isn't it? Well, you were right," she said, sounding desolate. "He hasn't come. Does that make you feel good?"

"Now, now, lassie," he said reprovingly. "You know how I feel for you. I only want what's best. Take my advice . . . pick up the pieces of your life and start again."

"Hope is all I have. Can't you understand? I won't let go of it. But even if I did . . . " Her voice faltered. Then she said more firmly: "I have to stay here. I can't earn enough money to support two children. Who would look after them while I was working? As for leaving them here, I couldn't bear to be parted from them. Besides, this is Jules's home. He has his grandfather. One day all this land will be his. Something will turn up for Ursuline. I don't care about myself. I just want to bring up my children properly. Things will change eventually."

"Then, lassie, Ursuline must attend the village school."

I heard a muffled sob behind me. That was when I discovered I wasn't the only one eavesdropping. My shame turned to concern. Ursuline looked so very sad. I didn't know much about children. What was I to do? Fumbling in my backpack, I found a bar of chocolate and handed it to her.

She gazed at me scornfully. She was a lovely child. There was a good deal of Sybilia in her features. Her red hair sparkled in the sun, her blue eyes shone with tears, and there were muddy streaks down her freckled skin. Silently I handed her a handkerchief, which she grabbed to dry her tears. Leaving her there, I scrambled backward out of the thicket and took the path up to the village. Suddenly I heard footsteps behind me.

"Here's your handkerchief," she called out.

I took it and thanked her.

"You're American?" she persisted in a tearful voice.

"Yes."

"My father's American."

Her English was wonderful. I told her so, and she glowed with pride.

"I can sing several songs from *The Wizard of Oz*," she added.

"One of these days perhaps you'll sing them to me."

"I might. Do you know my father?" she blurted out.

"No, America's a very big place with millions of people. I only know a very few of them. It's not like Taita, where everyone knows everyone."

"Mama's upset," she went on. "All the girls in the village go to school. Why shouldn't I go, too?"

"I don't know why, Ursuline," I said. "Perhaps because you're different from the other girls," I added.

"How could that be?"

"Well, you're half American. They're not."

She seemed pleased with that idea. She said: "Well, you're American . . . does that make us *buddies*?"

"Yes, of course."

She looked up at me and smiled. "You're my first friend," she said shyly.

She wanted me to tell her about America, so I talked to her for a while, then she scampered away.

"Her friend!" As I walked back I couldn't help wondering if I had agreed too lightly. Was I really her only friend? I felt saddened by her plight and burdened by the weight of my responsibility in light of her disclosure.

CHAPTER 54

It was half an hour before Father Andrews returned to the presbytery. I was expecting some sort of protest about my budding relationship with Sybilia. It was not long in coming.

"Tell me," he said, "are you a Catholic or Protestant?"

"Does it matter?"

"It might. That depends."

"On what?"

"On whether or not I have to bury you."

I felt shocked. "I get the point," I said. I wasn't in the mood to argue with him. Instead I stood up to leave, but the priest pressed me to stay and share a bottle of wine with him.

We had discovered three common interests: the English language, good wine, and sociological research. It was enough.

That night we sat for hours on his balcony, which looked up to the mountains. The moon was huge and lustrous, the air moist and heady with the scent of blossoms. We talked about Ireland and Corsica and the similarity of their problems; we discussed the island's wine industry and the sad lack of farming in the mountain villages, and how the shepherds were setting light to the forests to increase their grazing, and other inconsequential things.

It took me most of the evening to get around to something that had been bothering me. "Tell me about Ursuline," I said. "Doesn't she have any friends?"

"She's never had a chance to make friends. She's a sweet, spoiled, overprotected child who lives in her mother's shadow. Sybilia is worried about the inevitable victimization Ursuline will come up against if she mixes with village children. She's kept her out of school, so far. But the girl needs proper teaching."

"Is she the only child in the family?"

"There's a half brother. Rocca's grandson. The old man dotes on him. It's probably because of Rocca's influence that Jules will have nothing to do with his half sister. Rocca has never even acknowledged Ursuline's existence. The poor child is known in the village as the bastard. Jules has listened to the gossip, of course. The Rocca children don't even eat together."

What an absurd situation. I'd hoped her plight was better than that. I was still resenting the burden Ursuline had unknowingly placed on my shoulders. Her only friend, she had said.

"Of course Maria is good to the child," the priest was saying. "But she grows crazier daily. Don't worry," he added, noticing my expression. "Ursuline's a tough girl. No one's managed to break her spirit yet. She has her father's character, that's obvious. And why not? She's a miniature replica of him, from her unruly red curls to her freckled face."

Father Andrews seemed to think that he'd said too much. He clammed up and pushed away his glass of brandy.

"There's so much unhappiness in Taita nowadays. Most of it's caused by the war," he rambled on, as he often did. "At first it seemed that the occupation hadn't touched

Taita, but of course it had. The scars were there. You could not see them because they were inside the hearts of men—and their womenfolk.

"The men who returned from the Resistance were not the same boys who had joined up with so much idealism, and fought so bravely. Somewhere, among the killing and the tension, they became toughened and brutalized. I know of five cases of child battering in the village. Even making love can be an act of war if it's done with hatred and humiliation.

"Sybilia is one of the war casualties," he went on, surprising me. "What a strange, determined, introverted girl she's become. She's bitter, too. At night she cries herself to sleep. I know because Maria told me. Of course I shouldn't tell you this. I just want you to know that a second unfortunate liaison would probably destroy her."

Another subtle lecture. The priest was an expert.

"But why do they call her the *putana*?" I pressed him. "And who was Ursuline's father?" I had to know, and I sensed this was the right time to ask.

Father Andrews sighed: "She was the widow of an ex-Resistance fighter, who, as you probably know, was Rocca's son. She became involved with a young American intelligence agent: Captain Robin Moore. He left when the war ended, but she was already pregnant. She has waited for him ever since.

"The poor lassie. In Corsica you have the worst sexual repression I've ever encountered," he went on. "For a woman, sex outside marriage means irreversible social ostracism."

I couldn't pry another fact out of him. I left shortly afterward, but my curiosity was far from satisfied.

The next morning I wrote to the secretary of my faculty at Boston University, asking her to engage the Veteran's Administration to check through wartime army records and find the whereabouts of Captain Moore. I intended to tell him about his illegitimate daughter and force him to do something . . . anything.

The reply came a month later. No such person as Captain Robin Moore had ever existed. Yet, I knew, without doubt, an American agent had been parachuted into Corsica to organize the various Resistance groups.

One morning I spoke to the shepherd Antoine Romanetti.

He told me that Captain Moore was a very cautious man, thoroughly drilled in clandestine work. He'd carried this cautiousness into all his discussions. For instance, negotiations with the different leaders on various subjects had been kept strictly separate. No one knew more than they needed to know.

It seems that poor Sybilia had never even discovered his real identity. Of course, I wouldn't tell her this. It would be too cruel.

How refreshing Moore (for want of a better name) must have appeared to Sybilia, with his sympathetic manner, his frank and friendly ways, and the fact that he'd made her his close assistant; or so Romanetti told me.

All this must have impressed her deeply. Among Corsican men there has always been a deep, instinctive distrust of women. To a Corsican, a woman is dangerous and unfathomable. So then this smooth-talking agent dropped in and treated her as if she were his best friend.

So she fell for his line. Who could blame her? I could forgive her for imagining herself in love. But to ruin her life waiting for him? Well, that's another thing.

She erred once. So why not twice? It would be tempting to make her try.

CHAPTER 55

September, 1957

It was a beautiful morning. As the sun rose the maquis throbbed into Technicolor with patches of gold, orange, and red. Flocks of migrating woodcock and wood pigeons chased the morning midges. Blackbirds were rifling among the myrtle berries and stealing olives. A hare streaked across the terraces, startling a flock of partidges.

I was enjoying the view while I dug along the perimeter of the mountain slope overlooking the school. Although this particular stretch was on my schedule, it was not entirely coincidental that I was there on this particular day.

Below me, gaunt and old, stood the school of St. Augustine. It was state-financed but run by the church. It served two villages. In a small stone classroom, Sister Monica taught children of all ages, assisted by a young novice. Father Andrews gave weekly Scripture lessons. Today was to be Ursuline's first day at school.

Jules Rocca was the first to arrive, I noticed. There was no sign of Ursuline, and I suspected that Sybilia had kept her daughter at home, but five minutes later she emerged from the forest. She was walking stiffly upright, in a clean, starched dress, with a look of dread on her face. Her hair was tightly braided and wound around her head. Her fists were clenched.

I called to her and hurried down to the path to give her the geometry set I had bought on my past trip to the coast. She seemed extraordinarily pleased with it, although it was only a small thing.

Later that morning, at break, I saw her sitting alone in the clearing behind the school, eating her roll. The other pupils appeared to be ignoring her.

At one P.M. the school bell tolled and the children came running out. Jules was one of the first. He raced off down the forest path toward Taita. Obviously he intended to continue ignoring his sister as he had always done at home.

Eventually Ursuline came out. She looked serious, but not upset. She climbed up the bank and joined me at the side of the trench.

"My goodness, what a morning," she said.

"How did it go?"

"Oh, so-so."

She had an unusually low voice for a girl of her age: her mother's voice. To an outsider, I guessed she would seem precocious, but that was natural when you remembered that she spent her days with adults. She was tall for thirteen. At the moment she reminded me of a stick insect: long skinny limbs, huge eyes, and very little else.

We shared lunch, but she seemed preoccupied.

"What's a bastard, Dr. Walters?" she asked gravely, catching me unawares.

"Call me Jock," I said, playing for time. "Why d'you want to know?"

"You can tell me the truth, Jock," she said. "I have to know."

I explained as gently as I could.

"Is that all?" She stared at me haughtily, but her eyes were swimming with tears and she looked pale. "I expect that Mother and he were too busy to get married," she said. "You see, they both worked very hard in the war. Papa flew here from America to help free Corsica. He was a very brave man. He had to leave in a hurry to help free the rest of France. He was killed," she explained. "He was coming back to fetch Mother and me, but he was killed in the war. Yes," she added, her eyes looking at me wistfully. "For sure he's dead."

She bent her head, unwilling to let me see that her cheeks were wet with tears.

Two bars of chocolate later, she brightened up. "I asked Mama if Father was like you," she confided.

"Oh, yes?" I mumbled.

"She said you're taller than he was and a bit younger than he would be now. He had red hair like mine. Yours is dark brown, but you both have blue eyes."

She broke off and stared up at me. "You've got funny eyes," she said. "They're not like other people's eyes. They're too light."

"I see well enough," I snapped.

"Mama says your voices are very similar, and you are both very strong."

I decided to change the subject. "What did you learn at school today, Ursuline?"

"Corsican history. Tell me," she said, "who was the greatest Corsican who every lived?"

"Napoleon," I said, and watched her face take on an expression of contempt.

"No, it was Paola. Pasquale Paola. Never Napoleon."

"And why not Napoleon?" I asked.

"Napoleon was a great man, but more French than Corsican," Ursuline said excitedly. "Being born in Corsica does not make you a Corsican. To be Corsican you must be patriotic. You must love Corsica even more than you love yourself. You must do great things for your country and dream great dreams—just as Paola did.

"Mother says Paola is someone we need badly now," she

added. "He gave us laws that were more modern than anyone else's. After the French took over, he longed to free Corsica of foreign rule, but he never succeeded, even though he spent his whole life fighting for Corsican freedom. He was a great statesman and fighter. He made the world see how brave Corsicans are. In America, Paola was thought of as a hero, and three towns were named after him. Do you know where they are?"

"Don't you think you should be getting along?" I said wearily. "Your mother will be worried about you."

"Oh, all right." She left reluctantly. Shortly afterward I heard yells and screams coming from the forest. I raced along the path. At the edge of the glade I saw Ursuline surrounded by schoolmates, but far from beaten. She was kicking and hitting out with her fists. What a little tiger she was.

I was about to dive in and haul her out when I saw Jules racing back toward the children. A moment later he was in the midst of the fray, punching and swearing. He looked murderous.

I left them fighting back to back; I had a feeling that I shouldn't interfere. Together they were more than a match for the village toughs, but I hung around within earshot, just in case. Among the yells and shrieks and taunts, I heard Jules call: "Leave my sister alone! If you insult her, or if you touch her again, you'll have me to deal with."

So the Rocca children had found something to pull them together after all.

CHAPTER 56

Progress report to Prof. D. Miller
As I write this report to you, I am sitting in a tent beside my preliminary dig, overlooking the village Taita, which will be the object of my studies for the next few years. I've been crabbing around for a while now, and I haven't found my site. I'll swear it's here. Thanks for your confirmation of the

date of the artifacts. I knew the hand axes were Mousterian. Somewhere up here lies their ancient base—I'm homing in on it.

My village is exactly right. It's primitive—truly primitive. Most of their livelihood is pre-Neolithic. *Can you imagine? They actually* hunt *for much of their food: birds, wild boars, buck, rabbits—hunting is the principal pastime of most Corsican males. Their basic foodstuff—that is, chestnuts—is "gathered" by the women. (Strange to think that the hunting-gathering life-style could endure for so many centuries in Europe.) Of course, they also practice a little agriculture, but haphazardly and without much enthusiasm. They have a few vines and olives, introduced by Roman colonists centuries ago. They grow a few crops reluctantly—no more than they need to consume or barter. They herd sheep, and the women have spinning wheels to spin their yarn and looms, from which they weave a thick, warm fabric.*

The men are delightfully archaic. They boast that the only thing a Corsican man ever carries is a coffin. For the rest the women act as the beasts of burden. The men hunt, fight, sit around in cafes talking politics by the hour, and expect to be waited on hand and foot by their women, who do most of the work.

Traditional mores bind their life-style: examples are their traditional marriages, the belief in ghost funerals, their strange mourning rites, the vendetta (the word and custom originated in Corsica, incidentally), and the existence of mazzeris, *women who go into trances and predict death (accurately, if one can believe the local priest). My theory is that they're the direct descendants of the high priestesses of ancient Stone Age cultures. There's a famous* mazzeri *in Taita. Everyone knows about her, but I have not yet been able to find out who she is.*

When I find my site, excavating it is not going to be as easy as I'd imagined. First, there's no accommodation available in Taita. When winter comes I'll have a rough time sleeping out or lose hours each day traveling from an inn at the coast.

The locals have no intention of hiring themselves as laborers. That would be demeaning for a Corsican. Every man here is a prince. Even the French authorities have to employ "Macaronis" to build Corsican roads. I may have to import

Algerian diggers. This is complicated and requires permission from local authorities. Meantime, because of the difficult terrain, I have to carry all my equipment up and down a steep cliff to get here.

I'm hanging on here and will write again soon. As you probably guessed, the object of this letter is to enclose my expenses for the past three months. Please refund soonest.

Best wishes, Jock.

CHAPTER 57

October, 1957

I was excavating a cave overlooking a field above the forest when I heard a call: "Who's there . . . there . . . there . . . "

As the echoes ran around the mountains, I could sense the caller's fear but saw nothing. Below me was only a thick white mist stretching to the far horizon.

"Hello," I called.

A feeling of unease prompted me to abandon my dig and hurry down the hillside.

Incredible mist. So thick. Goddammit. I blundered into a ditch and fell heavily. I was being a fool, I thought. Yet something about the voice had reminded me of Sybilia Rocca. Could she be in trouble? I ran on and at last reached the forest where it was even worse. Visibility was down to a couple of yards, making it tough to follow the path. The mist seemed to press in and around me, choking sound. I began to feel disoriented. I had no idea which way to go, nor from which direction the cry had come. I shivered and swore. Then I decided to try to find my way back to my dig. It was typical autumn alpine weather, one minute so warm and the next freezing.

When I heard the river rushing over the stones, I felt relieved. I could follow its path upstream. I was on the way back when I heard a sharp scream of fright. It was far away and downhill. I set off down the bank again, slipping on sodden leaves.

I thought I heard a curse and a low moan. I wasn't sure, so I stood still, listening. There it was again, nearer now. But where? The sound seemed to echo from all around.

Where the hell is she? A shrill scream, suddenly silenced, turned my skin to goose pimples. I was sure it was Sybilia. I felt panic and a sense of futility. "What the hell's going on?" I muttered aloud. "Where the hell is she?"

Another scream. Surely she was not more than fifty yards away.

"Keep screaming," I shouted. "I'm trying to find you. Yell, for God's sake. Yell!"

I heard muffled groaning, then a stifled curse. Surely they were just beyond the dense thicket ahead of me. I charged through the bush, head down, and burst out, scattering twigs and branches. I was almost on top of them before I saw them.

It was Sybilia. She lay spread-eagled on the ground, her face covered with mud. Above her sprawled a filthy, unshaven man. He looked like a tramp, but he was probably a shepherd.

A split second told me everything: her eyes wide and staring with fear, her skirt pushed up around her thighs, her blouse ripped apart. Even in that moment of horror, I noticed how lovely she was.

I bellowed with rage and sprang on the shepherd, intent on beating him to a pulp.

He twisted aside and reached for his rifle. I flung myself at it and kicked it into the ditch. Then I grappled with the bastard around the hips and eventually flung him down. I was fighting a professional. Thank God I was still able to recognize that, in spite of my rage.

My right fist lashed out, and the shepherd ducked. We fell with flailing arms and legs into the bracken-filled ditch beside the river. Then we were scrambling around in the slimy mud, exchanging blows, fighting dirty with anything that came to hand. The shepherd knew all the right moves, and so did I. But I was younger and fitter.

After a few minutes the man's breath was rasping and his strength was failing. I caught the thick wrestler's neck between my hands, squeezed, and kept squeezing. Chest heaving, his face brick red, the man reached around and grasped a branch. He brought it down with a ferocious crack on my head.

That hurt. I nearly passed out but managed to hang on. Slowly I increased the pressure of my fingers and watched that ugly face turn from red to mottled purple.

The shepherd broke free, and for a few minutes we were wallowing in the mud again. Then a sudden, sharp swing of a dead branch caught me across the eyes. For a split second I could see only a red glow. The shepherd bolted into the thicket.

I found his gun and fired over his head. A flurry of panic-stricken birds soared from the branches. I guess the shepherd knew I wouldn't shoot him, for he kept going.

Sybilia had run a hundred yards downhill and collapsed behind a bush. She was mumbling a prayer over and over.

"Let's go," I said. I flung the rifle into a ditch and kicked some leaves over it.

She tried to stand but collapsed. Then she burst into tears. I helped her to her feet, but she keeled over again. After a few more tries, I caught hold of her and hoisted her over my shoulder. Together we slid down the riverbank.

Hours later, it seemed, we reached the mossy bridge. Trying not to lose my footing, I stumbled across. I was talking breathlessly all the time, trying to calm her. I can't remember exactly what I said, something about killing that bastard if it was the last thing I did.

By the time I reached the outskirts of Taita, Sybilia had recovered sufficiently to speak coherently.

"Put me down. Someone might see us," she complained.

I lowered her to the gound and steadied her. Blushing, she tried to pull her clothes together, but her blouse was irretrievably ruined.

"Here. Take my jersey." It was covered in mud. I wished I'd been wearing something warmer.

She was still shaking, so I took her arm.

"Where's the donkey? Where's Pierre?" she muttered.

"I'll look for him afterward. Don't worry," I tried to reassure her. "What were you doing in the forest?"

"Gathering chesnuts, of course. We're low in flour. Now I'll have to start all over again."

"And who was that stinking pig who attacked you?"

"How should I know? A passing shepherd, perhaps."

I gripped her arm tighter. "I'll find him," I promised.

"Oh, no. Don't interfere. I'm sorry—" She checked a sob. Then she gripped my arm and looked up at me imploringly. "I'm grateful to you. Truly grateful, but please don't get involved. This has nothing to do with you. Good-bye, and thank you again."

"I'll see you safely home," I said.

"No, really, you must let me go. How long have you been here? Three months? Yet you are still a stranger to our ways. Believe me, it would be better for you . . . for both of us . . . if you would let me go on alone. Please!"

"No longer a stranger," I argued. "Surely we're friends."

She did not answer. Regretfully, I watched her hurry away. Then I shrugged and went back to camp to clean myself up.

CHAPTER 58

I awoke to a feeling of intense discomfort. My bruises were coming out, and every joint ached. Sleeping out was a pain in the ass, particularly in October at this altitude, where it was damp and cold and the ground was stony. I was damned if I would admit that the shepherd was partially responsible for my pain and stiffness.

I sat up and pushed my head through the tent flap. It was still dark, and all I could see were the ghostly white shapes of bushes and stones covered with frost reflecting the starlight.

I dived back into my sleeping bag but couldn't stop shivering. It was too early to get up, but too cold to stay on the ground. Eventually I clambered out, pulled my trousers and sweater over my pajamas, and lit a fire. Half an hour later, crouched beside a roaring blaze, with a mug of hot coffee in my hand, I felt cheerful enough to watch the dawn break over the mountains.

I had a pretty good system for shaving: a mirror on a tree near the fire with a basin hanging below. When I peered into the mirror, I flinched with disgust. My face was swollen, one eye was almost closed, and I had a deep gash on my temple. My face was too tender to shave properly. After I'd cut myself twice, I abandoned the attempt.

The morning continued much the same as it had begun. My head throbbed when I tried to dig. The ground was frozen hard, and my fingers were numb with cold. Worst of all was my lack of concentration. I couldn't clear my mind of the image of Sybilia, stripped half-naked and screaming with terror. Uppermost was a disturbing sense of fear. What if I hadn't been there? What if it should happen again? Who would protect her next time?

I was puzzled by my concern. It was none of my business, I lectured myself. I was here to study the Taitans. This material was great stuff: the local whore, having broken the traditional moral code, was condemned to lifelong punishment, jointly and severally administered by a wrathful community. Cruel, but interesting. A valuable insight into primitive law enforcement. Any other concern of mine would be highly unprofessional, or so I lectured myself that frosty morning. Lust was forgivable, passion was not.

Eventually I decided to report the attempted rape to Father Andrews and wash my hands of the affair. The priest was not in the church, or in the presbytery, but a wrought-iron gate around the back stood open. I walked into a walled garden. Picking my way between rows of runner beans and chives, I found him on his knees, deftly plucking snails from the lettuces.

Father Andrews looked taken aback. Presumably this was his own private place. I had to admit it was pretty neat, with flowers and roses between the vegetables. It was a well-tended garden of about half an acre with a statue of St. Patrick at one end and a bench beside a fountain at the other.

"Good morning, Father Andrews," I called out.

"The top of the morning to you. What brings you from your work at this time of day?" The priest looked me up and down and grinned. "By God, the clinical Dr. Walters stumbled into a fight. Did you forget to mention you're an uninvolved observer?" Eventually he stopped laughing.

I forced a grin and told him what had happened as briefly as I could.

"I don't want to get involved with the villagers' squabbles," I told him, trying to sound reasonable. I could see by his face that he was disappointed in me. He'd spent much of the past few months trying to convince me that every man was my brother, not my laboratory animal.

"I'm here to record village customs," I argued in the face of his scowls. "It's not my job to push them into the twentieth century. Maybe it's your responsibility—I don't know. Do what you feel best. If Madame Rocca should lay a charge, I'm prepared to bear witness. . . ."

"Oh . . . you're prepared," said the priest. "Is it a matter of choice? Well, it's glad I am to see you're sufficiently human to help a maiden in distress. And a fine shiner you have for your trouble. All right. I'll let you scramble back into your ivory tower. I'll speak to Sybilia myself. Does that eye hurt much?"

"No." He could be infuriating sometimes.

"Come and have a bite to eat, Dr. Walters. You look as if you haven't eaten a good meal for days. Stiff-necked and gray-faced as an old woman you are, to be sure."

I couldn't resist the temptation of a hot breakfast. I warmed myself by the fire and listened to the priest's gossip as he bustled around the kitchen. Delicious odors kept teasing my nose: eggs sizzling in butter and cream, bacon grilling over hot coals, bread warming in the oven. The priest seemed to be in no hurry to hand over breakfast. I sat bemused and starving while he prattled on, describing the births and deaths and illnesses of his entire congregation.

A troop of Corsican police had arrived from Ajaccio in the night, he told me next. Inspector Rene Hiller was in charge. "A pompous man, between you and me," he continued. It was rumored that the young Bertoli, wanted by police for some crime in the mainland, was trying to see his mother, who was on her deathbed in Chiornia. Hiller was hoping to trap him unawares.

"Of course his chances are virtually nil." He pushed the plates to the side of the warming tray and began cleaning the frying pan.

He's a bumbling old idiot, I thought.

"I don't care for Hiller much," the priest went on. "He's a man without compassion. Or should I say without passion? Either way, he won't get much cooperation from the villagers."

"Breakfast smells real good," I hinted.

At last the priest pushed the feast under my nose. "By the way, who was it who attacked Sybilia?" he asked innocently.

"Who knows? A passing shepherd, perhaps. She'd never seen the man before."

The priest burst into harsh cackles of genuine mirth. "It was Ambrosini. The entire village knows about it. Sybilia knows him well. He's been boasting about your shiner and lying about your precise role in the drama. That man's a terrible crook."

He paused. "Strange people, the Corsicans. They guard their hates and grudges like they guard their goats. D'you think you're an island—something apart from all this? Let me put you wise. You're just as vulnerable as the rest of us, and Ambrosini's out to get you. So are his friends. So there you are, Dr. Walters. See how far you've slipped off your damned pedestal?"

"Tell me about Robin. Where the hell is he? What could he find anywhere else that's better than what he left here?" I felt I had to know.

"I doubt your curiosity is as scientific as you would like me to believe," the priest said. "Why don't you ask her yourself, since you're so interested. Just remember one thing—you've been hanging around for months now. Poking your nose into the villagers' affairs. You think you're invisible, a camera perhaps, something apart, but you'll surely find you bleed red blood—just like the rest of us."

CHAPTER 59

As I emerged from the presbytery, I saw Xavier Rocca loitering in the square. He strode over and clapped me on the back. His smile was compelling. Good humor oozed out of him. He ignored my obvious bruises and, to my astonishment, invited me to join him and his friends for a drink at the bistro.

An invitation to the White House couldn't have pleased

me more. This was the big breakthrough I had been hoping for, or so I thought at the time. I wondered if Rocca had heard about Sybilia's attack and this was his way of thanking me, although the subject was too delicate for him to mention. In my self-induced state of narcosis, I decided that was the case.

Rocca introduced me to several of his cronies, most of whom I'd seen around: there was Jean Pinelli, the cheese maker; Jean Padovani, the cabinetmaker, a careworn man with a twitching eye; Pietro Leca, the local blacksmith, who looked born to his trade with his big hands and enormous strength. Carlo Castelli, the cobbler, seemed to be wasting away from tuberculosis. There were deep grooves in his cheeks and a look of suffering in his dark brown eyes.

The small talk in Taita differed considerably from that of Boston, and I battled to join in, for the conversation centered about the rival clans of Corsican politics, and I soon discovered that allegiances were formed around clan personalities rather than bread-and-butter issues. Hunting and shooting were the other two topics of interest, and I tried to angle an invitation to join them, with no luck.

Consequently I was all the more astounded when Xavier Rocca, with an air of a conspirator, produced a bucket from behind the counter and solemnly gave me six Mousterian hand axes, which some children had collected for me, he said. He even fetched two of them to tell me exactly where they had found them.

Later, as I hugged the precious bucket, Rocca pulled me aside and told me that he had managed to persuade six leading villagers to allow me to excavate their land. He handed me a crude, hand-drawn map, marked where the children had found the hand axes, in the fields that I now had permission to excavate.

In one hour my opinion of the villagers had been knocked into a cocked hat. I was exhilarated enough to pay for drinks all around several times. My aches and pains dissolved in this euphoria and I remember thinking that Rocca really was one hell of a guy.

After that the party livened up. Castelli produced his accordion, and several men, including Rocca, sang and danced quite well.

Then, to my surprise, Romanetti the shepherd began to

sing in a hoarse, compelling voice. Perhaps it was the wine, but I had never before felt so moved. When I left at last, I was amazed to find that it was dark. We'd been drinking for hours.

Goddammit! I could squirm when I remember that day—even now. To be so naive—a mossback like me. Afterward, my views of the relationship between myself and the villages did an about-turn. While I was studying them, they were studying me, and I was damn near caught in the rip.

Of course, every man in Taita knew where the ruins lay. They deliberately sent me to excavate around the opposite side of the lake, about as far away from the ruins as I could possibly get. Months would be lost, archaeologically speaking, as I went digging southward. Anthropologically speaking, however, this time was invaluable, for I merged into the background as the village idiot, accepted, tolerated, but mainly ignored. This gave me inroads into the Taitan households.

CHAPTER 60

By evening I was feeling sick. My bruises were still sore, and I was once again in need of a good meal. Shivering and damp, I rifled in the wooden box, which was my larder, and found two stale rolls, hard as stones. I'd eat them both now and hope to buy something at the bistro next morning. Obtaining food was becoming an obsession. Some days I would return laden with all I could carry, only to find the bistro's shelves stocked with pies, eggs, sausage, and freshly baked bread. But when I took a chance, the shelves were invariably empty.

I sat on a stone and tried to munch one of the rolls. Eventually I dunked it in my coffee, and it promptly dissolved. Oh, hell!

Suddenly I saw a flicker of light in the darkness. I grabbed my night glasses, jumped on a rock, and scanned the maquis.

There was a lantern carried by hand, and it was moving purposely toward me. From time to time, I thought I saw the outline of the climber, but he or she was deliberately keeping out of sight.

As the figure neared camp I realized with a jolt that it was Sybilia. For a moment I felt an unreasonable hope. Was she coming to demonstrate her thanks? As she came closer I noticed that she looked so unattractive in her dowdy black clothes, her hair scraped back in a tight bun, her skirts long enough to cover the top of the clumsy men's boots she habitually wore. If I had not seen her naked, I would never have known how lovely her body was. I felt angry, both with her and with myself. I wondered what she wanted. At least I could offer her some coffee. I picked up a saucepan and flashlight and hurried to the river for water.

When I returned, I startled her. "I thought you weren't here," she stammered. Then she pulled herself together and smiled. "I came to thank you," she said. "And I brought you some food and, of course, your jersey."

I pounced on the basket. "Hey, but this is great." I couldn't believe my luck: sausage, pastries, fresh bread, olives, fruit, cheeses, olive oil—I unpacked it carefully and filled the larder.

"Wine! Hey! I'll tell you what. We'll celebrate right now. I've only one mug, but you get first sip." After a moment's hesitation and a quick glance around to make sure no one was watching, Sybilia crouched near the fire.

"You'll be racked with rheumatism like the shepherds if you persist in sleeping and sitting on this damp ground," she said, looking shy and very prim. "Haven't you noticed they are all crippled by the time they reach thirty?"

"I noticed they're ferociously strong." I fingered my eye tenderly and grinned. "Your English is really something," I said to bridge the awkward silence, although to tell the truth it was just a bit too perfect to be real. A few mistakes would have sounded less contrived.

"Yes, perhaps," she said, sipping the wine and taking care not to swallow much while pretending to be at ease. "I have an ear for languages. A gift which I neglect."

It was a chilly night. She shivered and pulled her shawl around her shoulders. "I came to thank you . . . for what you did. . . . You saved me, and I . . . I am grateful."

"Think nothing of it," I said lightly. "All this food . . . it simply wasn't necessary, although to tell the truth I'm grateful, too. So we're quits. I saved you from attack. You saved me from certain starvation."

"Yes," she said. "You do look thin."

"Sure am." I cut some bread on a large flat stone with an army survival knife, placed a wedge of sausage on it, and handed it to her, but she shook her head.

"Thank you, I supped at home quite adequately," she said primly.

"Supped"? Oh, heck! You need English lessons, Sybilia, and I'm volunteering for the job.

"Not supped," I growled. "That word's archaic. 'I ate,' or you could say 'I dined,' but that would really mean something pretty formal. Maybe you are formal at home, are you? Well, you've done your duty. I guess you want to go. It's cold and dark." I didn't seem able to get through to her, and that irritated me.

Sybilia made no move to get up. She flushed and bit her lip. I wondered what she wanted. "Tell me about your work," she whispered. "What exactly are you doing here?"

I was only too delighted to oblige. Heck, I was lonely, after all. I began at the beginning and took a great deal of pleasure in winding through my theories and my objectives.

Eventually she interrupted me: "Well, the fact that you've been studying our customs makes it so much easier for me," she said brightly. "Of course you will understand when I ask you, please, do not pursue this matter of my attack any further."

"Come again?"

"You were foolhardy to tell Father Andrews about the attack," she persisted. "Fortunately he is a most trustworthy person, and it will go no further. So please, tell no one. Let us remain silent, otherwise the consequences would be disastrous for me."

I frowned. What could I say? "Sybilia, I'm sorry. I took the easy way out because I didn't want to get involved. So I left it in the priest's hands, but of course you will bring charges."

"Why . . . no . . . I can't do that." She took a deep breath. "You see, I would be dishonored. Ruined! Do you understand?"

"Maybe I do. I think you're too damned scared to face up to the villagers. Or maybe you enjoy being called the *putana*. Are you some sort of masochist? Do you like being kicked around?" I knew that wasn't true. I wanted to hurt. Sybilia's placid acceptance of her fate was goading me into a harsh temper.

She gave a small cry. "Oh, how insulting." Losing her cool, she leaned forward and slapped my face.

Well, at least I got through to her, I thought. For a moment we stared at each other.

"How dare you insult me!"

"Sybilia," I began, trying to make amends. "I was trying to shock you into doing something about it. I want you to know what people will think if you don't bring charges."

"No one will know."

"Everyone knows. How d'you think I found out Ambrosini's name? He's been boasting around the village that he found you and me having it off under the bushes. I don't know if anyone will believe him, but they'll all have a go at you, because you're already *disonorata*. That's the word, isn't it? You could become the target for every horny shepherd in the mountains. Now either *you* bring charges, or *I* will."

I broke off, feeling confused. Sybilia was crying into her handkerchief, and I wasn't sure she was listening. Besides, I'd had time to remind myself that this had nothing to do with me. Every time I saw this woman, I lost my professional cool. She was distracting me.

When she was calmer I said: "Do as you wish, Sybilia. But don't kid yourself. You're outside local society because of something you've done in the past. Consequently your only protection is the French law. Believe me."

"Why are you so horrible? You have no right to say these things," she sobbed. "You don't know what you are talking about. It all happened long ago. People have forgotten."

"You know I'm making sense. You're not a fool."

She shuddered. Eventually she dried her eyes. "You saved me and I'm grateful, but that doesn't give you the right to lecture me."

"You're absolutely right. I can't imagine what got into me." I munched at the sausage and waited for her to pull herself together.

At last she said: "I've tried very hard to live down the past."

"Sybilia," I said carefully, knowing that it would be better to say nothing, "you've got yourself all socked in with this honor business. You're pushing yourself down—and for nothing. You won't regain your self-respect based on the villagers' opinions. They've got the lowdown on you. Although I don't know how or why. Put yourself above them. Somewhere so different that they can't judge you. And to start with, for God's sake, bring Ambrosini to justice. Don't waste time. I'll back you."

"You mean well, and you're a kind man, I can see that. I don't understand why you wish to involve yourself."

Because you're the most desirable woman I've ever met. Because you're quite special to me, although I'm not sure why—not yet. "Noble" would describe you rather well. You're also the saddest woman I've ever seen.

I decided to ignore her question. "Stand tall, Sybilia. Don't let them wipe their feet on you ever again." She picked up her basket and fled. I followed her for part of the way.

I wish I were someone different, I thought as I walked slowly back to my camp. I wish I could do more for her. As it is, I can only record and observe. That's all I'm good at.

It was a bad night. The sort of night that called for a drink. I raided my medicine box and finished off the brandy. I was still watching the following morning, sitting on a well-positioned rock with my binoculars, nursing a sore head and recording the comings and goings of the inhabitants before I settled into a new digging site. I saw Hiller return from Chiornia, accompanied by several police, with a prisoner in chains. Presumably they had caught Bertoli at last.

Later I saw Sybilia and Maria go to the presbytery, where Hiller was staying. I noticed that Sybilia's hair was dressed in a more becoming way around her face, and she was wearing a white blouse and smart shoes. Perhaps I'd gotten through to her after all. The women stayed there for half an hour, then they left.

Hiller took two police with him to the bistro. He was there for a while, but he emerged alone later. During that time I saw Ambrosini walk into the bistro. He was still there when Hiller left.

"What the hell . . . ? What the hell . . . ?" I mumbled to myself, feeling furious. In spite of my renewed determination not to interfere, I decided to pack up work for the day and see Hiller myself.

CHAPTER 61

Inspector Rene Hiller had cultivated a military bearing. He was tall and thin, clean-shaven, with shrewd gray eyes, neat, trimmed mustache, and boots like mirrors in spite of the dusty road he had traveled that morning. I found myself taking an instantaneous dislike to him, although I wasn't sure why.

As soon as I'd introduced myself and explained my mission, he lectured me in his cultured French on the folly of interfering in the purely domestic affairs of rural Corsicans.

I listened in amazed fury. *Shit. He's trespassing on my beat.* I wondered why I should find my own advice so contemptuous when heard from other lips.

"They're curious people," Hiller said, rubbing his hands as he warmed to his theme. "Primitive, savage, ungrateful. Dealing with a Corsican is like handling a keg of dynamite. You never know when it will blow up. Take my advice, don't get involved."

Encouraged by my silence, he added: "You might find yourself wiped out without mercy—just for interfering. In fact, if I were you, I'd move on."

"That's out of the question," I muttered.

"Ambrosini will be out to get you. So will his friends. Rocca would shoot you through the back, like a dog, just for touching his daughter-in-law. You went overboard and carried her home, or so I was told by the priest. Then there's my police. They're not French, unfortunately, but Corsican. They're inclined to shoot first and ask second. If you hang around here, stick to what you know and leave law and justice to me."

I tried to control myself. "Let's get to the point," I said. "Did Sybilia Rocca bring charges against him?"

"She did."

"So why didn't you arrest Ambrosini?"

The inspector was filled with his own self-importance and clearly enjoying himself. He simply pressed his lips together and smiled.

Angered by his attitude, I unleashed a barrage of accusations: "I fully corroborate her evidence: assault and battery . . . attempted rape . . . abusive language . . . polluting the atmosphere, he stank like an old goat. I can identify him positively, even by his smell."

"No doubt you could, my dear doctor," Hiller crowed, waving his hands like an animated octopus. "But Ambrosini just produced a dozen witnesses who swore he was in the mountains with them at the time of the assault on Madame Rocca and you. They also swore that Sybilia was touched in the head and regularly saw visions."

"Do you think I see visions?"

"Ah. Who knows? You have a certain frenetic look about you."

I sucked in a deep breath. "So what are you doing about it?"

Hiller hesitated. "What can I do?" He lifted his hands in an attitude of despair, but his face showed only satisfaction. "I must take the word of twelve villagers, all landowners—big fish in this stagnant little pond. We've added attempted rape and assault to a long list of crimes perpetrated by person or persons unknown in these barbarous backwoods. As for Ambrosini, he swears he scraped his knuckles in a mountain fall, and three more witnesses saw him do it.

"Don't take it so hard," Hiller said with cold triumph. "You're new here. In a few months' time you'll be delighted to let them get on with their lives their way. They're ignorant, intolerant, lazy, and not worth a glimpse of charity.

"Now, my dear doctor, let's think about lunch. If we were in Ajaccio, I could take you to some excellent seafood restaurants where they make the most delightful bouillabaisse, but as it is, Father Andrews's housekeeper is cooking some rabbit *en cocotte*. A change, at least, and the priest maintains a really fine cellar. He's promised to let me try his Clos Marfisi. Won't you join me?"

"Thanks, but no," I muttered. I turned abruptly, intending to leave without saying good-bye, but the inspector stopped me.

"One moment, Dr. Walters. You seem to me to be very naive. Excuse me for presuming to lecture you as if I were an older man, but perhaps I am more experienced in these matters. You're very taken with Sybilia Rocca, I can see. Don't lose your reputation, and possibly your life, for the sake of this temptress. Corsican women are renowned for their beauty, but untouchable.

"Did you know that three hundred of your compatriots disappeared in Corsica in the last war? Against orders they became involved in just such dangerous liaisons, and they disappeared. No clues. No corpses. Nothing! We have no leads.

"Sybilia Rocca is a whore. Her reputation did not come unearned, I assure you. In any case, all women are whores by nature. Some are cheap to come by, some want a lifetime's devotion and upkeep, plus a pension thrown in. Cheap or costly—it amounts to the same thing. Take a week off in Nice, why don't you? Forget Sybilia."

"You're mistaken. I'm not at all involved. It's a question of justice," I snarled. And with that, I turned and left hurriedly.

In the bistro the usual crowd of shepherds and landowners was gossiping at the tables on the terrace and drinking eau-de-vie. As usual, there was nothing to eat there. In the background the young shepherd Romanetti was singing a strange Corsican lament without accompaniment, the words and melody pouring out of him.

After the first raw brandy I found myself responding to the music. How strange it was: part Arab, part Oriental, a hint of Gregorian chanting; surely the sound went back to the very dawn of Mediterranean music. The untamed pagan voice seemed to hit me in the stomach. It was like a war cry! A challenge to emotions long submerged. As the song went on and on, I ordered another brandy and tossed it back.

Later, with a sense of being baited and trapped, I watched Ambrosini walk in. The shepherd sat at a table alone, which was strange in itself, since so many of the villagers had committed perjury for him.

Sobering to think that there is no shelter for American law here. In a way it's rather chilling. There's no one, absolutely no one, to see that justice is done. That creep is smiling to himself. Why not? He got away with it, didn't he? He'll try again. Next time I won't be there.

Was this the whole reason for the depression in which I seemed to be drowning? I've always reasoned myself out of bad moods and anger. I ordered another cognac and drank it slowly, gazing at the wall while trying to work out what was bothering me.

Ambrosini has knocked my theories into a cocked hat. Primitive law doesn't exist. The weak pander to the strong. The strong rule the weak. The essential goodness and justice of mankind is just a myth. There's no justice here. Consequently I feel angry and frightened. I've always sat back and let other people keep my world safe. Bands of highly skilled and trained lawmen. Now they're not here, so what am I going to do?

I waved to the barman, who placed cognac on the table. Then I looked up and saw, to my amazement, that Ambrosini was watching me and making a rude gesture with one hand while fingering his stiletto with the other. His smile was as vicious as the glint of the knife blade.

I lurched to my feet and flung my chair headlong at Ambrosini, catching him in the chest. As he fell, momentarily off balance, I thrust the edge of my hand against his neck, pinning him to the wall. His knife clattered to the floor. I'd got him this time. I homed in for the kill, both hands around his neck, my knee against his stomach. I squeezed with all my strength, enjoying the sense of satisfied hate and his flesh pulsating against my fingers.

Ambrosini was making weird choking noises. I heard him indistinctly beyond the roaring in my ears. I couldn't see too well. There was only that disturbing purple-veined face in a sea of mist. A face that must be obliterated. "Tell them you did it, you bastard. Tell them you did it."

It took four men to drag me off. I heard someone yelling hoarsely: "Let me kill the bastard. Let me at him." Then I realized it was I who was shouting.

Rubbing his neck and looking very pale, Ambrosini retrieved his knife and left quickly. The villagers dumped me onto a chair and returned to their tables without saying a word. I looked at them wonderingly—all Rocca's cronies. They knew what had happened. Every last one of the bastards.

I ordered a coffee. Still, no one said anything. I threw some cash on the table and left.

Incredible! Insane!

I was panting heavily as I labored up the track to the fountain. The autumn sunlight was blinding, but I felt cold and my head ached. What time was it, for God's sake? Only three o'clock. A bad time for drinking.

What the hell had gotten into me? Imagine acting like a Corsican. All passion and no sense. That's no way to carry on. Where's the logic in it?

I'd forgotten about Ambrosini. I leaned over the horse trough and ducked my head in twice. As I bent over for the third time, I heard footsteps behind me and swung around. Too late! The knife slashed my wrist as I flung up one arm. I managed to catch hold of it with my other hand, cutting myself deeply in the process.

"You're a glutton for punishment," I gasped as I knocked Ambrosini headlong with a vicious right hook. As he fell I kicked him in the stomach, but not hard enough. The shepherd ran, doubled up, into the cemetery, presumably en route to the forest.

I picked up the stiletto and examined it. A wicked-looking blade, sharp as a razor, with some words engraved in the local dialect. I'd work it out later, I decided as I thrust it in my pocket. Right now I was bleeding like a stuck pig. All the same, I was thankful for my military training. It had saved my life.

I turned back to the fountain and attempted to stop the bleeding with ice-cold water, but the blood kept flowing. I was beginning to feel faint. Looking around I wondered what would happen if I passed out. Probably nothing. I would lie there until I died or the pigs ate me. I wondered if I could reach the church.

Around the edge of the square people were loitering. They were watching me, wondering what I would do. No one came to my aid, but no one had helped Ambrosini, either. Silent watchers. *That was my job, wasn't it?* God, what a mess I'd made of everything. What a fool!

I heard someone calling: "Dr. Walters, come with me, please."

"I'm hallucinating," I said as Sybilia grabbed my elbow and supported me with her shoulder.

"Don't say anything, just walk," she snapped. "I thought you were different. I thought you used your head, not your fists. I thought you had some brains."

"I thought all that, too," I gasped. "Just shows how wrong we both were."

She guided me into the kitchen, where Maria clucked over me, stitched my wrist, oblivious to my pain, then bandaged me and gave me strong black coffee.

"I knew it was a mistake to bring charges, but you would have your own way," Sybilia said eventually in English. "You should have believed me. Madness! Now your life is in danger, and mine will be a living hell." Her two children hung around the doorway, eyeing me suspiciously.

It was clearly time to leave. Maria had packed a basket of food, which she handed to me without comment. Sybilia was silent, perhaps still too angry to speak to me. As soon as I could stand, they opened the door. I made my unsteady way up the goats' track to the camp.

Was that me? That crazy loon! What's come over me? I never lost my temper before. Or at least not like that. I never tried to kill a man. And why? Because he got away with something he shouldn't have gotten away with.

CHAPTER 62

November, 1957

My last box of matches, and the goddamn fire won't light. No food, but I could at least have a cup of black coffee if this frigging wood would catch. Just look at them down there! Chimneys smoking. Windows fastened. Selfish bug-

gers, every last one of them. I could die of cold, and they probably wouldn't find me until the spring. Even then they'd walk right around my corpse.

It was a dreary Monday morning in mid-November. It had rained for five days, and the maquis was a slippery nightmare of mud. The bushes, drenched and bedraggled, looked sadly beaten; the mountains loomed gray and somber under a leaden sky. I now understood why the shepherds were crippled with rheumatism. I stretched painfully and bent over the fire that I'd been trying to light in the mouth of a shallow cave. I'd been trying for over an hour.

I can't remember when I first started talking to myself, but it seemed to keep the silence at bay. I was still swearing at the damp sticks when a boy of about sixteen ran past. He was calling my name. He turned sharply at my answering shout and scrambled up the steep slope to the cave.

He was a tall, good-looking boy with black hair, blue eyes, and a fine-looking physique. He stood in the drizzle staring at me with a look that I could best describe as distant. I wondered what I'd done now. Then I realized that it was Jules. I greeted him as pleasantly as I could under the circumstances. He was carrying Maria's basket. My spirits soared.

"I've been searching all over for you," the boy muttered in French. "They all said you were digging down there, but you're up here."

I couldn't think of a reasonable reply to that. Besides, I was too busy delving into the basket: sausage, pies, warm bread. I offered him a pie, but he refused. Nevertheless, he hung around as if curious.

"The villagers say you are mad," he said, watching me eat. "They're wrong, of course. Grandfather says you're not mad. He's seen men like you before. You're like the American pioneers who discovered the West. We can't starve you out, so we might as well give you lodging and food. Madame Barnard is to put you up for the winter. We've arranged everything. You must see Grandfather at four on Thursday afternoon—down at the house."

"What's your name?" I asked him.

"Jules Michel Xavier Rocca. Do you want me to help you with that fire?"

"The wood's damp."

"For a small price I could deliver you some dry wood."

"Done," I said, feeling pleased. At least there was one entrepreneur in Corsica.

"One dollar?"

"Sure. Why not?"

Half an hour later the boy was back with a huge bundle that he had dragged up on a small cart. A shaggy dog wandered behind, looking wet and muddy.

"Would you like a beer, Jules?"

"Er . . . yes."

I finished out a dollar and a beer.

Jules moved swiftly and efficiently, with an expression of total concentration on his face. When he had lit the fire, he beamed with satisfaction at the blaze and sat back on his heels, gazing at me silently.

For a while he drank in silence. Eventually he said: "Grandpapa says you're the first of an army of invaders who will come from the Western world to pillage our history, our forests, and our women. He says eventually Corsica will be full of people like you enjoying themselves, while people like us work in the docks at Marseilles."

I didn't answer. I couldn't think of a suitable reply for a sixteen-year-old boy. Besides, Rocca was probably right.

"What's a plastic culture?" Jules asked after a while.

"Something that doesn't last, something cheap and shoddy and easily destroyed. I expect that's what he means."

"Is America like that?"

"No," I said firmly. "Perhaps your grandfather only sees what he wants to see. Your English is very good," I added to change the subject.

"Mother insists that we learn English. We have our own language. We don't really need another. Grandfather says there's no other language quite like it." After that, Jules lapsed into silence. I couldn't draw him out further.

When the fire turned to a pile of glowing embers ready for cooking, Jules stood up and left abruptly. He would not stay for breakfast. He was going hunting with the men just as soon as the rain cleared. They'd be back before Thursday, he promised.

The boy ran down the hill leaving me in a state of bemused elation. Things were going to get better. I had a feeling about it.

* * *

At four sharp on Thursday I knocked on the Roccas' front door. I was dressed in a pair of jeans, a clean shirt, and a windbreaker. I'd given myself a crewcut, and I was clean-shaven, though cut in several places. Under the circumstances it was the best I could do.

Xavier Rocca opened the door with a flourish and a smile. Standing beside him, I felt like a tramp. To start with, Rocca was taller than I, which was unusual. At six feet one I usually looked down on the world. Rocca's graying black hair and bushy mustache were perfectly groomed. His handsome but wolfish smile was reminiscent of wartime pictures of Stalin. His eyes, however, were glacial blue. When he smiled I noticed that his teeth were white and even. That was miraculous in a place like Taita. Presumably his short spell of plastic culture had introduced him to toothpaste and dentists. Right now he was dressed in his best clothes: black corduroy trousers and waistcoat, bright red cummerbund, and a white shirt with starched collar and a red-and-black-checked cravat. If anything, his clothes heightened the impression of veiled menace.

"Come in, come in," Rocca said in perfect French, in a deep voice that rumbled from his stomach. "Welcome to the Rocca household. Of course you've been here before, but that was in the kitchen with the women, so it doesn't count. Warm yourself by the fire, my friend." He poured two glasses of eau-de-vie and explained that Maria had made it herself.

"I believe I have to thank you for rescuing my son's widow. My son was killed in the war." He sighed dramatically. "The war destroyed many things for many people, but more for Sybilia than most. So now she stays here because she has nowhere else to go, assisting Maria with the housework in return for her bed and board. She is waiting, I believe. While she waits she is entitled to my hospitality, which includes my protection. *Just as you are,*" he said with emphasis. "Since you are here."

Everything he says is calculated, I thought. Nothing is wasted.

I looked around curiously, trying not to be rude but noting the hand-embroidered curtains and cushions, the sparse, homemade furniture polished to mirror surfaces, the piano, the paintings. Clearly the Roccas were well above the average household. On the table were plates of raw smoked ham and sausages arranged on squares of yellow pastry. There were dishes of olives, onions, and tomatoes swimming in the raw, hand-pressed olive oil. When we sat down to eat, everything tasted fantastic.

I didn't have to add much to the conversation. Every time I opened my mouth, Xavier interruped me. "Now, you sit there by the window," he said, "and watch the best theater in the world. The best! I've often said that to Maria. I've been to theaters in Rome, Paris, and once in Canada. There's nothing to beat the drama you see in this square. Today you have a private box, as it were. When the window is open you can hear every word. No doubt you brought your notebook, Dr. Walters. You may need it. There's a funeral on the way. You've been scribbling away at our weddings and our christenings for the past four months. The priest tells us we're to go into your book, to be published by your university. Makes us feel very important," he said with a touch of sarcasm.

"Perhaps I should explain . . . not everyone is aware of the social sciences," I began, feeling uncomfortable.

"Not necessary, not necessary at all, I assure you. The ways of the West are not completely foreign to us. Most of us here have business in the south of France. Well, at least a dozen Taitan families have financial connections there. They travel back and forth. Taita's lack of outside communication and facilities is largely a matter of choice. We like to enjoy our traditional Corsican ways. Here, each man is a prince—in his own way, of course."

I came to the rapid conclusion that Rocca was bluffing and playing with me. I grinned to show I could take it.

"I've been told there is a famous *mazzeri* living in Taita whose predictions have never been wrong. Everyone knows about her, but I haven't been able to establish her identity. Can you help me?" I asked.

Rocca frowned and then smiled again. "Do you believe in that nonsense?" He snorted with amusement. "I once went to a fortune-teller in London's Petticoat Lane. D'you know what she said? She said I would travel the world and marry money. I did, too."

Neat, very neat. I was distracted by the distant sound of knocking approaching the square. "It's nothing," Rocca said. "Just the funeral I mentioned to you. There won't be much to interest you: no mourners, no *voceri*, no family; just a very short service. A shepherd passing through. He leaves no kin.

"Well, now," Rocca went on. "You'll freeze to death up there, and we'll be responsible. Tell me, why are you camping out this winter, Dr. Walters?"

"I'm running out of time," I explained. "The journey to the nearest inn takes too long."

"We're not inhuman, Dr. Walters, even if it seemed so at times. The widow Germaine Barnard will put you up for the winter. She's our dressmaker. Oh, yes," he said as if on the spur of the moment, "you'll find her interesting. You'll be able to fill another notebook. Bed only, plus hot water and bathing facilities. Four dollars a week. Will that suit you?"

I gasped at this excessive demand but quickly agreed.

"From now on, you can buy your provisions at my store. Let us know in advance what you'll need. Oh, and by the way, we prefer dollars. Is that settled, then?"

Rocca clapped me on the shoulder. "I'll see the women don't neglect you. One or the other of them can take turns baking a bit extra."

I mumbled my thanks.

"I've heard talk that you will be bringing extra labor into the area. Is that true?"

I explained that I hoped to locate a good site. When I did I would apply for Algerian diggers since no one in Taita seemed interested in manual labor.

"A pity," Rocca said. "We're a law-abiding community. Such crime as may occasionally occur—usually a matter of passions running wild—are dealt with by the villagers. We take full responsibility. That's something you didn't understand," he went on. "I'm sorry you were knifed, but that's all been taken care of. You can feel perfectly safe here. We're a law-abiding community."

His expression was one of extreme kindliness. He might have been discussing Social Security pensions.

Law-abiding if you discount attempted rape, assault, near murder, I thought sourly. I decided not to bite the hand of the man who was about to feed me. No doubt I'd be shamelessly overcharged.

Xavier tried to persuade me to view the funeral from his window seat, but I wanted a closer look. I left shortly afterward.

Maria was waiting at the front door, smiling with her hand over her mouth, her eyes fixed on some point above my head as she handed me a basket of fruit. I knew better than to offer to pay for it.

I was glad to get outside. The meeting with Xavier Rocca had disturbed me. I felt dazzled by the man's magnetism. I could not help liking him, in spite of his lecture on justice and safety, which had been a bit hard to swallow. I grinned and rubbed my jaw reflectively. It was still sore.

By now the funeral procession had reached the square. There was a large open coffin devoid of flowers. Seven men in shiny black suits were shouldering the coffin, their rifles slung over their shoulders: Bonnelli, Padovani, Pinelli, Leca, Castelli, Cesari, Pascal, plus Jules. That surprised me. A dozen or more villagers trailed behind the coffin, their rifle butts rhythmically smashing the cobbles. There were no mourners, nor the traditional *voceri*.

I felt disappointed. This was my first funeral in Taita. The men passed solemnly into the cemetery, and I lingered by the gate. A few minutes later I heard footsteps behind me. I spun around, noting that my reflexes were improving, but it was only Hiller.

"You're lucky," Hiller said. "You're still alive."

"I guess so," I said with a laugh. "So what?" Hiller seemed a bit comic, like a character out of light opera. The local buffoon.

"Ambrosini claimed that you were making advances to Sybilia and that he warned you off with a black eye and a knife wound. That was why the villagers backed his false alibi. Later they decided you were telling the truth—mainly because of your splendid outburst at the bistro. Splendid in Corsican terms, that is."

"So what are you doing about it?"

"Not much I can do. Nearly all the village males were away on this hunting party they'd organzied. Now they all tell the same story."

"Which is?"

"That Ambrosini got in the line of fire. Stood where he

shouldn't have been standing, in front of the stag, which, incidentally, got away. Ambrosini got three shots clean through the middle of his back."

"And that's . . . ? I'll be darned." I felt a cold shiver of fear run down my spine.

Hiller sniffed unpleasantly. "Write it in your notebook, Dr. Walters. Publish it, for all I care. I've seven sworn statements from witnesses who saw the accident."

It was not necessary to peer in the coffin, but I did anyway.

That's why he wanted me here at four exactly. So that I could see the funeral. Yet this was arranged on Monday, and Ambrosini thought he was still alive. So much so, he even went on a hunting trip. My God, he was so dead, they even had the time of the funeral arranged.

I wandered down to the bistro feeling chilled to the marrow. I stayed there for a long time, but neither three stiff brandies nor the roaring fire was able to warm me.

CHAPTER 63

The following Monday I collected my suitcase from Father Andrews's storeroom and went to the address Xavier Rocca had given me. I wasn't impressed with the exterior view. It was a five-story building presenting the usual Corsican facade of dirt, peeling plaster, rotting wood, and several centuries of neglect. Nevertheless the building was constructed to last forever with granite walls two feet thick. Probably fifteenth century, I thought, wrinkling my nose at the smell of garbage coming from the back.

Still, the flat itself, a walk-up on the fifth floor, was in direct contrast with the damp, dark staircase. It was light, freshly painted, and clean. Madame Barnard, a sorrowful-looking woman with spaniel eyes, had moved out of her four-poster double bed into her son's single room, leaving me her magnificent, homemade goose-down mattress. I was too embarrassed to tell her that I was allergic to feathers, and consequently I sneezed throughout that winter.

On my first evening Germaine Barnard invited me to join her for a small sherry in her sitting room. Overstuffed, ornate pieces of furniture were so crowded together that it was hard to cross the room. The walls were cluttered with pictures of dead relatives, whom she addressed as if they were still alive and right in the room with us.

I discovered that she wished to "give me a reading." I wasn't sure what that meant, but I was left in no doubt at all that I was expected to pay one dollar first, which I promptly did.

She lit an old lamp on the mantel, fetched a dish from the kitchen, and poured some oil on the water. After that she seemed to be listening to voices.

She was, I discovered later, what they call in Corsica a *signadori*. She performed precisely the same function as a witch doctor in Africa, that of herbalist, soothsayer, spiritualist, and amateur psychiatrist. She was the expert in combating the pitiless *eye*—evil or otherwise. She also foretold the future and cured illnesses, especially mental ones. And she had a large and faithful practice in Taita. For a few days I thought I'd found the famous *mazzeri* of Taita, but I soon discovered my mistake.

"Corsica will take life, and Corsica will give life," she told me in a singsong voice. "I see danger, and I see death. I see you going over the seas and returning." Suddenly she pushed the dish across the table. "You should leave Corsica," she said. "Go home. You are going to cause too much trouble here." She put the dish away quickly, saying that she would pray for me.

Later, when we got to know each other better, she offered me breakfast at a more reasonable, all-in-one rate, but I wanted to be out of the house before dawn each morning, so we carried on as before.

Sometimes I slept in my camp, but in foul weather it was good to know that Germaine's deep feather mattress was there. Not that I slept particularly well anywhere. Frustrated lust was a new dimension in my life. When my frustration became almost unendurable, I took a fortnight's holiday in Ajaccio. But a short-term liaison with an air hostess did nothing to dispel my longing for Sybilia.

Occasionally we spoke to each other. The first time was one frosty morning in December. She'd been gathering pine-cones in the forest and emerged onto the higher pasture just as I was moving camp. The meeting was contrived, I knew. Her hair was brushed and gleaming, her eyes shimmered with promises her lips would never make. She was wearing a thin black dress that clung to her waist and was far too smart for gathering wood. Her face was pale, but her skin shone lustrously, and I longed to reach out and stroke the smooth slope of her cheek.

There was something so candid about her face. Perhaps because of the smooth wide forehead, the straight dark brows, the eyes set wide apart that stared into your soul. Yet when she was being devious I'd noticed she was unable to look at me. Instead she frowned, looked only at her hands and feet, and her long thick eyelashes would flutter down like the layered veils of a Moroccan woman.

That morning she was being devious. "What a surprise," she lied. Her lips were quivering as she tried to conceal a smile of triumph.

My invitation to coffee was accepted with icy disdain. She did not offer to help as I put up my tent and lit the fire.

"Is it worth it?" she asked. "What possible reward could be worth this discomfort? Do they pay you a great deal of money for your research?"

"Almost nothing," I admitted. "Particularly at the moment. I'm on a grant, but until I find my Stone Age site, I can't draw much of it. It's driving me crazy. Someone found those hand axes the priest gave me. They've been dated . . . proves my theory . . . "

I was panting as I dug in the tent poles.

"Man was here during the last ice age. Makes you think, doesn't it?"

"What are you talking about?" she asked sharply.

"If you're interested in archaeology, I'll give you a copy of my book," I said. "It explains the basics."

"I'm interested in books," she replied cautiously.

In my pack I carried an advance copy of *Learning from the Past*.

When I handed it to her, she gasped. "But this is your name," she said, pointing to the cover. "You wrote it? I misunderstood you when you said 'your book.' "

"It's okay. Happens all the time."

She turned the book over and burst out laughing as she looked at the photograph inside the dust cover. "But you don't look like this," she said. "Or perhaps you did before you came here."

When she looked at me, there was a completely new expression on her face. What was it? Admiration, I decided happily. Of course that was exactly why I'd given her the book. I was tired of being treated like the local loon.

"That book is paying for most of this. . . . " I gestured toward the equipment. "Now I'm writing a book about Taita, and Taita's past. About the people who lived here in prehistoric times and how some of their customs have lasted until today."

Suddenly she was interested. I spent most of that morning telling her exactly what I had told her before, but what she had obviously forgotten. Or maybe she'd never listened. This time she did, perhaps because the book was my banner of respectability.

Things seemed to be going my way at last. "I was thinking of packing up early and driving down to the coast to pick up the post and eat somewhere. Care to come along?" I asked as casually as I dared.

She shook her head.

"Sybilia, why are you content with such a god-awful life? Don't you ever hanker for something a bit better? You've let the locals brainwash you into believing that you don't deserve any fun in your life. You've paid your debt to society—whatever it was."

"You have no right to say that," she said angrily.

She stood up. For a moment she hesitated, absently kicking the turf with her thick boots. Then she scowled at me and grabbed her basket. "Thank you for the coffee," she flung over her shoulder.

Well, I blew that one.

I thought she'd never come back, but she did from time to time as I continued my frenetic search through the maquis. She seemed to have developed an interest in my work, and she was obviously learning English again, for her vocabulary now included words such as "snack," "buddy," "chuckle," and "nauseating." No doubt she was reading American books from Father Andrews's library.

In February the maquis turned white overnight with heath blossoms and wild almond trees. "We call it 'the white spring'," Sybilia told me one morning when she arrived with some pastries to find me wandering through the waist-deep flowers and smiling happily.

She, too, relaxed a little as we walked over the hillside, yet she was never completely open with me. There was always that lurking sense of secretiveness. She held back. Still, she was tantalizing. I could sense the sexuality behind her calm exterior: the passion, the voluptuous appetite, the craving to be loved. It was all there, waiting to transcend the barriers of village morality. She was like the early flowers: petal soft, dainty, waiting in fluttering awareness. Yet there was something detached and untouchable about her as well.

Among the flowers I stumbled across the ruins of an old Roman camp. I became wildly excited and showed it to Sybilia. She responded with stories of local Corsican heroes who had fought the Romans and won through cunning or bravery. The Romans, I discovered, were still very real to the Corsicans. It was as if they had arrived a generation ago.

Later that month mimosa trees made vivid splashes of yellow on the mountainside, and from then on the maquis changed color almost weekly. There were successive bloomings of spring flowers, reaching a peak in May with the glorious white, lilac, and yellow blossoms of the cistus bushes. By then my enthusiasm for this site had waned. I had dug and pickaxed my way through levels of Roman and pre-Roman occupation right down to Iron Age artifacts, and that was that. The site had been occupied on and off for plus-minus four thousand years. Not nearly long enough for my purposes, and I'd wasted months on the dig.

By July, I was ready to quit Taita.

I said as much to Bonnelli at Rocca's bistro, in a voice loud enough for Sybilia to hear. I could see her shadowy outline crouched over her accounts in the back room. I felt angry with her. Lately she'd been avoiding me—just when we were getting along so well, too.

"I'll be packing up one of these days. Don't worry, I'll give you a couple of weeks' notice of my intention to quit," I said as I paid for the day's food. "I'll be moving on in a southerly direction. Probably cross behind Mount Cinto and cut through the mountains toward the southeast."

Bonnelli showed no signs of interest, and Sybilia remained crouched over her books.

Although I hadn't found my Stone Age site, my anthropological studies of Taitan village life were more or less complete. It was a pity that I'd failed to find the *mazzeri*, or witness a vendetta, if you discounted Ambrosini. I'm not a quitter, but I knew that my frantic search here was unbalanced. I should've been able to accept defeat gracefully and move on. The same applied to my longing for Sybilia, which had become dangerously close to neurotic.

Perhaps I needed a spell in Boston, back where I belonged. So I told everyone of my intending departure, but I did nothing constructive about going. It was hard to sever the bonds with this strange village or to accept defeat. Instead I stored my gear with Father Andrews and took off for a month's underwater fishing.

I returned at the beginning of August bronzed and fit and somewhat saner, I thought. The following day I was once again excavating likely sites around the mountainside. Nearby, not so long ago, someone had stumbled across those Mesolithic hand axes and carried them down to Father Andrews. It was tantalizing, maddening, and perhaps crazy to leave when I was so close to success. And then, of course, there was Sybilia.

CHAPTER 64

September, 1958

The setting sun was reaching out to the mountains, lighting the rocks with crimson glows. Partridges called and whirled away in thick scrub, and from deep shadows half-wild goats and donkeys peered somberly at me. There were many birds, rising and falling in flight across the sun-drowsy maquis.

A perfect evening, but I was moping at my Roman camp,

thinking, *How can I ever leave this place?* I gazed at the half-ruined walls, some exquisite mosaics, a few pots and pans, and the remnants of my own fires. This was the scene of my biggest hope and eventual disappointment. I was feeling depressed, because I didn't want to leave Taita.

I feel at home here. That's the strange part of it. That's something new. I guess it's only because I'm identifying with the Corsicans. They have a sense of belonging that's instinctive. A Corsican is always intimately involved with his physical environment. But why am I thinking like this? To hell with the Corsicans.

All the same I was in no hurry to pack up as I gathered some sticks to make a fire and boiled some water for coffee. I had purchased my last supplies from the bistro that morning and made a big effort to be civil to Bonnelli, knowing that Sybilia was listening from the back room.

"So you won't want any more food, I suppose?"

A voice from behind me! It brought a glow of well-being with it. I'd been so busy getting the fire to draw, I hadn't even heard her footsteps.

"I was just thinking of you," I said.

"Oh, yes?" She began to pace up and down the narrow path between the trenches. She seemed ill at ease.

"Hey, what's the matter? Come and have some coffee."

She glanced shyly at me. "Where will you go next?"

I shrugged. "Haven't made up my mind. Have a last shot at finding a suitable site farther south, I guess."

"You haven't looked properly here."

"Haven't I? D'you know something I don't know?"

Now she looked guilty.

"I have to move on. You and I . . . well, we're getting nowhere, and you know how I feel about you. Besides, my work has come to a full stop. I can't find my site, although my instinct's never been wrong yet. It's here somewhere. I'll swear to that."

How restless she was, pacing up and down, rubbing her hands over her forehead. "Of course, if you found your ruins, you'd stay."

"But since I'm leaving tomorrow, that's not very likely," I retorted.

"Come with me," she said. "Just come. Remember to say that you found that place by yourself. Of course, you never would. You're on the wrong side of the lake. It's miles away. Come."

She hurried off in the direction of Taita. Did she really know what I was looking for, or would she lead me to another Roman camp? I stood up and watched her doubtfully, but she was charging ahead as if scared she might change her mind. Probably all for nothing, but I had to see . . . had to make sure. Grabbing a flashlight and a trowel, I hurried after her.

Amazing stamina. We went north through the maquis, using old goat tracks, along hairpin ledges and rocky slopes. We crossed a stone bridge at least five hundreds years old, moving toward the village. At the outskirts of the cemetery she made a detour and picked up the river north of her family's garden. After that we followed its route up steep slopes and slippery rocks where the river fell in a series of waterfalls.

I followed in awe. This was Rocca's land.

The sun set, but twilight lingered as we climbed higher.

Thank God there was a full moon, I thought two hours later, watching Sybilia, agile as a mouflon, scale a rocky outcrop.

I needed both hands now, so I thrust my flashlight into my pocket and tackled the gorge. Eventually I pulled myself onto the grassy ledge above the cliff. Looking to the right, I made out what looked like the ruins of a shepherd's hut and on the left another steep mountain crag. Far below were the lights of Taita—only a few dim candles flickering behind curtains.

Then, without warning, we were in the trees again. It was pitch dark with pools of dappled moonlight here and there, but still we followed the path of the river.

"This is all our land," she shouted over her shoulder above the roar of the river. Suddenly I was conscious of the night: the smell of the pine, damp earth and leaves, and the sudden sharp clatter of birds disturbed from their nightly solitude; the piercing cry of an owl as it rushed overhead into the dark sky.

At the edge of the forest we emerged onto a huge flat plateau edged on three sides by maquis. "This is where Ambrosini—" I broke off, remembering that I'd been trespassing the day I'd rescued Sybilia from attack.

"Yes. You almost found the place by yourself. They threw you off with those hand axes and maps."

"Why?"

"To get rid of you, I suppose. Rocca never wanted you on his land."

Far above I could see a cleft in the rugged mountain peaks surrounding them. For an incredulous moment I thought we were going to climb the slopes, but at the edge of the grazing land she walked into the impenetrable thicket and disappeared. Hurrying to catch up with her, I found an almost imperceptible gap in the shrubs and thorns that reached overhead to form a tunnel.

"Oh, God," she panted. "This is the way. I know it is, but the path's almost vanished. I remember this rock. I've passed it often enough, but it's years since anyone came here. This is all our land. Did you know that? Right up to the mountains, but in a narrow strip. Next to it is the land I brought with my dowry."

We came to the edge of the rushing river. It was strong but not deep, filled with reeds and icy cold. My feet were numb by the time we reached the other bank.

After that we climbed a steep slope and paused on the crest. Before me, glistening in the moonlight, was a vast granite bowl, surrounded on two sides by sheer slopes but falling away into darkness on our left. It seemed to be a drop of thousands of feet, but it was too dark to see properly.

"Now look," she said. "Over there."

Strange beings were crowded together in a gravel pit. Weird, terrifying stone figures were protruding from the earth at waist level, like ghosts rising from their graves. Ancient warriors, their faces imbued with fearsome authority, glared in the moonlight.

Suddenly I was running, stumbling, falling between the boulders, heading for the statues. I was only dimly aware of Sybilia's footsteps behind me. I walked around the statues, touching, stepping back in awe, worshiping the ancient primitive men who had evoked the human form with such mastery. They were frighteningly real with their prominent brows, coarse noses, heavy jaws, and small, tight mouths. There was an impression of sheer physical, brutal power about all of them.

I wandered around, touching them reverently, marveling at the formidable power of these ancient artists: the heads and shoulders were carved with skillful understatement and a sense of symmetry. There were smaller beings as well, with crude faces, flat-topped heads, and secretive eyes, fixing us with an impenetrable piercing stare. Each one was unique, but they glared with a shared antagonism. There were twelve altogether; some were set upright, some were lying on their backs, but all of them were superb.

At last I turned to Sybilia and said, "Thank you." Suddenly my arms were around her. I tilted her face up with my fingers on her chin, gazed at her long and earnestly. "I don't know why," I said hoarsely. "I can't begin to understand you, or why you waited so long, but thank you."

I tried to kiss her, but she pushed me aside roughly. She turned abruptly and then paused, as if wanting to say something but not knowing how. She pointed toward the shadow of a cave at the end of the quarry. "Go in there," she said.

I wandered into the cave like a man sleepwalking. Then I groped behind and caught hold of her hand, pulling her after me, sensing her fear.

I relit the flashlight, but it was ineffectual in the stygian depths. Perhaps the cave was unwilling to give up its secrets and fought back by pressing darkness on us. In the feeble beam I saw color and movement. I gasped and switched off the light. In that brief moment I had seen artistry as great as any modern painter, greater perhaps because of the economy of line. It was an illusion, of course. I knew that. A trick of the shadows, aided by my own imagination. I had merely seen what I wanted to see. Steeling myself to disappointment, I pulled Sybilia closer and eventually switched on the torch again.

"My God! Take a look at that." There was a massive bison, in shades of ocher, and it was charging over the ground, head lowered toward the hunters, a look of puzzled agony in its eyes. It was hauntingly alive. "I've never seen anything so brilliant, not in any cave paintings anywhere in the world," I whispered, feeling awestruck.

"There are more of these paintings farther back," she said.

I walked from one to the next as if in a trance, but gradually I became aware of the woman beside me and I flicked the flashlight toward her. She was shuddering violently. Her face had a strained, deathlike expression.

"What is it? Tell me what's wrong."

"This place is full of memories," she said.

As we walked back I noticed pieces of half-finished sculpture lying around, littering the cave. Compared with the ferocious power of the ancient statues, and the brilliant moving flow of the rock paintings, this work seemed pretentious and clumsy.

"Junk," I said aloud, and kicked a piece. "I'll get it out of here. Tomorrow."

Suddenly she burst into tears.

"You mustn't cry," I said gently.

Sybilia crouched down almost in a fetal position. "All for nothing?" she sobbed. "Michel and his hopes. And my hopes . . . We both tried so hard. He longed to be a sculptor. I wanted to be a wife. We both failed."

I felt her wet cheeks with my hand. I put my arms around her and pulled her against me.

"Poor, poor Michel," she sobbed.

I didn't know what she was talking about, but I sensed her uneasiness in the darkness, so I took her elbow and led her outside.

"Too many ghosts," she repeated with a shaky laugh.

The moonlight seemed blinding. In the reflected glow from the granite slopes, the concave bowl looked like the focal point of a ring of spotlights. I smoothed the ground and said, "Here. Sit here. It's dry."

She bent her knees and knelt on the sand. "I want to tell you about me. I want to tell you how it happened."

Torrents of words. I put my arms around her and pulled her against my shoulder. She didn't seem to notice. My lustful intentions were soon squashed in the trauma of her story. She told me of her grief when she was taken out of school to be married to a stranger. She recounted her efforts to make her marriage work, and then her war stories and how Robin rescued her from the Boche. Mainly she told me of how she loved Robin. She still believed he would come. To me that seemed amazing. I remember thinking, If I ever meet up with Moore, I'll kill the bastard. How could he leave her?

Afterward she lay in my arms, gazing at the sky, watching the moon sink slowly toward the sea, enjoying the silence and the shared intimacy.

"And now?" I said quietly. "It's time to forget the past. You're young and lovely, and you'll learn to love again."

"Love!" She laughed cynically.

For some reason her laugh annoyed me. I pulled her roughly toward me and kissed her. She gave a sharp cry and pushed me back.

"No," she said.

Her refusal was like a slap in the face. I felt furiously jealous of those ghosts from her past who still possessed her. She scrambled to her feet, looking hurt. "Here is your cave. Here are your statues and your precious bones. Don't lose them. I won't show you the way here twice. Remember to tell the villagers you found them by yourself." She left, and I lay back, feeling confused and angry. I felt sorry for her, but I felt even more sorry for myself. Sybilia was snared by the trauma of her past. She could never go forward, never forget.

When I next opened my eyes, the sun was streaming over the summit of Mount Cinto and I was quite alone.

CHAPTER 65

It was becoming lighter, and certain images were forcing themselves into my consciousness. I resisted them. I turned and buried my face in my pillow. That was a mistake, for the hay stuck in my nose and I sneezed violently several times. After that there was no point in trying to fall asleep again.

I lay and studied the painting on the ceiling above me. In the soft dawn light it was even more unbelievable, one of the most beautiful examples of prehistoric art I'd ever seen: a great bison charging a hunter against a backdrop of horses and deer. What was superb was the sense of power and speed so brilliantly conveyed in simple lines and natural pigments. Somewhere below me lay the artifacts and remains of the people who had created these paints. Maybe the bones of this very artist.

It was weeks since Sybilia had led me to the cave—my cave, as I thought of it now. I'd made some progress with the excavation, although not as much as I should have, mainly because I'd not been able to get any help. A report to Professor Miller was long overdue. I promised myself to write it as soon as I'd shaved. Meantime I lay in my sleeping bag reviewing my progress.

After finding the statues and satisfying myself that this was the site for which I had searched so long, my first step had been a visit to Bastia. I'd spend days wading through regional and national red tape in order to obtain a permit to import Algerian labor on a contract basis. I had come back disillusioned and depressed. It looked as if a long hard haul lay ahead before I'd get those diggers.

On my return I'd gone straight to the bistro and spoken to Bonnelli about local help, offering exorbitant rates; but no villager was prepared to demean himself by hiring out his labor.

Eventually I'd borrowed the priest's donkey, Matilda, and brought up load after load of spades, tools, wood, wheelbarrows, and everything else I needed. The first essential was to construct an office near the entrance to the cave. Then I'd sectioned off the dig. The thought of tackling the entire project single-handed was daunting.

At the end of a month, in a fit of pique, tiredness, and sheer frustration, I'd taken a holiday near Saint Florent. But I needed feminine companionship more than sun, so I went south to Ajaccio. Once again I cunningly booked into a hotel where they billeted air hostesses. Before long I was bedded down with a pretty, dark girl from Antwerp. But she was no Sybilia.

Enough daydreaming, I told myself sternly. There was work to be done. I climbed out of my sleeping bag and dived into the ice-cold river water. Then I went into my office to write the report I'd been putting off for far too long.

Dear Don,

I've completed my first excavations, and so far I've found two distinct cultures or time zones on this site going back to early Stone Age man, around twelve thousand years before the present. I don't know much about them yet, except that they may have worshiped the Mother Goddess, judging by the small stone idols they have bequeathed to us. (Three are enclosed for carbon-14 dating. They appear to be made of reindeer horn.) On a higher strata, I've found evidence of early Neolithic people, around eight thousand years before the present. With these more advanced tribes came a change-over to the more patriarchal concept of religion, as shown in the progression of their menhir statues in this very quarry (photographs and drawings enclosed). No more breasts and bellies. Instead they hewed larger-than-life figures displaying their meticulously carved weapons, glorifying and immortalizing man.

Hopefully the photographs and artifacts will enable you to unlock the major part of the university's grant. I've been using my own funds, and I'm getting near to broke. In the past month, for instance, I've purchased eight wheelbarrows, five pickaxes, trowels, half a dozen shovels, scaffolding and rope, and all my technical and drawing equipment.

The documentation of Taita and the villagers is proceeding splendidly, despite local attempts to block my research in every way. The villagers are—jointly and severally—the most baffling people. Their antagonism has increased since I found this site. I wonder why?

Regards, Jock

Writing the report had reminded me that the scaffolding was still piled up at the base of the cliff below Taita, waiting for me to bring it up to the site. I decided to go in the afternoon. I wanted to continue excavating all morning.

Later, when I went down to Taita and tried to harness the donkey, Father Andrews came out waving his arms angrily.

"Don't you think Matilda is looking a trifle wan?" he demanded. "She's been hauling your stuff up the mountains day after day without a rest."

I'd never given the donkey a thought. That's what donkeys were for, wasn't it? It looked much the same to me. "I'm sure you know its capacity better than I do."

"She's not an 'it,' she's a 'her,' and she's bushed. Give her a break. Go buy yourself a donkey. The Pinellis have a good, strong beast for sale."

I tried to explain that I didn't want to shoulder the responsibility for a living creature; I'd prefer to borrow.

"That figures," Father Andrews said.

Finally we hit on a compromise. If I would provide the cash for purchasing and feeding the Pinellis' donkey, Father Andrews would keep the creature in his field and take full responsibility for its welfare. I could "borrow" it whenever I wished. When I eventually left Taita, the church would inherit it.

"Oh, my goodness," he called just as I was setting off for the Pinellis' house. "How could I forget? There's a letter for you. It's from your publishers." He stood around looking anxious while I read it.

"It's good news," I reassured him. "My book is selling well, and I can expect a royalty check soon." He was pleased and invited me in for a glass of wine to celebrate. I'd never felt less like celebrating, but I couldn't disappoint him.

Shortly afterward I bought the donkey and left it in the field with Matilda. The following day I was once again carting gear up to my dig. It was getting monotonous. I had to talk to myself to boost my morale.

"I've found my ruins," I argued. "I'm sure I'll be given an additional grant to complete the dig. I'll notch up another triumph here, and without doubt they'll offer me the chair when Miller retires. My book is selling well, and I expect the next one will, too. If all this can't make me happy, there's something radically wrong."

Nevertheless, I couldn't convince myself that I was happy. I felt tired, and the new donkey was a mean brute. We were vying for leadership, and so far the donkey was winning. After all, he had teeth and hooves.

The sun sank into a wine-red horizon, the sea turned deep peacock blue, the mountains took on a luminous rosy glow with deep purple shadows. I let the donkey graze while I sat on a rock to watch the sunset. Dusk swept swiftly around me, and I succumbed to a sense of bitter loneliness.

The feeling had been creeping up on me for weeks, and I'd tried to overcome it time and again. It had something to do with the community I was studying so intently but which resisted me so completely. A world within a world—complete, whole, isolated, content. Never before had I become so involved and yet frustrated.

Last month, for instance, I'd been unable to sleep because Madame Barnard, junior, was giving birth to expected triplets. When they'd emerged just before dawn, the village had reverberated with happy cries, gunshots, and echoes of songs from the bistro. I'd curled up in my sleeping bag with a sense of having accomplished something important. What—for God's sake? What had all this to do with me?

I felt a part of them, yet I was apart. I would wake with them just before dawn, observe them stumble out to their fields or to the hunt, watch the women set about their daily chores, the typical hunting-and-gathering syndrome reminiscent of prehistoric man.

I would be there again at dusk, as I was now. This was a time when I became nostalgic, for then the villagers would wend their way home from mountains and terraces to open doors, warm baths, and even warmer welcomes. Delicious aromas would float from kitchen doorways. I would note in my cryptic shorthand the division of labor, the frequency with which they washed or bathed, what they ate, how long they slept. And all the time I would be wondering how to describe an integral part of their existence—their clannishness.

It seemed to me that here in Corsica all my preconceived ideas had been held up to scrutiny and found wanting. I'd been foolish enough to imagine that a simple, ancient lifestyle meant being primitive. I'd seen myself as the only modern and therefore civilized man on the island. Yet all that I had gained from my extensive education and twentieth-century background seemed pitiable compared with what they had.

Of course, Sybilia was an important factor in my perceptions. I could not help thinking that my fascination with and admiration of the Corsicans stemmed, in part, from my admiration of her. Slowly I was beginning to see that in Sybilia's eyes I had very little to offer, especially since she had already loved and been left by an American.

The crazy part was—I hadn't come here to study myself, but to study them, yet I was becoming increasingly introspective, and I didn't like what I saw.

I stood up abruptly and tried to bully the donkey out of the knee-deep grass where he was grazing. I reached the cave at last. After a quick scrub in the icy river, I dried myself and peered into the mirror hanging on the tree. Good God, I looked like a hobo. I decided to clean myself up, find something decent to wear, and go down to the bistro. Even Bonnelli's grim greeting would be better than nothing tonight.

PART V

CHAPTER 66

June, 1959

A glorious landscape—dew-fresh air scented with summer's sweet herbs: rosemary blooming in a dozen shades of blue; myrtle covered with snow-white flowers. Into it ran my favorite friend. She was on the way home from school, I knew. She was singing, and every now and then she gave a little skip. Her red hair glinted in the sun, and her blue dress billowed in the breeze. At almost fifteen Ursuline was gawky and tall. She showed promise of beauty, but she was still overly thin, with an elfin look about her.

"How was school?" I asked.

"Just divine," she answered. "Even Sister Monica's sarcasm was bearable today. Guess what?" Her eyes were sparkling with joy. She fumbled into her pocket and produced the outside shell of a chestnut. Delving into it with her index finger and thumb, she produced a ring. It was a particularly ugly signet ring.

"It's Raoul's," she said. "He gave it to me." Raoul was the grandson of her grandfather's friend, she explained.

I examined it with feigned interest. I couldn't help noticing that when Ursuline spoke of Raoul her skin began to glow, her eyes sparkled, and for no good reason she broke into giggles.

Did I realize that most of the girls in her class were already promised? she wanted to know. They would marry as soon as they left school.

"I can't think of anything more terrible, for them or for you," I told her. She wasn't interested in my opinion. She just wanted a listener. She babbled on about school and the future of the girls in her class. Her world! I'd noticed that over the past two years she had slowly become tolerated. I wasn't really listening to her now. I was thinking about her prospects. They didn't look too good. Perhaps I should try to help. It was the first time I'd thought about it. But she deserved more than Taita could offer her, I decided.

All the Rocca brains were wasted, I thought sadly. Jules, who had left school nearly two years ago, was halfheartedly helping on the land. Most of his time was lavished on the hotheaded subversive youth movement he had formed. Rocca was a bandit. Maria was half-crazy, and Sybilia's life had been thrown away. No doubt Ursuline would stay home and help her mother around the house. Suddenly I realized that the torrent of words had ceased. Ursuline's grave eyes were fixed on me. Some sort of a response was necessary.

"What was that you said?" I queried.

"Sometimes Mother is so unapproachable. Please talk to her about it," she said.

"About what?"

"Oh, talk about the absentminded professor. I just told you. I'm engaged. Raoul and I want to get married."

"Oh, hell, Ursuline. Don't talk such a lot of nonsense," I said.

"It's not nonsense. Most of the girls in my class are 'promised.' They'll be married next year. I've always liked Raoul best, and he loves me."

"Promised! What a stupid, old-fashioned idea," I fumed. "Besides, you're at least a year younger than the rest of them."

Ursuline put her arms around me. She was trying to get her own way. "But this time it's different. Jock, listen to me," she said, putting one finger over my lips. "Raoul and I have already decided."

Ursuline was being a fool. She must have a career. All Sybilia's frustrated ambitions and longings were to be fulfilled by her daughter, I knew. She would never allow her to marry in Taita, especially at this age. Even more chilling was the knowledge that no family in Taita would accept Ursuline.

"Jock, listen to me. Please talk to Mother," Ursuline persisted.

"Why should I? I'm entirely against this ridiculous idea. And your mother will be very upset."

"Why? Is it a crime to choose my own future? It's my life, isn't it? Somehow I'm going to show you and Mother that I have a mind of my own."

It was not a subject that would commend me to Sybilia. Finally I decided that this was one of the many problems Father Andrews was better qualified to handle.

CHAPTER 67

How could I talk to Sybilia about something so intensely personal? I was still a stranger, even if I was her daughter's confidant. Besides, I couldn't see much hope for Ursuline. Instead I explained the problem to Father Andrews, leaving him to cope as best he could.

The next morning a choirboy brought me a message from the priest. *A small talk in my garden—at once, if possible,* he had written. I hurried down from my dig, feeling cross.

As I had suspected, he intended that I should be present when he broached the subject with Sybilia. "What has all this to do with me?" I said, feeling exasperated.

"Nothing at all, except that you told me you could arrange a scholarship for Ursuline, and I want you to repeat the offer. Besides, it was you Ursuline went to, not me. She obviously trusts you."

Not long afterward we saw Sybilia outside the gate looking apprehensive.

"The poor lassie," Father Andrews murmured.

"You don't need me," I whispered uncomfortably.

Sybilia pushed the gate open. "Oh, my," she exclaimed.

The high wall enclosed half an acre of well-tended vegetables. Lettuce, cabbage, peas, and flowers grew in straight rows, with water sprayed from long hoses. The priest was wearing old dungarees, and he was raking leaves. He did not look much like a priest. Perhaps that was his intention.

"I had no idea . . . so well hidden." She smiled shyly at Father Andrews. Then she saw me, and her smile faded.

"My secret vice," the priest said.

"Vice?"

"Well, pride is a vice. I'm an efficient gardener, and I wouldn't like to put you Taitans to shame."

She laughed uneasily.

"Well, lassie," he said, indicating the bench, "did you know that Ursuline has been seeing Raoul Pascal secretly?"

She nodded.

"In that case, perhaps you also know that they've exchanged rings. A fine situation! They seem to be very headstrong—the pair of them."

She gasped, clutched her handkerchief over her mouth. "How could she be such a fool?"

"Well, I'm not breaking any trust, my dear. Ursuline asked Jock to speak to you. He, being unwilling to do that, fetched me to deputize."

I scowled at the priest. "It's just that Ursuline trusts me," I said lamely. "But I feel awkward interfering."

She shot a contemptuous glance my way.

The priest watched Sybilia anxiously. "Ursuline wants you to speak to Raoul Pascal's parents." He gave an unhappy laugh. "Now tell me, Sybilia, why didn't you explain these problems to her before?"

"She's only fifteen," Sybilia said.

"You always hide away from the things you can't face up to. You always have. At sixteen most of her class will get married."

"Yes," Sybilia said.

"Well, it's not the job of the village priest to act as a marriage broker, but I'll speak to the Pascals. I can but try."

"What's the point?" Sybilia said bitterly. "Xavier won't give her a dowry. He's made that clear enough. My land . . . Maria's land . . . Rocca controls everything. He won't part with an acre. He never forgave me. Besides, she's not his kin."

"Well, times are changing. Perhaps the Pascals will take an enlightened view and favor young love. They're rich enough. In any event, I'll throw out a couple of hints, and we'll see."

"I want her to be a teacher. I've always wanted that."

"After two years of formal schooling?" I said angrily. "She needs much more. Let her go to college. As a matter of fact, I've managed to obtain a scholarship for her."

"We both know who will be financing it. I don't want to resurrect old arguments," she said bitterly.

I shrugged and glanced at the priest.

"Evidently Ursuline has no such ambitions." The priest's voice was bitingly cool. "But what if she should change her mind? Would you be able to pay for her education?"

"No," Sybilia said hopelessly. "I've been saving for years. A few eggs here, a chicken or two. I can manage a part of it. Maybe in a year or so . . . Oh, dear God," she sighed. "There can't be anything more soul-destroying than failing your children."

"Well, I have an idea, but let's leave it until I've spoken to Raoul's family."

"What's the use? But thank you anyway." Sybilia hurried away.

"There, I warned you," I said to him. "It would have been far better if I had not been here. I should have kept out of this."

"Yes, you're right. I made a mistake," he said. "I'm sorry."

There wasn't much I could say after that apology.

"All the same," Father Andrews grumbled, half to himself, "I don't understand why two intelligent adults start acting like children the moment they get together."

It fell to me to tell Ursuline the facts of Taitan village life. It wasn't planned. It just happened that way.

Father Andrews saw the Pascal family. They were appalled by the suggestion and terrified at the thought of a scandal, he told me rather sadly. For some time they had been thinking of marrying their son to Castelli's daughter. Now they decided to push ahead with all speed.

The priest had seen Sybilia, and she was not the least surprised, he told me. They had asked Ursuline to be home at five that evening. The Rocca women and the priest would break the bad news to her and try to persuade her to enter a convent.

Ursuline looked exhilarated when she arrived at my dig around lunchtime. Her eyes were shining, her cheeks were flushed, and I noticed belatedly that she was turning into a woman. She would be lovely, I thought with a pang. I produced a roll and sausage for her and listened while she told me her news.

"This afternoon Father Andrews is coming to the house to talk to me. Mama will be there. And Maria." She giggled. "I'm not supposed to know what it's about, but I do."

She fumbled in her pocket and brought out a note. From the paper I could see that it had been smoothed and read and folded again many times. Yesterday Raoul had tossed it into her basket, she confided. It read:

Father Andrews has been to see my parents. Grandfather is talking to me about my future this evening. Forever yours, Raoul.

"Forever yours," she murmured. Her hand went up to her hair, which was hanging loosely over her shoulders. She pushed it back in a self-conscious, womanly gesture. Suddenly she reached forward and kissed me impulsively. "Oh, Jock, I'm so happy, I can't sit still." She leaped up and prowled around the excavation. Every now and then she clasped her hands and bit her lip.

"Ursuline, come and sit down," I said. So it was to be my lot to dampen that rapt expression. I felt like a heel. But how could I let her down?

"Ursuline, you've always been a brave girl," I began, "but you're in a singularly unfortunate position in that you don't have a dowry."

"No dowry?" Her eyes closed momentarily. "Does that matter?" Her eyes searched my face for reassurance.

"Yes, it matters," I said heavily. "If it were up to me, or your mother, you'd have a good dowry, but all the family's land—all that your mother brought into the marriage, and Maria, too, come to that, is in your grandfather's hands. He'll not give you a dowry because, strictly speaking, you're not his kin."

I couldn't look at her. Instead I gazed steadfastly at my feet. "As for me, I would willingly give you a dowry, but it would have to be in cash, not in land, since I don't have any. Perhaps there's some for sale. I could look around. I've done well this year." I felt so sad. At that moment I would have bought Taita for her, if I could.

Ursuline crumpled onto a boulder and sat there with her chin in her hands. Obviously she had never given the matter of a dowry a thought. "Raoul loves me for myself," she said after a while.

Should I carry on? It would be cruel to leave her hoping and worrying all day, I decided.

"It's not just a question of your dowry, Ursuline. Marriage in these parts is like a truce between clans. You have no father, therefore there's no family. Family ties are of the utmost importance in Corsica. Personally I find it archaic. But quite frankly I can't see you marrying anyone from these parts."

"Anyone?" she cried. "I don't want anyone. It's Raoul I love." She paused to gather her thoughts. "And Raoul?" she said abruptly, turning away so that I would not see her tears. "What has Raoul to say about all this? He's always known my situation."

"Raoul became engaged to Carlo Castelli's daughter last night."

"*Impossible! He loves me. You're lying.*"

"You do have other alternatives," I went on, ignoring her. "If you were an American child, you'd be told not to be absurd. Thinking about marriage at fifteen years of age is crazy. However, I know the customs here are different. I'd hoped you'd go to college in America." Was it wrong to press my own ambitions for her?

"As a matter of fact, I've succeeded in getting you a scholarship to my old school. Sybilia won't hear of it, but I'll work on her. Do you want to talk about it now or later, when you've recovered?"

"I'll never recover. This is all Mother's fault. I'm to pay the price of her foolishness."

"Listen to me, Ursuline, and stop feeling sorry for yourself. If Raoul doesn't want you without a dowry, then he's not worth having. Father Andrews wants you to be a nun. You've been accepted as a novice by the Sacred Heart Convent, near Ajaccio. You could be trained as a teacher and sent out as a missionary. You may be sent to Africa, or the Far East. When they put this idea to you tonight, I want you to remember my alternative. Okay?"

"Okay." She wiped her tears with the hem of her skirt and stood up. "Don't worry. I will never be a nun," she said. "Oh, Jock, I know you're trying your best. But Mother's wicked. I'm the evidence of her shame, so she wants to get rid of me."

She stood up quickly, burst into tears, and ran down the hill. I called to her, but she kept going.

Two weeks later, at eight in the morning, early in July, Raoul Pascal married Carlo Castelli's daughter. It was not a very good match, since Castelli was only a shoemaker. However, his daughter brought a small piece of property to the marriage.

"She's ugly," Ursuline said, watching the ceremony through my binoculars. "She's ugly and fat, and I hope he dies of misery."

"He won't," I said, "but she might. Have you noticed what a bully his mother is? By tomorrow she'll be the family servant. I wouldn't wish Madame Pascal on my enemy."

Ursuline began to giggle. The giggles became laughter. "Raoul looks so silly with that mustache he's grown." She burst out laughing again. "Yes, you're right, Jock. I'm lucky to be free of Madame Pascal."

She spent the day helping me, and I thought she'd come through the crisis very well. But I was wrong. A month later she told me that she had joined Jules's political group. They called it "Sword of the Nation." She had taken their pledge, and she was going to dedicate her life to Corsica's problems. "Far better to be a revolutionary than just an old maid," she told me. "Now I have a mission in life."

Over the next few weeks she learned to shoot, take photographs, and churn out leaflets on an old printing press. In her spare time she cooked and cleaned and carried provisions to the camp. Suddenly Ursuline had become a fierce patriot.

I understood her motivation. Her Corsican birthright was beyond dispute. It was something real and believable, and it was hers, so she clung to it. No one could take that away from her.

CHAPTER 68

August, 1959

Local members and leaders of the National Front were holding a series of meetings in the village square. It was about the war and a certain Major Ernst Krag, who had commanded the German occupation troops. I was not entirely clear what it all meant. The words "honor," "dignity of man," "freedom," and "revenge" were repeated ad nauseam. With frequent breaks, the meeting continued for over two days. The speeches were mainly in the local dialect, and everyone seemed to be voicing their opinions in turn.

It was harvesttime, but who cared? Corsican honor was at stake. Shepherds, farmers, tradesmen, and woodcutters neglected their work. Everyone had something to say.

In spite of almost total discord, there was at least one point of agreement: absolutely no one believed they should turn the other cheek. Something had to be done. But what? Some felt that Corsican justice was a matter of concern only to Corsicans. Others believed it was a matter of international concern. The dispute kept them arguing for two days and most of the night between. Finally it began to look as if those men with the greatest stamina would win the day.

I listened in to the meetings from time to time, particularly in the evenings when I had nothing better to do. I was struck by the high standard of rhetoric in men who were mainly uneducated.

Xavier Rocca craftily waited until everyone else had had their say before he set about winning their votes.

"I'm a reasonable man," he began tentatively. "Aren't we all? Let's face it, none of us here believe in fairy stories. Yet I seem to have been listening to a few here this evening."

He looked around contemptuously. "Here's one I've been listening to: it's about the possibility of the Western Allies restarting the war crimes trials for the sake of a few dead Corsicans.

"Well, my friends . . . if you kept up with the news, you'd know that the world is trying to forget about the war. We're partners in the Common Market. It's bad form to remember things people did sixteen years ago. Perhaps we should forget, too. Forget our children tortured to death; forget the insult to Corsica as the Boche defiled our island's soil. Is that what you want? What is it to be? Justice? Or forgiveness?"

"Justice," the assembly roared back.

"Well, my friends, you don't surprise me. After all, you're Corsican, aren't you? We've always taken responsibility for our own moral standards. Every Corsican householder has always been prepared to play the role of jury, judge, and executioner in times of trouble. We know in our hearts what's right and what's wrong. We've never shirked our responsibilities.

"If we were American, or British, and our daughter was raped, or our son murdered, we'd pick up the telephone and dial a number. That would be the beginning and the end of our responsibility. Justice is done for them by a team of trained lawmen who get well paid for it.

"Well, I thank God we're Corsican."

With his curious sixth sense of crowd mentality, Rocca knew that he had his audience right with him. He was working toward his climax.

"In Corsica, there's never been the triumph of one class over another. Our society is based upon a truce maintained between men who are free and equal. This truce rests upon our moral code and the acceptance of the dignity of man. *The breaking of this truce has always led to the vendetta.*

"But Major Krag came here with his fascist army and stripped us of our dignity—destroyed our honor, disregarded justice. I say there's only one way to deal with Krag, and that's the vendetta."

The vote was taken. Almost everyone was in favor of the vendetta. Xavier Rocca went off with the other leaders of the National Front to plot the hows and whens of the matter.

It was all great stuff, but since it was only theoretical, I couldn't see much point in it all. I was not aware that Major Ernst Krag and his family were touring Corsica.

CHAPTER 69

A strange phenomenon occurred in the village square at exactly four P.M. on the first Friday of that fateful August. I've never found a reasonable explanation of these events and I still get goose pimples thinking about it. Imagine the scene: The island was baking in a heat wave. I was excavating a cave in the blistering heat about two hundred meters above the lake. How cool the lake looked, glittering turquoise far below. I had a terrific hankering to plunge into it, but I'd trained myself to stick to my routine: stop work at four-thirty, make notes until five, and only then did I allow myself the luxury of a lazy crawl around the icy water.

That afternoon, however, I was disturbed by the sound of drums. An irregular beat! I remember thinking that the drummers could do with some training.

The sound seemed to be coming from the village square. I guessed the village youth were practicing for St. Augustine's Day, which they seemed to be tackling in earnest this year. Three weeks ago, to Father Andrews's astonishment and pleasure, Rocca had asked that the entire village be roped in to improve their patron saint's day celebrations. Whatever the reason for the drums, I wanted to record it, so I packed up early.

It was hard to hurry though the somnolent, moist air. The maquis was particularly lovely. Extreme heat had toasted the herbs to an indescribable fragrance. Several times I disturbed herds of goats and wild boars, but I didn't linger because the drums were quickening their beat and I was filled with a sense of urgency.

The square was cool, and I paused to thrust my head under the fountain. Then I turned to speak to an old woman sitting on the bench. "Why are they beating the drums?" I asked.

She jumped up, gave me a curious look, crossed herself, and hurried away. I didn't take much notice but sat on the bench and fished out my notebook.

Shortly afterward the drums increased in intensity. It was too much! The noise seemed to be coming from the Rocca house now, which was odd. Sure enough, the front door was flung open, and Maria Rocca came running out, cupping her ears with her hands. I could hardly blame her. When she ran to the center of the square and collapsed in a heap near the fountain, I jumped up in alarm. She moaned quietly and then started to speak in a curious, high-pitched, singsong voice, more like chanting than talking.

Was she ill? Had she received some bad news? I rushed to help her to her feet but found myself grabbed from behind by the priest. He surprised me with his strength.

"Leave her," he gasped. "She has these attacks from time to time, and I've found it's best to let them take their course."

I turned and saw that he looked worried. "Probably the drums," I said. "It's loud enough to give her a migraine. What's it all about?"

"What drums?"

Now it was my turn to look alarmed. "For God's sake!" I snarled. "Can't you hear the drums?"

"No!" He crossed himself silently. His expression of alarm convinced me that he was not playing the fool.

"What the hell's going on?"

"Jock, my friend," the priest said, "you are in mortal danger. You must come to mass. They say the spirits of the maquis beat the drums to herald a death. Sometimes, they say, the spirits come down from the mountains and perform a ghost funeral. Many older villagers have claimed to hear the drums, a few have claimed to see the funerals. The victim hears nothing, sees nothing at all."

Well, that was some huge relief.

"But you . . . you are not Corsican. They say that if you hear the drums, the spirits have taken you for their own. Come to mass," he repeated.

Superstitious mumbo-jumbo. I turned my attention to Maria Rocca, who was still chanting. I must admit at that moment I felt more elated than anything else. I had found the *mazzeri*. I should have guessed it was Maria—she looked the part exactly: her black hair was spread wildly over her shoulders, she stood pointing dramatically in the center of the square, her blue eyes fixed on nothing. She was obviously in a trance.

My understanding of the dialect is poor. It is a curious language, part French, part Genoese, some Latin, and some Berber. I only managed to catch a little of what she said, but she repeated herself several times. Piecing the words together, it went something like this:

"The drums are calling . . . the spirits are calling . . . calling him here . . . back to Corsica . . . back to die . . . to pay the penance for his crimes . . . the spirits are crying for vengeance, they will bring him back, his blood shall run on the cobbles. It will seep into the earth. They will not wait for long . . . sleep soundly, spirit of my son, sleep soundly, your blood will be paid for. . . ."

And so on. There was a good deal of repetition about blood on the cobbles, but that was about all there was, or all I could make out, until I caught the name Ernst Krag.

Suddenly Maria groaned and sat down on the fountain bench, holding her head. The priest took the stone cup hanging on a long chain and gave her some water, which she drank. She looked around, half fearful and half embarrassed. Then she stood up and hurried back to her house. The door slammed shut, and that was that. The villagers, who had gathered silently, began to talk to each other in undertones.

I felt exhausted, but thank God the drums were gradually fading into the mountains. It sounded as if a ghostly squad were marching away. I was left feeling light-headed.

The word had gotten around that I had heard the drums. People were staring, but not unkindly. I felt strange and very pleased with myself. So the famous *mazzeri* was none other then Maria Rocca, Sybilia's mother-in-law. Typical of them to conceal this information from me.

A quick survey revealed that of the twenty-five people in the square, only a few had heard the drums, one had seen the ghostly figure of the deceased Michel Rocca, wearing battle dress, and the remainder had seen and heard nothing, except, of course, for Maria's performance. However, they all remembered her past predictions, which, they claimed, had never been wrong, and were now eagerly awaiting bloodshed in the square.

I went on to question Father Andrews, who appeared to be humoring me, as if I were a mental patient. I took full advantage of this and persuaded him to reveal his precious and hitherto well-guarded research.

Because the priest thought it might help me back to reality, he actually showed me his bulky file on *mazzeri* and witchcraft. Of this, there was a large section on Maria, concisely and factually recorded.

"Maria Rocca is a good Christian," he insisted several times.

After we had shared a bottle of wine and eaten his excellent village-made bread and garlic polony, he told me the little that he understood. I've digested what he told me over the next three hours:

Maria Rocca was initiated into the ranks of the mazzeri *by an aunt when she was only thirteen. At the time she did not believe in witchcraft (and she tried not to believe in it later on). She dreaded experiencing these "nightmares," as she called them.*

At the age of twelve Maria was paralyzed, but no one could find out why. Eventually her condition was blamed on an attack of polio. She resigned herself to spending the rest of her life in a wheelchair. A year passed.

One night she was awakened by a voice calling her name, telling her to get up and walk in the maquis. She managed to stand, although her legs felt like rubber, to use her own description. Her aunt was waiting for her outside. She handed her a long stick, rather like an old-fashioned shepherd's crook.

They climbed into the mountains to hunt wild boar. Eventually her aunt pointed to one, and Maria struck it on the head with her crook. When they turned it over, Maria saw that it had the face of her aunt.

When Maria awoke in the morning, she found to her joy that she could walk, but her aunt died shortly afterward of cancer. Since then Maria claims to have had several visions, or trances, or whatever you like to call them.

Evidently a mazzeri *operates on behalf of her clan, as a mouthpiece of the collective psyche. She has only one function, that of predicting death. The priest, like the good Catholic he was, felt that if it was abnormal and if it couldn't be deemed a miracle, then it had to be Satan's work.*

To my mind, the explanation is nothing more mystical than Jung's shared subconscious, operating in birds and beasts (as instinct) and in people (as second sight and thought transference). Wolves and hunting dogs operate through mass communication. The termites' and the baboons' shared psyche has been brilliantly documented by Eugene Marais. The priest had some very convincing instances to suggest that it existed among the villagers.

There is a long study to be undertaken here, comparing local beliefs and sayings with those of Brittany and Wales, where phantom funerals have been seen within living memory. Perhaps I will tackle it when I leave Corsica. If I leave Corsica.

Now why was I feeling fearful? Why was it that I was loath to record my visit to Maria following her vision in the square? Was it because I was afraid that putting her words on paper would put the seal on them?

The truth was, I went to interview her and found her sitting in her kitchen, sipping tea. She did not invite me to have a cup with her, which was unusual. Instead she stared at my forehead with her strangely penetrating blue eyes and said: "Leave Corsica now. If you stay here, you will bring anguish and death. Go now. Leave the island. I'm begging you."

I decided that I needed a rest. The next morning I packed up early and went down the coast for a couple of days' underwater swimming.

It seemed to me there's no doubt at all that my brain had reached a level of consciousness where I could share the psychic unity of the mountain Corsicans. Either that or I was about to have a breakdown.

CHAPTER 70

St. Augustine's Day, Tuesday, August 28, was unbearably hot. The sirocco had strengthened during the night, and by morning it had reached gale force. Tempers soared as chimney pots tumbled and tiles ricocheted across the square. In homes, scrubbed and polished for the celebrations, dust infiltrated every crack and sabotaged the housewives' efforts. Tongues were coated, hair was grimy, and even the food tasted of cloying dust. Occasionally a strong gust would ring the church bell, making everyone uneasy.

The procession had lined up behind the church: the choirboys in their white smocks, the girls in their new white dresses. But before they could move into the square, the flowers, veils, statues, and even the priest's golden cope were streaked with grime. Everyone felt scruffy and cross.

I watched them, took notes, and hung about the village, feeling sticky and irritable, wondering if the saint's day celebrations were worth missing a day's digging. To my surprise, there were far more men than usual loitering in the square. Grim-faced and tense, they waited for the religious procession without a pious look among them.

Moving around, I mentally ticked off the names: Pascal; Pinelli the cheese maker, his soulful eyes glittering; one-eyed Giacobbi, who'd walked ten miles to be here; Castelli, looking thinner, if that was possible; then Leca, Padovani, and Bonnelli. I was surprised. The Roccas never closed the bistro. I was startled to see one of the Bertoli twins from Marseilles standing in the shadow of the chestnut grove. There were several strangers hanging around, too.

I'll never understand them. To think that this tough bunch could be so inspired with religious enthusiasm.

I made a few more notes in my book. Apart from the wind, the village looked glorious. Flags were flapping noisily from every window, there were little statues of the Virgin, St. Augustine, and his mother, Ste. Monica, in every nook and cranny. Flowers by the armful decorated every corner, and bunting hung across the square. Father Andrews looked magnificent in his gold alb and cope, his eyes gleaming.

He hurried toward me. "Quite a turnout," he muttered, unable to conceal his satisfaction. A sudden gust splattered his face with dust.

"I hate this goddamn wind," I said.

"Satan's breath. That's what I call it," said the priest. "It blows no end of mischief into men's minds. Seeds of lust and anger, grudges they'd almost forgotten. Everything flourishes when the sirocco blows. I'm glad you're here," he went on. "Naturally I've chosen the parable of the prodigal son. As you no doubt know, St. Augustine is the symbol of sinners and forgiveness. God pardons us all, if we repent in time. This is the day to remember the importance of mercy." He took his place at the head of the column, and the procession started off along its route.

Antoine Romanetti came up to me. He was dressed in his best black corduroy, his hair was plastered down with grease, and there was a bright polka dotted scarf at his throat.

"Might I trouble you to ring the bell?" he asked with old-fashioned courtesy. "I've wrenched my back, and it takes some pulling."

"Why, sure. Why not?" I felt pleased. It was the first time anyone had asked me to do anything.

"Be sure to hold on," Romanetti said gravely. "A sudden gust can whip you clean out of the tower. Give about two or three hard pulls every minute. That's what the good father prefers. You'll have a lovely view of the procession from up there."

When I'd climbed into the bell tower, I was surprised to find how high it was. I seemed to hang over the square. Literally a bird's-eye view, I thought, feeling pleased. I took out my notebook and found a handy ledge to write on. While waiting, I jotted down notes about the decorations.

After a while I remembered the bell. Without much enthusiasm, I caught the rope and gave a tug. Nothing happened! I tried again harder and managed to get a feeble clang. At the sound, a number of villagers looked up, and some of them started clapping and jeering. I distinctly heard Bonnelli say, "I hope that shit-bag falls out of there and takes his notebook with him."

I yelled back an equally obscene retort and instantly regretted it.

No one looked up, no one heard me. That was amazing. Belatedly I realized that the bell tower and the encircling buildings had created a whispering gallery. I could hear every word that was said in the square below, but they could not hear me at all. I felt foolish and sprang at the rope, forcing three good solid tolls out of the bell.

Leaning against the alcove, I saw the choirboys cross the square in a neat double line, looking cherubic in their white smocks. After them came six young men shouldering the statue, which, buffeted by the gale, was tipping at a dangerous angle. Then the young girls followed, clutching long white dresses with one hand while trying to hold their flowers with the other.

At that moment, a family who looked like tourists came puffing up the last few steps and onto the cobbles. They were being shepherded by Xavier Rocca with Guerrini and several other men I'd not seen before who were obviously Corsican. All were breathless as they leaned against the stone wall at the side of the square.

The tourist was balding, thick-set, and dressed in hunting gear: a safari suit, hiking boots, a Tyrolean hat with a feather in the side, his rifle slung over his shoulder. His skin was bright red, perhaps from the heat, and glistening with sweat. He was smiling broadly.

His wife was blond and pretty, with square shoulders. Only her hair was hanging lank and disheveled in a fashionable Brigitte Bardot style that gave her a slightly gaunt appearance. Their two daughters, who were about ten and twelve years old, were dressed alike in pink shorts and white T-shirts. They laughed delightedly at the sight of the flags and flowers. Shortly afterward they were thrust into the procession by a smiling Rocca. Their mother frowned, then shrugged and followed them.

The procession wound off on its circuitous route. They would pass along the clifftop to the waterfall, over the bridge, around the mausoleums to the back of the cemetery, and into the square again. This should take, in all, half an hour.

No one in the packed square appeared to be following the procession. I felt a twinge of unease when I saw Rocca take hold of the tourist's rifle, which he slung over his shoulder, while clapping the man on the back.

"Let me assist you. You're not as fit as a hunter should be," he bellowed. "Anyone can see that. Why, look. You're sweating like a pig and puffing like an old goat."

"My God," the tourist replied, ignoring the insult. "I thought I would only see mouflons on this precipitous mountain ledge. Instead I find a whole village." He gave a deep belly laugh. "Look at you all, so agile and fit, and no wonder, if you climb this way often." He was smiling, but it seemed to me that he acted uneasy. Why?

As the procession wound away out of sight, a hush fell upon the square. Something was wrong, but I couldn't work out what it was. I had the impression I was watching a play. A bad play! Perhaps because it all seemed so rehearsed, or was it because of the nonchalant groups of men gossiping together or merely waiting? For what? The only sound was the sighing of the wind, which seemed to have dropped considerably.

Suddenly I remembered the bells. I sprang up, grabbed the rope, and gave three sharp tugs, that nearly dislocated my arms.

As I let the rope go, something caught my attention. It was a cloud of dust streaming toward Taita in the valley below. Eventually I saw that it was a four-wheel-drive vehicle racing toward Taita. It could only be Inspector Hiller. Only he had that type of vehicle. Was Hiller coming to see the celebrations? Surely not.

"Well, Major Ernst Krag," Rocca's voice boomed out as if he wanted all the village to hear, "at last you see Taita. You'll meet a few old friends here from the war. Bonnelli, Leca, Castelli . . . well, just about everyone here was in the Resistance. Of course, many of them are dead. You'll remember Michel Rocca, my son, I expect. You had many conversations with him."

Major Krag turned deathly pale. He rubbed his hands together. Then he burst out laughing. "You're making a joke? Is that it? I've never been to Corsica in my life," he said loudly. "I haven't had the pleasure of meeting any of these gentlemen."

Krag! I searched for the connection. Then I remembered Maria's vision. *His blood shall run on the cobbles.* Jesus! They'd brought Krag here to murder him. I thought of Ambrosini lying in his coffin. "God help him! They're going to murder him in cold blood," I whispered.

I had to do something. Then I thought, *But why? It's their affair. I'm here to observe. What has all this to do with me? No doubt Krag deserves whatever he gets.*

But I couldn't stand by and allow this to happen. I raced down the spiral stone steps but found Romanetti blocking my way. His rifle was cocked and ready, three armed shepherds behind him.

"I like you, Walters." Romanetti's menacing stare belied his words. "But if you know what's good for you, you'll get back up there. You're trapped, so you might as well enjoy the show. It'll be over soon. That bastard will die today, and there's nothing you can do about it."

"Aren't you ashamed?" I asked. "A whole village out to murder a single man."

"Murder? This is a vendetta! Go back to your books, Walters. You've been asking enough questions these past two years. Here's the real thing, but I see you have no stomach for it."

"Not for terrorism. You'll all pay the price."

"We're more interested in imposing justice than saving our own skins."

"The war's over."

"The war will never be over."

I raced back and leaned over the balustrade. I was a spectator watching a horror movie. Inspired with the need to do something, I rang the church bell several times in rapid succession. Then I regretted my action. No one looked up, and the ringing seemed to bind me into an unholy alliance with what they were about to do.

At that moment there were shots from the side of the square. I saw Hiller standing at the edge of the mob, two policemen by his side. He fired again into the air.

"Thank God," I muttered.

The police were shouting, "Make way. Move off. Let us through," in the dialect.

Hiller was panting and red-faced. "Move away!" he yelled as he pushed through the crowd. When he reached Rocca's side, he called out: "In the name of the law, I arrest you, Major Ernst Krag, for crimes perpetrated against the French people." His voice cut like a gunshot. "Come on, hand him over," he added. "Major Krag's going to stand trial, and we'll see he gets what he deserves."

At these words, Krag abandoned all pretenses. There was a scuffle as he tried to fight his way toward the police. When his hand grabbed his hunting knife, Rocca, who was sticking close to him, squeezed his arm until the knife clattered to the ground.

"You won't be needing it again," he said.

A shepherd picked up the knife and thrust it into his pocket. Another took the rifle from Xavier and began to examine it.

This, more than anything, unnerved Krag. Suddenly his knees buckled, but he quickly regained his composure.

"What is the meaning of this charade?" he said. His voice seemed to be pitched too high. "This is a case of mistaken identity. I was never a major. Merely a corporal on the eastern front. I have never been to Corsica in my life before."

The crowd began to close in on Krag, pushing him toward the center of the square. Hiller was elbowed aside.

"Stop! In the name of the law," Hiller yelled, his voice high-pitched and ineffectual. "Xavier Rocca, hand over this man into police custody. This is my last warning."

Three service revolvers were pointing straight at Rocca's head.

"Three guns against this crowd," he sneered. "You may kill me, you may get one or two of my colleagues, but you, my friend, will be torn limb from limb before you leave the square."

Hiller faltered. He looked around and saw the truth of Rocca's words. At his command the police put their guns down.

The villagers pushed and pulled Krag toward the center of the square. They walked in total silence. All I could hear was the victim's rasping breath.

Krag seemed to have trouble moving his legs. Rocca crossed himself and took a long leather thong out of his pocket.

The women began to chant in their shrill, piercing voices: "Kill! Kill! Kill the Boche. Kill him." The young girls hid their faces and yelped in horror and excitement. Ursuline and Jules were agog with excitement as they clambered up a chestnut tree for a grandstand view.

"Major Ernst Krag, for your crimes against Corsica and Corsicans, you are to die," Rocca called out.

At these words, the German bellowed like a bullock being slaughtered.

Hiller, surrounded by villagers, watched from the back of the crowd. Rocca wound the thong around the major's neck. Two burly villagers grabbed his arms from behind. Krag's eyes opened wide in terror, his face turned purple as he gasped for air.

There was a sudden lunge forward from the crowd, a surge

that knocked Rocca aside. He hung on to the cord, but slowly he was ousted and forced away as the villagers moved in.

Now Krag was making strange, inhuman noises. His arms came free, and for a moment he seemed to be swimming in a human tide. Then he sank under it.

The crowd had taken over. It was intent upon tearing Krag limb from limb. There was a low, guttural moan, like the growl of some savage creature. Each one of them was caught in a strange metamorphosis—animals merged into one conscious will. They moved over Krag, growling softly, rummaging for blood, tearing the flesh.

I remembered the priest's words: Satan's beast! I shuddered.

At the edge of a crowd another act in the horror movie was being enacted, as Hiller tried to arrest Xavier Rocca. Under his unwavering stare, Hiller faltered, put down his gun, and looked away, to the jeers and laughs of the villagers.

"I'll be back with reinforcements," he said. "Next time you won't be laughing."

Rocca ignored him. He was looking for Sybilia. He found her and took hold of her arm, forcing her to look at him. "Your husband is fully avenged," he told her sternly.

"But you are alive," she said loudly. She jerked her arm free.

Rocca swore and turned his back on her. As he walked across the square to his house, Hiller took aim, then thought better of it. For the third time that morning, he put away his gun.

Suddenly the square was emptying. The shepherds blocking the stairs shouldered their guns and left. The women, heads hanging, shuffled away. The beast had disintegrated. From the distance the procession could be seen returning from behind the cemetery.

A dove cooed in the branches overhead, and I realized that the wind had stopped suddenly, as it usually did, leaving a breathlessly beautiful morning.

And I, who had been feeling sickened by the grisly scene, now felt bewildered by the sudden end to it all. An anticlimax! Was that it? No orchestration, no curtain calls, no applause?

I was wrong. From behind the cemetery the procession was returning. They were singing loudly, and I was struck by the beautiful voices of the choirboys. I caught the words "mercy," "forgiveness," and "penitence."

So much for mercy, I thought. All that was left of Krag was a pulpy mess of flesh and rags and two boots lying some distance away.

CHAPTER 71

November, 1959

The fall passed quickly. By early November it was clear that it would be a long, hard winter. I'd developed such an aversion to Madame Barnard's feather mattress that I made up my mind to rent a small cottage by the sea and spend the weekends there, catching up on the paperwork.

It seemed a good idea, but I wasted three weeks trying to locate the owners of various properties that appeared to be abandoned but habitable. Eventually I went to an estate agent in Galeria.

The agent found an ideal cottage nearby. My enthusiasm waned when I discovered that there were over thirty joint owners, all of whom had to be traced and their acceptance gained before the lease could be signed. After obtaining fourteen signatures I told the agent to forget the whole idea.

"Ah, well," the agent sighed, "that's Corsica for you."

Snow fell early that year, and the mountains took on a curious two-dimensional aspect. They looked like a theater backdrop, one range behind the other, going on endlessly from white to off-white to gray. The last peaks were just a faint gray smudge against the pearly sky. The countryside was white and fresh, too. It was all so beautiful, but for working purposes winter was a nightmare; weeks of sludge alternated with weeks of frozen ground. Digging became a punishment.

I caught the flu and then bronchitis from working in the

rain and sleeping out. One morning I found I was too ill to get up. I lay in my sleeping bag in the cave feeling sorry for myself.

Eventually Sybilia arrived to find out why I hadn't purchased my food. Like all healthy men, I've always felt sickness to be a weakness, and I felt ashamed.

I began by blaming Sybilia for avoiding me. When she denied this, I grabbed her arm and pulled her toward me. "You're driving me crazy," I muttered hoarsely. "I can't stop longing for you. Don't you have any feelings?"

She fought me off. She didn't have to try too hard. Rape isn't my style. Then she sat on a rock, stared at me sadly, and said: "I can't give you what you want, Jock. There's nothing left of me to give. Robin took it all. I feel . . . well, I feel empty; emotionally drained. You want sex, which is natural enough, but I . . . I can't explain."

I understood her. In a way, we were much alike. I'd always avoided intimate friendships with women. "All right," I blurted out this dismal morning, amazing myself. "Don't pretend you don't feel close to me. I'll settle for friendship. Now for God's sake, stop avoiding me."

Then I felt embarrassed. I grumbled on about the laziness of Corsican villagers who would not turn their hands to a day's digging no matter how much money was offered them.

"You don't understand us at all," she explained. "You just want to hire labor, not people. But if you would only explain about your work. Why not? You've never bothered with us. You behave as if we're imbeciles. Even schoolboys would be better than nothing," she babbled on in a torrent of anger. "If they thought for one moment they were doing something for Corsica, they'd volunteer. So don't blame us, blame yourself."

This stream of voluble patois took my breath away, and I had to spend a minute or two fathoming it out, by which time she'd calmed down.

"D'you think it would work? I mean, lectures—that sort of thing?"

"I already told you what I think."

A week later, when I had recovered, I gave in to Sybilia's nagging and planned a series of lectures. The priest offered me the library hall free of charge and promised to use his muscle to make sure that at least the front two rows were filled.

To my amazement, most of the village turned out. The hall was overflowing as I talked about Corsican prehistory and its unique artistic development.

At question time all the village men asked the same thing: Where exactly was I planning to extend my dig? They didn't have any real interest in archaeology, I discovered, although they were polite enough.

The lectures, which I repeated in three neighboring villages, brought a few schoolboys to volunteer their help, but after a month most of them dwindled away. Jules, however, became a regular helper. He worked hard, and this surprised me, for I'd often seen him drinking in the bistro, and I gathered he was lazy.

As the weeks passed I caught a glimpse of some of the traumas the boy was shouldering. Apart from the stigma of his mother's reputation, the Roccas were the most powerful and respected family in the district, in a country where ancient clan hierarchy still counted above all else. Family pride and honor was the basis of the Corsicans' traditional life. It overflowed into Corsican politics. With his father dead and his grandfather hiding in the mountains half the time, the onus was on Jules, at eighteen, to lead the family. He had to assert himself in the political arena. This meant that most of the district's youngsters would support him in whichever direction he went.

Consequently he was inclined to show off and swagger about the trenches, surly and uncooperative, while desperately seeking assurance from me. When we were working side by side, we had long arguments. His main preoccupation was Corsican politics and the economy. Jules maintained that Corsica had been cheated. The island did not receive its fair share of the nation's cash. Consequently there were no jobs for youngsters like him.

I tried to explain the background: Since Napoleon's days, large numbers of Corsican youth had entered the colonial service and eventually retired to the island with a good pension. Suddenly France had accepted a policy of decolonization. But Corsica was unable to provide alternative livelihoods, for there was no industry.

"So what's the answer?" Jules plagued me repeatedly.

"More capital investment; the rapid development of tourism and agriculture; new industries to create more jobs; better communication with France." I spent hours explaining basic economics to the boy.

Jules had other problems. He had been groomed to take over his grandfather's position as the local clan leader, but training was not enough. He had to prove himself the better man and come up with a viable policy, if he was to keep the communists at bay.

I began to worry about the boy. I talked about him to Sybilia one day when she came to help at the dig. "Why should Jules shoulder all this responsibility?" I asked. "Send him to the university. Let him be a boy while he's still young. He's missing his youth. I can organize an American scholarship for him. He's a bright boy."

Sybilia laughed at me. "He's not a boy, he's a man. He has inherited his responsibilities, together with this land and the birthright of being a Corsican. He cannot escape from it. Sometimes I fear you've missed the point entirely here. We're proud of our traditions, and we love our country."

"Sometimes you make me sick," I snarled at her. Without really being aware of it, I'd become fond of Jules, and I wanted to help him. As a bystander it was obvious that Jules's anger was leading him to anarchy. Before long he'd be in trouble with the authorities, I warned Sybilia.

"Since when has a Corsican run away from trouble?" she retorted. "Then he would not be Corsican."

It was my birthday. In the evening I decided to visit the bistro and stand drinks all around. I sat at a table drinking eau-de-vie while Romanetti poured out his soul in ancient laments. He gave himself completely to the music, his body vibrating with his song, his skin damp with sweat, his eyes burning with passion. His heartrending cry of love and separation laid a spell on the room. Gnarled old men remembered how it had been and wiped their eyes on their neck scarves. Even Bonnelli sat at the counter, his head held between his hands. The shepherd's cries seemed to intensify my own aloneness.

It was after midnight when I reeled off to the Widow Barnard's apartment, but the house looked twice as dismal in the moonlight. Stucco that had fallen from the facade, exposing red patches of rotting brick, looked like suppurating wounds. The smell of garbage and the garden privy turned my stomach, which suddenly revolted against the evening's abuse. I threw up in the gardenias.

Better to sleep at the cave, I thought, in spite of the cold. So I staggered up through the maquis, sobering rapidly as I climbed. The amphitheater, as I thought of the ancient quarry, was brilliantly lit by reflected moonlight on hoarfrost. On one side of the open arena was a huge shadow thrown over the ground. I hardly noticed it, until it moved. Then I heard a spade strike against granite. I jumped and moved to the shadow of a thorn bush. The figure of a tall man stood there staring at me in silence. He was dressed in black corduroy, his rifle over his shoulder, his spade in his hand. It had to be Xavier Rocca. There was no one else that big in Taita.

When my initial shock had passed, I stepped toward him and called out: "Hi there. Want to join the dig?"

He waved briefly and disappeared into the maquis, agile as a mountain goat.

I was too tired to wonder about it. I scrambled into my sleeping bag, slept soundly, and awoke to find the sun was shining the next morning.

CHAPTER 72

January, 1960

Since the execution of Major Ernst Krag, the Rocca household had been thrown into confusion. At first Xavier enjoyed the accolades of the village. Later he became moody. Not that he ever regretted his action. After all, he was not a man to shirk responsibility, but the harsh reality was that his life was ruined. He would have to head the local branch of the National Front as a guerrilla leader. Hiller would be back with a regiment of police and a warrant for his arrest. From now on he would never know a moment's peace, and there would be many nights spent out in the maquis. At sixty-five, he confided in me, he was too old for rough living. But what could he do? At least Michel could rest in peace.

Three weeks after Krag's execution Hiller returned, accompanied by twelve policemen, and marched to the Rocca house with a warrant for his arrest. Naturally he was not at home. The police posse had been seen as soon as they'd left the forest, which gave Rocca ample time to pack a hamper, stand several rounds of drinks with his friends at the bistro, and disappear into the maquis while the villagers gave him a hero's good-bye. He was seen by several children to climb onto a rock and stand gazing down at Taita, wiping his eyes for several minutes before entering the forest.

Hiller nailed large posters around the chestnut trees in the square and on the Roccas' front door that read, "Wanted for murder," with a life-size picture taken from his last election poster.

The new year began badly with shots around the square before dawn. Hiller had crept up unnoticed with a dozen armed police and surrounded the Rocca house. The first thing Xavier knew of them was a shot that shattered the front-door bolt, followed by the sound of boots pounding up the stone staircase.

Blear-eyed, but not blear-witted, in spite of the previous night's celebrations, Rocca grabbed his pants, his shotgun, and his knife and hid in a closet concealed by a curtain. The policeman, who was young and Corsican, ripped back the curtain, stared into Rocca's unwavering gaze, and slowly dropped his gun. So Xavier escaped out the basement exit in a police uniform several sizes too small for him. Once in the maquis there was no possibility of tracing him. He knew this, and so did Hiller.

Within a few hours everyone in the village knew of Rocca's triumph over that buffoon Hiller.

From then on Hiller stepped up the siege. There was no peace for Rocca. Every second day he was hotfooting out of Taita. It was a bitterly cold mid-January, and he suffered.

Hiller, too, was beginning to lose his urbane manner. He was overheard boasting to villagers that he would have Rocca before the month was out. "Just let him get within firing distance, instead of skulking in the maquis like a pig," was one of his favorite expressions, which he even tried on me once or twice.

On the first Monday in February, Hiller and his men returned from the maquis after another a fruitless search. Having supervised the change of guards, Hiller walked slowly down to the bistro for a cognac, as usual.

Two shepherds were lounging by the side sucking at their pipes. He nodded as he passed them.

At the turn of the road he saw Leca smoking his pipe and gazing over the valley toward Chiornia. "God! What a nation of layabouts," he was heard to mutter.

Rounding the bend, Hiller was amazed to see Rocca sitting on a rock by the roadside. He, too, appeared to be engrossed in the national pastime of gazing vacantly into space. What's more, he was unarmed.

You could literally see the surge of triumph running through Hiller as he pulled out his gun.

What happened next, only Hiller knows. I watched him intently, and I've thought a good deal about it since then. I guess his thoughts ran something like this:

At last I have the bastard.

I noticed he quickened his footsteps but stepped more lightly, no doubt hoping Rocca would not notice him.

He won't come quietly. He's as strong as an ox, and he'll run off into the maquis. But I could shoot him.

Hiller's footsteps began to stumble. He was walking more slowly now, as if to give himself time to think.

I'm trapped here. There's the shepherds behind me and the bistro ahead. The villagers are watching. How can I hope to arrest him single-handed? They'd never let me take him away. I'd be pulled apart, torn limb from limb, like that poor devil Krag.

Hiller was closer now. Close enough for me to see the anguish on his face. He looked badly scared.

Perhaps images of Major Krag's corpse, spead-eagled on the cobbles, flashed into his mind's eye.

Is it a trap? They all know I come this way every evening for a drink, so why is Rocca sitting there?

He was shaking visibly. The poor fellow! In the bistro we were all doubled up with laughter.

Shall I throw my life away for this scum? Who could blame me for being cautious?

Now he was almost beside Rocca, who was still pretending that he had not seen Hiller. The policeman glanced wildly over his shoulder. Retreat was impossible. There were three villagers blocking the track.

Hiller quickened his stride. Keeping his face averted, he hurried past Rocca.

"Hey there, Hiller," Rocca roared. "What's your hurry? Aren't you going to arrest me? Here I am. Take me! Unarmed as I am, I'm sure it will present no difficulties to you."

"I'm off duty today," Hiller mumbled. He shoved his gun into his pocket.

Hiller ordered a cognac. He sat silently at a table staring at his hands. He must have realized he was finished in Taita. From his expression, I guessed he'd lost his own self-respect, too. He left Taita very early the following morning.

Later that month the bistro began to run out of vital supplies, and Rocca, as usual, saddled Pierre with two large panniers and set off for the wholesaler at Galeria. On the way back, dusk fell while he was still in the Tetti forest. He was armed but relaxed, he told us in the bistro. It was a beautiful evening, and he passed the time by singing old Corsican laments in his particularly beautiful tenor voice. He was remembering in detail to whom he had sung each song and subsequently made love to. He had just reached "Dans Mon Ile D'Amour" when Pierre stumbled badly. Rocca was jolted half out of the saddle. At that precise moment a shot rang out and just missed him. As he rolled into the nearest ditch, a dozen more shots peppered the ground around him.

He was unharmed, he discovered, and pleased to see that his wartime reflexes had not been entirely lost. He let off a couple of rounds into the bushes and heard a yell of pain. Then he doubled back to the thickest part of the forest, where firs, brambles, and silver birch formed a near impenetrable jungle, and from there he made his way to the maquis.

Arriving home at midnight, he found that Pierre, too, had escaped unharmed, but that all the liquor had been taken from the panniers. The financial loss was bad enough; the loss to Xavier's dignity was worse. Even more dramatic was the knowledge that he was an easy target each time he set out for Galeria on his fortnightly buying trips. He would have to disassociate himself from the bistro. He even stood drinks all around and said good-bye to his patrons.

That night he was much more friendly toward me. I don't know why. Perhaps because he was half-drunk. He told me, in whispers, that Bonnelli was a rogue, and he would be bled dry if he were fool enough to put the cash into his brother-in-law's hands.

"There's only one person with enough sense and honesty to take over the bistro," he said, "and that's Sybilia."

"It must be very hard work running this place," I argued, amazed that he would trust Sybilia after all those years of contempt.

"Something you Americans have yet to learn," he said, slurring his words, "is that hard work keeps women out of trouble. Not one of them knows how to make good use of leisure time." He fingered his mustache thoughtfully. "It takes brains and integrity to use leisure wisely. That's why it's the prerogative of men."

CHAPTER 73

Inspector Hiller was once again in the village. He was investigating a bomb attack that had destroyed one of the immigrant farmers' barns around the other side of Lake Taita. Lately there had been several attacks against the *pieds noirs*, as the hated ex–Algerian French farmers were called. Hiller had taken up residence in the presbytery. Consequently Rocca was obliged to hold a family conference in the woodshed in the forest. It was a bitterly cold February. The family felt sorry for him huddled over the old wood stove. He looked older and so vulnerable.

Later that day Sybilia was full of compassion for Xavier. I marveled at her forgiving nature. He had spoken to Sybilia at length for the first time in ten years. From now on, he had told her, she would take charge of the bistro and the household cash.

"But what about Pierre Bonnelli, Papa?" she'd stammered. "He won't like me being in charge."

This was a business arrangement, Rocca had explained rudely. She could not call him Papa. From now on it was "Monsieur Rocca." After that he'd spent the next hour giving Sybilia exact instructions on how to set about her buying, how to make sure my needs were catered for, how to demand a cash discount from the wholesalers, how to check the labels and count her change.

He had promised to speak to Bonnelli, to warn him that Sybilia would do the nightly check on the bistro's takings, as Xavier had always done. In return for her trouble she could keep all the nonliquor profits for herself. Quite a nice little business, Rocca had pointed out to her.

Sybilia was thrilled. She told me she'd soon have enough cash for Ursuline's university education. She was still stubbornly refusing my offer of financial assistance.

The trip to the wholesalers involved a five-hour walk. Otherwise she could leave Pierre with relatives and bus to and from Galeria. But how would she manage boxes of liquor on the bus? she wondered. Eventually she discovered that walking for ten hours was not nearly as tiring as housework. She found the journey invigorating, even though it was a cold February.

For the first time in years she wandered around shops and villages, saw how old-fashioned and dowdy she was compared with all the other women. She marveled at the changes she saw. On her third trip she found an abandoned cottage near the beach. It was owned by an English family, she learned from the local agents. They were prepared to rent it to a reliable tenant. She hurried back to tell me about it.

By the end of the month the lease was signed. Sybilia agreed to refurnish and decorate the cottage for a fee. Soon afterward I received permission to employ twelve Algerian diggers. Sybilia volunteered to begin catering for them.

So there she was, a woman with prospects and cash in hand. It was great to see how she changed. Suddenly the sneers of the villagers did not seem so important. " 'Dogs bark, but the caravan moves on,' " she quoted to herself almost daily. She bought a new wardrobe and clothes for the family, including Xavier. Only Maria could not be coaxed out of her perennial black.

Sybilia felt as if she were at the start of a new life. It was as if she had joined the twentieth century, she told me.

I'm not a Catholic, but I went to church every Sunday morning, partly to feel a sense of oneness with the Taitans and partly to please my friend, Father Andrews.

The following Sunday I was sitting unobtrusively in the back row when I saw Sybilia come in. She was wearing a new navy-blue silk dress with a white lace collar and white cuffs. Her hair was turned under and held back with a navy band, and her hat was a straw boater. She looked tremendous. Envy and malice fairly dripped from the village women. The priest must have noticed. I blessed him for his unusual and spontaneous sermon on joy.

"I've been watching you all," he began in his deep, rough French with the Irish brogue he would never lose, "and I've been thinking to myself that God in his heaven must be sick and tired of the tiresome Corsicans who only seem to be happy when they are miserable.

"Is life a gift from God? That's what I want you to ask yourselves. The Bible says that it is.

"Now what if you were to give someone a present? Something precious. Suppose this person moaned about your gift, and far from bringing them joy, it seemed to make them utterly miserable. You might think you'd made a mistake and that this ungracious person didn't deserve anything.

"So I wonder, is that what God thinks? Where's your joy? I don't see much evidence of it. I see long faces and malicious gossip and a good deal of meanness.

"Sunday is God's special day, and to show Him that you are grateful I want you to try to be happy on Sunday. Come to church in pretty clothes, wear a smile, or if you can't manage a smile, wear a flower in your buttonhole. Show a little appreciation for this supreme gift." The priest went on at great length about joy.

What a hum of conversation the moment the service ended! Had this strange Irish priest taken leave of his senses?

Some even spoke of writing to the pope to complain.

CHAPTER 74

May, 1960

It was the twenty-seventh day of May. The weather was perfect, so I'd decided to take off a couple of days at the coast. Jules had promised to watch the dig. He was quite skilled at excavating nowadays, and it gave him an excuse to earn extra cash. I decided to go down to the bistro to pay my food bill for the month. With luck I might even persuade Sybilia to take a day off, too.

We were trying to balance the accounts when Bonnelli called out, "Hey! Guess who's coming?"

Inspector Hiller was looking even more pompous than usual. He was always a dandy, with his snowy cuffs a trifle long, his folded handkerchief aggressively evident, his carnation and trim mustache. Today he was wearing a bowtie.

I'd avoided him since the day he was set up by the villagers. I knew he'd seen me laughing in the bistro. I had no desire to talk to him today, either. Sybilia and I slipped into the back room, leaving Bonnelli to serve him.

Hiller sat at a table, placed his briefcase to one side of it, and handed Bonnelli his card. "Is Madame Rocca here? Good. Tell her I should like to see her now."

Sybilia walked out reluctantly. I noticed Hiller's frown when he saw how elegant she looked. She was wearing a black suit, and white shirt, open at the neck. I expect he was wondering why she had abandoned her peasant's skirt and shawl.

He did not stand when she approached the table. He appeared to be engrossed in his file. He flicked his hand toward the chair opposite. After a moment's hesitation, Sybilia sat down, frowning.

"Madame," he began quietly in French, "you seem to be surrounded with trouble. That's a pity. Xavier Rocca's lawlessness seems to have infected your children." Turning to Bonnelli, he ordered two coffees, waving aside her refusal.

"Your son, Jules, is running a subversive political organization, planting bombs on the property of French immigrant farmers. Did you know that? He was responsible for the bomb attack I'm investigating on Monsieur Bouet's farm on the other side of the lake."

Sybilia turned pale. "I'm sure you're mistaken, or you would have arrested him, Inspector Hiller," she said. "But I will speak to Jules. Now if you'll excuse me, I have a great deal of work to do."

"One moment, please. Your daughter, Ursuline, has joined his organization. It was Ursuline who carried the bomb into the shed. She's likely to blow herself up, along with her innocent victims."

Sybilia was badly shaken, and it showed. To tell the truth, so was I. I knew Ursuline had joined Jules's movement, but I never guessed she'd do more than clean the chalet and run errands.

"Did the French farmer identify my daughter?" Sybilia asked. "Have you come to arrest her?"

"I wanted to talk to you first," Hiller said, avoiding her question. "She's a pretty girl. I wouldn't like to see her in prison. She'd be ruined. I'd prefer to help her. Just as I want to help you. You are even lovelier than your daughter. Come, Sybilia, we've known each other for a long time. You're in serious trouble. You need an ally to bring your unruly family under control. Say the word and I will deal most leniently with your children." His hand slid over the table to rest on hers.

Sybilia started back and pulled her hand away.

What a pompous idiot. I'd like to punch his teeth in, but Sybilia can cope. I hope he's lying about the kids, but somehow I don't think he is. I've always suspected Jules and his gang might be linked to the bomb attacks around this area. I wonder if Hiller has any proof? Probably not. It's weeks since the bomb attack. He's bluffing Sybilia.

"How absurd you are," I heard Sybilia say. "I can't imagine how your leniency would alter our lives one way or the other."

"We'll see, we'll see." Hiller gazed at her lasciviously. "Rocca's getting old. Sleeping out in all weathers can't be good for him. I shouldn't be surprised if he died of exposure or pneumonia one of these bitter nights. He could be hounded into his grave."

"Monsieur Rocca seems to be quite capable of looking after himself," Sybilia said, smiling softly. "Particularly since you are so often off duty. Isn't that so?" She smiled mockingly.

"I see you have a sense of humor." His voice grated unpleasantly as he banged down some coins on the table and left.

Sybilia burst into tears the moment he left. She had good reason to cry. No comforting words from me were going to alter the truth.

"The children should get out of this cloistered village atmosphere and learn something of the outside world," I told her, adding that she mustn't let her silly pride stand in the way of her children's future.

Whichever way I put it, she wouldn't give in and accept my financial help. Jules would go into the army immediately, Sybilia insisted, and Ursuline would enter a convent as a novice, where she would be trained as a teacher. I couldn't persuade her to change her mind. Eventually we quarreled. Sybilia rushed back to the house, and I returned to my dig.

Both Jules and Ursuline were waiting there. They had guessed the reason for Hiller's visit and wanted my moral support.

"Don't expect me to condone your actions," I told them angrily. "You've done a terrible thing. Thank God no one was hurt. How would you feel now if a child had been crippled or blinded, or someone killed?"

"We were careful. The bombs were timed to blow up the sheds at night," Jules said.

"You had no right to take that chance."

Sybilia arrived, looking furious. She had intended to show the stern side of her nature, but she promptly burst into tears.

No one was hurt, they assured her when she had dried her eyes.

"How does Hiller know you're responsible?"

"Gossip. He's been asking around," Jules said.

"I never thought I'd see the day when I called you a coward," she said scornfully to her son.

The boy looked shocked.

"Yes, you are. Leaving bombs around for innocent people to be hurt. That's horrible, cruel, but worse than all, it's cowardly. And then to let your sister get involved. What sort of a man are you?"

"Mother, stop it. Say what you have to say without the overture. You're a bit melodramatic, don't you think?"

I longed to clout him, but Sybilia was running the show.

"Very well, Jules. If that's the way you want it. You're to leave Corsica for two years. Go and make your own way in the world. Join the Foreign Legion, or the civil service. That's my condition. Otherwise I'll turn you over to the police. You'll get ten years, or more. Perhaps that will knock some sense into you. I blame myself. I spoiled you because I felt guilty."

"But you don't understand, Mother . . ." Ursuline began.

Suddenly it became of vital importance to Jules and Ursuline that their mother should believe in them and be converted to their cause. She had to understand.

"The French are giving away our homeland to foreigners. To Algerian-born immigrants, the despised *pieds noirs* . . ."

"We can say good-bye to independence now that seventeen thousand ex–Algerian French immigrants have settled here . . ."

"Every day more pastureland is fenced off for scientific farming . . ."

"What is there here for us? No jobs, no industry, no chance to live and work in our own country. If we stay here, we'll be unemployed . . ."

Familiar arguments. We'd heard them before, time and again.

Sybilia was not convinced.

"It's true that we can't sell our olive oil anymore," Sybilia said to me later that evening.

I had come to the house to make sure that no one needed my help. Jules had already left. Ursuline was packing and crying bitterly. I tried to comfort her by promising to get her out of the convent within a year. "Just give your mother time to cool down," I told her.

Afterward I sat on the balcony having coffee with Sybilia. This was only possible because Rocca was hiding in the hills and Maria was in her room.

"We can't compete with the low prices now that the *pieds noirs* are producing so much. So the olives are rotting on the ground," Sybilia went on. "What's the point in gathering them? We can't sell our wine, either.

"The takings at the bistro are down because the men can't pay for their liquor. Too many families are leaving their homes. Our schools are almost empty. Oh, Jock, what's going to happen to the peasants?"

"Progress means change. There will be different kinds of employment. The old life-style is on the way out." There wasn't much point in trying to sound cheerful.

"I feel I've failed my children, Jock. I hope Jules will return with a new perspective on our island's problems. Ursuline will be better off with an education behind her. Then perhaps they'll be able to do something constructive to help Corsica."

What could I say? With a pang, I realized that I'd grown closer to those two children than to anyone in my life before. Now she'd sent them away. I'd be leaving, too, one of these days. I might never see any of them again.

This was not a night to be alone, I decided. I went down to the bistro and drank eau-de-vie. As I listened to Romanetti singing, I felt about as sad as I'd ever felt in my life.

CHAPTER 75

Sybilia had always taken refuge in her self-imposed standards and routine. She never had to worry about tomorrow since it would be a replica of today. This gave her some sort of comfort. But now everything was in a state of flux: first Ursuline left, sobbing bitterly; then Jules joined the army.

It was a lousy spring for everyone. Sybilia was depressed for weeks. I couldn't get through to her. I was determined to see Jules through the university eventually, but Sybilia wouldn't allow me to get involved in the Roccas' domestic affairs. She was like that. I reckoned that a two-year stint in the army wouldn't do him any harm. We'd see about the rest later.

After a few visits to the convent, Sybilia began to feel better. The nuns were kind to her daughter, and she was coping. The days passed, spring turned to summer, and Sybilia began to laugh again. I'd taught her to drive. How else could she transport the provisions to Taita? As it was she had to leave the jeep at the base of the cliff and make two journeys with a heavily laden donkey to get it all up to the dig. Now that I had fifteen diggers, requiring three meals a day, the catering was quite an undertaking. One day she told me that she had enough money saved to cover Ursuline's training, but she would wait a few months longer because she thought convent discipline was good for her daughter.

We were often together during that long, hot summer. She taught me the names of the plants and trees in the forest, I taught her scuba diving. I showed her how to excavate and explained the rudiments of archaeology. To my surprise, I discovered she was an accomplished rider. She had ridden with her brothers, she told me, so we borrowed two horses from a friendly farmer and explored the countryside.

For Sybilia nothing would ever be the same again. She was like a strong river, dammed too long by the imposed social curbs of her culture, which at last broke through.

We spent hours together, digging at the site, numbering and describing the finds, packing them. She became an efficient secretary, handling the correspondence with the French authorities and dealing with documentation and all the paraphernalia of an undertaking that had grown to mammoth proportions. Sometimes we corrected proofs of my book. She even helped me prepare a number of lectures. Weekends we swam and lazed in the sun.

We were together, yet we were also apart. I had never believed in a platonic relationship between a man and a woman, but she could not give of herself or show any type of physical affection. This was a source of constant irritation to me.

"Give me time," she would say when I broached the subject. If I persisted, she became angry. "If friendship isn't enough for you, then forget me," she would snap, and for a few days we would shun each other.

What's wrong with her? I asked myself repeatedly. It seemed that she was all snarled up in the past. There was a blockage, and she could not move forward. Understanding didn't make it any easier for me. I could forgive her for loving Robin and for waiting for him, but not for ruining her life—and mine.

CHAPTER 76

August, 1960

It was early August, and the weather was superb. I'd taken the day off from the dig. It was too damn hot up at Taita, and besides, I had other work to do. The morning had begun well with a hard chase after a huge, ungainly ray that had flapped around the bay. Then I had come across a slab-sided sargue, which I'd noticed crabbing around a rock in crystal-clear water not fifty meters from the beach. Suddenly there it was in front of me, tearing at soft fluffs of green seaweed. My harpoon transfixed it, a fluttering, broad silver disk. After that I'd caught some mullet and stowed it all in the deep freeze.

Later I was correcting proofs when I heard a knock on the door. It was a telegraph boy. The message from Boston University read: *Retiring at once due to ill health. The board has offered you the chair. Return soonest. Congratulations. Don Miller.*

My first reaction was a sense of loss. Should I go? I wondered. What possible excuse could I make, either to the faculty or to myself, not to take this opportunity? Besides, Professor Jock Walters sounded pretty good.

I began to mull over the problem. What if I left at once? What would that involve? I'd have to pay the Algerians the rest of their contract money—fair enough—give notice to the widow, Germaine Barnard, likewise no problem there. I'd promised a month's notice on the purchase of provisions. Well, a month would just about see me through.

What sort of notice do you give on love?

This was no time to get sentimental. Besides, there was no commitment between us. Sybilia had never been able to take the final step, so what was there to keep me here?

Once I'd decided, I felt better. I sat down and finished the corrections within the hour.

Shortly afterward I heard Sybilia returning. She'd taken the jeep to stock up the bistro's shelves. Feeling guilty, I hid the telegram in my desk.

Watching her, I wanted her badly, as usual. She was hot and perspiring, her hair plastered over her forehead, her face paler than usual from the heat, her eyes wide and very beautiful. When she was like this I loved the smell and the nearness of her. Just as well I'm leaving, I remember thinking. Life was too damn frustrating. At this rate I'd turn into a eunuch.

"I must bathe," she said. "Look at me. I'm exhausted. Or perhaps I'll swim. D'you feel like swimming?"

I turned away. I found I couldn't look her in the face. "You go. I'm busy."

She frowned, took my arm, and gazed at me quizzically.

"I'm just fed up with checking proofs," I lied.

"But what's wrong? Tell me what's wrong," she persisted as she fried the mullet I'd caught.

"I told you. There's nothing wrong."

"All right, have it your own way. I'm going to cheer you up with some special wine. It's out of our own cellar. I brought it from home this morning."

She was singing happily when I went off to shower.

"Where's the corkscrew?" she called out after a while.

"I dunno," I yelled. "Somewhere around."

I didn't realize my mistake at first. There was the sound of drawers opening and shutting, her happy singing, the fish frying, then silence. It took a while for the silence to sink in, and with it the knowledge that something was very wrong.

I went downstairs. As I'd thought, she had rummaged through my desk for the corkscrew and found the telegram.

She was so pale. She looked ill. I was surprised how hard

she was taking it, but I couldn't help feeling that it served her right. Virtue was all very well, but it could be stretched too far. She couldn't blame me for leaving.

"Professor Walters. Sounds good, hey?" I tried out a grin.

"Sounds good," she echoed, near to tears.

"Aren't you pleased for me?"

"Of course," she whispered. She pointed at my desk. "And those things?"

She was trying to change the subject. That was her way. I glanced at the relics of World War II I'd brought back from the dig that morning: a rusty dog tag and a few personal effects wrapped in an oilskin wallet. Nothing much. I said: "The Algerians dug them up when they prepared the ground for a new latrine. Did the war come this close?"

"No," she said. "Is that all there is?"

"A skeleton in bits and pieces. It's of no interest to me. I'll hand this over to Hiller next time I see him."

"He's in the village. I'll take it," she said. "I must go soon."

I frowned. I wanted her to beg me to stay. How upset she seemed. Her eyes were haggard. Suddenly she looked old. When she forced her face into a smile, it was even worse.

"It was always inevitable that you would leave," she said. She wiped her hair from her damp forehead with the back of her hand.

As she moved her arm, her breast swayed under her blouse, and I felt desire stirring again. Like a conditioned dog, I thought distastefully.

No one's ever affected me as she does. It's like being hooked on drugs or alcohol. I can't help wanting her, yet I can't have her. What's so goddamn special about her body, her sex appeal? There's plenty of other women around. She's like this damned island, she's penetrated my soul. I'm not free anymore. I should have left a long time ago.

I scowled with annoyance and with the necessity of saying the right and humane thing: "You could marry me. Yes, why not?"

"There are many reasons why not," she said, slumping onto a chair. "Mostly due to my past. There's Jules, Ursuline, Maria, the bistro . . . but primarily Robin." Suddenly she was sobbing, and I didn't react. It was over.

I felt relieved, almost happy. I drove Sybilia to the donkey and helped her pack the panniers. Now she seemed very controlled and calm. It was almost as if my leaving were of no interest to her, which was a relief. I arranged to see her the following day when she would deliver provisions to the Algerians.

Early next morning I set off for my dig, driving like a maniac through the Tetti forest, marveling at the splendor of the chestnut trees. Parking at the base of the cliff, I bypassed Taita. For the first time I saw a flash of a brown-gray pelt and the magnificent horns of a mouflon that streaked off into the maquis.

I felt pretty good. I was about as fit as I had ever been. My site had yielded five distinct cultures, from *Homo* Neanderthal to the later Stone Age. All had been documented and photographed. This was, without doubt, my best project to date. I grinned happily to myself.

As promised, Sybilia arrived in the midmorning, looking stern, uncompromising, businesslike. I recognized her efforts to put on a brave face and get me behind her. I respected her for this and felt grateful that she was taking it so calmly. Another woman might have acted differently, I thought.

When we'd finished unloading the food from the donkey, I realized that she was not going to make me some coffee as she usually did. All right. We could play this any way she liked, I decided.

She went up the hill and spent a long time poking around and talking to the diggers. She was probably avoiding me, but I felt glad I'd managed to stimulate her interest in archaeology. That was something, particularly since the ruins were on Rocca land. She'd have a good deal to do with the museum that would eventually be set up here. After a while I noticed she'd disappeared into the cave where we'd been working recently.

I hope she's not destroying anything important, I thought. From the clanging noises it sounded as if she were digging frenziedly, venting her anger on the gravel. Well, rather that than me. This was not the right time for a lecture on careful excavation.

An hour later she emerged from the cave and turned toward home. Then she hesitated and turned back, as if something had suddenly occurred to her.

"Jock, there's no need for you ever to feel guilty about anything," she said as if she'd read my thoughts. "I want you to remember that. I wish I had loved you more. If I had the time over again, I wouldn't hold back. No, not for a moment. I'm only sorry I waited so long and wasted so much time."

That seemed a strange thing for her to say. Later, when I heard the shots, witnessed the vendetta, and raced down to the square, I realized she had known at that moment she was going to kill Xavier Rocca. It was her good-bye to me.

PART VI

CHAPTER 77

September, 1961

It was the day before Sybilia's trial was to begin. The wind was blowing the first breeze of morning through the dusty room I'd rented in Ajaccio, where I would stay for the duration of the court case. Staring through the window, I watched the birds gathering on rooftops. I sensed their agitation and their restlessness. On the outskirts of the city the maquis was a staggering profusion of shrubs and flowers; their scent had been drifting around the city on these last torpid days of summer.

Last Sunday I had returned to Taita to watch the villagers make their annual mass exodus to the little chapel of Notre Dame de la Serra, on the Haut-Asco mountain pass. Father Andrews held a service, followed by an outdoor picnic in the hills. Taita, too, was languishing in a late-summer heat wave, just as it had been a year ago when Sybilia had taken the rifle and killed Xavier Rocca.

In my mind's eye I could see the square and hear the fountain trickling; I could see Sybilia standing there with the rifle and hear her sobbing.

After they took her away, I'd missed her desperately. She was being kept in a penitentiary run by nuns, where I hoped she was kindly treated. I'd tried to visit her several times, but she had refused to see anyone.

Eventually I had made an effort to get back to my work. I'd been about to leave Corsica to take up the chair of anthropology at my university. The faculty were eagerly awaiting my arrival. I knew I could not keep them on a string indefinitely. It took days of anguish before I decided to give up my career. Once I had resigned from my post at Boston University and given up my other commitments, I was free to research Sybilia's story in the hope of helping her defense.

Months later I felt that I knew her intimately, yet I was more baffled by her crime. Here we were, hours from the start of the trial, and I had no idea why she'd shot Xavier Rocca. Consequently the defense and I had been forced to agree on a plea of temporary insanity.

The morning passed slowly. I tried to work, but my concentration was nonexistent. I cooked lunch but had no appetite to eat. Eventually I decided to see Sybilia's defense lawyer again, although I did not have an appointment.

Advocate Charles Quinel, a top Parisian criminal lawyer, had been engaged with my financial backing to defend Sybilia. Quinel was a short, stout man with a remarkably cherubic face. If I'd had to describe him, I would have said "puddinglike." He was supposed to be the best, but nothing about him gave this impression. He looked more like a scoutmaster.

This was my impression once again when his secretary showed me into his office after only a short wait. These temporary rooms in the city were borrowed from a local colleague. They were old-fashioned and dingy, but to my mind Quinel fitted in very well. I wondered if his rooms in Paris made him look any more imposing.

When I told him of my fears, he did not offer any comfort.

"It's always difficult if you can't get the cooperation of the prisoner in the first instance," he explained.

I stared back, feeling hopeless. I had wasted a year in investigations and questions, but I had not found even a shred of evidence that might reduce her sentence or save her from the guillotine.

"You know what we're up against," Quinel began. "Henri Duval is a most able prosecutor; Pierre Vaquier is a gifted presiding judge. We face a formidable team of legal experts who have been influenced by the highest French authorities to ensure that the vendetta is never resurrected as a means of airing Corsican grievances. They intend to throw the book at Sybilia. They want the death penalty. The only hope we have is to fight for a life sentence instead of death."

I felt sick. This was not new to me, but with the trial about to begin it seemed even more terrible.

"If only we were in America. There she would at least be innocent until she's proved guilty."

Quinel looked at me and frowned. I was wasting his time. He wanted me to go, but I needed his advice, or comfort.

It's a different system, that's all, I reminded myself. Not better or worse. The case had already begun with a preliminary inquiry by a magistrate taking dozens of sworn statements by witnesses and making an attempted interrogation of the prisoner. Thus, the coming trial would only be a sifting of facts by the defense and the prosecution, conducted in public. The verdict would be delivered by the presiding judge, based on the votes of his assisting judges and the jury. It was all very thorough and very French, but much too rigid to establish innocence easily.

As Quinel showed me out of his chambers, I asked: "Could anything else save her?"

"Only new evidence of the most unexpected kind."

I lay awake that last night, obsessed with my failure and with Sybilia's anguish.

Just before dawn I fell into a restless sleep.

Sybilia and I were sitting in a cell. We could hear footsteps approaching. Sybilia's face was white as chalk; her eyes glittered. She looked at me and said: "You should have left me to die in Taita. Why didn't you?"

I felt overcome with guilt. The door swung open slowly. Father Andrews, his face heavy with sorrow, led in a small group of men: the prison warder, two guards, and a doctor carrying a black medical bag.

A wave of fear swept through me. "He's to blame," Father Andrews said, pointing at me. "He interfered." His voice echoed eerily down stone corridors, into the prison yard, and up into the mountains.

The scene shifted. I was imprisoned in the bell tower in Taita overlooking the square. Hooded men were dragging Sybilia toward the guillotine, which had been set up on the cobbles. The executioner stood there . . . waiting. The priest was mumbling the last rites. There was no time left. I had to get down there . . . had to save her . . . but Romanetti and the villagers were crammed into the spiral staircase, blocking my way.

"You must watch," the shepherd said. "See what happens when you interfere."

I turned and saw Sybilia pinned facedown on the guillotine. The blade descended in slow motion. The blood spurted on her white collar, staining it deep red. Panic-stricken, I screamed.

The noise woke me.

I got out of bed and made some coffee. It took some time to stop shaking. I kept telling myself that it was only a nightmare. The truth was, reality was just as chilling.

CHAPTER 78

On other visits I've always loved Ajaccio, with its many squares shaded by palms and plane trees, its wide avenues bordered by cafes and oleanders, and its old colonial-style buildings beside the picturesque docks. Today, as I walked moodily toward the court, the streets and buildings seemed to me like the backdrop to a comic opera. The theater doors were about to be thrown open, and a striptease show was promised: Sybilia exhibited, probed, and vilified.

In the antechamber of the court, the crowd gossiped and throbbed with the chatter of a social occasion. Most of Taita was present. Others had come from villages all over Corsica. Apart from the curious public, there were journalists, photographers, and harassed police officials, all shouting at once. The vendetta had created a storm of publicity in local newspapers, providing the raw material for countless arguments in the bistros and on street corners.

Xavier Rocca had been a famous wartime partisan, a "bandit of honor," guerrilla leader of the National Front, a traditional Corsican hero. The intimate details of a powerful family—its loves and hates and scandals—were about to be revealed. Everyone wanted to be there. God, how I hated them all.

I caught sight of Ursuline in her novice's habit and pushed my way toward her. I could not speak as a sudden wave of emotion undermined my calm. "It's horrible," Ursuline gasped. She looked grave and close to tears. In the past year she had lost weight. For the first time I noticed her fine bone structure, which was slightly more angular than her mother's. Her chin was more prominent, her nose longer, but there was still no doubt that she was going to be a beautiful woman. "Grandmother and I are staying in Ajaccio with relatives." She almost choked on the words. "She's coming with Father Andrews."

At nine sharp the doors were thrown open, and we were thrust into the courtroom by the crowd's momentum. As interested parties we sat near the front of the court, but behind us the public gallery quickly filled to overflowing. There were a few brawls outside as police held back the rest of the crowd. It became unbearably hot, and the stench of bodies from the antechamber flooded the courtroom while the babble of conversation grew louder.

On another occasion I might have admired the courtroom, with its brilliant red upholstery, carved oak benches, alabaster crucifix, and ornate ceiling. The sun's rays had set fire to the stained glass of the big windows. Rocca's rifle, which lay on the table at the front, was painted with blood-red light.

Just before ten there was a sudden hush as the doors near the rostrum opened and the legal teams began to enter. First came the advocate general for the prosecution, Monsieur Henri Duval, wearing his robe and torque hat. He was a tall, ascetic-looking man with thinning hair and an unhealthy pallor. His eyes were a strange dark brown, almost black, and they lent a hawkish appearance. He sat at a table to the right of the judges' rostrum and smiled coldly at his assistants, who now sat down around him.

I stared at him and was seized by anger. I knew his brief: Sybilia was an example, not a person, to be used as a deterrent. What did he know or care about the real person standing there?

Then the twelve jurists filed in, looking self-conscious and grimly determined to do their duty. Last of all came Charles Quinel and his two colleagues, who, like him, seemed insignificant amid the crowd.

When the prisoner was led in, I tensed and held my breath. Sybilia looked thin, almost emaciated, as she clutched the bar in front of her and stared around defiantly. She was wearing a plain, shapeless black dress with a drab V neckline. She wore no makeup, no jewelry, and her hair was brushed back in a plain bun. She had done nothing to make herself look appealing, but for me she stood there hauntingly lovely—a face that once seen could never be forgotten.

The court hushed and rose as the presiding judge entered with his five assisting judges in their red robes and hats. The president stopped at the seat in the middle. He was a surprisingly youthful-looking man, although he must have been in his sixties, with smooth cheeks and almond-shaped brown eyes. A clever face, I thought. He took the seat on a raised dais in the center, and his colleagues sat on either side of him.

By ten-thirty A.M. everyone was ready for the trial to begin, and the jurors took the oath. A clerk read the charges:

"May it please the president and members of the court, the Republic against Sybilia Rocca, the charge premeditated murder."

I felt Ursuline's hand tighten on my arm. I put my hand over hers and squeezed. "Chin up," I whispered.

The president looked at Sybilia sternly. He said: "You are Sybilia Rocca, born Sybilia Silvani, in the village of Chiornia, but now living in Taita."

Her tortured answer was hardly audible: "I am."

"Sybilia Rocca, you are charged in this court with the willful and premeditated murder of your father-in-law, Xavier Rocca, on the eleventh of August 1960. Are you represented, or do you require the assistance of a public advocate?"

Charles Quinel stood up: "The accused is represented, Mr. President . . . Charles Quinel, advocate for the defense."

The president nodded, and his pencil moved over his papers. Then he said, "Sybilia Rocca, according to this indictment, you walked across the main square of Taita at noon, carrying your father-in-law's rifle. You saw that he was sleeping on the bench, and you took aim. Monsieur Rocca woke and staggered toward you, but you fired six times, first wounding him in the arm and then the shoulder and finally the chest. Only when you had fired six shots and Xavier Rocca lay dead on the cobbles did you throw down your rifle. You ran to the church and put yourself under the protection of Father Andrews. That night, under cover of darkness, you fled to the maquis with the help of an accomplice. Later, on August fifteenth, you gave yourself up to the police at Xavier Rocca's funeral.

"You were taken into custody and charged. At the time, you made the following statement: 'I did not murder him, I executed him.' Do you now wish to withdraw this statement?"

Charles Quinel answered for her: "We do not wish to withdraw this statement. It was made freely and without coercion."

At these words a gasp rippled around the courtroom, followed by a few angry shouts.

"Silence in court, or I'll clear the courtroom."

The president made another note in his ledger. He turned to Sybilia and gave her a long, searching glance. "Very well," he said. "Sybilia Rocca, you are charged by the State with the crime of willful and premeditated murder. How do you plead: guilty or not guilty?"

"I refuse to discuss the question of my guilt. I acted according to the dictates of my conscience. I shot Xavier Rocca, and I am prepared to take whatever punishment the French courts care to mete out to me. I have nothing further to add to this statement."

Quinel was on his feet. "I act on behalf of my client to enter a plea of not guilty."

"Very well. The public minister may present his case."

The indictment by the president, the ornate courtroom, the red robes and tapestries, all seemed to shriek "inquisition."

Sybilia appeared to be in the grip of a death wish. Without any prompting from the president, she had proved herself to be sane, willful, and unrepentant. I didn't dare glance at Quinel.

When the prosecutor, Duval, stood up, his resemblance to a bird of prey was even more pronounced, for he had a habit of leaning forward in swift, stabbing movements, while his dark eyes darted from side to side.

"Mr. President, gentlemen of the court, this is a very

straightforward case," Duval began. "Sybilia Rocca shot her father-in-law with his own rifle, at noon, in full view of many good citizens of Taita and the local priest. She has never denied this, nor has she given the examining magistrate any reason for her crime. Throughout prior cross-examinations she has maintained an obstinate silence. I will not waste words condemning the prisoner's crime. Instead I will merely call my witnesses, who saw both the murder and know the family intimately."

I should never have rescued her. She wanted a quick death. I should have left her to die. Crazy thoughts! What the hell's got into me?

It was my helplessness that was mainly responsible for my morbid fears. I wanted to grab her and take her away, but I could not. At that moment I was keenly aware that all my resources might not be enough to save her from the guillotine.

CHAPTER 79

The first to testify for the prosecution was Carlo Castelli, cobbler of Taita. In spite of his slim stature, Castelli managed to convey an air of flamboyance. He walked and carried himself with an affected casualness, spoiled by frequent fits of coughing. He was wearing a brilliant red cummerbund and a matching cravat, contrasting with his peasant black corduroy suit. While being sworn in, he was full of bravado. This was all in a day's work for Castelli, or so his frequent shrugs seemed to indicate.

I listened impatiently while Castelli described the crime. He had been sitting behind the fountain enjoying the siesta and was the nearest eyewitness.

"You were a close friend of Xavier Rocca?"

"Yes."

"Had you heard of any quarrel or disagreement between Sybilia and her father-in-law?"

"Well, that's a strange question. Their life was one long

disagreement from the day she was married into the family. She was headstrong and arrogant.'' Castelli nodded contemptuously toward the dock. ''She and Rocca were always fighting—right from the start.''

''From the start? Could you be more explicit, please?''

Castelli gestured with his hands, palms upward. ''In the name of God! D'you expect me to remember all the Roccas' squabbles? I have my own problems. But as I recall, the first big confrontation was when that woman persuaded Michel to leave home and earn his living in Bastia. Rocca was heartbroken, what with Michel being the only son. After all,'' he continued, ''it's only right that a son should help his father on the land. . . .

''Well, she would have her own way. Michel was to be a famous sculptor. Village life wasn't good enough for her. We all knew the boy didn't have the talent. God knows his old man had tried hard enough to push him. But she insisted, and off they went to Bastia, where he worked as a stonemason. Then the war came, and Michel joined the Resistance, as we all did. I myself was the leader of a squad of fifty men. Well, I can tell you—''

''Quite, quite, but you were saying about their fights . . .''

''Next she wanted to join the Resistance. Big stuff, that was her. I remember her standing in the village square and looking at Rocca, daggers drawn. My word, yes. If looks could have killed, he'd have dropped dead that day.'' Castelli broke into a rare smile.

''Objection.''

''Sustained.''

The prosecutor shrugged diffidently and smiled at Castelli. ''Very well, Monsieur Castelli. Can you tell me if there was something specific and recent that they had quarreled about? Something that might have inspired this killing. After all, they had lived in this state of siege you have described to us for over sixteen years.''

''Yes.'' He hesitated and glanced toward his wife, who nodded. ''She wanted her daughter, Ursuline, to marry my son-in-law, Raoul Pascal, but Xavier Rocca wouldn't give her daughter a dowry. Ursuline was no kin of his, being illegitimate. Besides, she was living evidence of the disgrace that had dogged the Rocca family since the war.

''Sybilia begged him for a dowry, but he wouldn't give

in. He was an obstinate man. You couldn't budge him once he'd made up his mind. Well, Jules put the word round that when he inherited his grandfather's estate there would be a good dowry for Ursuline. Jules was fond of his half sister, but old man Pascal couldn't be budged. He didn't want the Roccas' scandal on his doorstep."

Castelli looked around anxiously at his wife, who signaled for him to continue. The president noticed, frowned, and made another notation in his ledger.

"I expect Sybilia blamed Rocca for being tightfisted."

All eyes turned to Sybilia, but she stared impassively at the wall over the judges' heads. There was no drama to be wrung out of her.

"So in your view, Sybilia wanted a dowry for her daughter strongly enough to commit murder."

"There's other possibilities," Castelli mumbled.

"Please continue."

"Mr. President, I protest," Quinel said. "We're not here to listen to rumors."

Once again there was a whispered consultation among the judges. Then the president turned to Quinel: "Since the prisoner has not contributed one word to her defense during the previous hearings before a magistrate," he said, "nor given us any reason for her crime, the opinion of this court is that we must listen to conjecture in order to discover her motives."

Castelli wiped his forehead with a handkerchief. He looked as if he were about to pass out. He began mumbling and was told to speak up. "A few years back, Sybilia was discovered in the forest in a compromising situation with Ambrosini, the shepherd. She pretended she was being raped, and the American archaeologist took her home. Ambrosini told us the real story.

"A few days later, Ambrosini was killed in a shooting accident during a hunt. Now, lately, she's taken up with this same American, Dr. Jacklyn Walters. He's been hanging around Taita for years, digging up ruins. Perhaps Rocca threatened her, or threatened Dr. Walters. Perhaps Rocca tried to turn her out. He always said that he would. Who knows? They had many reasons to quarrel."

It was Quinel's turn. "Were any of the rumors you have quoted to us anything more than idle gossip? You know that you are on oath, Monsieur Castelli. Can you swear beyond any doubt that Sybilia Rocca had actually engaged in sexual relations with Ambrosini or Dr. Walters?''

''No, of course not. People don't do that sort of thing in public, do they?''

The laughter from the public gallery was quickly silenced by the president.

Quinel continued: ''Are you aware that Sybilia Rocca brought a charge of rape against Ambrosini and that Dr. Walters has likewise sworn an affidavit about Ambrosini's attack? Inspector Hiller, too, has testified that Ambrosini had attempted to rape Sybilia Rocca. I suggest, Monsieur Castelli, that you are deliberately lying about my client's reputation.''

''It's not for nothing she was called the *putana*,'' Castelli retorted.

After that he became surly and uncommunicative, and shortly afterward, Quinel dismissed him. Rumors, conjecture, gossip, all of it. But nevertheless it was damaging evidence. The jurors' eyes reflected their opinions.

When Pierre Bonnelli, Xavier's brother-in-law, took the witness stand, I listened incredulously as he explained that Sybilia had always been known as the local whore and that she had lived up to her reputation. Rocca had often been on the point of evicting her, he explained, but he was softhearted and had pity on his grandchildren.

''What exactly is this scandal that dogged the Rocca family?'' the prosecutor asked Bonnelli. ''In this day and age, an illegitimate child is hardly considered that damning, particularly since the liaison occurred during the war.''

''They say her lover caused her husband's death,'' Bonnelli mumbled.

''Speak up, please.''

''It's well known that the American agent, Captain Robin Moore, deliberately sent Michel on a suicide raid in order to be rid of him. After that the two of them shacked up together in the mountains.''

A snicker rippled through the court.

Bonnelli's testimony went on for another hour. Because he was a member of the family, it was particularly damaging. Quinel declined to cross-examine him. By the time the court convened for lunch, Sybilia appeared to be all but condemned to death.

She was in a state of shock and had to be helped from the

courtroom. I felt equally shattered. As I'd feared, the trial was becoming a sham to confirm her guilt. I was gazing vacantly at the empty dock when Quinel approached me.

"It's looking grim," he admitted. "In a murder case it's rare for a witness to enter the box determined to falsely swear away the life of an accused person, unless, of course, they have an axe to grind or are themselves guilty. What possible reason could a harmless, sick old cobbler—or the rest of them—have to destroy Sybilia?"

"They're lying bastards, every last one of them. This is far worse than I'd imagined," I said.

Quinel shrugged. "I've tried again for bail, but it's no."

I walked into the anteroom of the court to find Jules and Ursuline waiting for me. Jules's eyes were blazing with fury. He had his arm protectively around Ursuline. When a photographer tried to snap them, he threatened to throw a punch at the man.

Ursuline was crying. "They're crucifying her," she sobbed. "It's all my fault. They're saying she did it because Grandpa wouldn't give me a dowry. If only I could help her. I'd do anything . . . anything . . ." She fumbled for her sunglasses and put them on.

"We all feel that way, Ursuline," I said sadly. "There's no reasonable defense against the murder charge. We're all fumbling in the dark. Why the lies? That's what I don't understand." I wished I could help her children, but I couldn't think of a single comforting word.

The afternoon's proceedings were as bad as the morning's had been. In turn a succession of witnesses—Leca, Padovani, and Giacobbi—swore that Sybilia was a whore, violently disliked by the family, while Xavier Rocca was a tolerant and compassionate man.

I could not banish a sense of horror as witness after witness pushed Sybilia inexorably toward the guillotine. I felt powerless to help her and desperately afraid. It all seemed so alien as witnesses gave way to emotional outbursts under the skillful tutelage of the eloquent prosecutor, who seemed to revel in their excesses.

Next the prosecutor called Inspector Rene Hiller. He mounted the witness stand wearing a shiny gray mohair suit immaculately pressed and a red-and-white-striped silk shirt with a starched white collar and all the trimmings. His straight black hair was plastered flat on his skull and shone like a mirror.

"Inspector," Duval began, "would you say that the murderous system of punishment known as the vendetta still lingers in isolated areas of Corsica, in spite of the French government's efforts to end it?"

"Hah!" he snorted. "Not just the French. The Romans tried to do away with the vendetta; then the Genoese. In those days it was already deep-rooted. For hundreds of years, successive governments have tried to do away with this terrible system. They never succeeded any more than we did. As a matter of fact, I'm something of an expert on the vendetta."

"You are?" The prosecutor suppressed a smile. "Would you describe to the court exactly what it is?"

"It's a sledgehammer method of enforcing good behavior among primitive people. It leads to the most frightful sequence of killings: men, women, and children. No one is spared."

"Would you say that the crime for which Sybilia Rocca is being tried is in fact a vendetta?"

"Without a doubt."

"Have you any idea why she killed her father-in-law?"

"The Corsicans are notoriously closemouthed about their vendettas. Their reasons for killing are not always obvious to outsiders. Some years back seventeen men were killed over a dispute about the ownership of a chestnut tree growing out of a wall. A savage spate of killings was set off quite recently by the death of a neighbor's dog. However insignificant the trigger, once passions have been unleashed by a vendetta there is total mobilization. Entire families can be wiped out. There's no distinction allowed between the innocent and the guilty. Half the time they don't even know what started it—a cow, a pig, a goat, a tree." He shrugged contemptuously.

"And how do you think the rest of the world should view the vendetta?"

"As the worst form of terrorism. Those who perpetuate this hideous crime are terrorists. The vendetta must be terminated at all costs."

"Thank you, Inspector Hiller."

Once again Quinel declined to cross-examine the witness, and when Hiller stepped down the court was adjourned until the following morning.

I watched Sybilia being led away with terror sinking into my bones. What chance did she have? If only she would change her attitude and at least plead her case in court. I'd been trying to see her for days, unsuccessfully. There and then I decided that I must see her. Surely someone would help me.

CHAPTER 80

I had to bribe my way into Sybilia's cell that night. It had cost me a great deal of money and time, but I had to see her. There was so much that I wanted to know. The trial was going badly. She must realize that. Perhaps at long last she would explain, or so I persuaded myself. The truth was I didn't know if she would agree to see me or turn me away, but the look in her eyes when the door swung open made me thank God that I had come.

"How long do we have?"

That was all she said as the door clanged shut behind me. I heard the key turn, the peephole slide back in place, and I felt some of the horror of the caged animal that Sybilia had become.

"An hour," I said.

She was dressed in a shapeless gray prison dress. She looked so young and so lost. A small wild creature, snared and doomed, could not have wrung more pity from me. She was frightened and deathly cold. I felt my love reach out and grab hold of her, wrap itself around her like a warm cloak.

"Jock," she stammered. Her teeth were chattering. "It's so cold."

I tried to warm her by rubbing her arms and wrapping her in a blanket, but she remained as cold as death. "I feel sick," she complained. I stared at the remnants of a warm and vibrant woman. "The doctor's been here three times. He says it's in my mind. There's nothing wrong with me."

Little wonder. She was so ashamed, being held up to public

examination and loathing. Her humiliation had become physical self-loathing to the point of nausea.

"I wish it were all over," she whispered. "I wish . . . but no, I won't spoil this hour." She smiled, and that was worse than when she looked sad.

I had never before seen her without a light in her eyes: that special glint, sometimes warm, sometimes reckless, shining with laughter or compassion or even anger. But it had always been there. Now it was extinguished. It was as if her soul had been taken away, leaving a living death. "I love you," I said. "I've always loved you, it took a long time to realize that. Now I love you more than ever before."

"Warm me," she whispered. "Don't blame yourself. Just love me now. I need your warmth. I need your life, here, inside me. I feel . . . I feel already dead . . . strange . . . as if the spirit of life has abandoned me."

I could feel it, too. Outside the moon was lustrous, the night throbbed with life and fertility. The air was vibrating with the richness of being. But here . . . Oh, God, it was like a dark pit. "No, never," I lied. "Never believe that. Don't say those terrible things."

I grasped her, too hard, deliberately hurting her, but she did not respond. Then I tried again to warm her, rubbing her arms, her feet, her back; but she remained ice cold. Yet her cell was warm.

But she had taken a gun and killed a man.

To me she seemed like a flower, plucked and carelessly discarded. She would shrivel and die. The pupils of her eyes were dilated and her skin was dry. She pushed her head against my shoulder, wound her arms around my waist, and hung on tightly. So tightly—like a drowning woman.

A moth came into the cell, attracted by the naked light bulb. It dashed against the bulb, burning itself, and fell to the floor.

"Poor moth," she whispered, and shuddered. "Night after night, more and more. I can't put the light out. I can't even cover it, it's so high. I am helpless here. I die with each one of them.

"Will you . . ." she began timidly. Then she hid her face against my shoulder. "If only . . . if we could only have one afternoon on the beach, at your cottage. Just one hour."

"We have this hour," I said gruffly. I wound my arms

around her and kissed her eyelids, smoothed her hair back from her face, wiped away the cold sweat that kept gathering on her forehead.

"Would you . . . Please . . . could you make love to me here?"

"Is that what you want?"

"It would mean so much to me."

There was no sound of footsteps. I could not hear the guard. The prison seemed very quiet. Was she the only living thing in this pitiful row of cells?

How can I make love to her in this deathly place? It could be a mausoleum and she a corpse.

Her coldness was seeping into me, and with it came her fear. It was a small thing at first, but it grew . . . a fear that knotted my stomach and my throat, dampened my hands and the soles of my feet. Yes, my feet were sweating like those of a frightened animal.

How could I? Yet I ached with the need to comfort her. Some of my life force must be pumped into this cowed, defeated woman. I took off my clothes and then hers. We both shivered. "Come," I said, and gathered her into my arms.

"I want to feel hot with love."

"I'll try."

"I want to feel passion. I want it to surge through my body, I want to live, one last time. How you used to want me. I wasted all that loving. Do you remember?"

"I remember. I'll never forget."

Why had I said that? It sounded like an obituary, and now she was shuddering at my words.

Never forget you . . . never forget . . . when you're gone . . . No, goddammit. No!

"If you love me, Sybilia, tell me why you did it. Tell me, or we're both lost."

She turned away and shook her head. "It all seems very long ago," she whispered.

I had a sudden moment of doubt. Perhaps she was mad. Perhaps she had taken the gun and shot Xavier and didn't know why or couldn't even remember.

"Don't think, just love me," she whispered.

I reached out and touched her cheek, and a strange vibration seemed to flow between us, a warm tingling that turned my skin into goose pimples. I could see from her face that she felt it, too. Her eyes became dreamy, her lips fell slack and half-open, her breasts rose and fell. Trembling, I laid her back upon her cell bed and pressed my lips over her breasts and stroked the soft white skin of her thighs.

I was becoming aroused. Unbelievable, but true. I bent swiftly and ran my tongue over her belly, heard the swift, sharp intake of breath and a half-formed cry, "Robin," quickly stifled as she flung her hand over her mouth.

I stiffened with anger and aggression. I was being used. I was only a surrogate for another man—the man she had loved to distraction. Still loved! Now it was all over. Everything she had ever wanted had been taken from her, first her freedom and then her life. So she wanted one last remembrance, by making love to me—or anyone? I pulled back and stared down at her.

Was that all I had ever been? An attempt to recapture Robin? And did it really matter? At that moment it seemed whatever she felt for me was trivial. I loved her—that was real and enduring, and she was imploring me to expunge her wounds.

"Jock, help me." A lost voice in the darkness of the night.

I leaned forward again and kissed her tenderly, felt her quiver and relax. I soothed her, stroked her, whispered promises and hopes.

Now she was stirring, her skin becoming moist and her breathing deeper; she closed her eyes and sighed with contentment.

Oh, God, Sybilia, I love you. I want to help you and understand you.

I sensed how much was being compressed into this one last act of love. It was as if she had risen out of the cold dark earth, quivering with the ecstasy of sensation, groping blindly for the light and warmth of life. She had uncoiled the bud of her womanliness for this one night. This night she would be reprieved.

So she gave herself to me, or Robin, fully and joyfully. Exalting in our shared ecstasy, we made love with an intensity of feeling I had never known before.

We only had an hour, and it was soon over. The scent of

our love filled the room. That was all that was left. I sheltered her in my arms and tried to make the magic last, but it was seeping down into the stone floor.

Her body became colder. Then she shuddered. I dressed her and wrapped the blanket around her. I felt that she was slipping back into her hell of fearful premonitions.

Afterward I could not remember all the promises I had made to try to cheer her. All I could see was the look in her eyes when I had to leave.

CHAPTER 81

The next day, Sybilia was not the same woman I had comforted in the cell. Her eyes deadened, her face rigid, she looked ill, but not afraid. She was wearing a black suit with a white blouse. I remembered when she had bought the outfit. It had taken me a long time to talk her into choosing it. Now it brought a lump to my throat.

I turned my attention to the proceedings and tried not to remember thc past.

"Call Maria Rocca."

There was an excited whispering in court as Maria approached the stand, leaning heavily upon her stick. There was hardly a person there who did not know that Maria was a *mazzeri*. With her long black hair, streaked with white, hanging down over her shoulders, she looked the part. Several people crossed themselves as she took the stand.

When the formalities were completed, the prosecutor said: "Madame Rocca, you have lived with the prisoner in your house for twenty-two years. That must have been a burden for you."

She turned toward him, gazed slightly above his head, and said: "No, why should it have been?"

Duval straightened up with a jolt as if he had been slapped. In prior examinations Maria had always seemed quite mad. Sometimes she raved about visions and the spirits throughout the investigation. For three consecutive days she had babbled on about revenge, which is what he had expected her to do this morning. Easy to send her over the edge again, he reckoned.

"Were you, madame, a witness to the death of your husband, Xavier Rocca?"

There was a long silence. Maria was clasping and unclasping her hands and muttering to herself.

"Did you, Maria Rocca, see your husband shot by this woman?" He pointed dramatically to the dock.

Maria looked around at the faces in the court. She gripped the rail tightly with her hands and stared toward the prosecutor. "I see a boy on a wolf's back. I see him holding a gun. I see his finger tightening on the trigger. I see the rifle pointing at my head." Her high-pitched voice suddenly stopped, leaving the courtroom eerily silent.

The prosecutor made one last try: "Maria Rocca, did you see Sybilia kill your husband?"

"They did not show me because of the lie," she tried to explain. "The lie in my head."

I noticed the prosecutor was smiling. I was sure that he had intended to show the court how her son's death and the resultant scandal had driven Maria insane. "No further questions," he said.

It was Quinel's turn, and he hesitated momentarily. I could read his mind. In this state of confusion, was there any point in trying to get through to Maria?

"Madame Rocca, this trial is a terrible ordeal for you, but I want you to try to remember when they first brought Sybilia to your house as a young bride. What was she like?"

"She was lovely. Full of joy. It was a pleasure to have her in the house."

"And later, when they brought her back from Bastia, during the war, after her ordeal of imprisonment and torture, was she quite normal, do you think?"

"Why, no. She went crazy for a while. She couldn't be with people. She shut herself up for weeks. I had to keep Jules away from her. She couldn't bear to see him or touch him. She'd suffered badly, and it took her months to recover."

"Would you say she was in need of psychiatric care?"

"I don't understand. She needed medical care badly."

"She was depressed. Do you think she was having a mental breakdown?"

"Yes."

"But the fact is she never received any treatment after suffering a breakdown caused by terrible bodily torture?"

"How could she? The Boche controlled the hospitals."

"Thank you, Madame Rocca. That is all."

"Call Madame Francoise Cesari."

She entered the witness stand like a prima donna taking a curtain call. With a pang of fear I recognized the dark, intent, semitic features of the famous *voceri* who regularly tore her clothes and rolled around the cobbles at funerals, whether or not she knew the deceased. Today she was wearing a smart black dress and coat, with a veiled hat and matching gloves, but the gleam in her eyes was as savage as ever.

Under the prosecutor's skillful guidance she explained how she had watched Maria's health and sanity fail after the killing of Xavier Rocca right under his wife's window. From time to time her eyes flickered triumphantly toward Sybilia.

Then it was Quinel's turn.

"Did you see Sybilia Rocca after she was rescued from the Italian prison?"

"No. No one saw her. She remained shut up in her room for weeks. Then Captain Moore took her away. He said it was to a place where she would be cared for, but the truth was they were shacked up in Romanetti's summer chalet. We all knew that."

"Why do you think Captain Moore didn't take her to the hospital?"

She laughed contemptuously. "We had no hospitals in the mountains. They were all around the coast in the hands of Axis troops."

"So although she was suffering from a nervous breakdown, she received no treatment?"

"That is correct."

"Could you describe Sybilia's attitude toward the villagers after the war?" Quinel asked softly.

"Stuck-up. Although she should have been humble."

"Would you describe her as aloof? A hermit?"

"Objection," Duval called out. "He's feeding her the words he wants to hear."

"Objection sustained."

"I will rephrase. Did she fit into village community life?"

"Her? No, never. She kept to herself."

She seemed reluctant to stand down when Quinel dismissed her.

The next witness, Madame Rossi, went through much the same routine. Then the court adjourned for the weekend.

I couldn't take any more. I stood up and pushed my way outside. All that spite. Why, goddammit? Why were they all against her? As I wandered aimlessly around the city, I was feeling terrible. My legs were stiff and aching, I had a splitting headache, I was plagued with the worst hay fever I could ever remember, and my stomach felt as if a lump of lead were stuck there. All classic signs of tension, I knew. My fear had become a palpable pain in the gut.

After walking for an hour I found I was repeating the same phrase monotonously without even realizing it: "God help her, God help her." As night fell, I decided to walk back to the court and try to bribe my way into Sybilia's cell again.

CHAPTER 82

Having tried unsuccessfully to see Sybilia again, I went back to my room and spent a frustrating evening going through my research into her background. I felt I knew her intimately. From her family and colleagues I had pieced together most of her past life. I understood what motivated her, I admired her, I loved her, but for the life of me I didn't have any idea what had possessed her to shoot Xavier Rocca.

Yet I was sure that this was not the action of a woman temporarily deranged, as Quinel was pleading for want of a better defense. After fiddling around with my notes for a while, I packed them away. I was getting nowhere.

At midnight there was a loud knock on my door. Father Andrews stood outside, looking tired and dusty.

"I could do with a drink," he said as he carried in a heavy

suitcase and dumped it on the floor. "I've been wrestling with my conscience, not knowing what to do."

He sat on the edge of the chair, looking uncomfortable. "As you surely know, the secrets of the confessional are sacrosanct, and I can never reveal them. But I can at least give you these papers, left in my care by Captain Robin Moore just before the Battle of Corsica began. I swore not to hand them to anyone except him, but he never returned for them. Realizing that Sybilia's life and liberty are at stake, I thought . . . I hope to God they help Sybilia in her hour of need."

He wouldn't stay long, and I didn't try to keep him. I couldn't wait to open the suitcase.

Inside were copies of reports detailing the day-by-day activities of Captain Robin Moore while he was in Corsica. I didn't know how much use they would be, but they did at least give me the name of his immediate superior in the war, Major Ronald Hartman. Perhaps he could supply some of the missing pieces.

It took me the best part of the weekend to locate the major, who was farming in the Scottish Highlands. I'd told him I was researching wartime intelligence, reasoning that I'd feel my way from then on.

I knocked on the front door of the beautiful stone farmhouse on Sunday evening. Hartman's wife, Pamela, insisted that I stay for dinner. Hartman and I settled into a large room with a high-beamed roof and chintzy sort of furniture scattered among mohair rugs and stone pottery.

Ronald Hartman was still trim and athletic. His white hair was crew cut, his gray eyes were stern, and I gathered that he was still very wrapped up in the last war.

When I asked him about wartime intelligence and his own particular outfit, he scowled. "Can't talk about that without another drink," he said, marching to the cabinet.

Pamela frowned.

"Pamela doesn't like me to talk about it . . . raises my blood pressure," he said. "My outfit was disbanded not long after it was created. Caused me a great deal of embarrassment. Most of the guys we had dropped were my friends."

After some prompting he told me about the pirate forces on the fringes of the many rival and warring intelligence services that mushroomed in World War II. Hartman was a founding member of the Special Air Service (SAS), by far the most celebrated of the array of "private armies" that emerged during World War II. "Between you and me, it's a bloody miracle any of us survived. When I think of the cock-ups we made, and the wrangling. Nowadays you remember the heroism and forget the spite," he said. "There were so many groups in competition . . . hating the sight of each other, overlapping, guarding their secrets jealously. . . . The British were the worse, I have to admit it." He laughed heartily.

Most wartime underground intelligence activity was controlled by the Baker Street–based Special Operations Executive (SOE), which ran French- and British-dropped agents in France. They were both disliked and distrusted by the British MI6, which rivaled the SOE guys. By far the most bitter rivalry, however, was between the SOE and General de Gaulle. The general claimed the right to control all agents and Resistance operations on French soil. To his bitter resentment, he was only allowed to drop his agents through British intelligence.

To add to this confusion, there were the Americans and their Office of Strategic Studies, run by General Donovan. He was infuriated by the reluctance of the British to see his American agents dropped into occupied France, and he had several head-on collisions with the British up to June 1944.

To get back at the British, the disgruntled Free French and the Americans got together on a few projects. The British weren't too keen on this alliance, and it was abandoned soon afterward when an Anglo-American intelligence force was created.

I wanted to know more—but Hartman was getting reluctant to talk further. Eventually I came to the point and admitted I was only interested in Corsican resistance.

He looked astonished. "Well, apart from the locals, Corsican resistance happened to be a one-man band. We—that is, the French-American alliance—dropped him in, and then we were disbanded."

"So where did that leave this one man you mentioned?"

He glowered at his drink. "In the crap. Naturally! Fighting his own one-man war, and he was damn good at it."

"You're talking about Captain Robin Moore, I assume?"

He was taken by surprise. Then he grinned. "Lieutenant

—not captain. He was a naval man. He was given the honorary title of captain purely for the Corsican drop. You see, he needed all the authority he could muster."

Navy! Well, that figured. I realized why all my detailed searches through military archives had drawn a blank. When he saw that I really only wanted to talk about Moore, he looked disappointed for a moment. Then he said, "You're asking about a great guy. Friend of mine, as a matter of fact, before he was killed. Missing in action—presumed dead, June 1944. Let's have another drink. I'm going to need it. I don't know about you."

Pamela called us to dinner. It took all my persuasion through cocktails, dinner, and coffee to convince them that Hartman had a duty to testify at the trial. I left with a feeling of trepidation. Now Sybilia would learn that Robin was dead.

CHAPTER 83

It was the seventh day of the trial. I had returned to Ajaccio and spent the previous evening with Quinel. As I ran a gauntlet of photographers to gain access to the courtroom, I was remembering our conversation.

Quinel told me that the prosecution had called a string of villagers who testified that Sybilia and I had been seen together frequently in various domestic scenes, quite apart from her involvement in my dig. Sybilia's new clothes and possessions, they argued, showed that I was paying for her services and consequently the family honor was once again being questioned.

"The prosecution has made a strong case," Quinel said. "But our turn is still to come. You're our only chance, Dr. Walters." He pointed toward Robin Moore's bulky reports. "I spent most of the night going through these. It will help a great deal."

As I took my place in the front row of the courtroom, there was a loud hum of interest. Everyone stared my way. The babble of conversation ceased abruptly when the two doors at the side of the raised dais opened. We stood as the judges came in. Then the prisoner was led in.

Sybilia's face was deathly pale, her eyes sunken with deep shadows underneath. Now that there was so little flesh on her face, her bone structure was more pronounced. She looked even lovelier, but dead. A beautiful but lifeless statue, cold as marble.

I shivered and looked away.

Quinel stood up and faced the judges. "If it pleases you, Mr. President, I shall open the defense case for Sybilia Rocca by calling my first witness, Major Ronald Hartman, now a farmer in the Scottish Highlands. Previously, Major Hartman was Captain Robin Moore's immediate superior officer. He tells me that Captain Moore was posted missing in 1944. I have only just been given access to Captain Moore's reports, which describe the actions of both himself and Sybilia Rocca during the war."

There was a sharp cry, but not from the dock. It was Ursuline who had burst into tears. Jules put his arm around her. I glanced swiftly at Sybilia. There was no change in her expression.

The prosecutor jumped to his feet. "Mr. President, I protest! What possible relevance can this evidence hold? After all, the man disappeared more than seventeen years ago. It can have no bearing on the crime."

The president shook his head. "We must overrule your objection. The prosecution has been at great pains to describe to the court the character and reputation of the prisoner. The defense must have the same opportunity." He turned to Quinel. "Please continue."

Quinel bowed slightly and waited as Major Hartman was led to the witness stand. He seemed strangely out of place in his World War II uniform, with all the medals for campaigns and bravery. His appearance and his British demeanor obviously impressed the court.

"Tell the court your name, please."

"Major Ronald Hartman."

"And you are now a farmer in Scotland?"

"That is correct."

"You must be a very busy man."

Hartman nodded.

"Why did you agree to fly over and testify at this court?"

"Friendship, perhaps, or a debt that was never fully repaid."

"A debt? Could you explain more fully to the court?"

"Certainly. In that file, if you have time to go through it, you will find enough evidence to convince you that Sybilia Rocca should have received France's highest award for bravery for her war work. That she was not awarded, or recognized publicly, is a matter of politics. Moore recommended the award, I sat on the file."

"Would you explain the reason for your actions to the court?"

"Surely. I'm glad of the chance to do that."

Major Hartman spent over an hour explaining the background to the Corsican operation and why the authorities had decided to play down the American-French intelligence liaison. In answer to Quinel's prompting, Hartman described Sybilia's precise duties in the war—of her bravery in returning to her post in Bastia in spite of the danger, and her heroism in not divulging information to the enemy, although she was subjected to the cruelest torture; of how she returned to her duty as communications officer during the Battle of Corsica, though crippled and mentally scarred.

"Scars she will carry for life, according to Moore's report," Major Hartman said briskly in a matter-of-fact tone, which made his testimony all the more horrifying.

Quinel picked up one of the files and faced the judges. "Mr. President, I beg the clemency of the court. There are various files here. One of them contains Robin Moore's daily report sheets during the period he was operating in Corsica. Although they have only just come into my possession, I can see that here lie the answers to many of the accusations which have been leveled at Sybilia Rocca by the testimony of various witnesses. I would therefore request permission of the court to recall several witnesses whom I previously declined to question."

"Permission granted."

"Major Hartman, would you kindly return to your seat but remain available for later questioning." Quinel cleared his throat. "Mr. President, gentlemen of the court, we would like to recall Antoine Romanetti."

The shepherd looked tired and even a bit scared. It was

hard to believe he was the same youth who had charmed the Taitans with his singing in the bistro. He looked older and rougher, his hair stuck out like straw. With his overlong arms and his brutish jaw, he looked like a lout.

When the oath was read he looked uncomfortable. He shuffled and twisted his hands while he gazed at his boots. He whispered an assent unwillingly.

"Tell the court your name, please."

"Antoine Romanetti."

"And your occupation."

"Shepherd."

"What were you doing in the war?"

"I joined the Resistance—naturally."

"Do you understand that I am going to ask you questions which will make you unpopular in Taita?"

"I have always been unpopular in Taita," he said truculently.

"Why is that?"

"I've always been free: a free talker, a free thinker! They don't like that in Taita. It's Xavier Rocca's stronghold." He looked up and then straightened himself as if a new thought struck him. "At least, it was. Now he's dead."

"Exactly." Quinel looked skeptical. "But you haven't been a free talker about everything, have you? There's something you've kept secret. Why was that, Romanetti? Were you afraid?"

"I don't understand." From Romanetti's manner it was clear that he was lying. He dropped his eyes, hesitated, and then shuffled his feet again.

"I want you to think back to that terrible day in April 1943, when Michel was captured," Quinel pressed on relentlessly. "You were the only person who spoke to Michel before he raced down to the bridge at Poggio where he was taken by the Germans. Why did he go?"

Romanetti took out a grimy handkerchief to wipe his forehead. "He wanted to warn Angelo."

"Why Angelo? Why not his leader, Captain Moore, or Barnard, or the others who were killed there that evening?"

"Well, it was Angelo he . . . the two of them . . ." His mouth trembled. "He loved Angelo instead of his wife, and the two of them made no secret of it."

"I see," Quinel commented dryly.

I glanced toward Maria, but she was staring stonily straight ahead.

"Did everyone know about this unnatural affair?"

"Oh, yes. They were always off in the woods together. They even held hands in public. Xavier Rocca didn't say much, but we knew it was only a matter of time . . ."

"Yes, a matter of time before what?" Quinel asked sharply.

"Well, I don't exactly know."

There was a long, pregnant silence, but Quinel decided not to pursue this point. Instead he said: "What did Michel say to you that evening?"

"He said that he was suspicious of his father."

"Explain to the court, Monsieur Romanetti—what exactly was going on that day?"

Romanetti looked resigned, as if he'd been waiting a long time for this question. He licked his lips and wiped his forehead again. When he began, his voice cracked. "Sybilia had reported that there was a convoy of arms coming along the Poggio road, en route to Saint Florent. Later she found out it was a trap. Instead of arms, the trucks would contain crack troops with orders to annihilate the Resistance. She contacted headquarters and gave the message to Xavier Rocca. Rocca kept the news to himself. He wanted to see his two bêtes noirs polished off in one neat operation, I suppose. At least that's what Michel and I suspected."

"Just a minute," Quinel cut in sharply. "What are you talking about? Who were Rocca's 'bêtes noirs,' as you call them?"

"Captain Moore and Angelo Serra."

"Yes, that figures. Carry on, please."

"Rocca didn't want Michel to be killed, so he invented the story of the parachuting scheduled for that night and the secondary convoy that was to go to Cap Corse. Of course, that was to get Michel, himself, and his friends out of the way. Only Michel became suspicious."

"Why do you think that was?" Quinel asked dryly.

As if anxious to get it over with now, Romanetti spoke faster, the words tumbling out. "Well, Rocca was too eager to take orders from Moore. He usually set up one hell of an argument. Secondly, we hadn't had a drop for some months.

It seemed an odd coincidence—or so Michel thought. Besides, the weather was foggy."

"Go on," Quinel said softly.

"Michel was angry. I remember that clearly. Normally he didn't talk much, but he wanted me to take his place and go into the mountains—just in case the plane came."

"And did it?"

"No, of course not. There wasn't a plane. It was Rocca's fabrication."

"So Rocca, not Moore, was mainly responsible for his son's capture."

"Without a doubt he was responsible, but he spread the word that Captain Moore had wanted Michel out of the way. I knew better. I tell you, I never felt safe in Taita after that. I used to watch my back."

"And why do you think Sybilia never told anyone?"

"I don't know. I've often wondered about that. I suppose it was to protect the family honor."

"Did you ever speak about this to anyone, other than Michel Rocca?"

"After the ambush, Captain Robin Moore questioned me several times, and I told him all I knew. Moore said we must keep quiet about it. He said it was important not to damage Xavier Rocca, because he was the leader of most of the Resistance. Moore told me he would record the matter in his reports, but that no one in Corsica would ever find out."

There was much more, but none of it was of any great importance after this disclosure. Romanetti looked exhausted as he stepped down from the witness stand.

The court was recessed for lunch.

CHAPTER 84

Major Hartman was recalled to the witness stand immediately after lunch. To a packed and emotional court, he told the story of Captain Moore, abandoned temporarily by his Allied commanders, fighting a lone battle to prevent the Corsicans from fighting each other, organizing raids for supplies, and keeping morale high, with Sybilia always at his side to warn him of the pitfalls of clan loyalties.

"So would it be true to say that Captain Moore made a few enemies during this period?"

"No, I should say that initially he won their support. He was that sort of a guy. Later, unfortunately, he became the scapegoat for the Allies' plan that Corsica should not evict Axis troops—a plan that the Corsicans refused to accept."

I could sense the sympathy of the public gallery and the jury as Hartman described how Captain Moore rescued Sybilia and took her into the mountains to nurse her. He explained Moore's daring strategy, which had saved Corté from being overrun by the crack German panzers brought from Sardinia and Sybilia's bravery in returning to duty as radio officer during the Battle of Corsica, although her wounds were not yet healed.

"Would you tell the court on what date you obtained these documents of Moore's, and the circumstances."

"Captain Moore was flown back to Britain twenty-four hours after Corsica was liberated. On the evening of October fifth, to be precise, Moore delivered his reports to me in London. He seemed shocked and tired. I gave him a week's leave. Then he was sent into occupied Normandy to help local inhabitants prepare for the invasion."

"Just like that?"

"Yes, of course. It was his job."

"Would you tell the court about your last meeting with Captain Robin Moore."

"I never saw him after that meeting. When his area was liberated, in June of forty-four, he telephoned me. He wanted two weeks' compassionate leave. He told me that he'd married a Corsican woman in Bastia on the very last afternoon before he was repatriated. Neither he nor Sybilia had their papers, and the priest told them they would have to legalize their marriage after the war. Moore had the impression that Sybilia was pregnant. He wanted to get back to her as quickly as he could."

Married! I sat dazed and shocked, staring at the dock. It

was not legal, but to Sybilia it was binding, and she was a Catholic.

"And what happened to Captain Moore?" Quinel was asking.

Hartman shook his head. "He was reported missing and never seen again. The Germans reoccupied his area briefly. A matter of days only. I never heard from him again, and he was posted missing, believed killed."

As Hartman left the witness box, Quinel turned to the judges; but before he could make his plea, the president preempted him. Picking up his gavel, he said, "The court is adjourned until Monday morning, September twenty-fifth, at ten A.M."

I stood up feeling elated and hurried toward the defense table. "This will make a big difference to her sentence—don't you think so?"

The advocate was leafing through the files. "There's a certain amount of sympathy coming out of the public gallery for her. Of course that's not where it counts, but up there . . ." He gestured toward the judges' dais. "Nevertheless, I think you might have got her sentence down to life."

A life sentence! I walked into the hot sun feeling dazed. God, no! Unthinkable!

There must be more I could do. I now suspected why Sybilia had shot Xavier Rocca, but I needed proof. I had to be alone. I had to think.

CHAPTER 85

I hadn't done much fishing for the past year. So now I swam out from my cottage determined to bring back something great, if only to restore my faith in myself. Close to the beach, the undersea scenery seemed strangely altered, more overgrown, denser. I soon reached deeper water and traveled between the rocks and seaweed as if through a forest.

A big fish—a corbeau, I think—was cruising across the silvery sandy floor. I dived after him with rough, careless swipes. The fish saw me, and with a flick of its broad fins and tail, it sped away. I cursed. I was out of practice, and my anger was getting the better of me.

I swam on for another half hour but saw nothing worthwhile. Then, out of the corner of my eye, I saw something dark move. In the shadow of a huge rock, another shadow swept forward. It came on, flapping over the sand like a great bird. Thirty meters away from me it sank flat on the sandy bottom: a dark, triangular shape with a long whiptail behind it.

It was a giant ray. As I approached it flapped away. I followed into water that became colder and darker. Enjoying the chase, I kept after it, trying to get in close enough to aim the harpoon through the thick layer of sinewy tissue between its two eyes. At the same time I had to avoid getting struck by its tail. At last my chance came. I aimed, steadied myself, and fired, but the spear shot off to one side, impaling one of the ray's wings. The fish left the bottom, turned, and shot straight at me.

I dodged away at a tangent as the fish zoomed past, its poisonous tail lashing too close, too fast. The ray surfaced and made for deep water, and I was swept along behind. I let out more line, but still I was pulled helplessly out to sea. It seemed to possess a ferocious strength, but eventually it tired and I began the long haul back to shore.

I felt better when I'd brought it in, flapping and lashing. There and then I cut off its dangerous tail and soon had the first slices cooking over a fire of driftwood.

Some of my pent-up aggression had died with the ray. I fetched some bread and wine from the cottage and tried not to think of what it would be like with Sybilia there. I thought about that last morning when Sybilia had brought the food and stayed to help with the dig. There was nothing sentimental about my recollections. I was trying to analyze every movement she had made.

Next morning I was up before dawn. I parked at the base of the cliff below Taita and continued on foot. By the time the sun rose, I'd reached my camp.

Autumn had filled the higher mountain slopes with a cold chill. Overhead the sky was paler, almost translucent. Small gray clouds, buffeted by the wind, clustered around the granite peaks. Flowers and herbs were sparse, and the shrubs had lost much of their foliage. The beauty and fragrance of the maquis was hibernating until spring. There was a great quietness about the land, except for the whining wind.

When I reached my camp I found that the stepping-stones across the river, laid so carefully in warmer months, were entirely missing. I cursed and waded into knee-deep icy water.

"Hey. Hey, you there. This is government property. Keep off."

Blue eyes appraised me coolly. A tousled blond head peered over the ledge, and a French rifle was imperceptibly aimed at my heart.

"Who the heck are you?" I called out without stopping.

"National Service guard, detailed to guard this barren patch. That cave there has been commandeered by the State. You may not believe it, but you're looking at a national monument, expropriated by the Department of Antiquities."

"I believe it," I said, grinning. "I discovered it."

"Oh, shit!" The boy's eyes widened, and his grin dissolved into dismay. "And you are . . . ?"

"Dr. Jacklyn Walters." I was angry to find myself out of breath as I climbed the last slope. Too much sitting around in Ajaccio.

"Yes," the guard said a few minutes later after he had skimmed through some papers. "You're on the list. Not many are, but you'd be amazed the number of people who'd like to be."

"Come again?"

"At night! Last night, for instance, although it wasn't the first time, a couple of crazy villagers climbed up here and started their own private excavation."

"Did you ask them why?"

"Looking for souvenirs, they said."

"Did you take their names?"

"No. Just sent them packing. There's been quite a few of them. They all want to dig up the past. They said you've been giving lessons—do-it-yourself archaeology. That true?"

"More or less," I agreed.

"Crazy! You and them both. You want some coffee?"

The boy looked lonely, and he was blue with cold. He led me to the mouth of the cave, where he had a fire burning in a jerrican with a tin of water near to boiling over it.

"How long d'you have to stay here by yourself?"

"Six-hour shifts. To tell the truth, it's not much better off duty. Nothing to do in Taita. Be glad when this is over."

"Which will be when?"

"I dunno. When they fence this place off, I suppose. I've heard it won't be long. We were moved up here when a visiting French archaeologist discovered one of the rock paintings had been painted over."

I leaped up and raced into the cave. The first painting, the one of a horse grazing among deer, was covered with a slash of red paint zigzagging across it.

In a state of shock, I hurried from one painting to the next, but the remainder were unharmed. I could probably restore that one later. Thank God the buffalo was still there, frozen into his moment of truth, as he had been for ten thousand years.

In the innermost cave, where it was almost totally dark, I found the place where Sybilia had been digging. I remembered wondering if she would damage a painting with stone fragments as her spade struck the stony ground. Then I realized without doubt what she'd been doing. I should have guessed before.

The priest was on his knees in front of the altar. He climbed stiffly to his feet, and I gathered he'd been praying for a long time.

I tried to control my temper as I strode down the aisle. "You knew. God damn you. You knew all the time. I blame you for this whole stinking mess."

Then I lost my cool, grabbed him by the cassock, and shook him. Father Andrews was a powerful man, with an Irish temper to match his strength. The next moment we were moving warily around each other, exchanging blow for blow.

I don't know which one of us pulled himself together first, but I remember feeling guilty as I watched the priest tugging his cassock straight.

"Unseemly, and childish," he panted. "Exactly what I would have expected from you."

"You're going to testify," I snarled. "You're going to tell the court every goddamned thing you know."

"Your blasphemous mouth will not in any way influence my judgment, Jock." He crossed himself. "I cannot reveal the secrets of the confessional. Neither you nor Satan himself could make me."

"Don't bet on that," I whispered. "You're hiding behind your priest's robes because you're scared. What are you scared of? The villagers? I'll have you subpoenaed."

"Sit down, boyo. Sit down and listen to me. You can't subpoena me. No court in the world would let you. Confessional secrets can never be revealed. D'you think I don't love Sybilia as much as you do?"

"Then why didn't you tell her?"

Father Andrews looked humble and sad. "I tried to, but she would not listen to me. Then, after a while, it seemed better to leave things as they were. If you hadn't come . . ."

"Don't waste time with excuses. You'll be there at the trial tomorrow morning if I have to drag you all the way."

"It's not so easy, Jock. All my information came to me under the protection of the confessional."

"Then find me an eyewitness. There must be one repentant heart among your black-faced flock."

"I'll do what I can. And I'll be there, I promise you."

"One eyewitness—just one. Find me that person."

The priest's black eye was swelling up, and his lip was bleeding. Without another word I hurried back to my dig.

CHAPTER 86

It was Monday morning, ten A.M. I took the stand amid a drone of public conjecture. I was carrying my sample bag, and as I put it on the ledge in front of me, I dared not look at Sybilia.

Would I be able to help her? Charles Quinel and I had

mapped out our strategy the previous evening. Quinel had also insisted that I get a decent haircut and wear a tailored suit. It was some time since I'd worn a tie, and I felt uncomfortable.

"Please give the court your name."

"Dr. Jacklyn Walters."

"I believe you are the author of several books. Would you list them to the court?"

I mentioned a few of them. Quinel had wanted to impress the court with my credentials, but this seemed to me to be a waste of time.

"What have you been studying in Corsica, Dr. Walters?"

"Structure and function in primitive-contemporary society and the link to Corsican prehistory. I've also been excavating a Stone Age site."

"I believe your work in this field has brought you worldwide fame."

"Perhaps," I muttered, adding: "Within a limited circle of social scientists and archaeologists." I saw Quinel scowl at me.

"Tell me, Dr. Walters, what was your precise relationship with Sybilia Rocca?"

"She was my assistant," I said. "She also ran the Rocca family's bistro in Taita and supplied my diggers with their food."

"Dr. Walters, the shooting of Xavier Rocca by Sybilia must have come as an intense shock to you," Quinel pressed on. "Quite apart from your natural anxiety for her, you must have wondered many times, why? Why did she kill her father-in-law?"

"I guess I did." I paused. "Yesterday I found out why."

A murmur ran through the court. The president rapped with his gavel, and there was silence again.

"Dr. Walters, will you please tell the court exactly what you were doing in Taita yesterday."

"I was up at my dig. The land's been expropriated by the authorities. There's a guard permanently on the site. Otherwise I might never have found these." I nodded toward my sample bag. "This evidence. . . ."

"I don't understand. What do you mean by 'never have found'?"

"For the past few months several villagers have been digging up there, looking for this evidence. The guards prevented them from finding it."

"Would you show the court what it is that you found?"

I picked up my bag. "Mr. President, may I have your permission to leave the witness stand and lay out the evidence on the defense table?"

"Permission granted."

I could not bear to look at Sybilia. I walked to the table, aware of the melodramatic interest I was creating, and opened my bag.

"This is evidence of a crime committed seventeen years ago. In June 1944, to be precise. Evidence that several villagers were anxious to find and dispose of, because it could involve some of them in criminal proceedings."

Suddenly angry shouts came from the public gallery. There was a scuffle as the police removed a man.

"Please continue."

"I remembered, too, how distraught Sybilia had been the night before in my cottage. I'd been so damned arrogant at the time. . . ."

"Please." Quinel held up his hand. "You're confusing the court. You say Madame Rocca was upset. Why was that?"

"The Algerians were digging a new latrine. They'd unearthed some relics from World War II. A rusty dog tag and a pistol. She saw them on my desk and asked me where I found them."

"And she was terribly upset?"

"I'd never seen her quite so shocked. At the time I thought—"

"It doesn't matter what you thought. What did she do?"

"Nothing then. She went home. The next morning, when she delivered the food to my excavation, she spent an hour talking to the Algerian diggers and examining the trench they were digging. I remember she climbed into it and dug around. I thought she'd found some more hand axes. Lately she'd become so enthusiastic. . . ."

"I see, but yesterday you thought otherwise."

"Yes. On Sunday I took a look around. In the back of the cave I found a grave with a small wooden cross erected over it. That's what she was doing that last morning before she shot Xavier Rocca—she was digging a grave."

I pulled the wooden cross out of my bag, held it up, and heard Sybilia gasp in horror.

"No! Oh, no! How dare you?" Sybilia's eyes blazed with anger. Her knuckles whitened as she clutched the rail. "You had no right . . . no right to touch it."

It was the first time she had lost her composure since the trial began.

"The prisoner must keep silent," the president said sternly.

Sybilia gave a long shudder and one sob. Then she bent her head and wiped her eyes with the back of her hand.

I pushed my hand into the bag and held up a rusty dog tag and a pistol. "These were the items Sybilia found in my cottage," I explained. "I found them buried in the grave in the cave. She buried them there alongside these few bones."

"No!" Her horrified scream echoed around the courtroom. "You didn't . . . you couldn't . . ." She was wild-eyed and white as chalk as we faced each other across the courtroom. She would never forgive me.

"Then I found this." I swung a gold chain with a Star of David on it. "Of course, she'd polished it up a bit," I added. "It had lain in the earth for sixteen years, but gold lasts longer than human flesh and bones. She found only a couple of neck vertebrae, probably beside the chain," I explained to a hushed court.

"She wasn't able to find all of the bones," I went on, trying to ignore her quiet sobbing. "But she'd put all she could find in this stone casket. Not much left of the full-blooded American man she'd loved more than her own life."

There were angry shouts from the public gallery as I removed the casket from my sample bag. Sybilia's sobs were louder now. Heartbreaking cries.

The president sighed and picked up his gavel and looked toward Sybilia. "Madame Rocca . . ." he began. She pushed her hand hard over her mouth and gazed back at the casket as if unable to look away.

"From this pathetic bundle of bones," I said, lifting the largest, "Sybilia pieced together the story of Captain Robin Moore's last hours."

I held it higher. "This is a pelvic bone. The correct name

is iliac crest. It's picked pretty clean by ants and worms. Of course, there was no coffin. You'll notice, Mr. President, the bullet hole. It's sort of punched in from the outside. Inside it's slightly beveled around the edge. This was from a shot fired by a high-powered rifle from a distance of about four hundred meters. The bullet shatterd Robin's hip as he tried to escape through the maquis. It must have hurt like hell and crippled the victim, but Captain Moore was a brave man, he kept going."

The prosecuter again objected, but again the president angrily dismissed his plea.

"It wasn't his only wound," I continued, louder this time to be heard above Sybilia's moans. "Gentlemen, this is a right shoulder bone, known as a scapula. Once again you'll please note the neat round hole. . . ."

"Stop it," Sybilia cried out. "Please. Please, Jock. No more. It's over. It's over, I tell you! Stop torturing me."

"The prisoner must keep silent or be removed from this court."

Sybilia pulled herself together and stood staring in horror.

"Then I found this skull," I said. "There are four bullet holes from pistols fired at point-blank range."

As I held it up, Sybilia moaned softly. She looked as if she were trembling on the very lip of hysteria. I had to push her over the edge. All that icy calm wasn't going to help her in a Mediterranean court.

"From these holes we know that someone, or more likely several men, held pistols to the back of Robin's head and pulled the trigger, blowing his brains out. A horrible death for a very brave man."

Sybilia screamed, a long, anguished scream. There was a sudden cry from Ursuline as her mother collapsed. A moment later she was carried out of the court. There was an angry buzz around the gallery, which was quickly stilled by the president. The jury looked moved, I noticed. Two of the women were dabbing their eyes.

Quinel jumped up. "President, with respect, could the prisoner be given medical attention?"

The court was adjourned. Half an hour later the president returned, and Sybilia was led in, looking contrite. "I'm all right, thank you," she said in reply to the president's query. "I'm sorry. It won't happen again."

Turning to me, the president spoke sternly. "I'm well aware of your tactics, Dr. Walters. You will kindly complete your testimony without any further melodrama."

"I apologize to the court," I said. "I didn't realize she'd be that upset. After all, she's seen these bones before, only she was all alone that time. Just imagine how she must have felt as she pieced together the story of her husband's last hours, how he dragged his maimed body through the maquis until he was cornered, shot like a dog, and buried without a funeral by her own father-in-law. She knew exactly what had happened. A horrible ending for the man she loved."

"Objection." Duval jumped up angrily. "There's no proof at all that Xavier Rocca murdered this man."

"Dr. Walters," the president said sternly, "this is my last warning. Answer the questions put to you *only* and refrain from extraneous comment, or I shall hold you in contempt of court."

Quinel was smiling quietly. "So, Dr. Walters, on the morning of the shooting, Sybilia Rocca had just retrieved from the Algerian diggers her common-law husband's bones and a chain. She took his remains and buried them together with his pistol and dog tag, which she had found on your desk the previous evening?"

"Exactly so."

"Then she went down the mountain, took Xavier Rocca's gun, and shot Captain Moore's murderer."

"Objection!"

"Sustained."

"Thank you, Dr. Walters," Quinel said, but his words were almost lost in the tumult from the public gallery. "You may step down.

"My apologies, Mr. President, gentlemen of the court," Quinel continued. "Please bear with me. I am about to call to the witness stand an eyewitness to the murder of Captain Robin Moore."

CHAPTER 87

The villagers watched uneasily as Maria hobbled painfully to the witness stand, eyes blazing with anger. I could see that the truth about Michel's death had hit her badly.

"You are Maria Rocca, widow of the deceased Xavier Rocca?" Quinel began when he had dispensed with the formalities.

"Yes." Her voice was low and vibrant and carried well—a stage voice when she chose.

"Madame Rocca, could you repeat, how long has your daughter-in-law, Sybilia Rocca, shared your home with you?"

"On and off for twenty-two years."

"Happy years?"

She snorted. "Happiness? What's that? I put no store by it. I do my duty."

"Very well. That's good. You must know her well."

"I do. I know her very well."

"Would you say that until this event took place she was a good person?"

"The kindest, sweetest girl that ever lived." For a moment her eyes moved restlessly toward Sybilia with a look of infinite sadness and despair. "I wronged her."

The president thumped his gavel on his desk. "Madame Rocca, kindly confine yourself to answering the questions put to you. You may continue," he told Quinel.

"Madame Rocca, please tell the court all that you can remember of the night of June fifteenth, 1944."

"I will try," she said simply. "It was the night Ursuline was born.

"The men were gearing up for a hunt all evening, but I never knew what it was about. Later, when it was dark, a knock came on our front door. Xavier went to open it, and I heard a voice saying, 'He's nearly here.' Then the door shut. By the time I got to the window, Xavier was standing by himself at the bottom of our front steps. Then he whistled: three short, sharp whistles. That had been his signal in the war. I watched the lights go up in the windows around the square and saw the men hurrying out of their front doors. Like dogs! Xavier's dogs. That's what I used to call them.

"They went down the cliff face. Sybilia was calling for me to fetch the midwife. She was in labor with Ursuline, you see. So when Pietro Leca came to the door to fetch Jules, I told him to wait there until I came back.

"I went to fetch Madame Rossi, and when I returned I found Leca had gone, taking Jules with him."

"And then?" Quinel prompted her.

"I felt frightened. I knew something was wrong, but I had to wait for the midwife. As soon as she came, I went after the men to bring Jules home. I could see their lights spread out through the maquis."

Maria was woman of powerful imagery, I discovered. Within a few minutes of listening to her, I was back in Taita watching Robin's last, hopeless, desperate flight through the maquis.

She paused and glanced worriedly toward Sybilia, as if she had just remembered her presence. She said: "To cut a long story short, they drove him up to the old quarry.

"Castelli saw me coming. He pushed me aside. He said, 'This is men's business. This is the vendetta. Keep away, Maria.'

"I told him to give me Jules, but he refused, so I went on toward the cave."

Quinel interrupted her. "Madame Rocca, was Captain Moore dead when you arrived?"

"No, he was alive. He was exhausted, moaning slightly, but lucid."

"Did you hear him say anything?"

"He spoke to me quite clearly. He said, 'For the love of God, help Sybilia.' "

"Was that all?"

"Yes. Jules was crying. It's like a dream," she said. "Now I remember, the boy on the wolf's back." She closed her eyes but recovered when the warder handed her a glass of water.

"I begged them not to kill Robin, but Xavier said that Michel must be avenged. Moore was shot up badly, but they were still lusting for blood. Pinelli was there, and Padovani . . ."

There was a sudden uproar in court. Men were shouting, and a woman screamed, "She's mad. She should be put away." The woman was removed bodily by two hefty police guards. It was Madame Padovani.

"I also saw Pascal," Maria was reciting, "Romanetti, Giacobbi, Castelli, Leca, Bonnelli . . . all the village elders. Moore was at the end of his strength. He'd lost a lot of blood.

"Romanetti didn't want them to kill him. I remember he said, 'Let him go. He'll probably die anyway. If he lives, he'll never come back here. He helped us in the war. Why are we killing him?'

"Xavier shouted, 'For Michel.'

"Romanetti said, 'You killed Michel.'

"Of course, I should have realized then. Xavier gave him a punch that knocked him unconscious. Then he put the pistol against Robin's head and said to Jules, 'I'll show you how to avenge your father's death and your mother's honor.' Then he shot Robin, and I grabbed Jules.

"The villagers left as quickly as they could. Xavier took a spade and began to search for a place to bury the corpse. I ran home with Jules. He was silent all the way. I remember how heavy he was. When we got home he said, 'I'll never be afraid again, Grandma. When I grow up I'm going to kill all the bad men. Like this: bang, bang.' For days afterward he went around pointing his wooden gun and saying, 'Bang, bang.' Sybilia never knew. When she got up a week later, he'd grown tired of that game and found something else.

"Still, he was never the same again," she told a courtroom stunned into total silence. "He used to be such a happy child, always laughing and kind to everyone, but after that he became surly and bad-tempered. He was almost three years old and he soon forgot, but I think it was there in the back of his mind."

"Madame Rocca, why did you keep silent for so long?"

"I respected my husband. He never forgave Moore for making Sybilia pregnant and bringing disgrace to our family when Ursuline was born."

"And you never told her. You let her wait all those years, never losing faith, but always believing that Robin would come?"

"I believed Xavier when he told me that because of her, my son was killed. Now I know it wasn't like that at all."

She looked around at Sybilia, a fearful, lonely old woman begging for forgiveness.

"Thank you, Madame Rocca. You may step down."

Maria stumbled on the stairs, and Jules jumped up to help her.

After silence had been restored, Quinel consulted his assistants and then stood up to address the court.

"Mr. President, I should appreciate the leniency of the court. Bearing in mind that this evidence has only just come to hand, I should like to change Sybilia Rocca's plea. She is undoubtedly guilty, but of homicide with extenuating circumstances. I plead a *crime passionnel*."

The president stood up. "The court is adjourned until ten A.M. tomorrow morning to consider this plea in the light of the new evidence," he said, and left hurriedly.

Sybilia seemed to be in a state of shock. She made no move to leave as the guard took her arm and shook her.

Another adjournment, another night to spend alone in the cell. Would she make it? I watched Sybilia moving as if sleepwalking out of the dock to her cell.

CHAPTER 88

This was the last scene of the drama. Prosecutor Duval, tall and predatory, had taken the floor. His confident bearing made me cringe.

"Mr. President, gentlemen of the court, I too feel moved by the story of Sybilia Rocca. Her tragedy has touched my heart, as I know it has yours. Nevertheless, we must not allow our emotions or our pity to cloud our judgment. She took the law into her own hands, and she shot a man as a reprisal. Whichever way you look at Madame Rocca's—Sybilia's—vendetta, one point is clear: murder is wrong, it is punishable by law, and the law must be upheld. If it is not, we could be thrown back into the hell on earth that this small island once was, when entire villages were wiped out as reprisals for long-forgotten crimes. The vendetta must never be allowed to flourish again, not even in cases where the law has failed to prevent wrongdoing."

Masterly oration, superb timing, total confidence—and no wonder, I thought bitterly as I listened to a performance that would have won a Tony if we were in a theater instead of a court of law.

At several points the prosecutor, in his lengthy final address, actually resorted to histrionics, speaking with tear-streamed eyes of Maria's love for her husband and the desperate loneliness that had finally brought the poor old lady to the sorry mental wreck the court had witnessed. It was all good stuff, but predictable, and it was clear that although the prosecutor had the law on his side, public sympathy was running against him.

That wasn't enough, of course. Not nearly enough. I felt that I had failed dismally. My evidence had been designed to bring about Sybilia's collapse. Unfortunately I'd not rung as much anguish out of her as I'd hoped. Apart from the one lapse, she had remained in full control of herself. Sybilia was too proud and self-possessed. I'd wanted her to sob her heart out, until even these stern-eyed patricians were prepared to bend the rules for her.

At last it was Quinel's turn. He stood up tentatively, almost as if he were uncertain of what he would say. I felt I hated him at that moment. What was it to him? Just another case. His reputation was hardly at stake, since everyone knew it was a bad case; but Sybilia was fighting for her life.

"My friends," Quinel began hesitantly, "you've heard a great deal about duty and law and the code, but very little about mercy or understanding, without which there can be no justice.

"There wasn't very much justice for Sybilia Rocca in Taita. Because she loved without a legal license, she endured irreversible social ostracism. She became an outcast.

"As for her bravery and her patriotism . . . well, gentlemen of the court, that was quietly forgotten. There was no medal, no praise, not even a thank-you note from the government. This tragic woman never complained. She simply made the best of a bad job.

"Between the spite and the jealousy and the lies you've heard from witnesses in this trial, you've probably pieced together her true story for yourself. It goes like this. . . ."

Quinel led the court through Sybilia's story, starting with the young, sensitive girl suffering from an arranged marriage until the birth of Ursuline.

"So strong was the bond between them that Captain Moore sensed she needed him and that she was carrying his child." Quinel continued. "He applied for compassionate leave to legalize their marriage, and made his way to Corsica. But there was to be no happy ending for the couple who loved each other dearly. While Sybilia lay in labor, Xavier Rocca, inspired by fear and guilt, called on his wartime squad to help him destroy Captain Moore. Rocca had already blamed him unjustly for the capture of his son, Michel. Now he was afraid that Moore would tell the truth about his fiasco, and he would lose his political support. So he summoned his village cronies to a macabre hunting expedition.

"Let's look at it from the villagers' point of view. What was in it for them? Sybilia Rocca, lovely, coveted, but disgraced, returned to Taita to have her child, much to the villagers' interest. No one would marry her now, but they all awaited their chance. Sybilia was earmarked and labeled the village whore. They did not want a foreigner to take her away.

"So when Xavier Rocca called on the villagers to help him destroy this young American agent, they readily agreed. They believed his story about Michel's death, and, as we have all heard, they also blamed Captain Moore for trying to push home the Allies' strategy during the occupation.

"Together they stalked him through the mountains and brought him to bay in an old quarry, where they shot him several times through the back of the head at point-blank range. They buried him there without a proper grave, and that—to all intents and purposes—was the end of Captain Robin Moore. A sad end for such a brave man."

In the dead silence that followed his words, Ursuline suddenly burst into muffled sobs and buried her head on Jules's shoulder.

"It was not the end for Sybilia," Quinel said softly. "There was nothing so merciful for her. Instead she waited—and waited. Almost everyone in the village knew that Captain Moore was dead and buried in the quarry, but no one told her. They watched her hoping, year after year. She never gave up hope. She knew beyond any shadow of doubt that her Robin would never let her down, and she was right. After a decade she began to recognize that he must have died. But how?

"Then Dr. Jacklyn Walters came and started excavating around the cave where Moore was murdered. Jointly and severally the villagers tried to keep Dr. Walters away from this place. But eventually his workers uncovered the personal effects which Sybilia recognized one night on Dr. Walters' desk.

"The next morning she went up to the trench where they were digging for a new latrine, and she uncovered these few shattered bones."

Quinel mopped his brow. I knew he was gearing up for the climax of his plea.

"Now what was Sybilia to do? I want to ask you that question, gentlemen of the court. Was she to go to the police? Would they nail up a few more posters? You all know that Rocca had been wanted for murder for some years, yet he was still at liberty *and living at home most of the time*.

"So was she to go on living in the same house with the monster who murdered the father of her child—the man she loved?

"Sybilia had relied on State justice before. Now she knew that she had only herself to rely upon. That, my friends, is the terrible sad truth of the matter.

"It is the duty of the State to impose law and order, but what if the State fails? What then? Surely the onus falls upon the individual. For what is the State? It is merely the collective will of the people—an extension of our own innate desire for justice, freedom, and righteousness. If the State fails to provide these basic requirements, then the responsibility falls upon our own shoulders. Then each one of us must stand up and be counted. Our moment of truth arrives, as did Sybilia's.

"How many times in the war crimes trials has the plea 'I only did as I was ordered' been rejected as not sufficient justification to commit a crime? The moral behind that rejection is that each man is responsible for upholding goodness. We may all have to face such a moment of truth: a moment when we must stand up for what we believe in, even at the cost of our lives, or lie down and submit to evil. Sybilia chose the former."

Quinel walked to his table and sat down. He looked drained. The public seemed to be stunned into silence. The president toyed with his pencil. The jury stared at Sybilia. Everything had suddenly come to a halt.

Then, in the silence, a woman stood up and called out, "I demand justice for Sybilia Rocca. I demand—" There was a scuffle. The police gripped her arms, but as she was led from the court, another cried out: "She's not guilty. Let her go!"

"Free her!" The cries now reverberated through the courtroom.

Five minutes later, when order had been restored, the president leaned toward Quinel and said, "And your client? Is she to be given her opportunity to make a personal statement? It is customary, as you know."

Quinel looked toward Sybilia. At first she appeared to be on the point of refusing. Then she gripped the rail and began to speak in a whisper.

"Speak up," the president said.

"Please . . . please . . . would someone arrange a proper burial for Robin Moore's remains, with a proper service? And please, put some flowers on the grave from me. And Jock, you had no right to dig up his grave. Those bones should never have been treated as exhibits for this trial. They are his mortal remains. You had no right . . . no right at all."

She looked around. "Thank you. That's all I have to say." She leaned heavily against the bailiff as she was helped back to her cell.

The police were filing into the courtroom. Clearly they were taking no chances of further disturbances as the trial drew to a close. They clustered around the doors and fingered their batons in the aisles.

When the judges walked into the courtroom, the silence was ominous. To me it felt like every movement the president made was in slow motion; every facial expression signified doom. He seemed to spend an hour or so rearranging his papers, then he began to speak:

"I don't remember when I last felt so compassionate toward any prisoner that I have sentenced in the dock. The murder of Xavier Rocca began, in my opinion, long ago, in times when Corsica was ruled by clan reprisals and consequently no one could walk safely on this island.

"That is precisely why the vendetta, this terrible Corsican tradition, cannot be tolerated. We all know that in cases where the law has failed to punish wrongdoers the individual cannot and must not take the law into his own hands. No court can tolerate this, however great the original wrong. If we were to do so, we would be in danger of returning to the days of anarchy and savagery, and the survival of our society would be threatened.

"Therefore . . ." He paused. "I give no credence to the defense advocate's pleas of her innate right to take on the role of jury, judge, and executioner. Quite simply and without mincing words—*she committed murder*—and as such she will be judged accordingly."

He paused again, drank some water, and turned over a page. I buried my face in my hands. I couldn't bear to watch Sybilia. My mind was in a turmoil. Could she appeal? I tried to remember how the French legal system worked, but I felt dazed and upset.

"However," the presiding judge continued, "we commend her defense advocate for his plea, and we are far more sympathetically inclined toward the prisoner than might normally be the case. France has always felt that there is a thin dividing line between a criminal act and an act of passion. The *crime passionnel* is one with which we are familiar, and it has always been humanely dealt with by French courts. In view of the fact that Sybilia Rocca suffered a great and desperate loss, after a life of great sorrow, the view of the judges and jury of this court is that she is guilty of murder with extenuating circumstances. We feel, therefore, that her sentence should be minimal."

He turned toward the dock to make the judicial pronouncement.

The prisoner rose. "Sybilia Rocca, the judgment of this court is that you are guilty of the lesser charge of homicide, committed while you were under considerable emotional and mental strain. For this crime of passion, you are sentenced to three years' imprisonment, one of which you have already served while awaiting trial, the remaining two to be suspended for three years."

She was free. Free! I let out a roar of applause that was lost in the tumult in the courtroom. Even the police could not prevent the spontaneous cheering and clapping and stamping as Sybilia stumbled out of the dock.

As I fought my way toward her, through the well-wishers, the press, and her family, I paused for a moment. Who needed me? I was, after all, an outsider. A watcher!

I hung back and tried not to grin with embarrassment at the moving scene enacted in the courtroom. Sybilia had her arms around Maria, Ursuline, and Jules—the wounds of three generations were healed at last. Sybilia was smiling, although she still looked dazed. She wanted to embrace them all at once. Then she turned to thank Quinel.

They sure as hell didn't need me butting in on them.

I felt ridiculously emotional as I stumbled through the antechamber and pushed my way out into the blinding sunlight. Funny how good news can be as physically devastating as bad news, I thought. My legs didn't work properly, there was a lump in my throat and tears in my eyes. I hoped to God no one was looking as I leaned against the pillar and dabbed my eyes vigorously, mumbling to no one in particular, "Thank God she's free, and thank God it's over."

I'd run the full gamut of emotions these past few weeks, and now I had a desperate need to get back to my work. I pushed aside a photographer and was about to rush down the steps when I heard Sybilia call my name.

This was my moment of truth, I thought with a flicker of wry humor tinged with fear. I could turn round right now and walk back into the trap of loving and caring, or I could keep going. I'd paid for my intrusion into their lives, hadn't I? I was a free agent. There was nothing at all to hold me here. For the first time in my life, I didn't know what to do.

EPILOGUE

August 15, 1962

Dawn in Ajaccio: a mauve twilight behind eastern mountain ranges. In bars and cafes around the docks, waiters were hosing pavements and tables; washing was being strung from windows across narrow cobbled streets; fishing boats were moving swiftly from the quayside and chugging out to sea. The city was waking.

I'd been standing on the steamer's deck leaning over the railings since before dawn. I glanced at my watch. It was eight-thirty. The ferry should have left half an hour ago. "Who cares," I muttered, then laughed. I couldn't help remembering my first baffling month in Corsica and my agony at the pointless delays, the frustration of dealing with people who had no clear concept of time, and all those early disappointments that often drove me to despair.

I remember a shouting match with a shepherd. The old man had been herding his goddamned smelly goats down the only route through a narrow mountain pass, and I was compelled to drive my jeep at a goat's pace. When I had exhausted my vocabulary, threatened to run over the entire herd, and eventually acknowledged defeat, the shepherd had said:

"I pity you, my friend. Time is your enemy. Now as for me—I savor each moment and live happily in the here and now. Well, we all have our enemies. You carry a watch, while I carry a rifle."

That was more than seven years ago! Now I was going home to Boston to see my family, sort out my affairs, and attend the launch of my latest book.

If, as I hoped, my book should jolt the world into recognizing the beauty and importance of the Corsican culture, then it might repay a part of the debt that I owed the island. It was a book about Corsica. I'd poured my heart into it. Somewhere, among the digging and the loving and the agony, I'd grasped the island's emotional thread. I would never let it go.

After musing for a while, I decided that "passion" was the closest word I could find. In Corsica I'd learned about passion—a passion for honor, for loving, for morality, for living. A total passionate involvement with the environment and with every moment of every day.

I felt it now, in the railings vibrating under my fingers, the town basking indolently in the sun, the boat heaving, the sea lapping against the bow, gulls swooping and crying—a moment in time, pure and priceless.

The ferry was moving, as the horn signaled our departure. A steward walked along the deck toward me carrying a basket decorated with herbs from the maquis. The pungent scent filled me with longing, and for a moment I had a crazy impulse to rush back to Taita.

The note, in Ursuline's handwriting, read simply: *To Sybilia and Jock Walters: Come back soon. Best love from all of us.*

I thrust the note into my pocket. Still I lingered, watching until the outline of the immense mountains faded, as sea and sky merged into one empty canvas.

Then I smiled to myself, slung the basket over my arm, and went down to the cabin to join my wife.